IN THE SHADOW OF LOVE

(SHADOW SERIES BOOK 2)

J.E. LEAK

CERTIFIABLY CREATIVE LLC

Copyright © 2022 by J.E. Leak

All rights reserved.

This book is a work of fiction. Any references to historical events, real people, or real places are used fictitiously. Other names, characters, places, and events are products of the author's imagination, and any resemblance to actual events or places or persons, living or dead, is entirely coincidental.

No part of this book may be reproduced in any form or by any electronic or mechanical means, including information storage and retrieval systems, without written permission from the author, except for the use of brief quotations in a book review.

ISBN 978-1-955294-02-7 (eBook Edition)
ISBN 978-1-955294-03-4 (Paperback Edition)
Library of Congress Control Number: 2022900023
First Printing February 2022
Edited by Pam Greer

Published by Certifiably Creative LLC
Ocala, Florida
press@certifiablycreative.com

Printed and bound in the United States of America

To my wife.

SENSITIVE CONTENT

This novel contains instances of PTSD from war experiences. While it is not the central theme of the story, it is woven into the tapestry of the characters' lives, and I am mindful that for many, such forewarning is appreciated.

CHAPTER ONE

May 1943: New York City

It won't be long now, Kathryn kept thinking as they walked arm in arm toward the bedroom door. The road had been winding, and not without its bumps, but the time had come. They were finally going to consummate their relationship. The air crackled with the anticipation of an opening night set list. The sensation sent a chill skittering up her spine. The feeling was so palpable, she was tempted to look around for the audience, sure the whole world was watching and lending its energy to their mission.

No one else was watching, though. It was just the two of them, finally, about to share something that had been building and, until now, had been denied for weeks. They'd put their previous relationship behind them. It had no bearing on who they were to each other now. Tonight would propel them forward and complete their transformation into a couple. No more teasing, no more truncated foreplay. This was it. It was happening.

At first, the realization made her nervous. That was odd. She'd had more than her share of lovers, and while every relationship differed, she'd never had so many stops and starts on the way to the inevitable union. This night would be a triumph of patience and perseverance for both of them.

She relaxed as the night wore on, and her nerves turned to fascination. A new lover was always interesting, but none more so than this one. There was an element of danger that both excited and frightened her. They'd forged a successful working relationship, and she worried this next step might compromise it. Too much was at stake to let sex get in the way. She wouldn't let it, that's all.

Tonight was the culmination of weeks of curious, but limited, exploration, and it had ended in an evening of wining, dining, secret seductive touches, and longing looks. At long last, they were at their final destination—the bedroom. After they entered, Kathryn kicked the door shut without looking.

She closed her eyes, stepped out of her heels, and pulled her long dark hair to the side, exposing the back of her neck and the zipper of her dress. As the zipper pull descended, warm lips painted a trail of light kisses from the nape of her neck and around to her collarbone. Her dress slid from her shoulders and to the floor. She reached out to the shirt in front of her and began liberating buttons from their holes with a seductive glance before each one. The glance was not a question of consent but a promise of things to come. Almost there.

A shaky exhale made her pause. Kathryn looked into nervous eyes with understanding. She pressed her body close in a comforting embrace, hoping her strength and confidence would calm her suddenly anxious soon-to-be lover. Through the thin material of her slip, she could feel the pounding heart that, to her surprise, seemed to resonate more fear than excitement. She kissed a flushed cheek and whispered, "We'll go slow."

A bashful nod.

She carefully slid a hand down an unfastened waistband but didn't get very far before a choked voice whimpered, "Don't." A nervous breath. "Stop."

Kathryn hesitated.

"Please. Stop."

"Don't stop, please? Or please, don't stop?" she asked playfully.

"I can't. Please." A strong hand gently stopped the seduction. "Please. I'm sorry."

Her assignment for the Office of Strategic Services, Marcus Forrester, was nothing if not consistent. He thrived on the foreplay but never went beyond, verging on panic the moment intimacy seemed near. Kathryn was grateful for that and amused at the rejection. That didn't happen to her. She kept trying though. He wanted her to. He liked it, he promised. But Kathryn had her doubts. She wondered if, one day, he'd actually let her touch him intimately or if he would ever touch her that way. How bizarre, their little game, but thank you, Howard.

She smiled, as Jenny Ryan's childhood misinterpretation of the line *hallowed be thy name*, from the Lord's Prayer, popped into her head for a brief moment of respite from her current situation. She'd gotten used to her former assignment occupying her thoughts at the most unusual times. Marcus Forrester was supposed to cure her of that as she worked her way deeper into his life to uncover his traitorous sins, but it didn't work. Jenny still lived in her heart as a constant comfort—hope to her usual doom. She hadn't seen or heard from her since they parted at OSS headquarters. It seemed so long ago, and she missed her, despite vowing to move on. A month was a long time, wasn't it?

She fully expected the plucky ex-reporter to show up to a rehearsal at her nightclub gig at The Grotto, hands behind her back and lashes fluttering over undeniable green eyes as she tilted her head and pointedly asked, "So, what exactly does *got to you* mean, and how do I cash in?"

Instead, she hadn't heard a word, which she supposed was for the best. Jenny was an assignment while the OSS looked for her deceased father's medical research files. Kathryn got too close. Cared too much. It got messy emotionally, but they had made their peace with each other before they went their separate ways.

In the rare moments when Kathryn was honest with herself about it, she was disappointed. Her parting comment, that Jenny had gotten to her, was meant to be bait, even if she didn't realize it at the time.

She accepted Jenny's decision not to contact her, and she found serenity in the choice. It was for the best, now that they both worked for the OSS.

Kathryn periodically asked her OSS handler, Colonel Forsythe—casually, of course—how the new recruit was doing, and he would always say something to the effect, "Miss Ryan is a very hard worker, creative as hell, and already making substantial contributions to the war effort in Morale Operations." Kathryn would hide her proud grin behind her coffee cup, but she knew she wasn't fooling anyone. Colonel Forsythe least of all.

When she thought of Jenny, which was more often than she cared to admit, it was not with angst and guilt, as she had before because she failed to preserve her beautiful, normal life, but with a feeling of satisfaction that Jenny had found her niche. She was making a difference. Kathryn knew that would make her happy, and she realized that's all she really wanted for her. In some small, unexpected way, she was responsible for a piece of her happiness. She liked the feeling. Quite an odd turn of events. Guilt had turned into pride. Miraculous! The demons must be sleeping on the job.

A sense of calm had entered her life without so much as a *How do you do?* as it brushed by her usually alert defenses. It wasn't the apathetic calm that she was used to—the one that wore disdain behind its back—but something better, like she'd crawled one step higher than she'd ever stood before, and the air was a little cleaner. Even her time with Forrester seemed effortless. They'd moved seamlessly into their new roles after Jenny, thinking she was saving her, turned her gun over to the police, causing Forrester enough trouble that he considered taking her life with his own hand. This would forever be known as the *gun incident*. He thought better of her execution, and she continued playing the good little mistress while he became more open and trusting than ever.

Despite his claim that their business arrangement was now a friendship as well, he started acting like they were a couple, with her as his absentee wife. He doted on her in public and in private, frequently dining and dancing with her at supper clubs. He'd even taken to having her on his arm at charity functions, a previous no-no, in deference to his wife. All pretenses had fallen away in that regard, and it seemed he'd do anything to be seen in public with his favorite girl. He always looked around, making sure he was noticed, that *they* were noticed. She wondered if it was leading up to something. Something in his business world, that is. It had already led up to something in his personal world, and to that end, he promised this night would be the night she was waiting for. She would have put off this night forever if she could.

He'd stopped their usual *sex-for-dysfunctional-lovers* game right after the night of her aborted murder. He treated her differently after that, more like a cherished partner than a plaything on the payroll. He had not asked her to perform for him since. Instead, he took a more interactive role in their physical relationship, actually touching her, and allowing touch in return, but nothing more intimate than adolescent petting, not even kissing on the mouth. She found his pseudo sex life utterly fascinating, even while not minding it a bit. This was her job, after all, nothing more.

She wondered what he was thinking, how he derived pleasure from such a frustrating exercise in denial, but, honestly, she didn't want to know. If his big lead-up to the evening wasn't to finally have sex with her, she wondered what on earth he had planned.

After he stopped her seduction, she took in a silent breath and reeled in her adrenaline-induced excitement. It wasn't sexual arousal she felt but the promise of power. Control. Triumph. That's what sex was to her. Partners always mistook it for passion. What else would they think? It was an honest mistake and one she let them make. It only added to her satisfaction. They couldn't know it was a release for her anger, a panacea for helplessness, and a victory where none other was possible. She had come so close this time to dominating Forrester. She longed for the pleading look in his eyes as she held his release hostage to her whim. The harder they come, the harder they fall. It was crude but true. Putty in her hands. That's what her lovers were. She would have laughed at her arrogance if she hadn't proved it true again and again.

"I have a surprise for you," Forrester said brightly, recovering quickly from their oft repeated termination of affections. He removed his dinner jacket and replaced it with a rich maroon velvet smoking jacket. "Here ..." He passed her a silky black robe with an absurd feathery trim. "Put it on." She complied, and he held out his hand. "Come."

That wasn't likely. Kathryn took his hand with a fake smile.

He led her through the cavernous halls of his Long Island estate to the room Kathryn liked to call the whorehouse. This is where he indulged in his sexual fantasies.

He should have been a Broadway producer. The room looked like a small, intimate theater, with a bed center stage. Behind the bed was a large mirror, reflecting the scene for the best possible view. Kathryn knew that another girl had taken her place in his little voyeuristic sex game, and she offered a silent apology to the stand-in. The whole setting was absurdly over the top, and Kathryn was glad she no longer had a role there.

She wondered what he thought his sexual quirks did for her as a partner. If she really *was* interested in him sexually, like she pretended to be, his rules would result in total frustration. Maybe he didn't care. Maybe he thought she would have no trouble finding sexual satisfaction elsewhere whenever she wanted it. He already thought she had a lover, despite her protests to the contrary.

He led her into the mostly dark room, which really amounted to a half room, as the entryway deposited them into a stage-level theater box, complete with low, warm footlights and swooping velvet curtains. There were two seats instead of the usual one, and she supposed she was going to be part of the audience for his little show for a change.

He disappeared for a moment and then came up behind her in the shadows, which startled her, as his warm breath reached her neck before his hands settled around her waist. He held her close.

He motioned toward the bed. "Look."

The lights slowly came up to a comfortable but appropriately moody level, revealing two incredibly beautiful women on the bed, one blonde, one redhead, dressed in surprisingly tasteful lingerie, considering.

"They're for you," he whispered, obviously pleased with himself.

She chuckled, as if he was kidding. "Both?"

His smile crackled in her ear. "If you like."

"Mm," Kathryn said, as she assessed the two scantily clad women. She was unsure of his intent, though, and she looked sideways at the extra chair and then to the women who were staring seductively back at her.

"You can watch, or you can join them if you'd like," he whispered softly as he stroked her cheek. She didn't have to accept, but Forrester seemed to like the idea of it, and no one would have to twist her arm. The night was turning out better than expected.

"You're sure you don't mind?"

He responded with an incredulous expression. "Silly of you to ask, isn't it?"

She grinned in agreement.

"One thing ..." He took her trailing hand and entwined his fingers with hers. "Do me a favor."

"Hm?"

"Let them ... take you." He leered his meaning. "Just let them."

She moaned her approval as she spared a glance at the beautiful women. "My pleasure."

She entered stage left wearing a smirk, her back to Forrester. She'd seen women pressed into this kind of service by hardship or coercion, and she could tell them immediately. There would be fear and shame in their eyes, and their body language would struggle not to betray a mind screaming for escape. These women, however, were not of that variety. Kindred spirits? For now, perhaps. They were all on the same page tonight, and no one was doing anything against their will.

She turned to face the seating section, where the low footlights were casting an eerie shadow on Forrester's face from below. The two beauties slithered off the bed and began their seduction. She held out her arms in supplication and, as requested, just let them take her.

She supposed Forrester imagined himself as those girls, devouring a woman he desired but unable to bring himself to try. She soon found herself on the bed wearing nothing but a smile and two very attentive women. She didn't even mind Forrester watching. In fact, it felt triumphant. It wasn't the complete victory she envisioned, but it would do, and the benefits weren't too bad either.

Warm bodies pressed against hers with a velvety softness only another woman's gentle curves could supply. For Kathryn, this was a world of pleasure that men could only watch from the outside with their fantasies and egos. They could mimic the actions but never attain the innate intimacy that only the feminine psyche allows.

She stared directly at Forrester with eyes that, for the first time in his presence, registered true arousal, as the blonde and redhead greedily caressed her naked body with hungry hands and intimate kisses. He could never compete with that. Maybe he knew that. Maybe that's why he never tried.

Freud would have a field day with the lot of them, she imagined. A mouth found a particularly sensitive spot, and Forrester disappeared from her vision and her mind. She gave in to the pleasure, allowing herself, on this special night, to be consumed.

CHAPTER TWO

It didn't start out like a life and death situation when Jenny stopped by the manufacturing plant to interview some striking workers, but the strong hand wearing the front of her shirt around its fist told her otherwise. A large man with one eyebrow, who reminded her of the cartoon character Bluto, was breathing down her neck. She turned her head to escape his foul breath and swore she'd never eat a pastrami sandwich again. She was too stunned to be frightened. There were plenty of people around. Surely, none of them would let the man hurt her. Surely.

She looked in every direction, wondering when someone would step in to save her. No one stepped forward. Instead, the small group of strikers turned their backs and formed a human wall, blocking the altercation from view. The last to turn away was the striker who agreed with her dissenting opinion of the organized work stoppage only moments before.

In contrast to the inexplicable trouble in which she usually found herself, she didn't have to wonder how she got into this mess. She went looking for it.

For weeks, she'd followed the rumors of a strike at the manufacturing plant across town, and now that the strike was a reality, something had to be done. Quitting her uncle's newspaper, the *Daily Chronicle*, made her an ex-reporter, but she was still a patriot, and the country was still at war. Marcus Forrester owned this plant, and she was sure he was behind the strike. It fit right in with the investigative piece she'd started on the man when she thought he'd ordered her father's death. She never did prove that, and it was ruled an accident, but she'd uncovered enough to know that his angelic philanthropist persona was a ruse. Instigating a strike in his own plant would tick the traitor box. Kathryn Hammond, his fake mistress, all but confirmed that he was a criminal, and Jenny wasn't going to let it slide if she could do something about it. Reporter or not.

She took the long way to the office for her shift, just to gauge the mood of the strike, and couldn't resist stopping when she saw a lone striker off to the side, looking disgruntled at the whole situation. A group of women workers were barred from the plant by a sea of angry men, some carrying signs, some just waving their fists. Jenny hoped talking reasonably with the lone striker might make him receptive to her concerns. To her surprise, it did. He claimed the whole strike was started by a small group of bullies who intimidated the rest of the workers to join in, either out of fear or an irresistible mob mentality.

She'd almost convinced the man that if he got enough of the workers together who felt like him, they could raise a united voice against the few reprobates, and this strike would be over, enabling machine parts that were desperately needed to roll off assembly lines again.

Just as she came to the best part of her *do it because the country needs you* speech, the man's eyes drifted over her shoulder, and fear replaced interest. Only then did she hear the gravel crunching under the head bully's size eleven feet.

"What's goin' on here, Charlie?" the large man asked with a suspicious scowl.

"Nothin', Butch. Just talkin' to the pretty lady."

Jenny internally rolled her eyes. Butch. Seriously?

"And what are you doin' here, dolly?" Butch asked, turning his gaze on her.

"None of your business," she said, and turned her back on him.

"Another uppity broad," he said, spinning her around and grabbing her by the front of her shirt. The material ripped before a button gave out, and she winced as his nails dug into her chest.

"Let go of me!" she screamed, as she tried to push against his shoulder. Her arms weren't long enough to reach his body, so her hands wound up sliding ineffectively down his thick, sweaty forearms. She pulled at his wrist, but it felt like an immovable block of concrete. She struggled briefly, but his grin said he liked it, so she stopped. She couldn't escape his grasp on her own, so she turned to the stunned striker by her side.

"Help me!"

He didn't move. He shifted his wide eyes from her to the menacing hulk towering over them both.

"Charlie!" she screamed, hoping his name would awaken the human part of him she hoped was lurking somewhere inside. His eyes snapped back to her, and she thought he was moving to help, but, instead, he looked up past the struggle in front of him and stepped back in reaction to a small group of men quickly approaching.

Jenny nearly wilted in relief. No way Butch would hurt her in front of witnesses. She almost smiled in his face. It was the evil sneer that told her this wasn't a rescue—not here, not with his men.

Now was the time to panic. Where in the hell was Popeye and his can of spinach?

She watched the men form their wall again and realized there was only one thing left to do—scream her brains out.

"Hel—" The rest of the scream was cut off by a huge hand covering most of her face. In fact, it not only covered her mouth, it also covered her nose, and what little air she could inhale smelled like—ugh, she didn't want to know. She began struggling again. When she began kicking, he thrust her backward against a truck, its door handle stabbing into her back. His fist felt like a hammer against her chest, and the more she struggled, the harder he pressed. The men surrounding them did nothing. She couldn't breathe. Panic turned to hysteria, and she pulled helplessly at the hand covering her face. Her eyes filled with tears, pleading for him to at least let her breathe. Did he know she couldn't breathe? The sick pleasure in his eyes told her he did. The phrase *curiosity killed the cat* never seemed more appropriate. She was sorry she ever convinced herself that two miles out of her way wasn't *that* far off the route to the office.

The ringing in her ears grew louder, and she felt lightheaded. Passing out in this mob was the last thing she wanted to do, but on the other hand, maybe he would let her go and she could at least breathe. She feigned passing out moments before she actually would have and heard a dull thud followed by a choked groan. She wasn't sure if it came from her own throat, as the hand over her face disappeared and she hit the ground, or Butch, who she realized was suddenly doubled over, with a long arm growing out from his crotch.

Jenny blinked into the sun from her position on the ground and saw a silhouette of her savior, bathed in a halo of bright light. Singing angels would have made the vision perfect.

"Get to my car!" came a stern command.

She knew that voice.

Kathryn Hammond had a viselike grip on Butch's crotch from behind. He fell to his knees as his face turned purple.

"You bitch ..." he croaked through gritted teeth. He turned his head and stared at his own reflection in Kathryn's sunglasses before succumbing to an even tighter grasp. He groaned in pain and flailed an arm in her direction, to no avail.

Jenny looked to her right. The hostile crowd was moving in. One man was almost at Kathryn's back, and she couldn't even yell *look out* before Kathryn extended a leg straight into the man's chest, sending him sprawling onto his backside in pain. Jenny wasn't going to leave Kathryn to the wolves, so she looked around for something she could use as a weapon. Another man came crumbling to his knees in front of her from a flying elbow to his jaw.

"The longer you stay here, the longer I have to hold these guys off," Kathryn said. "Go!"

Jenny scrambled to her feet as Kathryn released her hold on Butch. He hit the ground, hip to shoulder, with a thud and a slow, wheezing cough. "Y ... you ... you'll ... pay ... for ..."

"Yeah, yeah, yeah. Put it on my tab."

Kathryn raised her hands in defense, turning slowly, as more of the crowd pressed in. "Come on now, boys," she said, cocking her head at the moaning bodies on the ground. "Is it really worth it?"

Jenny sprinted to the car a few yards away while keeping an eye on Kathryn, who seemed to have the situation well in hand. The men stopped moving in and took stock of the situation. Jenny brought the car to a skidding halt a few feet away, sending dust and gravel billowing into the air. She flung the driver's door open and slid over to the passenger side in perfect synchronization to Kathryn's feet-first dive into the driver's seat.

Kathryn hit the clutch and the gas at the same time, slamming the car into gear and spewing gravel into the faces of the angry crowd. She quickly turned the wheel, hand over hand, forcing the door shut of its own volition. She cursed under her breath as the car lost traction in the loose gravel, but the wheels finally found purchase on asphalt and they took off, tires squealing, at full speed down the road.

Jenny had one hand on the dashboard and one hand clutching the handle on the passenger side door as she stared wide-eyed and speechless out the windshield.

Kathryn had a one-handed white-knuckled grasp on the steering wheel as she effortlessly shifted through the gears. "Are you all right?" she asked hurriedly, turning her attention to Jenny, then to the rearview mirror, then to the road ahead and back. "Are you all right?" she said with more urgency when Jenny didn't answer.

"Yes," Jenny said hesitantly, then, "*yes*," with more authority, as she looked down and removed her death grip on the door to hold her shirt closed. Her chest stung and was bleeding from Butch's grasp, and her back was killing her, but she was alive, thanks to Kathryn. She looked her way. "Thank you."

Kathryn's jaw was set, and her eyes behind her sunglasses shifted like a hawk on the hunt, seeing everything, as she scanned the road in front and in the rearview mirror behind them. Determination was pouring off in waves, and Jenny looked away, hoping that intensity was not going to turn into a lecture about her stupidity. No one had to tell her she'd screwed up.

Kathryn made a final glance in the rearview mirror and pulled over. Jenny closed her eyes, bracing for whatever was coming. She heard Kathryn shift in her seat and felt her slide closer. Jenny opened her eyes to see a hand coming toward her, and she instinctively flinched, Butch's paw still fresh in her memory.

Kathryn quickly withdrew her hand. "Sorry." She removed her sunglasses and tossed them on the dashboard as she drew an arm over the back of the seat. "You're hurt," she said, pointing at the blood-stained shirt.

Jenny peeled her hand from the dashboard and covered her chest. "I'm fine."

"You're bleeding. You're not fine. Let me see."

Jenny looked at her hesitantly, aware of her aversion to blood, and tightened the grip on her shirt in a futile gesture of privacy. "Wouldn't that be a bad idea?"

"I'm too torqued off to pass out, believe me. Come on." She moved closer. "Let me see."

Kathryn was all business, with a little impatience mixed with her concern, but not anger—not at her this time anyway. Jenny parted her shirt to Kathryn's sympathetic hiss.

"Son of a bitch," she said.

Butch's nails had dug two short but significant gashes in the hollow between Jenny's breasts, just above her bra line. Blood seeped from the uncovered cuts, and Kathryn quickly averted her eyes and pulled the shirt back over the wounds with an unsteady hand. "Okay. Let's go clean that up." She slid back to her side of the seat and retrieved her sunglasses.

"It's nothing," Jenny said, as she pressed her fist into the wound to alleviate the stinging and stop the bleeding. "I've got to get to work."

Kathryn looked at her in disbelief, then turned her head and put her sunglasses on. "You've got to get that taken care of, and then we're going to the police. That ape could have killed you."

"He wasn't trying to kill me. He was just trying to scare me."

Kathryn turned, peering over her glasses. "Oh? Was it fear that caused that curious blue tint to your oxygen-starved face? We're going to the police, and if you don't, I will."

"No police."

"Jenny—"

"I'm okay."

"What if I hadn't been there?"

"Look, Kat. Thank you for the rescue—" She was going to breeze on to her point, but having one's life saved was nothing to gloss over. "Thank you," she said again sincerely. "Really." She took Kathryn's hand from the gearshift. It was trembling. "Are *you* all right? You're shaking."

Kathryn took her hand back, holding it up like it belonged to someone else. "Must be the adrenaline. It's been a while since I physically accosted someone."

Jenny wasn't sure whether she was being serious or trying to lighten the mood, but lightening the mood didn't seem like such a bad idea.

"Accost a lot of people, have you?"

Kathryn looked again at her trembling hand. She opened and closed it a few times and gave it a good shake. "Like I said, it's been a while."

Jenny grinned and shook her head. "I can't believe you grabbed that guy by the nuts."

"Think I'm gonna skin a knuckle on his ugly mug? Besides, once you shut off the flow of blood to his brain …" She made a sour face. "Remind me to sterilize this hand when I get home."

They both chuckled and exhaled calming breaths in the subsiding rush of the incident. Jenny finally relaxed into her seat.

Kathryn put a hesitant hand on her shoulder. "Are you sure you're okay?"

Jenny exhaled again and let her head fall back. "Yeah. Stupid." She paused. "Thank you for not yelling at me."

Kathryn looked at her quizzically. "I'm not your keeper, Jenny. What you do on your own time is your business. I don't think you need a lecture from me about how volatile that situation is. I'm just glad I was there to help."

"I should have gone straight to the office. Instead, I—" she left the sentence hanging and rubbed her forehead. "Stupid."

"Once a reporter," Kathryn said with a grin, but Jenny knew there was nothing funny about what she'd done.

The impact of what had happened, and what could have happened, had Kathryn not been there, welled up in her like a rising tide. "God." She put her head in her hands as the tears came out of nowhere.

Kathryn anticipated a breakdown when reality set in, and she was at Jenny's side with her arms around her in an instant when it happened. "Shhh. It's okay. You're okay now. I'm here. You're okay."

Jenny responded to her gentle cooing by melting into her offered shoulder.

"Shhh. You're okay," Kathryn continued. "You're safe now." She tightened her embrace. "Safe."

She stopped her gentle rocking, stunned by the emotion she was feeling. Never had she felt more useful or more at home than with her arms around Jenny Ryan, protecting her from the big, bad world. Traffic buzzed by, and the engine continued to hum, oblivious to her revelation. She closed her eyes and rested her head on the soft, fragrant blonde hair, wishing for the moment never to end.

Jenny shifted slightly and pushed away. "Jeez, I'm sorry."

Kathryn wanted to say, *stay here*. "What's the matter?"

"I'm being a baby," Jenny said, as she wiped away tears.

"Don't be ridiculous. You've just been attacked by a man who outweighed you three to one. He could have snapped you like a twig."

Jenny stretched her back and winced. "He nearly did."

"Yes, he nearly did."

Kathryn slid back into the driver's seat, trying to hide her anxiety over what might have been. Her trembling was more than just adrenaline over the confrontation. It was fear, but not for her life, for Jenny's.

When she saw the brute put his hand to Jenny's face, she was afraid she wouldn't reach her in time. Her heart nearly stopped when he slammed her against the car and she went limp. That's when the adrenaline really hit her and she felt as though she could tear the man apart with her bare hands.

She glanced at Jenny, an absentminded gesture of reassurance, and found her looking her up and down curiously.

"What were you doing there, anyway?" Jenny asked, taking in the denim work shirt and soft cotton pants. "Moonlighting at the factory?"

Kathryn smiled, looking down at her casual attire. "Cleaning day."

Jenny raised her brow, and Kathryn knew it was because that didn't answer her question. Her appearance involved a phone call from the OSS and a recruit in surveillance training in over her head when she saw her blonde charge for the day stepping into possible trouble. Unsure of what to do, she called in for instructions. Kathryn happened to be the nearest source of help, so she was called out to assess the situation.

Having lied to Jenny during her assignment to her, she was loathe to do it again, so she told her the truth.

Jenny paused a beat, then shook her head. "Trainees are tailing me?"

"Don't take it personally. If you move into field training, you'll do the same."

"Ugh." Jenny put her head in her hands again. "That means my boss knows where I was and what happened."

"Probably."

"Will I be fired?"

Kathryn looked at her wristwatch. "Technically, you're not on the clock yet."

"I'm such an idiot."

She patted Jenny's leg with a reassuring smile and glanced in the rearview mirror for any sign of a tail or trouble. "You'll be fine."

Jenny looked behind as well. "Are we in the clear?"

"Seem to be." Which was unusual. Forrester generally had someone lurking, watching—guarding, as he liked to call it. Some guard. A few more minutes with that crowd and she would have been in deep trouble as well. Maybe he really did trust her and had called off the watchdogs while he was out of town. No matter, she still had to be cautious, just to be sure.

Jenny offered another glance back, and Kathryn realized she was reacting to her furrowed brow and inaction.

"Take me to work?" she asked.

"First, we get that taken care of." Kathryn pointed at Jenny's chest. "We'll just make a quick stop at a clinic."

"Honestly, Kat, it's just a scratch. What are they going to do there?"

"Give you a rabies shot?"

"Ha ha." Jenny peeked at the wound. "Hm. Maybe." She smiled. "Seriously, though, they're going to clean it up and put a dressing on it. I can do that."

That was true. "Are you sure you don't want to go to the police? They're all good friends of mine now. I'll make sure they treat you well."

Jenny laughed, and Kathryn was glad she recognized it as a joke about her part in the gun incident that briefly made her a murder suspect.

"I don't want to go to the police," Jenny said. "I think I've done enough antagonizing for today, if you know what I mean."

Kathryn did know what she meant, and she was right. Going to the police wouldn't accomplish anything. It must have been the shock of finding Jenny in such dire straits that blinded her to the fact that the police should be kept out of it. She mentally shook her head. All rational thought seemed to flee where Jenny was concerned.

Forrester was behind the strike, she knew. It was an attempt to break the union, and a little money thrown at some disgruntled employees went a long way toward stirring up already high emotions. She hoped no one got her tag number in all the excitement, but only time would tell, and she would cross that bridge with Forrester if and when the time came.

Jenny was silent, and Kathryn glanced over to see disgust and disappointment clouding her face. "Are you okay?"

"I shouldn't have been there in the first place. What happened was my fault."

Kathryn bristled. She shouldn't have been there, that was true, but there was no justification for a three-hundred-pound thug to attack a defenseless woman, let alone one she was growing fond of. Just the thought of the man's brutal hands on her brought on a flash of rage, and she couldn't contain it. "That guy had no right to attack you!"

Jenny turned away. "Please don't yell at me."

"I'm not ye—" Kathryn cut herself off, realizing she was doing just that, and reeled in her emotions. "Sorry. I just—" She bit down on the nonexistent excuse. She couldn't admit that she was entirely too protective and liked the job.

"I just want to go to work and forget this ever happened," Jenny said. She adjusted her collar and fiddled with a button hanging from a rip in the fabric, not really comprehending why it wouldn't stay fastened. They both looked down at the torn, bloody shirt.

Jenny gave up trying to make it look presentable and cursed under her breath.

Kathryn faced forward and put the car in gear. "All right, let's find you a new shirt, clean that up, and then I'll take you to work. Okay?"

"Where are we going?"

"My place."

CHAPTER THREE

The distinct smell of ammonia filled the air as Jenny followed Kathryn into her apartment, which was a shame, because she was looking forward to experiencing every nuance of her living quarters, and she was pretty sure ammonia potpourri was not the norm.

Kathryn's was the only apartment above a three-car garage in the short but deep building tucked in between two taller buildings on Jane Street, in Greenwich Village.

A long expanse of honey-colored hardwood flooring defined the living room area, and Jenny followed the line of its planking until it was interrupted by a rolled-up carpet and a bucket with a mop handle protruding from it in the center of the room.

"Sorry," Kathryn said, sliding it to the side with her foot. "Real glamorous, huh?"

"Well, there's more to life than glamor."

Kathryn gasped and put a hand to her heart. "Say it ain't so." She grinned as she slipped off her shoes and then tilted her head toward the long hall. "Come on, let's get you a shirt."

Jenny slipped off her shoes while she pulled her pale green blouse from her skirt. The apartment was bigger than she thought from the outside but not as big as it could have been because of a beautiful grand piano taking up a good portion of the living room. It was a Steinway, with a hand-rubbed satin finish on its mahogany body rather than the customary black lacquer high gloss. The warmth of the wood blended beautifully with the warm hues and cool color accents of the living space.

She entered the bedroom after Kathryn, who went to the closet and opened the door.

"Pick anything you like. I need to make a quick telephone call, and then I'll get the first-aid kit."

After Kathryn left the room, Jenny unbuttoned her shirt and took in the space with curious eyes. The walls were a soft yellow that complemented nicely the muted flowered drapes that adorned the windows. An antique armoire with a full-length mirror was on the far wall, and adjacent to that was a vanity with a collection of small glass bottles dotting the surface. She smelled traces of Kathryn's perfume, which made her remember their first meeting in the ladies' room of The Grotto. That seemed ages ago, and she realized she didn't know Kathryn any better now than she did then, only that there remained an undeniable pull whenever they were together. Whether they were on good terms or bad, she wanted to be near her.

She heard the low murmur of Kathryn's voice from the living room and remembered that voice telling her that she'd gotten to her. It had been a month since that confession, and Jenny had given up hope that Kathryn would contact her to explore that further. Kathryn was in a tough spot because of her assignment to Forrester, so she'd left it up to her to renew their friendship. When she didn't, Jenny understood it was just too complicated, or perhaps she still couldn't forgive her for the gun incident.

Fortunately, she'd been so busy with her new job that she didn't have time to dwell on the loss of their friendship and the potential relationship she'd felt forming between them. Seeing her again, though, Jenny sensed no trace of the anger that had torn them apart, and she had renewed hope for their future, one that found her standing in Kathryn's bedroom with her shirt unbuttoned.

Continuing her glance around the room, she noted a dresser and a matching set of nightstands residing on each side of a woven bamboo headboard that loomed over a very comfortable looking bed. She quickly turned her attention to the closet before her mind went some place her body might not be welcome.

She let her shirt fall from her shoulders, which left it hanging listlessly from her elbows. As she leaned into the closet to make a quick selection, Kathryn came back into the room.

"I don't know whether I have a Band-Aid big eno— whoops," Kathryn stopped short, looking up from the box in her hand. "Sorry."

"Don't be sorry. It's your house." The scene was a mirror of one that had occurred at her house, when she walked in on Kathryn putting a shirt on, but Jenny waited in vain for the continuation of that scene. "Isn't this where you say you're not used to seeing half-naked women in your bedroom?"

Kathryn smiled but avoided looking her way as she crossed the room and set the first-aid items on the nightstand beside the bed.

"You're right," she said, sitting on the bed and making eye contact. "I'm not used to seeing half-naked women in my bedroom." She leaned back on one elbow and crossed her legs. "If there's a woman in my bedroom, she's usually *completely* naked."

Jenny was momentarily stunned at the inviting gaze and its accompanying smirk and decided two could play at that game. "Is that a prerequisite? Because I could—" She stuck a thumb under her bra strap, lifting it slightly off her shoulder.

Kathryn laughed and patted the soft white material of her seashell-embossed duvet cover. "Here, let me take a look at that." She sat up and reached for the first-aid items.

Jenny gave up on the closet and obeyed, walking the few steps to the bed.

Kathryn handed over a sterile gauze pad and the antiseptic. "You clean. It'll hurt less if you do it yourself."

Jenny sat and took the items, soaking the pad with antiseptic. She sucked the sting through her teeth as she applied the cleanser to her wound. "Says you. Ow."

Kathryn echoed the hiss. "Sorry." She tore open another gauze square and picked up the roll of white medical tape.

"Damn," Jenny said as she dabbed at the cuts. Two tracks of raised welts crowned with two short ragged gashes were still trying to bleed. "I think this is going to leave a scar. Jerk."

A flashback of the attack washed over her. His filthy hands were on her face and she couldn't free herself. The momentary panic sent a jolt through her system. Her chest tightened and her breath caught.

Kathryn's hand gently touched her shoulder. "What is it?"

"I hated feeling so helpless."

"It's an awful feeling."

Jenny nodded, keeping her emotions in check. Remembering Kathryn's strength during the attack gave her strength now, like victory would always be possible, even when it seemed hopeless. "The way you took care of that guy, I can't imagine you being helpless."

Kathryn smiled. It was an odd smile, Jenny noticed, all knowing and melancholy because of it. Her eyes widened, and then she mentally slapped herself as the story she'd heard about Kathryn's imprisonment by the enemy overseas hit her like a brick. How could she have forgotten that! Of course she knew what helplessness felt like. Jenny could hardly believe it was true. It was so far removed from the woman sitting on the bed beside her getting ready to tend her wounds that it was impossible to picture her in such dire circumstances. "I'm sorry," she said.

"For what?"

Jenny was glad Kathryn couldn't read minds. "For messing up your day."

Kathryn chuckled. "If rescuing a pretty girl is the worst thing that happens in my day …"

Jenny's eyes lifted, and she sat a little straighter. Kathryn called her pretty.

She cut off a strip of white tape and attached it to a folded piece of gauze. Jenny reached for it just as Kathryn leaned in to position it over her chest.

"Oh," they both said simultaneously as their hands collided.

"I thought …" Jenny said, flustered, thinking that Kathryn was handing her the bandage.

"No, I … oh. Here." Kathryn offered the bandage, now hanging limply from her finger.

"No, no," Jenny said.

They played hot potato with the dressing for a moment, both insisting the other do the deed until, finally, their hands were a tangled bundle of tape, gauze, and fingers.

Kathryn laughed. "Nuts."

"Shit," Jenny said, as they both gave up on the mangled dressing.

Kathryn gently peeled her fingers free. "Here, let me make you a new one."

Jenny straightened out the tape. "It's okay, I've got it." She placed the bandage firmly in place over the wound and tried not to lament the lost opportunity of Kathryn's hands between her breasts. She almost laughed out loud at her desperation.

"Are you sure you don't want someone to look at that?" Kathryn asked. "That's a lot of blood for such a small wound."

"It's fine. I'm a slow clotter."

A faint crease of worry appeared in Kathryn's brow, and Jenny tried not to shake her head. Kathryn had one heck of a maternal streak hidden beneath that cool exterior. It was flattering, but, at the same time, annoying, because it made her feel even younger than her twenty-four years, and appearing younger was not the impression she wanted to give.

"You need to relax. It's just a scratch. It'll heal in no time. Look …" She turned, letting one side of her draped shirt fall from her shoulder, purposely exposing most of her chest in an effort to prove she was no mere child. "Clean bandage, no blood."

. . .

Kathryn couldn't help but grin as Jenny playfully leaned her ample bosom in her direction. It was obvious what she was trying to do, and she had to hand it to Jenny for her tenacity. Nearly at heaven's gate less than an hour ago and here she was, on the make already.

She found it endearing, as she did most of Jenny's seductive antics, and she turned her head before the blush creeping up her neck reached her face.

She gathered the discarded bandage wrappers. "Pick out a shirt."

Jenny stood and shrugged her blouse over her shoulders. Kathryn could tell Jenny was disappointed that she didn't want to play.

It wasn't that she didn't want to play. It actually took a great deal of restraint not to gently cradle her breasts in her hands and place soothing kisses on each one. She missed Jenny. She missed her honesty, her ambition, her kindness, and, yes, her endless attempts at seduction, but most of all, she missed her starry-eyed optimism. She didn't let tragedy and guilt define her as she had. She allowed purpose to carry her forward, with hope at her heels trying to keep up. Kathryn's purpose carried her forward into darkness. Jenny was the light leading her out.

It was selfish. She could only drag Jenny down with her. She'd told herself that over and over. For Jenny's own good, when her assignment to her was over, they would be over. The longing for her would cease. It was a product of her own making, after all—the legend she'd created to draw Jenny into her web while she completed her assignment. She'd done it dozens of times, but this time was different. The longing didn't cease. She pretended it had, because she was good at pretending, but the moment she saw her in danger, all the lies fell at her feet and Jenny was her beacon of hope again.

Staring at her back while she gazed into her closet with her hands on her hips, Kathryn wanted to embrace her from behind and kiss her soft neck. "I missed you," she'd say, and Jenny would turn in her arms for a long-awaited kiss. Kathryn closed her eyes and admonished herself. Hold her in your heart, not in your chains. She took a silent deep breath and let it out slowly before getting back to the matter at hand.

"See anything you like?"

"Crisp white shirt or crisp white shirt?" Jenny said with a smile.

"Hm. Not exactly the back room at Loehmann's, is it?"

"And for some reason, I thought it would be."

"You'll be disappointed to know my taste in clothes is pretty pedestrian, I'm afraid. Sorry."

Jenny chuckled. "Hm, I must have missed that day. You're always so impeccably dressed. I was expecting evening gowns and tailored suits and such."

"You want to wear an evening gown to work?"

"No, I just—" Jenny looked over her shoulder, and Kathryn smiled to let her know she was kidding.

"The gowns aren't mine. They belong to The Grotto."

"Seriously?"

"Mm. I have a few, but there's no need to keep them here. The others, Nicky gets from various designers around town. I'm just the prêt-à-porter singing mannequin."

"Nice work if you can get it."

"No complaints from this working stiff. The bulk of my personal wardrobe is at Forrester's estate right now."

She would wear a set of clothes out there, and more often than not, Forrester would have a set that he preferred laid out for her. Her clothes never seemed to make it back home. She hadn't realized how empty her closet had become.

"I've all but moved out there, it seems."

It had been Forrester's idea. Part of their new arrangement. Taking into consideration her penchant for independence, he offered her free rein of one of the guesthouses on the estate. She thanked him for his generosity, but if she was going to have free rein, she knew she would be most effective in the main house.

She convinced him that the only reason she wanted to be at the estate was because he was there, a statement that seemed to warm his icy, murderous heart. She would reside in the main house, separate bedrooms, he insisted, with an adjoining door. *Mi casa es su casa,* he announced proudly. She thanked him again but informed him that when he was away, she had no desire to stay in an empty house, adding flattering musings about the weight of his absence making the house cold and unwelcoming.

He ate it up, commenting on her strength while being drawn in and boosted by her apparent weakness for him. Her life was hers, he assured her, except—reminding her of their agreement—that his needs took precedence, to which she replied, "As they should."

"I don't spend much time here anymore. Marcus has been quite the homebody lately, so I'm glad he's out of town this week. It gives me a chance to give this place a little attention." She looked around with affection. "It's not much, but it's home, and I miss it."

Jenny turned her attention back to the closet at the mention of Forrester's name, and Kathryn sensed she didn't like the casual use of his first name. She made a mental note to refrain from doing that in her presence and rose from the bed to help find her something to wear.

Unable to resist, she casually brushed her hand along Jenny's lower back as she passed. "Let's see what we have here."

Jenny flinched at the touch.

"What is it?"

"Ticklish."

From the wince and sharp intake of breath, Kathryn knew she was lying, and she dared her to do that again with a pointed glare.

"I got slammed into the truck door handle," Jenny admitted.

"Let me see."

"Kathryn—"

Another glare had Jenny lifting her shirt to expose her back.

The area was already starting to discolor. "Dammit, Jenny, where else are you hurt, and don't you dare lie to me."

"In order of appearance ... chest, pride, back, skinned knee, elbow, scraped palm," she held it up. "That's all."

Kathryn looked up from the upheld palm with wary eyes.

"I swear."

"That back injury is nothing to play around with, Jenny. There could be internal dam—"

"Internal damage to the kidney," Jenny interrupted. "I'm well aware of that. I will be ever vigilant for unusual abdominal bloating, lightheadedness, and God forbid, blood in the urine. Will that make you happy?" She paused. "And did I mention a bruised ego to go with that wounded pride?"

Kathryn knew Jenny was trying to lighten the mood, but concern and lingering anger over the man's attack got the better of her. "Just because you're a doctor's daughter does not make you a doctor."

Jenny pulled down her shirt and looked away.

Kathryn didn't think her concern was unreasonable, but she realized she could have expressed her anxiety in a less confrontational manner. She smiled regretfully and pulled back the hand she was going to place on Jenny's shoulder as an apology. "It doesn't make you a nurse either," she said with a softer voice and a teasing lilt. "But you talk a good game."

"Yeah, that's me," Jenny said bleakly. "Maybe you should pick out a shirt for me." She moved away from the closet.

"Jenny—"

"It's okay," Jenny said. "You're right. It's nothing to fool around with, but I'm fine. I promise. Just find me a shirt and I'll be out of your hair."

All levity was gone from Jenny's voice and demeanor, and the disappointment in her eyes cut Kathryn to the core, because she'd put it there.

"If I pick out a shirt, will you promise to stop looking at me like I just kicked your dog?"

That drew a smile, and Kathryn almost felt forgiven. Almost, but not quite, as Jenny's smile disappeared again, and she didn't answer.

"I've upset you."

"No."

Kathryn ducked her head to find Jenny's eyes. "Sure?"

"Mm-hm. Just a traumatic day."

Jenny was lying again, but Kathryn let it go. She glanced at her boring closet and shut the door. "Not into crisp white, obviously. That's all right, I've got just the thing." She went to the dresser and pulled out a light knit crewneck pullover in deep sienna. "This should fit you perfectly." She held it up to Jenny's approaching form. When she reached for it with polite disinterest, Kathryn pulled the shirt away.

"You're sore at me."

Jenny crossed her arms. "I'm really not, Kathryn."

"Did I mention I abhor it when people lie to me?"

"No, but I kind of got that impression a moment ago."

Kathryn arched a challenging eyebrow. "So ... are you sore at me?"

Jenny uncrossed her arms and exhaled as she leaned her elbow on the chest-high dresser beside her. She wanted to say *yes and no*. Perhaps she was overreacting to Kathryn's protective nature, but she wanted so badly for her to ... to what? Take her seriously? Take her to lunch? Take her out to the ballgame? Take her period? All the above, she supposed.

She turned her head as she composed exactly what she wanted to say and came face-to-face with a small silver-framed black-and-white photograph of a woman that looked very much like Kathryn, albeit a few years older. She had a young child on her shoulders, and their faces were mirror images of joy, as their matching dark hair swirled in the wind while the older woman held up the youngster's hands in victory. Jenny smiled. That had to be Kathryn and her mother. "You don't have to answer," she became aware of Kathryn saying. "I know I've upset you, and I know I'm not the easiest person to get along with, but it's only because I worry about you, and—"

"What are you talking about?" Jenny interrupted, her annoyance evaporating somewhere between Kathryn's childhood photo and her apologetic face. The contrast of the exuberant innocence in the image to the pensive face before her, weary beyond its years, reminded Jenny again of Kathryn's horrible capture by the Germans, and she reprimanded herself for giving her grief over something stupid and petty. She just saved her life, and petulance was her reward?

"When you're not yelling at me, you're very easy to get along with," she said with a grin, hoping Kathryn could tell she was no longer upset. "And not too hard on the eyes either." She offered another grin before turning serious. "I'm sorry, Kathryn. I'm being obnoxious, which isn't an uncommon occurrence. I try too hard, and then I'm just *shocked* when things don't go my way. I tend to find myself irresistible, you know."

Kathryn laughed and shook her head. "You're too much."

"I hope you mean that in a good way."

"The best way."

Kathryn was smiling. Jenny took pride in her accomplishment and marveled at the years it took off Kathryn's appearance. "You've got a beautiful smile."

Kathryn pressed her lips together in an attempt to suppress the grin.

"Well, don't stop!" Jenny said, as she tugged on Kathryn's hand. She watched Kathryn's eyes settle on the black and white snapshot. She resembled the woman in the photograph even more now, the lighter moment completely changing the angular planes on her face.

"Is that your mother?"

"Mm."

"She's beautiful."

The smile instantly faded, replaced by a shadow that brought the previously shed years with it. "She died when I was 14. Killed by a drunk driver." Kathryn pursed her lips and shook her head. "I don't know why I said that last part. As if the manner of her death defined who she was in life."

"What was she like?"

Kathryn lifted her eyes to her and then to the photograph. She closed her eyes.

"She was warm and gentle. Intelligent, beautiful ..." She smiled. "Patient. The kindest soul I've ever known."

Jenny let the words linger in the air until Kathryn opened her eyes and looked at her again. She was reminded of the comfort she found in Kathryn's arms when she was upset about her father, but she didn't feel they were back to that point yet, so she just took her hand instead.

"I'm so sorry."

Kathryn nodded and looked away briefly. When she looked back, all traces of grief were gone. "We all have a story."

"I'd like to hear yours one day."

"And so you shall." She handed her the knit pullover. "Try this on."

"Thank you," Jenny said softly. She intended it to be for the pullover, but still lost in Kathryn's mesmerizing eyes, it encompassed so much more, and by Kathryn's open gaze, she knew she felt it too.

"I didn't mean to snap at you," Kathryn said. "I don't ever mean to snap at you. I just —" She cut herself off and shrugged regretfully.

"I know you don't," Jenny said. "You're just concerned, and that's awfully sweet ... it really is. It's just that it makes me feel like you think I'm a kid." She paused and shifted, suddenly feeling very childlike. "And I don't want you to think of me as a kid."

Kathryn's posture physically softened, and she reached out to tuck an errant strand of hair behind Jenny's ear. "I don't think you're a kid. Believe me."

Jenny couldn't hide her skepticism.

"*Believe* me," Kathryn emphasized with a grin as her hand slid gently down Jenny's arm.

Jenny felt the gesture to her very core and felt goose bumps rise on her arm where Kathryn touched her. Her eyesight faltered for a moment until she finally focused on the hollow at the base of Kathryn's throat, where she was mesmerized by the fluttering heartbeat evident in the shadows of the soft skin. Kathryn had to know the effect she was having, and Jenny had no intentions of letting the moment pass unacknowledged or unchallenged. She shed her ruined blouse and let it fall to the floor as she took the offered pullover.

"But do you think I'm a woman?"

. . .

Kathryn swallowed as her eyes drifted down, taking in Jenny's perfectly proportioned, toned, compact frame. "Of course," she managed to say calmly in the face of a very enticing bra clad torso. She hoped her pounding heartbeat didn't show through her lightweight shirt.

"Well ..." Jenny reached up and traced Kathryn's jawline with her index finger, stopping momentarily at the tip of her chin. "That's a start." She turned and flung the borrowed top over her bare shoulder as she left the room and walked down the hall to the bathroom with an exaggerated sway to her hips.

Kathryn watched Jenny's gorgeous back leave the room, and she soon found herself staring into empty space. She exhaled the breath she was holding as her eyes drifted to the photo on the dresser. "*She* finds herself irresistible? Good heavens. She ain't the only one."

A knock at the front door drew Kathryn out of the bedroom. As she exited the room, she offered a glance down the hall at the sound of running water behind the closed bathroom door. She traversed the length of the living room and parted the wide horizontal wooden slats on the front window to see Smitty's car on the street below. She hadn't seen much of him since her new arrangement with Forrester took effect. He'd been put on his own assignments, which kept him busy and away from her, and she knew he was probably having withdrawals over not seeing her on a regular basis. She had to admit, she missed him too.

She absently adjusted her shirt, as if she had something to hide, and opened the door with a welcoming grin. "Hi, handsome."

"Hi, dollface," he said, as he removed his hat and gave her a kiss on the cheek. "How's things?"

"Twice as good as they were yesterday but not as bad as they could be tomorrow," she said, stepping aside to let him enter.

"Do you know where Jenny Ryan is?"

Kathryn closed the door and followed him into the room, putting herself between him and the bathroom down the hallway. "Gee, Smitty. It's swell to see you too. Why do you ask?"

"She's AWOL uptown. Folks are getting worried."

"So you came to me?"

He grinned. "I came to you because I miss your funny face. Jenny Ryan's whereabouts are merely a curiosity to me."

"I already called in. She—"

Jenny's quick, light step coming down the hall interrupted her speech, and Smitty's eyes widened. Kathryn's heart rate quickened. Please let her have that top on.

"Say, Kat—" Jenny began before she realized there was someone else in the room. "Oh. Hello."

"Well," Smitty drew out, his brow planted firmly in his hairline as he watched Jenny smooth the pullover over her skirt waistband.

"It's not what you think," Kathryn said, relieved that Jenny was dressed, at least.

"What do I think, Kat?" he asked with a smirk.

"Yeah. What *does* he think, Kat?" Jenny chimed in.

Kathryn chuckled and rubbed her forehead. "Jenny Ryan, meet John Smith."

Jenny held out her hand. "How do you—" She stopped, recognition playing across her face. "Say, you're that fellow from that night. The accident. You took us to the hospital."

"That'd be me."

"I never did get a chance to thank you."

"No thanks necessary."

Jenny noticed he was looking affectionately at Kathryn as he spoke, and she, in return, had an odd grin on her face.

"Smitty is our resident hero," Kathryn said. "He's my partner. He watches my back."

"Was your partner," he said, a touch of melancholy in his voice.

Jenny saw something between them, a history that went beyond a working relationship. She found herself envying it. Not in a jealous way, more like a longing, wanting to have that closeness to convey whole conversations and a range of emotions with just a look. She had that with Bernie, but she wanted that with Kathryn. John Smith was a lucky man.

Kathryn placed a sympathetic hand on Smitty's chest, and Jenny marveled at the instant comfort it appeared to bring him.

"So," Smitty said, "What *is* going on here?"

Jenny decided it would be best if she let Kathryn tell the tale, so she looked expectantly in her direction to find she'd already taken the lead.

"Jenny found herself in a bit of trouble. It got a little dicey. A blouse gave its life to the cause, and I'm just lending a hand."

"You're being modest. She saved my life."

"Lucky you," Smitty said, but he was looking at Kathryn when he said it.

"Yes. Lucky me," Jenny said.

"I was just getting ready to drive her uptown."

Smitty frowned. "It's not Friday. You shouldn't go to HQ."

Jenny looked to Kathryn for clarification, but she paused a beat before answering.

"If they're watching, then they already know she's here. It won't make any difference. I'm just driving her to her ad agency job, for all they know."

"Are they watching?" Smitty asked.

"I didn't see them today."

"I'm sorry," Jenny interrupted, "who's watching whom and why?"

Kathryn looked to Smitty, as if she needed permission to explain. He merely shrugged, as if it were up to her.

"Sometimes Forrester has me followed."

Jenny reflexively clenched her fists. "Why?"

Kathryn looked at Smitty again. "Because he can."

It was a stupid question. Of course he would try to possess her. "Look, if it's going to get you into trouble, I'll call a cab."

Smitty looked at his watch while Kathryn hesitated. "Haven't you got a rehearsal pretty soon?"

Kathryn glanced at the clock on the bookcase. "Nuts," she said under her breath.

"It's okay," Jenny said with a raised hand that didn't quite reach Kathryn's arm. "I'll take a cab."

"I'll take you in," Smitty said, asking permission with a quick glance to both. "Do you mind?"

Jenny smiled. "Handsome man, friend of yours ... not at all. I'll get my things."

"Thanks for doing this, Smitty," Kathryn whispered as Jenny walked down the hall to the bedroom.

"Didn't my mom give you that top?"

"It was too small."

"I didn't think so."

"Well, you wouldn't. You gave her the size."

"Like I said ..."

Kathryn shook her head.

Jenny emerged with her purse. "Okay."

"I owe you a ride uptown."

"I'll hold you to that."

"I'm sure you will."

Kathryn found herself at an awkward goodbye again, made even more awkward by Smitty's very interested gaze. Jenny seemed hesitant too, but she moved in for a quick hug, which Kathryn accepted, albeit self-consciously, much to Smitty's amusement.

"Thanks for the rescue," Jenny said with a wink as she backed away. "Shall we?" She touched Smitty's arm as she passed on the way to the door.

Smitty gave Kathryn a *get her* eye roll, and Kathryn gave him her well-practiced *don't start* look in return. He followed Jenny out the door and down the steps.

"So, John, how long have you known Kathryn?" Jenny began before they were even out of earshot. Smitty threw a mischievous grin over his shoulder, and Kathryn thumped her head on her doorjamb. "Ugh."

Sending them off together was a bad idea. She could just imagine Jenny with her thousand questions and Smitty with his smart-ass replies. She was doomed.

CHAPTER FOUR

Kathryn had barely entered the club when the bartender, Bobby, handed her the telephone.

"For you, Miss Hammond."

"Thanks." She tucked the phone between her shoulder and chin as she rolled up her sleeve. "Yes?"

"That kid," Smitty's irritated voice began without ceremony, "did not shut up from the second we walked out of your apartment till the second I left her inquisitive rear end on the sidewalk in front of headquarters."

Kathryn laughed. "You volunteered."

"Mother mercy. Why didn't you warn me?"

"She has to be experienced to be appreciated. What did she talk about?" Like she needed to ask.

"Well, let's see," Smitty began, as if a synopsis of *War and Peace* were to follow. "First, she asked about you, then she asked about you, and when she got tired of asking about you, she asked about you some more."

Kathryn grinned from ear to ear, partially because she knew Jenny would get no satisfactory answers from Smitty and partially because she was flattered. The mental image of Jenny chewing her lip as she decided which tact to choose in her futile expository effort was almost as clear as the mental image of Smitty's aggravated face on the other end of the line.

"And what did you tell her?"

"I fed her a steady diet of 'ask her yourself.'"

"Good boy."

"She's got it bad for you now, Kat. Do me a favor and don't sic your conquests on me so soon after you've ravaged them. It leaves them in that delirious *I must know everything* haze."

"I didn't ravage anyone."

"Uh-huh. A helping hand always necessitates a trip to your apartment in the middle of the afternoon to exchange clothing. You forget who you're talking to."

"For your information, Sherlock, she got herself into some trouble—"

"What a surprise!" he broke in.

"Down at the plant," she finished slowly.

"Yeah, she probably opened her big mouth."

"Smitty?" she said patiently, not appreciating his venomous glee.

He paused at her odd tone. "Yeah?"

"If I had ravaged her, do you think she would have had the energy to talk your ear off all the way up town?"

There was silence through the receiver, and she imagined him conjuring up a mental image of the act in question.

"Smitty?"

"Kathryn?" he said, as if he were surprised she was on the other end of the line.

"Yes?"

"Is that you? Because if I didn't know better, I'd say that last remark was meant to be humorous."

"I was just helping her out of a jam."

"I'm not even going to ask you how you got involved in that."

"Just lucky, I guess."

"So she said."

There was an uncomfortable silence, and she sensed his disapproval.

"It was pure happenstance, Smitty."

"Did I say anything?"

"Not in so many words."

"You know where your boundaries are."

"I do. Thank you."

"Okay, then."

She was glad it was a definitive statement rather than an accusation. It was obvious he was worried and still had lingering doubts about the wisdom of any relationship she might have with Jenny Ryan, but she had to give him credit for his attempt to mask it. His reaction also gave her a sense of Jenny's frustration with her displays of concern, suddenly recognizing how easily they can be misconstrued as a lack of confidence in one's abilities. She made a mental note to be more aware of Jenny's sensibilities in that regard and vowed to be more conscious of her own.

"I'll be careful, Smitty."

"I know," he said. "By the way, she told me she has a ride home tonight and not to worry about it."

"Oh."

That was disappointing and confusing. Maybe Jenny felt she had been pawned off on Smitty, mistaking the gesture as relief rather than necessity. Maybe she had barked at her one too many times. She couldn't really blame her if she wanted to wash her hands of her. Their relationship, such as it was, had not been the smoothest, and no one gets unlimited chances to get it right.

"Anyway," Smitty said, "I hear the band warming up in the background. I'll let you get back to it. I just had to vent."

"Thanks for sharing. Glad I could help."

"How long will you be home this time?"

"Forrester is out of town until Friday, so the rest of the week."

"Call me when you're free for dinner. I'm having withdrawals."

She laughed. "Will do."

"See you soon, honey."

. . .

Rehearsal was slow and plodding, with Dominic Vignelli overseeing the addition of two new songs to his club's lineup. He could be very particular about the arrangements on occasion, and today was one of those days. Fortunately, he had the perfect bandleader for his temperament. Jimmy Laine had the patience of a saint when it came to the club owner's particular sense of what should be.

Kathryn kept her mouth shut as she watched Jimmy rearrange timing, key, and tablature in an attempt to satisfy Dominic's cheery interpretation of a relatively moody song. Jimmy was the third bandleader in her relatively short tenure at the club, and she had learned there was no point arguing the composer's original intent with the boss. He had fired people for less, and while she had no fear of being fired for speaking her mind, she knew it was a fruitless argument.

Thankfully, Dominic didn't interfere often. He paid handsomely to have the best people around him, and, for the most part, he let them do their jobs. But when he had a vision, he had a vision. Sometimes the results were brilliant, like the song they had hammered out earlier in the day, but other times, Kathryn just had to grin and bear it, all the while cringing at the sacrilege of it all.

The background singers gathered for the four-part harmony arrangement, and the group went about their work like the professionals they were, much to the delight of the boss.

CHAPTER FIVE

The telephone rang on Jenny's desk, interrupting her work on a black propaganda article about Nazi troop movements. She knew it could only be one person. "Jenny Bug!" Bernie said through the handset.

"Hi, you!" Jenny said. The photographer was cheerful as ever—a constant in the universe—and one of the few things she missed from the *Daily Chronicle*.

"Are you running that ad agency yet? You've got a secretary, for crying out loud! *Please hold for Miss Ryan,*" he said and then giggled.

"She's the secretary for the department, Bernie, not my personal secretary." She looked up and winked at the OSS employee parked at the desk adjacent to hers. He smiled as he gathered some papers and disappeared into the busy office, leaving her to her phone call.

She had never lied to Bernie about anything in her life—ever—and while she knew he was as patriotic as the next guy, he was not really one to keep his tongue when the drinks flowed, and that made her decision to deceive him about her employment a little easier to swallow. It was for the good of the country, after all.

"Sure you don't want to come back to the *Chronicle*?" he asked.

"Ever since you left, your uncle has been grumpier than a horny toad in a shoebox."

"And how is Cal?" Jenny asked about his southern boyfriend.

"He's wonderful. We miss you."

"I miss you too. It's just been crazy with the new job and everything."

"Say, listen, why don't I come over for a late lunch?"

She had to think quick. "I've already had lunch. Why don't I come over to the *Chronicle* tomorrow? I've got to make nice with Uncle Paul anyway. The benefit is Friday night."

"Jeepers crow, that's right. You're his date."

"Well, I don't know about that. I'll see if I can patch things up. I'm still plenty ticked."

"A month is a long time to hold a grudge, even for you."

"He was wrong, Bernie. He's just too damn stubborn to admit it."

Bernie paused, and Jenny knew he was biting back a comment about her stubborn streak.

"You know he'd give you your job back in a second. He hasn't even filled your desk. It just sits there …" He paused dramatically. "Like a barren reminder of your once radiant light."

Jenny chuckled. "Are you sure you don't want to come and work here? We could use your particular brand of BS on our latest account." Who knew lying was so easy.

"Ha, ha. Those Madison Avenue dopes can't afford my brilliance."

"Pardon me while I get a shovel. It's getting a little deep in here."

She heard Bernie's laughter trail away from the receiver as someone called his name in the background.

"Nuts. I've got to run. Tomorrow at noon?"

"I'll be there."

"Love ya, hon."

"Love you too, sweetie."

"Final run-throughs!" Jenny heard someone shout as she entered the nightclub section of The Grotto. She could see Kathryn taking her place on stage in front of the microphone as the bandleader raised his hand and counted a silent rhythm in the air. She saw Dominic sitting at a table in the back, newspapers, receipts, and ledgers spread before him in controlled disarray. He pulled on the cigar wrapped in his thick forefinger as he stretched out his legs in apparent satisfaction.

Jenny moved over to where he was sitting and gently placed a hand on his shoulder. "Hi, Mr. Vignelli," she whispered.

"Ah, Miss Jenny," he said in a hushed tone, a little startled. He seemed confused for a moment at her presence on a late Monday afternoon, when they were closed, but he ventured a glance at the stage and smiled.

"Sit down here," he said, as he closed the ledger book and moved the papers aside.

Jenny complied. "The band sounds fantastic."

"A special arrangement," he said, beaming with pride.

Jenny's eyes drifted to center stage, where Kathryn performed her craft flawlessly, clad in her staple white blouse and a tight-fitting navy blue skirt.

"Listen to her," Dominic said. "Now listen carefully to the music." He tilted his head toward the sound.

Jenny did her best to tune out Kathryn's vocal, and to her surprise, she found the band appeared to be playing a totally unrelated song to the melody Kathryn carried so effortlessly above them. She looked at Dominic in amazement. "Wow."

"Mm-hm. She alone carries the melody."

Jenny knew very little about the mechanics of making music—other than she couldn't carry a tune without the music to keep her on pitch—but even she knew this feat was impressive, especially with a band playing something else in your ear.

She felt a spring of pride well up in her. This amazing singer was a friend of hers. She'd be more than a friend if she had anything to say about it. She turned to Dominic to speak and found him staring at her with a knowing smile. She blushed and felt she owed him an explanation for her presence.

"Kat owes me a ride home tonight."

Dominic's grin widened, telling Jenny all she needed to know about his comprehension of the situation.

They watched the rest of the set in silence until the last song, when Dominic turned to her.

"You like?"

"Well," Jenny said, trying to think of something to say without offending the man. "I don't think I've ever heard 'Stormy Weather' so ... optimistically cheerful."

"Ah! Perfect!" he said. "There is enough sadness in this world, no? You want to be blue? You go to the club across town." He thumbed dismissively over his shoulder. "We are happy here." He clasped his hands together. "Nothing but happy."

A lovely sentiment, Jenny admitted to herself, but an upbeat version of "Stormy Weather"?

"She hates this arrangement," he said, pointing to Kathryn, who was smiling valiantly through cheery note after cheery note, sung in perfect harmony with the backup singers.

Jenny laughed out loud, imagining Kathryn suppressing an eye roll, and then quickly covered her mouth and a muffled apology.

Kathryn went through the motions of the song but felt nothing for it. Dominic had sacrificed the emotion of the lyrics for the joyful exuberance of the arrangement. Kathryn had done the same in her own life.

Every day she played along, dragging the appropriate emotions from memory to appear moved on the outside, but she cared for very little, except for her music. In her music, she could feel again. Live again. Music was truth, and from it poured her soul. For her, it was the purest form of communication she'd found. So much so, she felt inadequate expressing herself any other way.

She was momentarily annoyed with Dominic. His bastardized

creation interfered with her only source of joy. Her irritation was interrupted by a familiar laugh, warm and inviting. Okay, so music wasn't her only source of joy. Her heart lifted at the sound of Jenny's laughter, and her mood lightened immediately. She finished the song and, with it rehearsal, and left the stage, making her way to where Jenny and Dominic were engrossed in conversation.

"Hi," Jenny said with a full-faced grin when she arrived.

"Hi. What are you doing here?" Kathryn replied coolly, then regretted her tone, which came out all wrong, in an attempt to mask her delight at finding Jenny at the club.

Jenny's enthusiasm seemed unaffected. "I'm here to take you to dinner, and then you're going to drive me home."

Kathryn raised a surprised brow. "Oh?"

"That was the deal, right?" Jenny asked in a tone that said the only answer was yes.

"Well, yes. That was the deal." Dinner was new, but she didn't mind at all. "I didn't expect you. Smitty said you had a ride home."

"Yes. You."

"Ah."

"Have you made other plans?"

"Oh, no." Kathryn smiled cheerfully, overcompensating in the opposite direction. "Let me change and I'll be right down."

"Lovely job today, Kathryn," Dominic said. "Thank you."

She threw a warm smile over her shoulder as she walked away, no longer irritated by the song. "Anything for you, Nicky."

"Judas priest," Jenny said, watching Kathryn descend the stairs from her dressing room. "Pedestrian my—" she left the rest of the sentence to Dominic's imagination.

"You don't like?" he asked about Kathryn's attire.

"What's not to like?"

Kathryn wore a perfectly tailored dark gray jacket and skirt, with a matching thigh-length cape that draped from her broad shoulder pads. A billowed red blouse with small white polka dots peeked out from her suit's low-cut collar, and a beautiful sterling silver brooch embedded with red stones surrounded by delicate silver rose petals resided on her oversized lapel.

"Pedestrian?" Dominic asked.

"She claims to have pedestrian taste in clothes."

Dominic nearly choked on his drink and gestured at Kathryn's approaching form. "That beautiful lady wouldn't know pedestrian if she tripped over it on the sidewalk. She was born to wear clothes, and she has only the finest." He admired the outfit. "Her clothes are designed especially for her, you know. Part of our arrangement." He nodded, as if Jenny knew what he was talking about. "Now, if only you could convince her she can keep them." He smiled and stood as Kathryn reached the table.

"Absolutely stunning, my dear," he said, as he needlessly adjusted the cape and brushed an imaginary speck of dust from her shoulder.

"Tell Anita it's beautiful. Ready, Jenny?"

"Mm-hm."

"Good night, Nicky."

"Have fun, ladies."

"Oh, we will," Jenny said.

Kathryn threw a glance over her shoulder to find Dominic shaking his head with a grin.

CHAPTER SIX

The supper club was more expensive than Jenny's first choice for dinner, but one look at Kathryn in her haute couture best and she knew Wan's House of Noodles would not do.

Kathryn released her cape from the oversized buttons hidden under her large lapels and handed it to the waiting coat check girl as the hostess prepared to lead them to their table.

"I've got to make a quick phone call. Be right with you," Kathryn said. Jenny nodded and followed the hostess to the table.

It wasn't a large club—nowhere near the exclusivity and opulence of The Grotto—but it held a special place in her heart as one of her father's favorite hangouts. They would have dinner together or just meet for drinks at least once a week.

She hadn't been back since his death, fearing a lack of strength against a loss still too painful to bear, but she took Kathryn dressed to the nines as a sign. Tonight was special, a new beginning. She wasn't sure how she knew it would be okay, but she did, and maybe, part of her had to admit, she just wanted to show off her date. She felt invincible, comfortable, on home turf, and she figured she could use every advantage she could get.

. . .

In Kathryn's experience, any place with the word lounge in the title usually had sleaze oozing from every floorboard, but she liked the intimate nature of this one. The Blue Note Lounge was one of the nicer clubs of that ilk, and while not particularly fond of her memories of the working conditions, she appreciated the experience afforded her by singing there occasionally in the early days of her career in the city. Not much had changed, including the piecemeal nature of the band on stage.

Even in the dim lighting, she was aware of heads turning as she made her way to Jenny's table, and she ignored the looks, as she always did, focusing instead on Jenny's bright face, illuminated by the small lamp on the table. Her smile stretched ear to ear, and Kathryn couldn't help but feel her delight and respond in kind.

The band had just finished a number when a waving trumpet from the stage caught her eye and momentarily distracted her from her destination. Tommy Wallace was one of the best horns in town. The eternal boy with a quick smile and boundless energy. He also had a heroin addiction that caused him to lose his job at The Grotto. Rumor had it he was now clean, his first child his inspiration.

She made a detour toward the stage and smiled as she recognized a few of the musicians. The band, at its core, was made up of steady session players that made the sound cohesive, but the rest were fill-in drifters or fellows looking for a second chance. Tommy greeted her at the base of the stage with open arms.

"T," she said as she embraced him. "How are you?"

He knew what she was asking. "One day at a time, gal. One day at a time."

"That's it, man," she said with an encouraging squeeze to both arms. His eyes were clear and his demeanor told her he was indeed clean—for now. She'd never seen anyone as hooked as he was stay clean for long, but she'd always heard parenthood was a life-altering experience. Never planning to test that theory, she could only hope for his sake that it was.

"Sit in?" he asked, thumbing toward the stage. "Be just like old times."

"Dinner with a friend," she said, tilting her head in Jenny's direction.

He looked over her shoulder and wiggled his eyebrows in approval.

Kathryn glanced at the empty microphone on stage. "Who's your stand-up?"

"Bill Connelly."

"Good grief," she said, looking around in case he overheard. "Who's holding the leash these days?"

"The clarinet."

"Good choice. Subtle. It's working, I take it?"

"Eh." Tommy shrugged. "The acoustics are so bad in this place, no one notices. Besides, folks come here for the four-star food, not the music."

"Nonsense. I heard the boys when I came in. Tight. Good group."

"You should come jam with us sometime, angel. We could use a real artist at the loudspeaker for a change."

The empty microphone came to life with a distinctly annoyed clearing of the throat as Bill Connelly glared down his nose at the AWOL trumpet player. Tommy acknowledged the cue with a wave and a covert roll of his eyes.

Kathryn embraced him. "Have fun," she whispered in his ear. "You look and sound great. It's so good to see you."

His look of appreciation told her it meant a lot that she cared.

She weaved her way back to the table, and Jenny's smile broadened, something Kathryn didn't think was possible. She almost looked over her shoulder to see what was so wonderful.

"Friends of yours?" Jenny asked.

"I've worked with some," Kathryn said, as she tucked her skirt under her legs and settled into her chair.

"You worked here?"

"Sporadically. A long time ago."

Jenny knit her brow. "Well, I've been coming here for ages. I think I'd remember you."

"I doubt it," Kathryn said as she glanced at the menu. "Completely forgettable performances all."

Jenny snorted audibly as she picked up her menu and dropped the subject. Kathryn could tell by the subtle shake of her head that her answer annoyed her.

"So, what's good here?" she asked, unable to think of anything else to say.

"Everything."

Kathryn cringed into her menu, hoping Jenny would have more than that to say. She would soon regret that wish, as Jenny went on to dissect the menu: every dish's pros and cons, what she liked, what she didn't like, what her father liked, her aunt liked, her uncle, and on and on. When the menu ceased to offer a subject of conversation, she hit the latest on the food rationing front, droning on about the virtues of white potatoes verses sweet potatoes, and somehow winding up on government subsidies to the watermelon farmer. She was mercifully interrupted by the restaurant owner.

"Miss Ryan!" Joe Radcliff beamed. "So good to see you again." He hadn't even taken the appropriate two breaths before the obligatory, "Terribly sorry about your father."

Kathryn lifted her eyes to Jenny's face, as the statement lingered too long without further elaboration or reply.

"Hi, Joe," she said, causing Jenny to look her way in relief.

"Kathryn!" He turned with equal enthusiasm. He leaned in close, stealing a peck on the cheek. "Please tell me you've left that pretentious club on the hill and you want a job."

"Just dinner." She smiled at Jenny, who now seemed unaffected by the remark about her father.

He straightened. "Well then, just for you—" He snapped his fingers at a waiter, who appeared immediately. "A bottle of our finest, on the house, for my two favorite ladies. Red or white?"

Kathryn deferred to Jenny.

"White."

"Very good." He snapped his fingers again, though he needn't have, as the waiter was already on his way, snapping his own fingers, which set off a chain reaction of some unspoken *get the best wine in the house, pronto* train.

Joe placed his hands on their shoulders, creating a bridge between the women. "Enjoy." He gave a squeeze and headed for a table across the room. "Mrs. Haines—" his voice trailed off.

"We're not his favorites anymore," Jenny said with a mock pout as she watched him go through the identical greeting with whom she assumed was Mrs. Haines.

"Nor will we get the finest wine in the house," Kathryn said.

A waiter showed up with the bottle in question, and Jenny raised a brow at the vintage.

"Look at that ... it *is* the best wine in the house."

Kathryn registered the same surprise. "Well, well. Joe must be getting soft in his old age."

Jenny accepted the sample glass, sniffing and sipping like she'd done it a thousand times before. She nodded her approval, thanked the waiter by name, and Kathryn realized she probably had done it a thousand times before. Her pedigree was showing, and it made Kathryn smile.

Jenny raised her glass. "Here's to new beginnings."

"How many times are we going to start over?"

"Until we get it right."

Kathryn smiled and clinked Jenny's glass with hers. "I'll drink to that."

They ordered their meal, and Jenny tried to think of something to talk about that didn't make her sound like a babbling idiot. Engaging Kathryn in a conversation that required answers in paragraphs instead of simple sentences wasn't easy. So far, their relationship consisted of flirting, emotional turmoil, and life and death scenarios. She never felt more alive than in Kathryn's presence, but she never felt more intimidated either. Kathryn was gorgeous, talented, self-assured, and what the hell was she doing here with her? They had nothing in common. They both worked for the OSS, but they couldn't discuss that in private, let alone in public. Disregarding the frantic rescue at the plant, this was their first casual get together since the gun incident, and Kathryn seemed reserved and distracted.

The stage held her interest, where the band was about to launch into a new song, and Jenny wondered if an evening at a supper club was a mistake. The song intro started, and Kathryn smiled in what Jenny assumed was recognition and then turned away with a smirk as the singer began his part. When Kathryn's eyes locked with hers, the smirk faded and her face relaxed into a vacant daydream. The glow of the small lamp on the table revealed none of the facial tension of the moments before, and Jenny warmed to this peaceful Kathryn, a woman she'd only seen in repose on her couch.

The suspended moment lasted so long that Jenny felt self-conscious in the public setting. She had no idea how it was affecting Kathryn's libido, but Jenny had tingly feelings in inappropriate places, and a warm rush to her face made her glad for the low lighting in the club.

When would Kathryn look away? Jenny tried to make it a staring game, but when her arousal increased and her breathing became shallow, she broke eye contact and reached for her wineglass. She had to think of a conversation topic fast.

"That John is a nice fellow," she said, and then took a sip.

Blue eyes blinked, and the tension returned to Kathryn's face. "Yes."

"He loves you, you know."

"I love him too."

"No, I mean he *loves* you."

Kathryn reached for her own glass but left it on the table and merely twirled the stem between her fingers. "I know."

Her reply was apprehensive, and Jenny took the hint to drop that line of questioning.

"I'm afraid he doesn't care much for me."

"Why do you say that?"

"I can tell."

Kathryn chuckled. "That must have been some ride across town. What did you talk about?"

"You, mostly. Not that I got anything out of him, mind you, but sometimes what you don't say says more about the subject than what you do say."

"Is that right?"

"Mm-hm." Jenny said. "And I'm pretty good at reading people."

"I see. And are you reading me right now?"

"Loud and clear."

Kathryn raised her brow. "And what am I thinking?"

Jenny made a furtive glance around them and then leaned in for privacy. "You're thinking, my God, when did this woman steal my heart?"

She didn't know if it was the wide-eyed horror or the hard swallow that surprised her more, but Kathryn seemed paralyzed.

"Oh, dear," Jenny said, leaning back. "That hit a soft spot."

Kathryn blinked, as more tension gathered on her brow.

Jenny's confidence slipped with every passing uncomfortable moment. She had nothing to lose, so honesty seemed like the best option. "I realize I'm talking nonstop and monopolizing the conversation, but you're not saying anything, and I'm a little nervous."

She was happy to see Kathryn smile at that.

"What have you got to be nervous about?"

"Oh, only that I'm having dinner with the most beautiful woman in town."

Kathryn looked away with a snort of disapproval as she shifted in her seat. "You don't get around much."

"You know," Jenny said, as she straightened her already straight dinner napkin across her lap, "I'm getting a little tired of having my compliments thrown back in my face. If you're not careful, I'll stop giving them."

Perhaps she needed to work on her delivery, because by Kathryn's concerned expression, the humorous intent didn't come through. Jenny slid her glass of water across the table. "You don't corner the market on dry humor."

Kathryn smiled, and Jenny was glad she recognized her own dry humor turned on her. It didn't change her attitude, however.

"There are a lot of beautiful women in town," she said, modest as ever.

"And you're one of them." Jenny stared her down, daring her to disagree.

Kathryn nodded in resignation. "Thank you."

"There. That wasn't so bad."

Her brief triumph disappeared when Kathryn's head tilted appraisingly and her eyes gave her the once over.

"I don't think I got the chance to tell you this afternoon, but that top looks great on you."

Jenny glanced down at the borrowed knit pullover and smiled. "Thank you."

"It brings out the subtle reds in your hair."

Jenny touched her hair, liking the direction of the conversation. "No one ever notices the subtle red."

"That's probably because they're mesmerized by your beautiful eyes."

Jenny slid her hand to her neck as heat rushed to her face. "Kathryn," she whispered, looking around in embarrassment, as if Kathryn had shouted it from the rooftops.

"It's true," Kathryn said.

Jenny squirmed under Kathryn's intense gaze. "Thank you."

"That compliment-taking business isn't always so easy, is it?"

"I'll live."

Kathryn continued looking right into her, it seemed, and Jenny's heartbeat quickened while that wave of arousal swelled again. She tried not to give into it, but when her nipples hardened against her form-fitting sweater, she knew she'd better start a diversion before Kathryn caught on. She crossed her arms to hide the obvious and leaned onto the table, casually glancing at the stage. "He's got a nice voice."

"Mm."

Kathryn continued staring, and Jenny was a last-ditch effort away from suggesting a more private venue for their evening.

"Is that singer leering at you?"

"Probably."

"Is there a story?"

Kathryn finally turned down the intensity, flicking a dismissive glance at the crooner. "There's always a story."

"Care to share?"

"We were both backup singers at The Grotto."

"You were a *backup* singer?" Jenny asked in disbelief. "What a waste."

"Not too long ago, most singers were backups," Kathryn said. "Music was all about the band. You can thank the AFM's ban on studio recordings for singers finally getting their due. Evidently, they don't consider singers musicians, so the ban doesn't apply to us."

Jenny stared back blankly, more out of surprise than a lack of understanding. Kathryn had just uttered four whole sentences, one after the other.

"American Federation of Musicians," Kathryn clarified.

"Not a fan of unions at the moment," Jenny said. "Especially ones that don't consider you a musician."

"Well, when the strike began a year ago, it was because of the inequality of pay to exposure. Gigs were becoming scarce for the musicians because canned music is everywhere … radio, films, jukeboxes … who needs a live band when you can reach for a record?

"I mean, the real rub is the radio station. More than half of all music broadcast is from recordings. That includes songs, serials, commercials …" she ticked the items off on her fingers. "They have unrestricted use of those recordings, jukeboxes too. It's all about royalties."

Jenny tried not to smile. She loved listening to Kathryn go on about something mundane for a change.

"The kicker is that with the demand for canned music on the rise, the record and transcription companies were throwing millions at the industry, boosting the federation's coffers, and still they issue a recording ban. Wrong approach, if you ask me, but that's Petrillo for you." She shook her head at the union leader's stubbornness. "He's killing the big band, and he just can't see—" Kathryn stopped abruptly. "Sorry, that was incredibly boring. I don't recall you asking for a dissertation on the state of the musicians' union."

"Not at all," Jenny said, embarrassed that her dreamy stare had telegraphed boredom. "It's fascinating."

"Uh-huh. What was your question again?"

"You were going to tell me why that singer is leering at you."

"Good heavens, I did go off, didn't I?" She picked up her glass of wine and settled back into her chair. "He thinks I got him fired from The Grotto."

"Did you?"

Kathryn chuckled into her drink. "He got fired because he can't sing on key."

Jenny looked to the stage. He seemed on key, but what did she know.

"Listen carefully," Kathryn said. "Listen to the arrangement. Just before he hits his note, the clarinet hits it first. He's taking his cues from there. He couldn't stay on tune otherwise."

"Is that bad? I mean ... it sounds okay."

"Sure," Kathryn said with a shrug, "if you can find a band to play that game and a club owner who doesn't care. That's not The Grotto."

It occurred to Jenny that she had insulted Kathryn by saying that someone of such obvious inferior talent was fit to sing for public consumption.

"Sorry, I didn't mean—"

"Don't be silly. As long as he's not on a stage with me, I couldn't care less what he does or how he does it."

Jenny noticed that her attitude was hostile, and she wondered if there hadn't been something between them at one time. He was handsome, and the women in the audience paid him more attention than his vocal abilities deserved because of it. She wouldn't ask Kathryn if she had more than just a working relationship with him, but she apparently couldn't hide the thought from her wrinkled brow.

"There's no personal history there," Kathryn said, as she picked up her drink. "Not really."

"Not really?"

"He had a standing bet with the band that he could get me into bed. His attempts became tiresome."

"And?"

"And he lost a lot of money. I don't sleep with people I work with."

Jenny sat back in her chair and grinned. "Well, thank goodness we're not working together."

Kathryn's eyes snapped up from her drink as she swallowed a laugh. "Why, Miss Ryan, what are your intentions this evening?"

Jenny smiled innocently. "I don't know that I have any, Miss Hammond."

"Hm, how unusual."

Just the thought of an evening that involved more than a courtesy ride home brought another wave of heat, and Jenny dropped her eyes to her glass and pushed it around in small circles.

"Slumming, Kat?" she heard a deep male voice say. A hand appeared on Kathryn's shoulder. It was Bill Connelly, fresh from the stage, holding a drink.

"Yeah, Bill. Slumming's a habit of mine," Kathryn replied in a bored tone. "Nice gig for you."

"And you said talent like mine wouldn't fill a thimble and that I had no hope of ever headlining."

"If I recall correctly, Bill, my hand was squeezing the life out of your manhood in response to your hand on my ass, and when I said fill a thimble, it wasn't your talent I was referring to."

Jenny raised her brow and suppressed a snort.

"Why, I—" He laughed uncomfortably as he looked helplessly her way. "She's such a kidder."

"Yeah, a real comedian," Kathryn said impatiently, "and if you don't stop rubbing my shoulder, in the very near future, you may be able to reach those high notes. It could take your career in a whole new direction."

There was something playfully evil in Kathryn's voice, and Bill Connelly removed his hand like it was touching fire.

"I did say you'd never headline, though, and here you are, so I sincerely apologize for my lack of vision."

"Well, I— Joe!" He said awkwardly as the club owner approached. "Look. It's Kat Hammond."

"I know," Joe said. "Have you convinced her to sing?"

Joe's suggestion didn't sit well with the crooner. He shifted uncomfortably and put his arm around the owner's shoulder, trying to stammer out a reason Kathryn shouldn't sing.

"Joe, you don't understand. Miss Hammond is a perfectionist. She doesn't sing anything without practicing it for at least two weeks in advance."

Jenny realized it wasn't a compliment, but Kathryn took it with her usual indifference.

"She's incapable of spontaneous musicianship, you see."

Jenny eyed Kathryn for a reaction and found none. She looked back to the smug lounge lizard and regretted ever giving him a compliment. "Listen you," she said, fed up with his attitude.

Kathryn threw her napkin on the table. "Excuse me a moment, will you, Jenny?"

Bill Connelly moved behind the club owner as Kathryn rose from her seat, no doubt afraid for the existence of his future children. She headed toward the stage as Joe grinned ear to ear.

"Hey!" Bill said, slightly panicked. "You can't do that. You have a contract."

She threw a dismissive smirk over her shoulder and continued on.

"She can't do that, Joe," he said to his boss.

Joe ignored him and rubbed his greedy hands together as he wandered to the bar to enjoy the show. Bill dropped into Kathryn's empty seat and stared forlornly at her back. "She can't do that," he said more to himself than Jenny. "She's got a contract. She opens her mouth on that stage and she's as good as unemployed."

Jenny was sure Kathryn knew what she was doing, and she didn't see what the big deal was from Bill's point of view. Whether Kathryn violated her contract with The Grotto was no concern of his, but as she watched him pull out his handkerchief and wipe a field of sweat from his brow, she realized he feared for *his* job, not Kathryn's. His eyes shifted nervously from Kathryn, about to go on stage, to his boss, waiting at the bar.

"Oh, baby!" Tommy Wallace beamed as he jumped to his feet and offered his hand. "You just made my night, sugar."

Kathryn let him pull her up on stage to the complaint of the bass player.

"What is this, amateur night?" he said. "It's bad enough we have to be sidemen to the likes of Bill Connelly."

"You ain't from around here, are you, brother?" the drummer said while extending his hand. "Hi ya, honey."

"Good to see you, Drum," Kathryn said with a grin as she shook his hand. She always found it amusing that his name was Drummond and he played the drums. She nodded and waved to the rest of the band before turning and offering a questioning glance to the leader, who was also the piano player.

"What's your pleasure, Kat?" the pianist asked from across his instrument.

"I don't want to be too much trouble. What's next on the sheet?"

"'Blues in the Night.' C."

She exchanged a smirk with the pianist at the C major key—the kindergarten of keys, and perfect for Bill Connelly—and held out her hand for a look at the arrangement. She extended a long, shapely leg behind her as she reached across the piano to take it, which brought a low hum of approval from the audience and a wolf whistle or two.

The bass player rolled his eyes as she took the music. She understood his apprehension, having seen her share of singers stand front and center, fumbling with sheet music as they tried to bluff their way through an unfamiliar arrangement. That wouldn't happen tonight. She offered him a curt smile and returned the arrangement to the pianist. She'd seen all she needed to see to fake with the best of them.

"How 'bout B flat, and make it sassy. I'll follow you. I know you're used to that around here." She offered a glance in Bill's direction to snickers of agreement from the band.

"Don't you worry about us, honey," the leader said. "You just sing … we won't let you fall."

She nodded. This was either going to be brilliant or a disaster.

Tommy was already on the edge of his seat in anticipation. He spared a glance at the bandleader, his body language begging to lead the way. The pianist abdicated control with a salute and let his trumpet player lead the way, which made Kathryn more comfortable. Tommy was a born leader, with the smarts and the personality to pull it off. He bounded to the front of the stage, taking his place beside her as he enthusiastically offered final instructions to his mates and orders to watch him for the changes, because he was familiar with her phrasing. He turned to the doubting bass player. "Get ready to go to school, junior." He lifted his trumpet and winked at Kathryn. "Let's make some magic, angel."

She cocked her head. "Take me there."

Tommy fitted the mute into the bell of his horn, and he and the rest of the brass section blew a raucous intro while the drummer caressed the high hat cymbals with his wire brushes.

Jenny stared in awe as the music brought Kathryn to life. Her face relaxed into a grin of pure pleasure as she mouthed *yeah, yeah,* to the wah-wah of Tommy's horn.

"That's my song," Bill said like a petulant child, loud enough for the table beside them to look.

Kathryn's smooth vocals complemented the bright horn, but Bill Connelly wasn't impressed.

"Wrong key," he said smugly, as Kathryn started in an unexpected harmony to the band's B flat. Jenny shot him an irritated glance, wishing he would just shut up. She was glad to see the people around them giving him the same dirty looks. His comment appeared to result more from wishful thinking than a genuine notion that Kathryn would start singing off key, and his annoyance turned to resignation when her voice blended perfectly with the mellow hum of the clarinets and trombones. He watched in utter fascination as she executed the song with technical perfection.

Jenny paid more attention to the arrangement than she normally would have and noticed the horn player watching intently for the vocal changes. By the time they got to the second chorus, they were no longer following Kathryn—it was more a blend of give and take as the musicians got a feel for each other. They spoke a secret language of nods, glances, and subtle facial expressions, and after singing her part, Kathryn stepped aside, letting each musician improvise his verse before they all came together at the end like they'd been playing together for years. Jenny hadn't seen Kathryn so relaxed since the night she entertained the troops at the armory, but even then, there was a latent emotional undercurrent pervading her performance. Not this time. This was pure pleasure, and everyone in the room felt it.

Jenny beamed with pride as she glanced at the disgruntled crooner at her table. To her surprise, he no longer seemed upset but amused at Kathryn singing about a man's propensity to break hearts. She flicked her eyes to the stage and found Kathryn throwing an intimate smirk in Bill's direction, the kind of smirk that says more than just casual history. Kathryn wouldn't have lied to her, would she? Jenny banished the thought in an instant when Kathryn left Bill to his musings and looked her way with a wink and a full-faced grin.

Jenny melted.

When the song ended, the crowd whooped and hollered for more. Bill shot a worried glance toward his boss at the bar, who, by his enthusiastic applause, could not have cared less about the displaced crooner's insecurities. Joe Radcliff had a hit on his hands, and the energy in the room was intoxicating. He wanted more.

Bill stood to plead his case as Joe arrived at the table. "I can't follow that, Joe!"

"You're right, Connelly. Scram. Take the night off."

"You can't—"

The club owner tore his eyes away from Kathryn's shapely backside as she offered her thanks to the band and silenced him with an annoyed look. "I'm getting a little tired of you telling me what I can and can't do, Bill," he said. "Beat it ... like now."

Bill looked at Jenny in desperation, and for the first time that evening, she felt sorry for him. She did her best to convey her empathy with a sympathetic tilt of her head, but he stormed off, intercepting Kathryn just before she reached the table.

"This is my gig, Kat," he said as he confronted her.

She chuckled. "It's still your gig, Bill."

He grabbed her by the wrist, and Jenny flinched, ready to take action.

Bill let go immediately when Kathryn's eyes drifted menacingly to his hand.

"Is there something else, or do I have to help you out of my way?"

He wisely stepped aside and allowed Kathryn to return to the table.

Amidst a wildly applauding audience, Joe clasped his hands in prayer and clutched them to his chest. "I'll give you anything ... your own band, your own dressing room, ten times the dough snob central is paying you. What do you say?"

"I told you, Joe. I've got a job," Kathryn said, as she sat and arranged the napkin on her lap.

Joe turned to Jenny. "If you've got any influence at all, I'm begging you."

"None whatsoever."

"Ugh, Kat, you're breaking my heart here. The crowd adores you. Is there *nothing* I can do to change your mind?"

"Afraid not. You had your chance." She smiled and shifted her focus to Jenny. "Only if you're *very* lucky do you get a second chance."

Jenny mirrored the smile. "Or a third."

"Low blow, Hammond," Joe said. "How was I to know? Quiet little mousy thing you were, making like part of the scenery." He looked her up and down, appreciating the woman she'd grown into. "Who knew?"

Their dinner salads arrived to interrupt the head-hunting, and Joe reluctantly acquiesced. "You were fantastic, Kat. Dinner on the house, and anytime you want to take the stage, it's all yours."

"Thanks."

Jenny watched the owner walk away and leaned in with a whisper, "You? A quiet little mousy thing? Blending in with the scenery? What was he, blind?"

Kathryn chuckled. "I told you, utterly forgettable. My first go-around here was more about selling drinks than singing."

"Selling drinks?"

"I'd sing, and in between sets, my job was to mingle with the crowd, get them to buy drinks. That's why I was hired, but at the time, I was underage, and, of course, it was during Prohibition, so it got, well ... shall we say ... messy."

"Prohib— Say, how old were you, Kat?"

Kathryn smiled. "Underage."

"Don't tell me," Jenny said, "you were tall for your age."

Kathryn flashed a dazzling grin. "I was."

The rest of dinner was uneventful and decidedly more comfortable, as both women relaxed into easy conversation. After dinner, coffee was a long, drawn-out affair, as neither was in a hurry to end their evening. It was Kathryn who finally looked at her watch, and Jenny regretfully agreed it was time to call it a night.

As they made their way to the exit, a well-dressed man approached Kathryn and presented his card.

"Your performance tonight was exceptional," he said, "and I would like to represent you. I'm talking a recording contract, radio, headlining tours, the whole nine yards."

She took his card. "Thank you, Mr.—" She found the name on the card, "Mr. Carmichael, but I'm afraid I have no need for your services." She handed back his card and put her arm around his shoulder, directing him to the stage. "But do you see that young man with the trumpet? His name is Tommy Wallace. Under the right hand, a brilliant future awaits him. You'd be wise to speak with him."

Mr. Carmichael reluctantly let one prospect go for another, and the women continued their trek to the exit, stopping at the cloakroom.

"I can't believe you turned that guy down," Jenny said, as she helped Kathryn fasten her cape to the buttons under her jacket lapels.

"I haven't time for that nonsense."

"Nonsense? The shot at a successful career in music?"

Kathryn raised a brow. "And here I thought I was successful."

"You know what I mean."

"It's not for me, Jenny."

"Miss Hammond?" the maître d' interrupted. "Telephone for you."

"Popular girl," Jenny said.

Kathryn agreed with a self-deprecating grin and thanked the maître d' as she took the call.

"Yes?" she drew out, knowing it could only be one person.

"SOS, Kat," Smitty said in a whisper.

She could almost hear the smile in his voice, so she knew he wasn't in any immediate danger. "Where are you, and what do you need?"

"I'm downtown at the records archive, Building 2, on the fifteenth floor. There's a new guard playing Boy Scout, who is entirely too serious about his job. I need a distraction."

"In or out?"

"Out."

"Elevator?"

"Yes. To the right."

"Stairs?"

"I got it covered."

She looked at her watch. "Can you hold out for fifteen minutes?"

"You're an angel," he said before hanging up.

Kathryn turned regretfully to Jenny. "Sorry. Duty calls." She looked up at the maître d', who was hanging up the phone. "Could you ring a taxi, please?"

"Is it dangerous?" Jenny asked, stalling the maître d' from his task with a raised hand.

"I don't think so. I need to cause a commotion."

Jenny put her hands behind her back, head held at an innocent tilt. "Need help?"

Kathryn paused, finding her irresistible. "You don't mind?"

"Are you kidding?"

There was a large reception in the ballroom off the main lobby in the building where Smitty was trapped, and they easily slipped through the crowd unnoticed. Kathryn removed her gloves and picked up a nearly empty bottle of champagne on her way past the open bar. She motioned Jenny to follow her down the terrazzo-floored hall as she made her way to a self-service elevator closest to the stairs.

Jenny looked both ways down the hall, stepped into the elevator, and straightened her jacket. She had the eerie feeling that a mugshot was in her near future.

Kathryn paused with her hand on the safety cage handle. "Are you sure about this? I can let you out right now."

"No. I'm in," Jenny said, and then paused. "Is what we're doing legal?"

"Having second thoughts?"

"None at all."

She trusted whatever Kathryn was doing was for a good reason, and she had to admit that participating in something that she sensed was just shy of unlawful was exciting. The mix of apprehension and adrenaline made an exhilarating combination, and she braced for whatever she was getting herself into.

Kathryn took a cigarette from her silver case and dropped the case into her purse. She pushed the button for the appropriate floor and slowly pulled the control lever toward her, starting the elevator on its ascent.

Jenny ventured an uncertain glance at her partner in crime and wondered how one causes a commotion with a nearly empty bottle of champagne and a cigarette.

"Now what?"

"Have a drink."

Jenny complied and then passed the bottle to Kathryn's outstretched hand. She took a swallow and returned the bottle.

"Have another drink."

Jenny did.

Kathryn watched the elevator's progress until it got to the tenth floor. "Would you like to kiss me?"

Jenny almost spit champagne all over the doors in front of her. "What?"

"Would you like to kiss me?" Kathryn repeated, as she watched the floor indicator arrow move steadily toward their target floor.

"Yes?" Jenny said tentatively, not sure if it was a request or just a general question.

"Follow my lead."

"Okay. Anything that involves kissing."

Kathryn chuckled as she slowed the elevator and stopped at the twelfth floor. She slid the safety cage to the side and opened the door. Before Jenny could move, she found herself simultaneously kissed and waltzed into the hallway where she barely heard the security guard on duty register his complaint.

"Say, folks, this is a private—" He stopped short, realizing it was two women kissing. He was speechless for a moment, and Kathryn positioned their bodies so that the guard turned his back to Smitty's escape route. Jenny saw Smitty peek his head out the door at the end of the hallway. He gave a thumbs-up as he headed for the stairwell a few feet away.

Kathryn broke the kiss, settling her arm around her shoulders, as she pretended to sway drunkenly on unsteady legs. "Ah. There you are," she said to the guard, her speech slurred. "Take our bags to room three thirty-six, please." She leaned in for another kiss.

"Stop that!" the guard said. "That is disgusting."

"This?" Kathryn held up her unlit cigarette. "I know. Nasty habit. I've been trying to quit, but—"

Jenny slipped her hand behind Kathryn's neck and silenced her with a kiss.

"Stop that!"

Jenny broke their kiss. "Listen, you—" She did her own drunk imitation by stumbling slightly and using Kathryn's left breast for balance.

"Pardon me," she said to the breast.

"Quite all right."

The guard pointed at the elevator. "You need to get off this floor right now."

"Shh," Jenny said in an exaggerated whisper. "You'll wake the children."

Kathryn held up her cigarette. "Do you have a light?"

"Off!" the guard shouted.

Jenny untangled herself from Kathryn's arm and left the champagne bottle in her care. She turned to the guard and played with his tie. "Say, you're cute when you're angry."

"Stop that!" He brushed Jenny's hands away. "If you don't leave this instant, I will be forced to remove you!"

Kathryn moved in and put her hand on his shoulder. "Promise?"

"Out!" He hustled them into the elevator, slid the safety cage door shut, and with one fluid movement, reached through the gate, pushed the ground floor button, and quickly withdrew his arm before it got caught in the closing door.

"Hey! Watch the merchandise!" Jenny said, as she stayed ahead of the door's path until it slid shut.

Kathryn laughed and pushed the control lever forward, starting their descent.

Jenny took the champagne bottle from her hand and emptied it with a long swig. She'd dreamed about kissing Kathryn Hammond since the day they met, and their kiss, however brief, proved she wasn't the only one.

"Stop me if I'm out of bounds," she said, as she cupped Kathryn's face with her free hand and gently guided their lips together in a heady mix of anticipated pleasure and champagne-induced abandon. Kathryn did not stop her.

The kiss was soft, sensual, and, to her surprise, mildly desperate, if the moan from Kathryn's throat meant anything. Jenny didn't remember dropping the champagne bottle, but she heard it clank at her feet as Kathryn's arms encircled her and deepened their kiss.

As much as she wanted the kiss to go on, this was not the place or time. Jenny pushed away and casually straightened her skirt as they passed the eighth floor. She pulled a compact and lipstick from her jacket pocket and corralled a smudge of lipstick with her finger before reapplying and handing the items over to her slightly disheveled elevator mate.

"Victory Red, for when I feel bold, you said."

"Remind me to make suggestions more often," Kathryn said, as she cleaned up her own smudged lipstick and then applied the color and returned it without further comment.

Jenny slid the doors open when they reached the ground floor and strode out with her head held high.

No sooner did Kathryn put the key in the ignition than Smitty popped up at Jenny's window.

"Hi ya, kid."

Jenny jumped and put a hand to her chest. "Jeepers, you startled me. Hi ya, Johnny."

She could tell by the scowl on his face that he hated being called Johnny, and he immediately looked at Kathryn as if she'd told her to call him that. Kathryn laughed and held up her hands in innocence.

"Quite a performance," he said, dripping with condescension.

Kathryn leaned forward. "You're welcome."

Jenny didn't appreciate his tone. "You're out of there, aren't you?"

Smitty glared at her and then addressed Kathryn. "I think I'm outnumbered."

"Then perhaps you should run along now," Jenny said with a shooing wave of her fingers.

"Now, now, kids," Kathryn said.

Smitty laughed, as if the whole point of his act was to get a rise out of her, and patted her on the shoulder. "Nice job for your first diversion, kid," he said. "See you tomorrow, Kat, and thanks. Both of you."

Kathryn leaned back in her seat and chuckled with a shake of her head. "Night, Smitty."

Jenny thumbed out the window at Smitty's departing form. "Get him. He interrupts *our* evening, we save his sorry butt, and he gives us flak for our method."

Kathryn grinned. "He's just—"

"Jealous, is what he is," Jenny interrupted.

The ensuing pause let her know that Kathryn didn't think Smitty was the only jealous one. "He's saved my sorry butt enough times to warrant some slack. He's a great guy, he really is. I couldn't ask for a better friend."

"Well, as I said, he doesn't think much of me."

"*I* think a lot of you. That'll be enough for him."

Jenny's annoyance floated away. "Does that mean you think well of me or you think of me often?"

Kathryn started the car. "Yes."

Kathryn was thankful Jenny didn't mention their impromptu kissing session on the ride home. They kept to safer subjects, like making fun of the security guard and appeasing Jenny's jealousy over her assumption that she had more than a past working relationship with Bill Connelly. She squelched that misconception with stories of Bill's lecherous ways and musical misadventures. Jenny laughed at herself, and Kathryn loved how she forgave herself easily for her shortcomings. She should probably take notes.

She didn't plan on kissing Jenny in the elevator, but she looked so adorable and so eager to carry out her first spy-like activity. She also didn't expect Jenny's kiss on their descent and just barely resisted pressing the stop button to finish what they'd started, but she decided their first sexual encounter would not occur while propped up against the wall of a stalled elevator. No, it would be special, tender, unrushed, and uninterrupted, befitting the relationship she hoped would grow from it.

She'd fought against her desire to keep Jenny in her life. A relationship complicated an already complicated goal: Get back to the war, pay her debt to the dead. She didn't believe in signs, or fate, or destiny. Only stolen moments. Why then, did Jenny have her thinking about things like relationships and the future?

A mental checklist with things Jenny needed to know if they got intimately involved occupied her mind. Kathryn didn't make lists. She took lovers for kicks or as a means to an end. Their emotional well-being was the furthest thing from her mind. Until now.

Before she knew it, she was idling in Jenny's driveway.

"Would you like to come in?"

Kathryn could tell by the serious tone and the controlled intensity of Jenny's eyes that if she went into the house, she would not leave anytime soon. She would not have a friendly cup of tea, or make small talk, or sleep on the couch. In fact, she was pretty sure she would not sleep at all.

She glanced in the rearview mirror as a stall tactic rather than an actual concern, and Jenny turned around, peering into the night for whatever or whomever Kathryn may have been looking for.

Kathryn chuckled. "You know, you really need to cultivate your casual glance."

"Like this?" Jenny ran her eyes seductively up and down Kathryn's seated form. "Is that a casual glance?"

"No. I think that's what's called a mental undressing."

"Why does that sound like more fun than it actually was?" She propped her arm up on the back of the seat. "As you said this afternoon, if someone is following you, they already know you're here, so what's the harm in coming in?"

Kathryn offered another glance in the rearview. Jenny was right, and she wasn't shy about her intentions.

"I don't think we were followed."

"Did you look?"

"No, but I'm sure you did. Were we followed?"

"I don't think so."

"So?" she said, tilting her head with a subtle glance at the house.

Kathryn felt off balance and couldn't think. The list. What was on the list? She couldn't remember. Jenny's desirous eyes and the memory of her kiss lured her recklessly into the unknown.

She got out of the car without another word, and Jenny almost tumbled onto the driveway in her haste to get out of her side. She passed Kathryn on the sidewalk and then fumbled with the key in the lock on the front door. Kathryn smiled and placed a calming hand on her back. Jenny paused, took a breath, and then opened the door and stepped inside.

She methodically put down her keys, removed her coat, took Kathryn's cape, and put them both on the hall tree. Then she faced Kathryn dead-on and pinned her to the wall with another kiss, this one hungry and purposeful.

CHAPTER SEVEN

Kathryn started laughing into their kiss, and Jenny pulled back, disconcerted.

"What's so funny?"

"You're so impatient."

That was an understatement. Jenny entwined her fingers with Kathryn's, raised their hands until they were above Kathryn's shoulders against the wall, and leaned in, pressing her breasts against Kathryn's warmth. She'd barely kissed her, yet her body reacted as if they were long-lost lovers. She'd imagined lust in her fantasies, but moments away from turning fantasy into reality, she felt out of control. Her body craved this person, and the sensation was as intoxicating as it was frightening.

"I know you came into this house for one reason," Jenny said, her voice low and husky. "I don't want you to get away, so I'm going to show you what you're missing before you change your mind."

The seduction Jenny had planned evaporated in an instant when Kathryn reversed their positions. Jenny's arms were now overhead and pinned against the wall, and Kathryn's mouth was beside her ear.

"Do you really think you could stop me if I wanted to leave?"

Kathryn's warm breath in her ear erased the shock of the surprise reversal, and her desire grew until her rhythmic breathing became halting pants. "Do you want to leave?"

Kathryn pressed closer, brushing her lips down the side of Jenny's neck with a deep inhale and then back up to her ear. "Not at the moment."

"Mm, good." Jenny moaned, as Kathryn's lips and soft exhale on her skin made her knees weak.

The inability to touch Kathryn pushed her already considerable arousal to the point of madness. Kathryn brought her open mouth just within kissing range, but offered a mischievous grin instead and slowly kissed her throat, down to her collarbone. Jenny's body hummed like a tuning fork, and her legs stopped pretending they could bear her weight. Her bruised back didn't appreciate their dereliction of duty.

"Let go," she said into Kathryn's ear.

"Oh, believe me, I won't hold back," Kathryn said between kisses.

Jenny shifted. "No, let go ... my back."

"Oh, God, Jenny. I forgot."

"It's okay. I just can't stand anymore."

"I'm so sorry. Are you okay?"

"I'm fine. Don't stop," she said with a grin, now that she had two hands free to wander over Kathryn's gorgeous body.

Kathryn backed off, immediately repentant. "I'm sorry. Are you all right?"

"Kat, relax. I'm fine."

Worried eyes stared back at her, and Kathryn turned away with a hand to her forehead. "What am I doing?"

Jenny put a reassuring hand on Kathryn's back. "If you've forgotten, let me remind you," she said, moving in to pick up where they left off.

Kathryn pulled away and seemed disoriented. "This isn't going to work."

Jenny frowned. Seriously? "Sure it is," she said, hoping she masked the desperation rising in her gut.

Kathryn retrieved her cape from the hall tree without making eye contact. "I'm sorry."

"Wait. Kat, what are you—"

"I've got to go. I'm so sorry."

The words hung in the air long after Kathryn dashed out from under them, not even closing the door as she hurried down the walk to her car.

Jenny put her hands on her hips, dumfounded and frustrated, as she watched Kathryn's car peel out of her driveway in reverse, the scene framed like the story of her life inside the constraints of the doorjamb.

Kathryn waited until she cleared the third block of empty lots before she turned the corner and pulled over. She turned off the car and slammed her palms into the steering wheel. "Ugh! What am I doing?"

She wasn't sure if she meant running or sleeping with Jenny Ryan. There were a million reasons she shouldn't sleep with her, and no reason she should, other than the selfish satisfaction of scratching a sexual itch.

She closed her eyes. How dare she think of Jenny as a sexual itch. She was more than that. Much more. Too much more, and that was the problem. She had tried to let her go, but she couldn't stop thinking about her.

When she saw Jenny crumble to the ground beneath the hulking menace of the violent striker, her indifferent heart burst through its heavily defended wall, vowing, from that moment on, to do anything to protect her.

Sleeping with her would not protect her. A relationship would not protect her. She would only hurt her. She'd already negatively affected her life, and they weren't even in a relationship yet. Because of her, Jenny had been injured in a car accident, nearly had her head blown off, lost her job, and was now working for the OSS, which would very likely put her in harm's way. She couldn't imagine the emotional wreckage she would exact on her should they embark on a serious relationship. She couldn't deal with her own baggage, let alone inflict it on someone else.

She should run. She didn't deserve Jenny. She'd only bring her misery. What did she have to offer?

"Nothing," she whispered, as she rested her forehead on the steering wheel. "Nothing."

Treasured moments with Jenny played in her head like a movie: Jenny's annoyed, upturned face morphing into astonishment the first time they met, her shy smile when she presented the single yellow rose as a thank-you, her seductive smirk as she ran her foot up her thigh on the couch, her radiant blonde profile backlit by the golden rays of the morning sun at their first and only breakfast together, and her beautiful green eyes glistening with pride during their dinner earlier in the evening.

A tear fell down her cheek as the visions overwhelmed her. Jenny made her feel again—want again. To not have her in her life seemed unbearable, but she would endure her loss like she'd endured so many others.

Standing on Jenny's doorstep, Kathryn closed her eyes and exhaled a shaky breath. She bucked up for anger, frustration, and the final brush-off as Jenny slammed the door in her face. She didn't blame her, and she would take it because Jenny deserved an explanation before she walked out of her life.

She straightened and knocked.

The door swung open too quickly for a pleasant greeting. Jenny's stern silence was expected, but not her appearance. She was barefoot, with her blouse hastily untucked from her skirt and frustrated green eyes peeking out from behind freely flowing waves of unpinned blonde hair. She tucked her hair behind her ears and then crossed her arms.

"You know, I'm a big fan of hot and cold running water, but this is getting a little ridiculous."

Kathryn stared at her. She looked so wild, restless, and alive. One look and she didn't want to walk away. Her heart raced and her fists clenched in restraint as she fought the urge to take her in her arms again and kiss her.

"May I come in?" she said instead. "I'd like to talk."

Jenny uncrossed her arms and theatrically motioned her forward with an outstretched arm extended toward the living room. "Yes, by all means, let's talk." She held the position while Kathryn walked past. "That's what we need ... more talking."

The door slammed behind her as she entered the living room, and then Jenny strolled past, chin held high in displeasure, on her way to the large bay window, where she jerked the curtains shut. She turned around and glanced at her sideways as she headed toward the couch.

"What?" she said of Kathryn's conflicted expression.

"You look ... beautiful."

Jenny stopped and pointed at her. "You really need to make up your mind, because you're driving me crazy."

"Sorry."

"Yeah, you've said that a lot tonight." She continued to the couch and plopped down. "What do you want to talk about, Kathryn?"

Kathryn didn't know where to begin. She wasn't sure she should even try, which exceeded Jenny's tolerance level at that moment.

"Well, that's fascinating, Kat," Jenny said into the silence. "I had an interesting day as well, momentous in fact. Let's see ..." She looked to the air. "I almost got killed by a human gorilla. His name was Butch. That's so stereotypical, isn't it? Butch. Then I was rescued by this really amazing woman. She was incredible. You really had to be there. Words can't describe."

Kathryn raised her eyes. It was a warning, but Jenny was too bothered to care.

"Then what, you ask? Oh, then I lied to Bernie about my job. First time in my life I've ever lied to him." She shrugged. "Quite right, actually, because he can't keep his mouth shut. That was the right thing to do, wasn't it?"

Kathryn looked away.

"Then I had dinner with my beautiful guardian angel." She leaned forward, seeking Kathryn's eyes. "You remember her, the one who saved me earlier?" She leaned back, sarcasm dripping from every word. "Did I mention what a swell gal she is? We even pulled off a caper—we're a great team," she said, as if she was a radio announcer. "We had a terrific time, and we were really hitting it off until she gave me the air and left me on my doorstep, with nary an explanation."

Kathryn's instinct to run was the right one, and this time she wouldn't stop to entertain normal things like relationships. Jenny wouldn't put up with her, nor should she. She turned for the door without a word.

"Wait!" Jenny jumped up. "Don't go. I'm sorry." She tugged on Kathryn's hand. "Wait. I'm sorry. I'm ..." She softened her demeanor. "I'm really sorry."

Kathryn set her jaw in irritated humiliation. "I came back to give you an explanation, but I can see that was a mistake."

"No. It wasn't. I'm a jackass. Please stay. I'm sorry."

Kathryn resisted, but Jenny's beseeching eyes and gentle stroking up and down her arm melted her resolve.

"Please?" Jenny said. "I'm sorry ... let's talk." She led her to the couch and sat on the floor at her feet. She put her hand on her knee and rested her chin on it. "I'm all ears."

She was irresistible, that's what she was, and Kathryn tucked her hands under her thighs to keep from running them through Jenny's hair. She needed a clear head, and touching Jenny only muddled her thoughts.

"I'm sorry about Bernie ... that you had to lie to him."

Jenny shrugged. "Occupational hazard."

"And I'm sorry about your back. I didn't mean to hurt you."

Jenny made a *don't be ridiculous* face and lifted her head. "Kat—"

"I don't ever mean to hurt you," Kathryn finished quietly, hoping Jenny understood the scope of her statement. She didn't protest further, so Kathryn went on. "Which is why I wanted to talk to you ... to explain ... about me, my life."

Jenny's open, serious gaze invited Kathryn to continue. She began with the easiest subject.

"The first thing I want to address is work-related. The nature of what I do makes it difficult to have a relationship."

"Because of Forrester? Like that?"

"Well, I was speaking in general. Forrester isn't really a problem in that regard."

"Because?"

Kathryn hated admitting this consequence of their interaction. "For some reason, he already thinks you're my lover."

Jenny's brow lifted in surprise. "And how did that happen?"

"Haven't a clue, but because of that, you may draw some attention. If he watches me, he may watch you, and I'm sorry for that."

"Okay," Jenny drew out. "But if he thinks we're together, he's already doing that, so what we *actually* do from now on makes no difference."

Kathryn paused, realizing protecting Jenny from her would not protect her from Forrester. "True."

"Good to know. Next?"

Jenny's nonchalant approach to barriers nudged Kathryn's glimmer of hope. "Next, you have to understand that my first responsibility is to my assignment, and that doesn't bode well for relationships."

"So," Jenny began hesitantly, "you're saying the OSS has rules about relationships while under assignment? Because I missed that chapter in the manual."

"Well—"

"I mean," Jenny interrupted, "I can see if you're on assignment with Forrester, for example, and you're in a relationship, say personally, with someone else ..." She offered a longing look and batted her eyelashes. "That might affect your interaction with Forrester, and that would be bad. I understand that."

Kathryn eyed her warily while suppressing a grin. The kicker was coming.

"So, what are the rules, and how do we get around them?" Jenny asked as she rubbed her hands together diabolically.

Kathryn chuckled. Jenny was either fearless or naïve. She sensed a bit of both. "The OSS doesn't have any set rules about that. I'm sure my superiors would prefer I have no strings, but my personal life is my personal life, as long as it doesn't interfere with—"

"So, this is *your* rule," Jenny said with a lilt of relief in her voice. "You find it hard to juggle business and pleasure, is that it?"

Kathryn shook her head and wondered how she'd ever get through the next part if Jenny couldn't even let her get through the easy part. "I'm a professional. I know the difference between business and pleasure."

"I see." Jenny slid her hand from Kathryn's knee to her thigh and beyond until it rested on the side of her hip.

"So, um ..." Jenny's other hand began a slow but steady journey up Kathryn's other thigh as she raised herself on her knees. "You find that your personal relationships are negatively affected by what you do for the government. Is that it?"

Kathryn gripped her thighs tightly to stop herself from grasping Jenny's shoulders and pulling her into a kiss. She calmed her ragged breathing before answering. "It depends on whether the person I'm having a personal relationship with knows the difference between business and pleasure."

"And in your experience, do they?"

"No."

Jenny pressed her body as close as physically possible, given her position. "I, uh, I'm kind of new to the spy game, but—" She lifted her chin and tentatively kissed Kathryn on the lips, then stopped, looking into her eyes for a reaction.

All thought left Kathryn's mind as desire gathered in every sensitive spot in her body and urged her to take action. Jenny probed her lips further, and Kathryn let her into her mouth. Oh, how she wanted this. She freed her hands and tangled her fingers in cascading blonde hair. She drew Jenny into a deeper kiss, and gentle exploration gave way to restrained hunger, as pent-up need overtook them both.

It was an unfamiliar place for Kathryn, disarmed by her own desire and sexually out of control. Her thundering heart and uneven breathing fed the ache in her core, and she longed for Jenny's touch.

She hovered over Jenny on the couch, with no memory of dragging her there, and she knew this was the point of no return. It scared her. She couldn't have this. Not now.

"Like I said," Jenny said breathlessly, "I'm new here, but I'd say that was pleasure."

Kathryn sat up, trying to corral her selfish need and remember why the hell she came back. "Do you know what you're doing?"

Jenny raised herself on her elbows. "Say, I'm new, but I'm not *that* new."

"That's not what I meant. Can you handle the business end of my life?"

"You said you don't sleep with Forrester."

"Yes, but that's not to say that won't change or that I won't be reassigned. Then what?"

"I'd cross that bridge when I came to it."

Kathryn cocked her head in disapproval. "When you're in the middle of the bridge is no time to find that it won't support you."

"You're right."

"So?"

"So, then, I guess it would depend on how strong our relationship was. You see trouble, I see potential."

Kathryn smiled. "I'm going to be presumptuous and say that I have more experience in this matter."

"Maybe so, but we're just having a hypothetical conversation about a hypothetical relationship."

"Oh," Kathryn said, arching a brow. "Hence, that hypothetical kiss."

"Exactly. Do I need to apologize for that?"

"I found it rather enjoyable, actually."

"I don't know," Jenny said, feigning dissatisfaction. "I think the jury's still out on whether you even like me."

Kathryn's eyes softened in a subtle apology for her actions, past and future. She ran her hand through disheveled blonde hair and smiled. "Case closed."

Her declaration only confused Jenny. "Look, you've already said Forrester's not a problem. We work for the same people, but we don't work together, and we've established there are no rules governing our actions, so what's the problem?"

Kathryn brushed a hand across her forehead, caught between wanting a future, however improbable, and saying goodbye because it was the right thing to do for Jenny. Work wasn't a problem. It was just an excuse on the way to explaining personal shortcomings exacerbated by emotional baggage. Even the most forgiving person would run in the opposite direction if she revealed herself.

"Normally," Jenny went on, "I'd take the nickel and buy a clue ... you're not interested. But you're here, and from that amazing kiss, I know you're interested, so you can understand my confusion."

Kathryn understood completely, and Jenny's confusion wasn't far from her own. She knew what she had to do. If she gave in to her lust, Jenny would interpret it as something else, which was a complication she could do without. She would lay out the inevitable relationship disaster and let Jenny see the truth for herself.

"I told you once that I liked you too much."

Jenny smiled. "Which on the surface seems like a plus, but I've come to see that things are not always as they seem."

"Which is precisely my point."

"Then I think I'll shut up now, because this is one point I don't think I'd like to make for you."

Kathryn chuckled. If only they'd met at another time, under different circumstances. If only she were a better person with more to offer. "I'm not very good at this," she said. "I don't express myself very well ... obviously."

"Nonsense, Kathryn. You express yourself every night on stage, and it doesn't get more vulnerable than baring your soul to a room full of perfect strangers."

"Well, it's easy to hide behind a song, and believe me, if I knew a tune to cover this situation, I'd be singing it."

"As long as it's not 'Let's Call the Whole Thing Off,' I wouldn't mind a bit."

Jenny's sense of humor made opening up a little easier, and the truth would do the rest.

"Seriously, Jenny, I don't know how to have a relationship. I'm selfish, egotistical, and brooding. I don't know much about having fun, or being charming, and if it weren't for music, I don't think I could express a genuine emotion if my life depended on it. You deserve so much more than that, more than I can give you. And it's not that I don't like you, and it's not that I'm not attracted to you. I just don't think I'm any good for you—" Jenny opened her mouth to speak, but Kathryn stilled her with a raised hand. "I'm not telling you this as a subject for debate. That's just the way it is, the way I am, and because of that, I'm not going to let you get involved with me. I'm not going to drag you down to the hell that is my life, and I'm not going to let you make a fool of yourself trying to convince me otherwise. One day you'll see it's for your own good."

There was a moment's silence, as Kathryn's monologue dispersed into the stillness of the room.

Jenny blinked. "Wow. I'm speechless."

Kathryn chuckled, not expecting that response. "Do I get a prize for that?"

"Yeah, me, if you can get out of your own way."

"Haven't you heard a word I've said?"

"Kathryn, you've done your duty, told me all the things to watch out for, done everything you can to dissuade me, and I'm still here, ready, willing, and able. I could go on, point by point, and disagree with everything you just said about yourself, but I have a feeling you already know they aren't true. You're afraid of something, and it can't be hurting me, because I can take care of myself. There's more going on here than the line of bull you're casting, and things would go a lot smoother if you would just be honest with me, or at least be honest with yourself. What are you afraid of?"

Too many things. Too much to hide, too much to deny, too much to admit. She wasn't ready to deal with the emotions weakening her resolve, and Jenny, seeing right through her, was not helping. Walls went up and common courtesy lost its persuasion. "If I wanted to be psychoanalyzed, I'd go to a head shrinker."

Jenny pursed her lips. "Sorry."

Kathryn exhaled a regretful breath and shook her head. "No. I'm sorry. I—" She rubbed her forehead. "I'm just not a generally pleasant person, I promise you, and that—" She waved her hand, indicating her rude comment, "is a perfect example of why *we* are not a good idea." She got up to leave.

"What are you doing?"

"It's not going to work, Jenny."

"Kathryn—" Jenny grasped her trailing hand and pulled her back to the couch. "So you're a mean ol' bitch and I'm a pushy little pain in the ass. If you can put up with that, then I'm sure I can put up with ... whatever it is you're afraid I won't put up with."

Jenny had her hands on her again, and Kathryn wanted to kick herself for the affect it had on her. She melted under Jenny's ministrations and relaxed onto the couch.

"I'm an adult," Jenny said. "Please stop deciding what's good for me and what I will and won't put up with. When I've had enough of you, you'll know it."

Kathryn never wanted that day to come, and it surely would if they started something. The best way to prevent it was to avoid it altogether. She looked at her feet to hide her cowardice.

"Oh dear," Jenny said, "so very serious."

Kathryn raised her gaze. "It is serious, Jenny."

Jenny tilted her head. "Does it have to be?"

"What are you saying?"

"Well, let's face it ... we're not picking out china patterns here. We hardly know each other. Certainly not well enough to warrant such trepidation on your part."

Kathryn admired her honesty.

"Now, I'm pushy," Jenny went on, "but I'm not oblivious. I know a lost cause when I see one, and we aren't one of them. Frankly, you baffle me. Despite your actions, I'm pretty sure you at least enjoy my company. Now, if I'm wrong—"

"You're not wrong."

Jenny smiled. "Look, I think we could be good friends. I also think we could be more than friends."

She waited for a response, but Kathryn didn't dare, for fear she would agree.

"You've admitted there's something between us. You came in, you left, and you came back. You're about to bolt out of here again, and I have a sneaking suspicion you'll be back *again*. Maybe not tonight, because after all, a girl has her pride, but you'll be back. And if you don't come back ..." Jenny grinned and did her best Humphrey Bogart impersonation as she quoted his speech from the end of *Casablanca*. "You'll regret it ... maybe not today, maybe not tomorrow, but soon, and for the rest of your life."

Kathryn was damned if she did and damned if she didn't. Jenny was the most open and straightforward person she'd ever met. She'd made her feel again, and hope again, and though they were the worst traits for the road ahead, she would never forget Jenny for that. A pang of loss swept through her, and as if Jenny sensed she needed comfort, she took her hand.

"Kathryn, if there's anything I've learned in this past year, it's that our hold on this mortal coil is tenuous at best and relationships are overrated. If I see someone I'm interested in, I'm going to act on it, and if they're interested too, then bully for us—drinks all around. I don't think I'm being conceited when I say I think there's something between us. To ignore that in the best of times would be a crime, but in this age of uncertainty ..."

Perfect logic Kathryn couldn't refute.

Jenny cupped her cheek and leaned close to her lips again. "Come on, Kat. What's all this doom and gloom? It's just sex. I'm not sure why you feel the need to torture yourself. I'm attracted to you. I think we could have some fun, and I told you once before, no strings, that's not what I'm looking for, and obviously neither are you. So, what say we have a little fun, hm?" She slid her hand down the side of Kathryn's face and kissed the cheek that it once occupied. "Just one night," she whispered and then kissed just below her ear. "Just for fun, hm?" Kisses followed the path of her hand, now resting on a very warm chest.

Kathryn sat motionless, trying to wrap her head around Jenny's new *just sex* attitude. Here she was, trying to protect her from emotional catastrophe, and all she wanted was casual sex. Was it a new attitude?

She thought back to Jenny's birthday night, on the same couch, in the same position, when Jenny tried to tell her the same thing. She wasn't listening then. She was too concerned about the assignment and too wrapped up in the same foolish fantasy about a future, but now it all seemed so clear. She just wanted sex. Why was she surprised? It was always about sex, and she was the biggest perpetrator of all. Jenny was no different. Why should she be? It made her angry, a familiar feeling where sex was concerned, but why? To be angry with Jenny was ridiculous. The situation was perfect, a dream come true. The anger quickly turned to relief. Jenny had the good sense not to get emotionally involved with a relative stranger, especially one so damaged as her. Sex for fun? Sex for enjoyment, with no ulterior motives? Finally, someone who understood that sex wasn't a three-letter word for commitment. She felt relieved, like a weight had been lifted. She chuckled at the lengths she'd gone to, all because of some ill-conceived notion that she had to protect Jenny's innocence. Ha! Innocence? Jenny knew exactly how to live life and seemed more and more like an old hand at seduction. What had come over her? Relationship? Love? Future? Good grief. Madness.

Jenny heard the low rumble of laughter echo through the chest under her lips. "You find the most interesting things amusing," she said, having had Kathryn laugh twice now at her seductive advances.

"I'm sorry," Kathryn said, as she sank further into the couch and settled her arms around Jenny's waist. "I've been awfully silly, going on and on about heaven knows what."

"Ah," Jenny drew out in delight. "You surrender?"

"Completely. Do what you will with me."

Jenny backed off to get a better look at Kathryn's face. "Are you serious? This is okay?"

"Recreational sex with no strings, promises, hearts, or flowers?"

Jenny grinned. "As long as you respect me in the morning and promise to come to my rescue should the need arise."

Kathryn ran her hands up Jenny's waist and slid them under her pullover. "Sounds like a swell bargain to me."

Jenny's body hummed with Kathryn's touch on her bare skin, and she gazed lustfully at Kathryn's waiting lips. She felt the zipper release on her skirt under Kathryn's direction, and she leaned in for a kiss.

"Do you like my brooch?" Kathryn asked to her approaching mouth.

"What?"

Kathryn's eyes drifted to the pin on her lapel, and Jenny's followed.

"Uh, yeah. Pretty."

"Take it off."

Jenny eyed her suspiciously. "Okay." She fumbled with the catch, but once free, she held it up. "Next?"

Kathryn unbuttoned the top button of her tailored jacket and, in one quick flick of her wrist, removed a scarf she'd strategically draped about her chest and held in place with the brooch. She tossed it over her shoulder, and Jenny watched, wide-eyed, the red and white material flutter to the ground.

"You have got to be kidding me!" she said. "Your blouse was just a scarf and you've been half-naked the whole night?"

Kathryn grinned. "You've got a broad description of half-naked." She slid her hands under the knit pullover and up the length of Jenny's torso until she got to the sleeves. Jenny's arms lifted automatically, pulling the top off. Kathryn's fingers slipped under the bra straps, and Jenny reached behind to undo the catch.

"No, let me," Kathryn said, pulling her closer until the straps fell listlessly over her biceps.

Kathryn's light touch followed the straps down, sending tingles up Jenny's spine. She maneuvered her arms out of the straps and pulled the bra down, releasing her breasts to Kathryn's rising mouth.

Warm lips enveloped the sensitive flesh of her nipple, and she threw her head back with a moan. She'd waited so long for Kathryn to touch her like this. She didn't even notice her freeing the clasp on her bra until it was tossed haphazardly over the back of the couch.

As quickly as her mouth was on her, Kathryn backed off, but this time it wasn't trepidation. She caressed the other breast and gently brushed the hard nipple with her thumb. "So beautiful," she said, and the words sent a warm rush to Jenny's core.

She closed her eyes, waiting for Kathryn's mouth to devour her. Nothing happened. When she opened her eyes, she found Kathryn gazing into her soul with what she could only describe as awe. Jenny had never felt so desired, and she didn't dare blink or look away, for fear the spell would break.

The awe on Kathryn's face turned into a slow grin. "For future reference, this—" she raked her eyes up and down her torso, "is half-naked."

"I stand corrected," Jenny said, reaching for the rest of the buttons on Kathryn's jacket. She needed to see her. To touch her.

Kathryn lifted one arm behind her head, evidently content to watch her free the buttons with shaky hands.

Jenny was nervous but determined. Her casual sex routine was a load of bull, but she could tell that Kathryn's reticence was due to some mistaken impression that she was a fragile flower with limited sexual experience who couldn't handle the demands of such a worldly woman.

Well, she'd show her. She was no fragile flower. The other stuff was true, but every expert was a beginner once. Kathryn might be a love 'em and leave 'em kind of gal, but Jenny sensed there was more between them. Kathryn cared. A lot. If she didn't, she would have had her way with her and disappeared already. This was her chance to calm Kathryn's fears, and to be honest, a few of her own, about moving forward with a relationship.

With the buttons undone, Jenny parted the jacket to reveal already erect nipples on mounds of luscious, soft skin. She was perfect. Jenny lifted her eyes to express her appreciation, but the dark lust roiling behind Kathryn's intense stare silenced her.

Dress rehearsal was over. Jenny raised the back of her hand to her lips to remove what was left of her lipstick, but Kathryn stopped her.

"No," she said. "I want to see it all over my body."

Jenny swallowed. She'd never think of lipstick the same way again. With her fingertips, she lightly traced the smeared path she'd already left on Kathryn's neck until she got to her chest and stopped. Kathryn's heart hammered beneath her hand, and for the first time, Jenny realized the power she possessed.

She was going to give Kathryn Hammond the greatest night of sex ever.

Kathryn didn't often give herself over to passion. Sex was usually a means to an end. Pleasure was a byproduct sometimes, but most often, that was reserved for self-satisfaction or the random romp with an attractive stranger, just to blow off steam.

It was different with Jenny. She was drawn to her from the beginning. At first, she thought it was pity. She was the poor patriotic kid with the dead traitor father unwittingly snared in a government fishing operation.

But then pity turned protective, as if sparing this one person undue pain would bring her one step closer to redemption.

It wouldn't. There was no redemption for her. She didn't deserve it, and she didn't know why being near Jenny made her want it, but Jenny made her want many things she shouldn't. She made everything better, even thoughts about herself, which, considering her horrific past, was extraordinary.

The war compressed time into small windows of grace surrounded by uncertainty and death, but Jenny's presence made her forget about the war and life's impermanence. She wooed hope from its musty trunk and rolled the future before her like a technicolor dream of possibilities.

Kathryn never thought she'd feel those things again, and from such an unexpected source. Their roles were reversed now. She was the naïve one, dreaming of the impossible, and Jenny the realist. There was no promise of tomorrow. Only today. Only this moment. Jenny wasn't wasting her moment, and she wouldn't either. She would enjoy this night as if it were her last.

She memorized Jenny's face as her trembling hands unbuttoned her jacket and revealed her breasts. She longed for her touch and hoped Jenny didn't mistake her smile for an arrogant smirk.

For the first time in years, she savored the intimate reaction of a sexual partner exploring her body for the first time. It was a vulnerable moment, even for her, despite her experience, but she felt safe with Jenny. Seeing herself through her eyes washed away the detritus of her dirty past, and she basked in the purity of Jenny's wonderment.

Jenny slowly traced the shape of her breasts with hesitant fingers and looked up, almost for permission, before placing gentle kisses everywhere but where Kathryn needed them.

Kathryn closed her eyes and arched her back instinctively into Jenny's touch with an audible exhale, hoping she would take her into her mouth soon.

The anticipated pleasure drove her mad, and she was moments away from grabbing her own breast when the kisses stopped.

Jenny hovered above her face, lips parted and eyes hungry like hers. Kathryn lifted her head to meet her lips, but Jenny pulled back. "What is it?" Kathryn said huskily, as her eyes danced between desire and concern.

"Do you want me?" Jenny whispered.

The answer burned like a fire in Kathryn's belly. "I want you." She lifted her head with parted lips for her reward but came up empty when Jenny pulled out of reach.

"Do you want *me*?"

Kathryn searched questioning green eyes and found herself there. Found the truth there. "I want you, Jenny."

She gently cupped her face in her hands and guided her to her waiting mouth. The kiss started gently but quickly turned intense, as neither held back.

Jenny feared one more second in Kathryn Hammond's passionate embrace and she wouldn't need anything but the kiss to push her over the edge. She wanted this to last. She wanted to give Kathryn a night she'd never forget, and that certainly wouldn't happen on a sofa in her living room. With strength she didn't know she possessed, she extracted herself from Kathryn's heavenly lips and strong arms and scrambled to her feet, impatiently holding out her hand.

"Come on."

She didn't have to ask twice. Kathryn was on her feet in no time. They left a trail of clothes on the way to the bathroom until they stood naked and kissing outside the shower, waiting for the water to warm. Ever practical, Jenny offered Kathryn a shower cap to protect her perfectly coifed hair, and Kathryn chuckled as she pulled pins from her hair and let it fall out of its victory rolls and onto her shoulders.

"Do you think I care about my hair right now?" she said between kisses.

"Silly me," Jenny said, and tossed the cap aside.

Once in the shower, the sensation of skin on skin, slick with soap, raised arousal to a new level, something Jenny didn't think was possible.

Kathryn pressed her long, naked torso into her back as her arms encircled her. One hand caressed a breast, and the other slipped over her pelvic bone on the way to her inner thigh. Jenny shot her arms out to their full extension as she propped herself up on the shower wall to keep from crumbling.

Kathryn's beautiful hand explored every inch of her breast, and

Jenny watched as her excited nipple played hide and seek with long fingers as they alternately soothed and teased. That hand disappeared and joined the other on her hip, as Kathryn rested her cheek on Jenny's shoulder blade and slowly lowered herself to her knees, placing gentle kisses on her path downward. She pulled her closer with a hand against her abdomen and continued kissing down the back of her thigh.

Jenny was having a severe case of stimulation overload. Hands and kisses seemed to be everywhere, making her momentarily lose touch with reality. "What are you doing to me?" she whispered, not realizing she'd spoken out loud until her question was answered.

Kathryn removed the hand from her abdomen and caressed her hip. "It seems I caused you some pain earlier. I think I need to make up for that." She ran her hand down Jenny's backside. "May I touch you?"

Just the suggestion forced a moan from deep within. "I think I might die if you don't."

Kathryn's hand slid between Jenny's legs.

The tiles complained with a squeak as Jenny tightened her grip on the shower wall for support. "Mmph," she said on a clipped exhale. "Okay." She gasped. "Restitution is good."

Kathryn ran her fingers slowly along the length of her folds.

"*Yes*," Jenny said breathlessly.

"Hm. Sounds like you like this." Kathryn repositioned her hand, eliciting another unintelligible groan. "Or was it this?"

"Guh—Kat, God—okay." Jenny didn't trust her legs to hold her any longer. She needed to lie down before she turned into a liquid mass and washed down the drain. "Bedroom. Now."

The change of venue was merely a convenient place for Jenny to recover, having found her release almost immediately under the weight of Kathryn's warm body and hard thigh pressing between her legs as they fell into bed. A year without a sexual partner was definitely too long.

When she caught her breath, and the world came back into focus, it didn't escape her attention that the pleasure thus far had been very one-sided.

"That was unfair."

Kathryn propped her head up on one hand and smiled as the other hand connected glistening water droplets on her chest. "How so?"

"I've been trying to seduce you for weeks, and you just waltz in here and all my best-laid plans go right out the window."

"Is that a complaint?" Kathryn said, as she slowly moved her hand down Jenny's torso.

Jenny rolled into the touch, her passion ignited once more. She lifted herself on still shaky arms and straddled Kathryn, who was now lying on her back beneath her. "Not in this lifetime."

She slid her hands up Kathryn's body, pausing briefly to encircle her breasts. Kathryn was mirroring her moves, causing Jenny to lose her concentration. "Stop, Kat," she said with a giggle.

Her plea did nothing, so she grabbed Kathryn's wrists and pinned them above her head to the pillow. "Stop it," she drew out playfully.

A flash of wild intensity widened Kathryn's eyes, and Jenny immediately loosened her grip, remembering the same disoriented panic from the night on the couch when she startled Kathryn from sleep and she drew a gun on her. "I'm sorry. Did I hurt you?"

The wild intensity disappeared, and Kathryn's arms relaxed. "Kiss me, silly."

"My pleasure."

As the kiss intensified, Kathryn tried to free her wrists. Jenny knew it wasn't a serious struggle. Kathryn could have thrown her over in a matter of seconds if she really wanted to. Instead, her body writhed beneath her and the kiss grew desperate, as if it would never be enough. Moans came from deep in Kathryn's throat, and Jenny broke away, pulling out of range with a mischievous glint in her eye. She leaned in and then pulled away again when Kathryn opened her mouth to receive her. She was in control now.

Kathryn raised her head as far as her pinned wrists would allow, trying to recapture Jenny's lips. When she couldn't, her mouth twisted into a crooked grin, recognizing a good old-fashioned tease.

"You're a little bit evil, aren't you?" she said.

Jenny smiled. "I learned from the best."

She had to admit, Kathryn intimidated her, never more so than when it came to sex, but seeing her respond under her touch gave her confidence she'd only pretended to possess before. She leaned just close enough to brush her lips across Kathryn's waiting mouth before retreating.

Kathryn lunged forward, briefly tasting her before falling back onto the pillow. "Please kiss me."

When Jenny didn't respond, the writhing intensified and polite pleading turned breathless and desperate. "Please," she said.

Between Kathryn's begging and her gyrating hips pressing on her passion-inflamed center, Jenny couldn't hold back any longer. Despite her upper hand, she finally released Kathryn's wrists and slid to a prone position, where their horizontal repose made all things equal. Kathryn exhaled an approving purr as Jenny's body came down to meet hers in all the right places. Jenny moaned as Kathryn tangled her fingers in her hair and entwined their legs as if she would never let her go.

The kiss was hungry, and their hips ground together in perfect rhythm. Jenny couldn't tell where she ended and Kathryn began. She was lost in the rising passion of their desperate embrace. She lived only for Kathryn at that moment. Lived only to please.

"Tell me what you like," she said, when she finally broke for air.

Kathryn mildly protested the interruption before mumbling her answer. "What I don't like would be a shorter list."

"Okay. What don't you like?"

Kathryn pulled her into another kiss, stopping only briefly to reply. "Nothing."

"Mmm," Jenny hummed as their lips were reunited. She cupped Kathryn's cheek before dragging her fingertips down her neck, across her collarbone, and to her chest, where she encircled a breast to muffled moans of approval with every brush of a sensitive spot. Jenny took mental note of the pleasure map and continued her path down the long midsection until Kathryn's thighs parted for her hand. Her fingers reached the slick folds of Kathryn's warm desire, and she slowly followed the increasing sounds of pleasure until she slipped two fingers inside. Kathryn tore her mouth away from their kiss as a breathless cry escaped her open mouth and her head thrust back into the pillow.

With her other hand, Jenny stroked Kathryn's upturned face, astounded she put that rapture there, and found her fingers taken into her mouth as Kathryn moaned her appreciation over and over. Kathryn's approval was addicting, pushing her lust and physical stamina even farther than she imagined possible. For some reason, she thought Kathryn would be the silent type, in total control at all times, especially during sex, given one's vulnerable position, but she couldn't have been more wrong.

Kathryn pressed into her hand, and she gave her what she wanted, massaging her need until measured exhales of pleasure turned into incessant moans of desperation. Addicted to Kathryn's escalating craving, Jenny cupped the soft fullness of Kathryn's breast and took it into her mouth. She suckled and teased the hard flesh between her teeth, and Kathryn arched into the sharp jolts of pleasure. Jenny stopped, afraid she was hurting her.

"I'm sorr—"

Kathryn quickly clutched her shoulder. "I'll tell you when to stop," she said between gasps. "I'll always tell you when to stop."

Jenny understood, and it spurred her on to new heights of arousal just thinking of the possibilities. She continued the rough teasing of the nipple in her mouth and rolled the other between her fingers, with an eye on Kathryn's limits. She pinched harder than she would have thought comfortable for anyone, but Kathryn's twisting body and exalted cries of *"Yes!"* at every effort proved intoxicating. Never before had someone responded so intensely to her touch, and now she held the ecstasy of the most sensual creature she'd ever encountered in her hands.

She slid her body the length of Kathryn's, settling her shoulders between her open legs. She ran her hand up Kathryn's soft inner thigh to more moans of pleasure and followed with a trail of kisses that ended when her mouth enveloped the swollen flesh at the end of the line.

"God ... *yes!*" Kathryn cried out as she convulsed into Jenny's hot tongue. "There. *Right there.* God. *Yes!*"

Kathryn couldn't tell what Jenny was doing exactly, and she didn't care. Her mouth was on her, her fingers were in her, and every movement sent a wave of renewed ecstasy like a warm drug injected into her veins. She was so ready to come it hurt to be touched, but pain and pleasure had become the same, and her body craved the fire. The pressure built and burned until she couldn't stand it. She was lost in the rapturous insanity of sexual abandon, and it took her a moment to realize that the desperate cries of passion filling her ears were her own voice, unfamiliar in its pleading. She tried to quiet herself, the sounds seeming wholly absurd in their intensity, but she found her body's response beyond her control as Jenny's mouth suckled and teased—gentle, then hard—and her fingers filled her again and again in a steady rhythm. She had been taken to the brink quickly, but she held on, unable to take more, but unable to deny that she wanted the madness to last forever.

She was panting almost to the point of hyperventilation, and wait, was she whining? She pinched her own nipples, seeking more stimulation, or less—God, she didn't know anymore—and then Jenny plunged her fingers deep inside and curled them up until she pressed hard against the hallowed spot that made her body and mind explode in pleasure.

She arched rigidly into Jenny's touch as she desperately clawed the sheets with one hand and gripped Jenny's shoulder with the other, a signal she hoped was understood as *don't move!* Jenny didn't move, and she cried out her release seconds later, as they both clung to each other and let the searing rapture have its way with them.

A blinding white light lifted Kathryn on a wave of exploded bliss.

Her body convulsed and shuddered, and she let out a final moan of relief before her voice and her breath were taken from her. She tumbled weightlessly into an endless abyss. She rode out the spasms, clinging desperately, gratefully, to Jenny until the urgency subsided and she relaxed, spent and breathless, her heart beating wildly.

Jenny trailed soft kisses from her inner thigh, to her breast, to her shoulder, where she rested her head. She placed a hand on her heaving chest, moving in soothing circles as if to calm the pounding heart beneath it.

Kathryn released an exhausted exhale, still struggling to catch her breath. When she finally managed to make her hand obey her command to move, she placed it over the one on her chest, stilling it. "You lied to me."

She felt Jenny stiffen at her side.

"You said you weren't good at anything but shooting."

Jenny relaxed with an exhaled chuckle and entwined her fingers in Kathryn's. "Well, it must be you, because I assure you, no one's ever responded to me like that before."

"You're obviously not making love to the right people."

"I couldn't agree with you more."

Kathryn seconded that. She couldn't remember the last time she felt so safe and so free under someone else's control. For that matter, she couldn't remember the last time she *wanted* to feel so safe and free *or* under someone else's control. She kissed the top of Jenny's head. "Are you all right?"

"Are you kidding?"

Jenny snuggled closer and draped her leg across her thigh in a mindless display of possession.

Kathryn kissed her on the head again and settled her head back into the pillow. She wiped the sweat from her brow with the back of her hand as "Gosh" came out in a feeble exultation of her night.

Jenny kissed her hand. "I told you once that I'd seduce you, and then I'd have you under my spell."

Kathryn let out an easy laugh. "I love—" To her horror, she almost said *I love you* and stumbled over the unconscious impulse.

She continued instead with, "That about you." Adding, "I love your sense of self," to make her cover complete.

Jenny chuckled, tilting her head up to see her expression. "Is that a polite way of saying I'm conceited?"

"It's self-confidence, not conceit."

"Well," Jenny said, as she settled her head back in its cradle, "that's what you get for being a spoiled only child. You never outgrow that whole-world-revolves-around-me attitude."

"You wear it well. I like it." Kathryn squeezed tighter, making sure the *I love you* rolling around in her head stayed put. That just couldn't be. She didn't even know what love was. She certainly wasn't going to give into the cliché of saying it for the first time during pillow talk.

"Wait a minute—" Jenny lifted her head. "Like it? A few seconds ago you loved it."

Kathryn laughed. "I love it," she said, and planted another kiss on Jenny's head. She wanted to change the conversation to divert attention away from her uncharacteristically clingy behavior. "Are you sure you're all right? I think you got the short end of the deal here."

"Hey, I came twice. Poor you."

Kathryn rolled on top of Jenny and arched a seductive brow. "The night's not over."

Jenny feigned apprehension. "You're going to kill me, aren't you?"

"What a way to go," Kathryn said with a grin.

CHAPTER EIGHT

Jenny didn't remember falling asleep, but she rolled onto her side and blindly reached for Kathryn to make sure it hadn't all been a dream. She found an empty space next to her in the bed and, for a brief disoriented moment, thought that it had been. "Don't even tell me," she whispered.

"Don't even tell you what?" Kathryn whispered back, as she stood behind her at the edge of the bed, buttoning her suit jacket.

Jenny rolled over, relieved to find she hadn't hallucinated the most incredible night of sex she'd ever had. "There you are."

"I'm sorry. I have to go."

Jenny lifted her head and looked at the clock on the nightstand. "Good grief, it's five-thirty in the morning. Don't you sleep?"

"Not a lot. I didn't want to wake you."

"Who was sleeping? I passed out."

Kathryn smiled. "I believe you did at that."

Jenny casually draped one arm behind her head, trying to look as alluring as possible. "Are you sure you can't stay a little longer?"

"As much as I'd like to—" Kathryn's eyes drifted to Jenny's exposed breasts. "I can't." She turned and picked up a hairbrush and some bobby pins from the vanity behind her and held them up. "May I?"

"Be my guest," Jenny said. She watched in amazement as Kathryn put the bobby pins between her pursed lips, brushed her disheveled hair into submission, exchanged the brush for a rat-tail comb, sectioned her hair, and back-combed it to support the victory rolls she made next.

She executed a salon-worthy do in a matter of minutes, and Jenny wondered if her talents ever ceased. "It takes me two mirrors and twenty minutes to do that."

Kathryn primped her work in the mirror. "Not one of my better efforts, but I was distracted."

She straightened as she turned back to the bed and adjusted her jacket on her shoulders, an action Jenny recognized as a final gesture before one leaves a room. She didn't want to appear too needy, ever vigilant against Kathryn's flight response, so she exhaled regretfully and threw the covers back, reaching for her robe. "I'll walk you out."

"No, no," Kathryn said quickly. "Don't move. I want to remember you just like that."

Jenny lay back on the bed, naked and uncovered now, one knee bent, one arm over her head, the other across her abdomen. "No fair. I have to remember you with clothes on."

Kathryn smiled, tilted her head in sympathy, and slowly began unbuttoning her jacket. She paused and raised a seductive eyebrow as the jacket slipped gently from her shoulders, revealing her bare breasts.

"Ugh." Jenny rolled to her side and buried her head in the bedding as she convulsed with desire. "You're killing me." She hugged her pillow. "You'd better get out of here before I barricade the way out."

Kathryn smiled and kneeled on the bed. She leaned in close and brushed her lips against the side of her cheek. Jenny felt her inhale deeply, and when Kathryn exhaled the breath into her ear, Jenny's eyes rolled back in her head. She cupped her hands around Kathryn's face and captured her lips in a passionate kiss.

Kathryn groaned regretfully, and when she pulled back from the kiss, Jenny could see her eyes were clouded with the same desire as her own.

Jenny's body was on fire again, demanding a repeat of last night, and Kathryn's flight risk be damned, she wasn't beyond begging. "Please stay," she whispered.

Kathryn's eyes darkened and her breathing picked up. Jenny's body celebrated its victory with a wave of anticipatory goose bumps.

Kathryn closed her eyes. "I can't." Without hesitation, and without giving Jenny the chance to say please one more time, she gave her a final kiss on the forehead, whispered "Bye," and quickly buttoned her jacket as she got up and headed toward the bedroom door. "I'll talk to you soon," she said without turning around.

Jenny lifted a hand goodbye as the door quietly closed. "Take care." Then, "Thank you," added as an afterthought. She stared at the towel swinging from the hook on the back of the door and cringed. "Thank you?" she said to herself. "Brilliant."

She heard Kathryn gather her things in the foyer and slip out the front door. Jenny lay motionless, processing the previous evening, not quite believing she actually seduced Kathryn Hammond. "Holy shit," she said on an exhale, as she sank back into her pillow with a very satisfied grin.

Kathryn couldn't think of one good reason to get out of Jenny's bed, but she knew there was one. Somewhere. Only reflexive discipline gave her the strength to end that final kiss. Her body was out of control, and her mind had to put an end to that.

Sheer force of will propelled her out of the house, into her car, and on her way home. She couldn't shake the feeling that she had done something wrong. Wrong for Jenny, wrong for her, wrong for the success of her job at the OSS. But it sure didn't feel wrong last night. In fact, it had never felt so right. The roller coaster of emotions, from trepidation to surrender, left her floating on schoolgirl giddiness.

In the light of the dawning day, Jenny's one night of fun was a revelation. What she felt was a true connection, not mindless recreational sex. She was an expert at that, and last night wasn't it.

The resulting high and lack of control frightened her, and she reached blindly for her treasured indifference to bring her back to earth. She wrapped it around her like an impenetrable cloak and convinced herself that, in the relative scheme of things, their moment was perfect in its brevity. Overwhelming *because* of its brevity. Just one night. Just like Jenny had said. One night of fun. It was as advertised, and then some, and she was going to keep that notion close and repeat it often, because the alternative seemed so impossible. She was falling in love.

CHAPTER NINE

*J*enny rolled out of bed, unable to fall back asleep. She showered and donned her robe and then wandered into the kitchen to start some coffee. Mission accomplished, she shuffled down the hallway in her slippers, on her way to the front door to retrieve the morning editions. She did a double take as she reached for the door. Kathryn's red and white scarf was draped neatly around a hook on the hall tree, and the beautiful silver brooch was pinned to it through a note.

Something to remember me by, it read. *I now have a broader definition of fun. Thank you.* The last word was underlined. The note was signed with a sweeping K and sealed with an openmouthed lipstick kiss.

Jenny smiled as she unpinned the note and reverently lifted the delicate scarf from its resting place. "As if I could ever forget." She buried her face in the sea of red and white material and inhaled deeply, pleased to find Kathryn's scent still lingering there. The memory of their night together was something she would always cherish, but her apprehensive lover left something tangible. That told her maybe she wasn't so apprehensive anymore. "I've got you now, haven't I?"

She set the note and pin on the foyer table and then dramatically wrapped the scarf around her neck a la the Red Baron and proudly stepped outside to gather the papers from the lawn. Starting with the *Daily Chronicle*, she spread the pages on the kitchen table and settled in with her cup of coffee. The paper had gone on without her—not that she expected anything less—but egos are demanding little creatures, and hers was no different. She patiently waded through each section and each article on her way to the part of the paper that would be most impacted by her absence: *Arts and Entertainment*.

Jenny almost dropped her coffee cup when she unfolded the section and found a small photograph of Kathryn Hammond staring back at her from the *Around Town* column, under the headline Grotto Chanteuse Wows Downtown Crowd. She quickly scanned the article, all the while cursing her uncle as she remembered Bill Connelly's warning about the consequences for breach of contract at The Grotto. "How in the hell did you find out about this?" she muttered, as she prepared to read for content. "And how in the hell did you get it in the morning edition?"

She had to admit, it was a great article, one she wished she'd written. It extolled Kathryn's virtues as one of the town's finest singers and plugged her nightly shows at The Grotto every chance it got, but her concern over Kathryn's job tempered her pride. She put a hand to her forehead and uttered a curse. "She's going to think *I* called the paper. Mr. Vignelli is going to fire her, and that's going to screw things up with Forrester." She paused, trying to think of a way to fix things, even though she knew in her heart it was hopeless. More cursing ensued.

It was déjà vu all over again. She took a calming breath and ran down her options. She could confront her uncle, but she hadn't spoken to him in over a month, and nothing she could say would change the fact that the paper was already out there. She could call Kathryn and apologize, but she probably wasn't home yet, and that still wouldn't keep her from being fired. The only other player, the key player, in fact, was Dominic Vignelli. She would get a hold of him as soon as possible and explain the circumstances at the Blue Note, hoping he was the understanding sort.

Smitty climbed the stairs leading to Kathryn's apartment and was about to rap on the door when he heard an odd sound. He paused and listened, then smiled, welcoming back a habit absent for far too long.

"Knock, knock," he said as a courtesy, swinging open the door she'd left unlocked for him.

"Hi, handsome," Kathryn said with a grin as she came out of her bedroom, tucking a white t-shirt into her dark olive fatigues. She kissed him on the cheek and continued her path into the kitchen. "Want some coffee?"

Smitty did a double take at the clothes and the demeanor. "Were you humming when I came in?"

"Was I?" Kathryn said over her shoulder as she poured her breakfast into a cup. "I hadn't noticed."

"Yeah, you were, and you are uncharacteristically cheerful at this ungodly hour."

"Seven thirty is not ungodly. Five o'clock is ungodly, and I should know because that's what time I got up." She turned and leaned against the counter, an odd smile pulling at her lips.

"Nightmares again?" he asked sympathetically as he approached, unsure of her expression.

"The exact opposite." She grinned, offering him her cup, as if she were handing him back his words and the memories that went with them.

He took it for what it was worth and nodded. "I see. Explanation to follow, I'm sure."

Kathryn smiled and reached into the cupboard for another cup. "I'm sure."

Smitty knew the answer would come in its own time, and pushing would not hasten the disclosure, so he watched her fill her cup and ran his eyes down her tall frame. "What's with the duds?"

"I thought I'd put in for mission training," she said into the hollow counter space beneath the cupboard.

He noticed she didn't turn to face him as she delivered this news, which told him she expected an argument about it, and he would not change her mind.

"Why?"

On cue, she turned and defended her decision with an air of confidence. "Because I have experience and I think I could impart that knowledge to the incoming recruits."

"I know *that*, but why now?"

Kathryn didn't answer immediately. Instead, she stalled by grabbing her black turtleneck sweater from the kitchen table and slipping it over her head. "I'm tired of running, Smitty," she said, guiding her hair out of the confines of the top. "I'm wasting the skills I have by hiding behind some mental crutch when I could be making a valuable contribution."

"Kat, you already make a valuable contribution."

"I could do more."

Smitty shook his head, but she looked away so she didn't have to see it as she turned down the collar and smoothed the ribbed sweater over her torso.

"I'm just putting in. It doesn't mean Walter will approve."

"Sure he will. You were one of the best."

She looked up at his use of the past tense. "My point exactly."

He could only assume her sudden change of heart had something to do with her night, a night that was undoubtedly spent with a certain young blonde. "The kid's really something, eh?"

She paused at the shift in subject matter, and then smiled and patted his cheek as she brushed past. "No, Smitty, she's just like all the rest ... a party girl looking for a thrill ride."

He stared at her back as she picked up her purse and her cup of coffee from the counter. "You're kidding."

"Nope," she said as she headed out of the kitchen and toward the stairwell. "I'm relieved, actually. That never would have worked long term. They never do."

If Smitty didn't know better, he would say there was a sting of hurt in her tone.

She didn't wait for him to get the door. "Coming?"

"Yeah."

Smitty slowly raised his hat and settled it firmly on his head. Jenny Ryan was no fool. She hadn't known Kathryn long, but she already knew how to get what she wanted. "You played that right, kid," he mumbled to the air as he turned off the light and shut the door behind him.

Kathryn was lost in her thoughts on the ride to the training center, and Smitty was respectfully silent, content to let her have her space. She snuck a look at him and smiled. She loved the way he watched without looking and spoke volumes without saying a word. This morning, the confident set of his jaw telegraphed his wisdom without effort. She could only shake her head at her futile attempt to deceive him *and* herself. Jenny had gotten to her, changed her, as she knew she would, and, as usual, Smitty sensed it long before it was even a consideration in her mind.

"Can't fool you, can I, Smitty?"

He smiled. "Never, doll."

She bowed her head with a grin, accepting his insight as a comfort.

"Are we sharing?" he asked.

Kathryn knew her involuntary ear-to-ear grin told him everything he needed to know, and she relaxed into her seat, crossing her legs against the sudden arousal spreading from her center at the mere thought of Jenny.

"Of all people, Kat, why her?"

Kathryn thought about giving him some dismissive remark about fantastic sex, but she was captured long before that, and what she felt for Jenny deserved the dignity of the truth. "She soothes my soul, Smitty."

Kathryn sensed his questioning glance, and without returning it, felt her answer accepted, as he turned his attention back to the road without comment. After all of his protests and warnings against getting involved, his acceptance proved that he knew a losing battle when he saw one, and she could almost sense a physical change as he turned his efforts to damage control.

"It might get complicated," he said.

His comment tempered her enthusiasm but not her determination. "I know."

"Do you really believe she's just looking for a good time?"

"Right now, I'm having a hard time discerning between fact and wishful thinking. I honestly don't know." She paused. "I hope not."

"Well, how did the morning after go? Couldn't you tell?"

"I didn't stay to find out."

Smitty turned his head in amused disbelief. "You chicken!"

"I know," Kathryn said and briefly buried her face in her hands, hiding the blush warming her cheeks. "I feel like a high-schooler."

Smitty shook his head. "You've got it bad, gal. What has she done to you?"

"I don't know," she said, realizing how uncharacteristic her behavior must seem to him. In the end, perhaps she was just being foolhardy. "Maybe it's just great sex and I'm reaching for the brass ring."

"Don't sell it short, Kat. Not if it makes you happy."

She loved him for supporting her, even though she knew he had his reservations. "Does it sound too clichéd to say that I've never felt this way before?"

"Yeah, but what's a cliché between friends when there's great sex involved?"

She smiled, growing more comfortable with her burgeoning attraction and Smitty's ability to accept it. Was this what love felt like? Floating on air, able to take on the world? Suddenly, everything seemed possible.

"I want to tell her everything about me."

Smitty raised a doubting brow, but it didn't matter. The way Jenny looked at her, it was as if she wanted her to tell her everything, her gentle green eyes begging for it so that she could tell her it was okay. "I think she can take it. I think she'd understand."

Kathryn could see the scene so clearly that she almost swore it had already happened. The car hit a pothole, shaking her out of her reverie, and head cleared, she attributed her mirage to foolish idealism, reaching out in desperation from under a life defined by tragedy and regret.

Smitty was non-responsive this time, as he let her process the reality of what she was saying. Her shoulders slumped as her expectations fell, but she remained silent, with everything she didn't want to acknowledge encompassed in her vacant stare.

"But what if she doesn't understand?" he finally asked.

She exhaled regretfully. "Yeah."

"Are you ready to risk it?"

Her eyes closed as the memory of their night together drifted through her mind, painting the corners with warmth and hope. When her eyes fluttered open, she had made her choice. She would run just a little longer. "Not yet."

CHAPTER TEN

*J*enny held the telephone receiver in one hand and pushed some files around on her desk with the other, looking for her keys. "Bernie, I'm sorry. I can't make lunch, I'm running late."

"What a surprise!" he said.

"Ha ha," Jenny said, "not you too. I just hung up on Aunt B because I couldn't get her off the phone. I'm surprised she hasn't called back and given me what for."

"And how is dear Aunt B?"

"Fine. She was riding me about making up with Uncle Paul before the benefit tonight."

"Well, since he's your ticket in there, that's a good idea. I thought you were coming over to do that?"

"I am—" She opened and closed her desk drawers in her frantic search. "But I'm late. Dammit, where are my keys?"

"Jacket pocket."

She reached for the jacket on the back of her chair. "Bingo! Thank you."

"And my reward is that you stand me up for lunch. I'm hurt."

"No, you're not," she said with a smile as she tucked the receiver between her shoulder and chin and put one arm into her jacket sleeve. "I'll come see you before I leave, and, boy, have I got news for you."

"Can't wait."

"See you in a bit, hon." The receiver was in midair and on the way to its cradle before Bernie managed to utter his goodbye. Jenny was rushing out of the office when the secretary held up her phone with a hand over the mouthpiece.

"For you, Miss Ryan."

Oh no, Aunt B's wrath. She stopped mid-step and leaned back into the office. "If it's a woman, I'm not here."

The secretary nodded in the affirmative, indicating it was a woman, and politely reported Miss Ryan unavailable. Jenny waved a thanks and took off at a trot down the busy hallway.

"Would you like to leave a message, Miss Hammond?"

"No. Thank you, Lorraine."

Kathryn hung up the phone and looked quizzically at the receiver. The old 'hand over the mouthpiece' was never as effective as people thought. Jenny didn't want to talk to her. She felt the heat rise to her face as she recognized the familiar brush-off, one she had used more times than she could remember.

She realized that she hadn't really taken Jenny's lackadaisical attitude seriously, but faced with the reality of it, she could hardly ignore it. For some reason, this panicked her. Maybe it was because she was so familiar with the pattern, or because she was unaccustomed to being on the losing end, or for the simple reason that it mattered this time.

"Kat—" Bobby leaned closer, like someone who had said her name more than once before she noticed him and looked up. "Dominic would like to see you in his office."

"Thanks, Bobby."

He eyed her suspiciously as she tucked the phone away under the bar counter. "You okay?"

"Fine," she said with a smile, swinging her hips around the end of the bar. "Don't I look okay?"

"More than okay, as usual," he said, returning a grin. Kathryn playfully tugged on his sleeve and headed toward the boss's office.

"Ah, good afternoon, Miss Kathryn," Dominic said when she entered. He folded the newspaper he was reading to the *About Town* section and handed it to her. "You are a very popular woman. Should I fire you for breach of contract?"

She smiled as she scanned her article. "If I had a contract, I suppose you should." She flipped the paper over, looking for the author. "No byline."

"It is a very good article. Mentions us several times. Reservations have increased already, and you are not even singing tonight."

"I'm sorry about that, Nicky. You're not mad, are you?"

He made a sour face and looked up from under his furrowed brow. "Don't be foolish. I know you have other obligations. It is never an issue, you know that."

"Thank you, but I mean about singing at the Blue Note."

"As you say, you do not have a contract."

"But I sense you have something to say about it."

"You are a very talented lady. Too talented to spend your career in this nightclub. One day you will move on to bigger and better things. I am just testing the waters, as they say, wondering if you are testing yours."

"I'm very happy here, Nicky. You know my unique situation, and you're more than good to me."

"I am indebted to you, Kathryn. There will always be a place for you here."

She shifted uncomfortably. "You don't owe me anything. Anyone would have done the same."

"Well, that anyone was you, and I don't want to hear anymore nonsense from you."

She held up her hands in surrender, and he took the opportunity to switch gears.

"Your young friend called me this morning. She was very worried for your job."

Kathryn tried to remain neutral, but from Dominic's knowing grin, she'd failed utterly. "That was sweet."

"Yes. Very sweet."

He looked at her expectantly, but she certainly wasn't going to confirm what she feared he already knew.

"Well, I'm glad you're not upset about the Blue Note, but I'll make it up to you just the same."

"Get out of here." He waved dismissively at the door, rejecting her offer as unnecessary.

She tossed the paper on his desk. "Ciao, Nicky."

Jenny found it odd riding the elevator to her old floor at the *Daily Chronicle*. Odd, yet familiar, in a way that told her she no longer belonged here. She waved to old friends as she strode through the busy office, giving hugs to the few who made the effort and hurried small talk to others, as she tried to say as little as possible about her new job, in an attempt not to lie to her former colleagues.

She passed by her still empty desk as she approached her uncle's office and tapped lightly on the door, entering when he lifted his head and smiled at the sight of her.

"Well, well!" He rose to greet her.

"Hi, Uncle Paul." She made her way to the side of his desk and embraced him.

"I wondered if I'd ever see your shining face again."

"No, you didn't," she said, playfully slapping his belly. "Nice article this morning." She pointed at the open paper on his desk.

He chuckled. "I thought that might get your attention." He disengaged himself from her arms and made his way behind his desk, lowering himself into his large leather chair with a self-satisfied groan.

"You're lucky Mr. Vignelli is so easygoing," she said, losing a little of her good humor. "Kathryn could have lost her job."

He peered over his glasses. "Then she shouldn't do things that put her job in jeopardy."

Jenny bristled at his comment, which carried the slightest hint of condescension in its delivery. He did it on purpose to get a reaction, and she wasn't going to give him the satisfaction.

She pushed some papers aside to sit on the corner of his desk. "So, how did you hear about this?" She tapped her finger on Kathryn's article.

"Someone called it in last night." He removed his glasses and casually tossed them on his desk. "Thought it was news, for some reason. Friend of yours?"

"Hardly. Bill Connelly." It had to be him. She picked up the paper and stared at Kathryn's picture, quickly setting it aside when she realized she couldn't hide her infatuated grin. She rubbed the back of her neck and got back to the matter at hand. "A man of limited talent with an axe to grind."

"Miss Hammond only brings out the best," he said.

"Anyway," Jenny drew out, trying to ignore his attitude.

Her uncle wisely changed the subject, smiling as he leaned back and clasped his hands across his stomach. "I hear through the grapevine you've got a nice ad job."

Jenny knew who the grapevine was, and she'd specifically asked him not to say anything. "Bernie's got a big mouth."

"It gets even bigger when you threaten to fire him if he doesn't talk."

"Nice, Uncle Paul. You could have just asked me."

"I didn't think you were speaking to me."

"Well, I'm here—" She absentmindedly repositioned a pencil, taking responsibility for her part in their estrangement. "I guess I am."

"Your job is waiting for you whenever you're ready." He glanced in the direction of her empty desk, as if she'd made an unspoken apology.

"I'm not coming back to the *Chronicle*, Uncle Paul." She was on the defensive, which made it sound like a warning, which caused her uncle to lean forward and clasp his hands on the desk in front of him, a gesture she recognized as trouble.

"Then why are you here?"

She realized the situation could easily spin out of control, so she reached over and touched his tense hands. "Do I need a reason to come see you?"

He eyed her warily, and then his face hardened as the dawn finally broke on her intentions. "The benefit." He pulled his hands from under hers. "You're here because of the benefit."

Jenny watched him stare at her in disbelief, and she knew this visit would not go well.

"You think you can just waltz in here, bat your eyes, and you're forgiven?"

"Forgiven? Me? Forgiven for what?" It was a knee-jerk reaction to the unexpected turn in mood and a reaction she regretted when her uncle abruptly stood and glared at her. His body blocked the light from the window and cast an ominous shadow on her smaller form. "Uncle Paul—" She held up her hand and slid off the desk to get out from under his gathering storm. "I didn't come here to fight with you."

"No, you came here to make sure you were still invited to the benefit tonight, and I'm here to tell you, you are not."

"Why, because I don't want my job back?"

"Because you haven't made the slightest effort to square things with me until now, and you're only here now because you want something."

"That's not—"

"Don't you dare deny it, young lady," Paul said with a warning finger.

It was obvious he was hurt, but whether that hurt stemmed from their neglected relationship or because of her change in occupation was unclear. She supposed it was a bit of both. "I was going to say," she drew out slowly, trying to remain even-tempered, "that's not entirely true."

As her uncle stood, hands on hips, waiting for her explanation, she had a sick feeling in the pit of her stomach. The guilt of arguing with her father—words of anger, the last communication they shared—rose in her throat like bile, and she swallowed hard. After vowing never to make that mistake again, she had let this estrangement go on for over a month. Regret filled her eyes, and her uncle melted to it, as his demeanor softened and he awkwardly reached out to her.

"Hey."

She gladly accepted the comfort of his embrace. "I'm sorry, Uncle Paul. I love you. I don't want to fight."

"I love you too, kiddo." He gave her an apologetic squeeze. "Let's forget all this nonsense and call a truce, shall we?"

She gave him an extra squeeze before releasing her hold. "Gladly."

"Good." He stepped back behind his desk and settled into his chair. "Janie can fill you in on everything you've missed." He started riffling through some files on his desk. "Thought you might be interested in this—" He held up a folder.

"Uncle Paul, I'm not coming back here."

He dropped the file and clasped his hands across it. "So much for burying the hatchet."

"It's got nothing to do with that. My change in employment is not a reflection on you and has nothing to do with spite."

"You have a bright future here, Jenny."

"Thank you for saying that, but it's just not for me."

He glared at her. "Just like that? Suddenly, it's just not for you. You're too good for the newspaper business now, is that it?"

Jenny knew her uncle to have a quick temper, but something else was going on here, and whatever it was, she was not going to feed it. As gently as she could, she tried to backpedal gracefully. "It's not like that. I've just chosen another field, that's all."

"Oh, yes, advertising. There's a noble profession," he said sarcastically, "much more respectable than the *news*."

"Uncle Paul, you cannot be serious. This is not about me leaving the paper."

"I built this paper for you, Jenny."

"Don't you lay that at my feet. You built this paper as a big up yours to Granddad."

"What do you know about it?" He stood, eyes wide and seething, causing Jenny to step back. He stabbed his finger into the folders on his desk. "I fought and scraped and sacrificed for everything I have. What have you worked for? Born with a silver spoon in your mouth and every opportunity handed to you."

Jenny felt the words like a knife in the heart. Who was this man, and what had he done with her uncle? She was momentarily stunned, never realizing how bitter he was at the lifestyle he was born into yet denied. He *had* scraped for everything he'd gotten, spite spurring him on, success at any cost, all to show his father he could. It never occurred to her that he would take her departure so personally. His words were cruel, with an edge honed by resentment. She didn't deserve that, no matter how large a chip he bore.

She remained speechless, and her uncle seemed as shocked as she at the words falling out of his mouth, but he made no attempt to take them back or to soften the blow. They lingered in the air like poison gas until Jenny thought she might suffocate. Her slow death was interrupted when her uncle broke eye contact and turned his attention to the organized chaos on his desk.

Jenny stood abandoned in the middle of the office, too hurt to comment without crying, too proud to allow the pain to show. She turned to leave, but before she could reach for the doorknob, she felt her uncle's hand on her shoulder.

"I'm sorry, Jenny. I didn't mean it."

Unable to turn around to face him, she paused and bowed her head. Gathering as much forgiveness as her wounded psyche would allow, she tried to part with some semblance of civility, but her vow not to part in anger was severely tested. "I know. I'm sorry too." With that, she left the office and gently closed the door behind her. She imagined she had quite a look on her face, as, out of the corner of her eye, she saw her former coworkers following her progress down the aisle from under cautious brows, making no attempt to speak to her or say goodbye.

"Hey, Bug!" Bernie beamed as Jenny made her way to his desk in the basement of the *Daily Chronicle*. She was still smarting from the run-in with her uncle, but she tried to smile anyway, a futile gesture that wouldn't fool her friend, who reacted immediately. "Uh-oh. Things did not go well upstairs, I take it. No go on the benefit tonight, eh?"

"Worse than that," Jenny said, as she glided straight into his open arms.

He gave her a squeeze. "What could be worse than that?"

"Oh, he basically told me not to choke on my silver spoon as I waltz effortlessly through all the open doors that have defined my existence on the planet thus far."

Bernie stepped back to get a look at her face. "He what?"

"Swell, huh?" Jenny patted his arm and sat on his desk, her deflated posture saying more about her emotions than her cynical words conveyed.

"Jeepers." Bernie crossed his arms and shook his head as he took a seat next to her. "I can't believe he said that." He paused. "Even if it is true."

Jenny snapped her head in his direction just in time to see the grin spread across his face. Her sour mood lightened, and she chuckled with him as she leaned her head on his shoulder. "I miss you."

"I miss you too." He craned his head to the side, seeking her downturned eyes. "Are you okay?"

"Yeah, don't worry," she said, knowing what he expected. "I had my cry in the elevator."

Bernie put his arm around her shoulder and pulled her closer. "He loves you, Jenny. You know he does."

"I know. I just ... I know he's got a temper, but jeez. Was that really necessary?"

"You know he didn't mean what he said."

"I guess."

"Stop it. You had to work harder than anyone in that office just because the two of you are related, and no one knows that better than he does."

"That's true."

"He just misses you."

"Well, he's got a funny way of showing it."

"The gals in the office say he sometimes just sits and stares at your empty desk with a forlorn look on his face."

"He does not."

"It's true."

"Really?"

"Mm-hm. And to ease his pain, he calls in some new intern and chews them a new behind."

"Lovely."

"Yeah, he's a giver."

Jenny shook her head. "Still. Ouch."

Bernie hopped off the desk and into his chair. "So, what's your big news?"

"My what?" She blinked. "Oh!" She raised a hand in disbelief that she'd almost forgotten, and her face lit up, warming from ashen grey to slightly embarrassed pink, with an accompanying self-satisfied smirk. She leaned forward, making a quick scan of the busy office, and whispered to make sure she wouldn't be overheard. "I seduced Kathryn Hammond last night."

Bernie gasped. "You did not!"

"Shhhh!" She looked around, feigning alarm before grinning proudly. "I did too."

"And?"

"And," she drew out incredulously, "what do you think?"

"From the look on your face? Holy cow."

"You said it, brother."

"Holy cow," he whispered again. He leaned forward and scooted his chair to Jenny's knee. "So, is she your girlfriend now, or what? And what about the evil boyfriend? How does that work?"

"The evil boyfriend is apparently very liberal, and girlfriend status has not been achieved, but I will do my best to change her mind."

"What do you mean, change her mind?"

"She thinks we're just having sex."

"And whatever gave her that idea?"

"Hey, a girl's got to do what a girl's got to do."

"Jenny!" Bernie smiled and shook his head. "What if she doesn't want to be in a relationship?"

"Oh, she's in a relationship. She just doesn't know it."

Silence was Bernie's cautious reply, and Jenny felt the need to defend herself. "She's just scared of commitment, and I'm going to show her that she doesn't have to be scared of me."

"Maybe she's scared *for* you. Did you ever think of that?" He glanced around the room before leaning even closer. "She does have a mobster boyfriend, you know. Liberal or not, a man's a man, and sharing is not always high on the list of acquired social graces ... I don't care what Kathryn Hammond claims."

"Kathryn can handle Forrester, and I can take care of myself."

Bernie's jovial mood vanished. "Be careful, Jenny."

She exhaled a heavy sigh and looked vacantly into the busy office, finally offering an empty grin and a half-hearted wave to a familiar face across the room.

Bernie put a comforting hand on her knee. "I'm sorry, sweetie. I just don't want you to get hurt."

"I know." She took his hand. "Crummy day, that's all."

"I've got something to cheer you up." He patted her hand before abandoning it for something in his top desk drawer. "As head staff photographer of this fine publication—" He rummaged through loose grease pencils and empty film cartridges. "I have certain perks." He found what he was looking for and held up an envelope. "Like being entitled to bring one guest to tonight's benefit."

Jenny's eyes lit up, and she clasped her hands in exaggerated worship. "My hero!"

CHAPTER ELEVEN

An array of popping flashbulbs momentarily blinded Jenny when Kathryn took Forrester's offered hand and unfolded herself from the backseat of his Packard limo. Her heavily beaded gold gown slinked obediently behind as it landed with a solid thud at her feet, following her step to the curb.

Her hair was up, exposing her graceful neck and shoulders, making her seem taller and even slimmer than usual.

She enveloped Forrester's arm at the elbow and smiled like she truly cared when he covered her hand with his. They made the short journey up the red carpet like a deliriously happy Hollywood couple arriving at the Oscars on the big night.

She was a walking statuette, Jenny thought, as she watched from over Bernie's shoulder in the crowded photographer's row. He leaned in to take his shots, and for a few fleeting moments, she had an unobstructed view.

"Wow, she looks gorgeous," Bernie said over his shoulder, as he reached in his pocket and secured a new bulb to the flash harness on his camera.

"I didn't know she would be here," Jenny said, transfixed but dismayed to see her new lover all over Forrester.

Bernie turned in disbelief. "Jenny, he's one of the chief contributors ... one of the reasons this foundation even exists."

"I know." She shook her head. "I don't know what I was thinking."

He grinned and turned his attention forward, waiting for the next car to arrive. "I don't know what you were thinking either, but I know what you were thinking with."

She slapped him playfully on the back. "I'm going in."

"Sure, leave me here, slaving away, while you go inside and knock back champagne."

"Gotta love the perks," she said with a wave as she blended into the throng of well-dressed people entering the large hall.

She took the coupe of bubbly offered upon entry and worked her way to the second-floor balcony for a better view. Making herself comfortable, she leaned on the railing overlooking the ballroom and watched the city's top dignitaries mix and mingle with the celebrity and stuffy medical set, all in the name of charity.

It wasn't hard to spot Forrester. He was the one surrounded by the small tribe of drooling men in black-tied monkey suits, as the beautiful woman on his arm quickly became the center of attention.

Kathryn held a coupe of champagne in one hand as the other alternated between the crook of Forrester's elbow and the air into which she drew very animated gestures to embellish whatever story she was telling. Jenny watched curiously. This was a woman she'd never seen before. Kathryn was smiling and laughing, unabashedly fawning over Forrester when she wasn't playfully touching the arm of some other man in the group, all under Forrester's watchful and approving eye.

He smiled proudly, his hand on the small of Kathryn's back, just above her scandalously low-cut dress. It made Jenny want to turn away in disgust, not sure if her revulsion was his arrogance or Kathryn's masquerade—*if* it was a masquerade. If it was, she was good. Too good. Frighteningly good. It was unsettling, but she couldn't turn away. She kept waiting for a slip, just a glimpse of the woman she called lover the night before.

Perhaps drawn by the intense stare, or perhaps by happenstance,

Kathryn looked up and found Jenny's uncertain green eyes boring into her. There was a momentary pause, long enough for recognition, but not long enough to elicit a reaction. Kathryn went on with her flawless performance and never again lifted her eyes above room level.

Jenny got the drift—she was to be ignored. She also didn't like it. Her reaction was foolish, and she caught herself immediately. She didn't know what she expected, but Miss Jekyll and Miss Hyde was not it. She closed her eyes, admonishing herself for being selfish, and tried to put herself in Kathryn's position. Forrester was a dangerous man, and Kathryn had warned her about the complications of a relationship. Assignments always come first, she reminded herself, as they should.

Jenny pulled her eyes from the scene and spotted Bernie at the bottom of the stairway, accepting his own coupe of champagne. She left the irrational jealousy at the top of the stairs and descended to greet him.

He hoisted his glass to hers as she negotiated the final step. "Cheers, cutie."

"Cheers. Did you get some good shots?"

"Honey, good shots are all I take. Come on, help me—" He grabbed her hand. "It'll be just like old times."

Jenny didn't mind the distraction, and she slipped easily into her typically charming self, seamlessly arranging photo ops for her friend. They managed to avoid her uncle, but all good things must come to an end, and as Jenny caught a fleeting glimpse of Kathryn and Forrester, a large form stepped into her line of sight and she heard Bernie utter, "Uh-oh," under his breath.

"How did you get in here?" Paul demanded sternly.

Jenny wrapped her arm around Bernie's bicep in defiance. "I'm Bernie's guest."

Paul cut his eyes to him. "You are fired, Roth!"

Bernie had his camera in one hand and a glass of champagne in the other, and Jenny knew he would have dropped either one, or both, had she not immediately given him a reassuring squeeze and stepped between him and her uncle.

"Uncle Paul," she said in controlled anger, "if you fire him over this, I will never speak to you again." She paused for dramatic effect. "And you know I mean it." The two stared at each other, each daring the other to back down.

No words passed between them, and Jenny considered this a victory. She stepped aside, making room for the apology. Paul's gaze drifted past her shoulder, and his eyes fell on the half empty glass in Bernie's hand. The apology was issued Paul Ryan style. "Don't you need two hands to take pictures?"

"Yes, sir," Bernie said, handing the glass to the nearest waiter before making himself scarce.

Jenny watched Bernie's back disappear into the crowd before turning to her uncle again. "What is wrong with you?"

He reached for her arm. "You're getting out of—"

"Paul," a deep voice came from behind, with an accompanying hand on the shoulder. "So good to see you. How have you been?"

Her uncle turned, revealing Forrester's stout frame to her view and two familiar hands wrapped around his arm. Jenny hoped no one would move so she wouldn't have to face Kathryn, not sure she could pull off casual indifference at this close range.

"Marcus, a pleasure." Paul extended his hand and smiled graciously, as if nothing had happened and Marcus Forrester was his best friend.

Jenny eyed her uncle with contempt and wondered if she was the only one who could carry an honest emotion from one moment to the next. Bodies shifted as they greeted, and Jenny caught sight of Kathryn's eyes, which were firmly fixed on Paul with a distinct if-looks-could-kill glare. Jenny's confusion was interrupted by the continuing courtesy of introductions, with Forrester all but brushing Paul aside as he extended his hand in her direction.

"This must be your lovely niece. Jenny, correct?"

"Yes, sir," she said, politely returning the nicety, "pleasure to meet you." Her stomach churned as their palms met. She was touching the man who had taken countless lives, if not directly then by proxy, and touching the hand that does God knows what with the woman she now calls lover. She released his hand with a misleading smile and joined the ranks of the emotional chameleons.

"I believe you know Miss Hammond." He stepped slightly to the side and extended his hand in presentation.

Jenny knew he thought them to be lovers, and his crooked smile seemed to condone it, as if they needed his permission and he had graciously agreed, making him the master of their fate. She hated that he thought he was in control. She briefly entertained taking Kathryn in her arms and kissing her right there, in front of him, in front of everyone. Show them how Kathryn craved her touch, begged for it, even. Instead, she stood mute while he had the audacity to present her like a prized cow.

"Yes," Kathryn said. She offered her hand quickly. "Jenny. Hello."

The way Kathryn said hello, warmly, with detached innocence and no hint of their recent intimate past in her voice or manner, calmed Jenny immediately, and she momentarily overcame her revulsion for Forrester. She accepted her hand and smiled in relief. "Kathryn."

Jenny noticed Forrester and her uncle watching with interest. Forrester looked like the cat that ate the canary, and her uncle looked like he'd like to punch something.

Bernie appeared, holding up his camera, eager to show the boss he was doing his job. "A picture, folks?"

Her uncle briefly glared at him for the interruption before putting on a fake smile for the lens.

As the group stood shoulder to shoulder for the photograph, Jenny choked on the irony of the situation. Not so long ago, she would have given anything to be face to face with the evil man to her right, to know intimately the woman by his side, and to feel the satisfaction of knowing the work she was doing could change the course of world events. But instead of a sense of accomplishment, the weight of the responsibility pressed on her fragile calm and she realized the seriousness of her position. She silently thanked Kathryn for her cool example, for without it, she was sure she'd have fallen apart.

Bernie slipped away with his captured images, and her uncle turned to Forrester to excuse himself. "Good to see you again, Marc." He turned his false smile to her. "Jenny, may I speak with you for a moment?"

She passed her champagne glass from one hand to the other and stood her ground, purposely disregarding the implication of his outstretched hand. She had no desire to publicly humiliate him, nor did she want to listen to his heavy-handed monologue of what she could and couldn't do. She felt it best to defuse their volatile situation and avoid a confrontation altogether.

She put on an artificial smile of her own. "Why don't we just enjoy ourselves this evening, Uncle Paul? That other matter will wait until tomorrow." She placed a conciliatory hand on his arm for good measure, an action that saw him tense visibly.

Despite her best acting, the discord did not go unnoticed, and Forrester stepped into it. "So, Jenny," he said as he put his arm around her shoulder and led her into the milling crowd.

Kathryn exchanged silent daggers with Paul as Forrester walked away with Jenny.

"What were you thinking, Paul?" Kathryn whispered sternly, when she was sure they were out of earshot. "You hired us to keep her away from Forrester, and you bring her here? I recall getting the third degree from you for less."

"I tried! She wasn't supposed to be here."

Kathryn shook her head and then turned to catch up with the pair.

"Please," Paul said as he reached out, eliciting a warning look. He pulled his hand back, warning noted. "Just—" He glanced in Forrester's direction but, evidently, didn't know how to finish what he wanted to say. "Please."

There was something in his eyes. It was more than just fear. It was desperation, far out of proportion to the danger posed in the crowded room. Kathryn nodded and quickly took her place at Forrester's elbow.

"It really makes no fiscal sense," she heard Marcus say as she joined the pair.

"That really depends on which side of the line you're standing," Jenny said with an aggressively polite tone. "Don't you think?"

"The double-edged sword of the union," Marcus said, catching her up on the conversation.

Kathryn affected disinterest with a raised brow. "Oh, my, I leave you alone for a second and already you're talking business."

"I'm sorry, my dear." Forrester put his hand around her waist and she dutifully melted into his side.

"No, no ... go on. Don't mind me." She smiled innocently, as if it was all beyond her. "Something about fiscal sense and double-edged swords."

Jenny looked for a sign from Kathryn—a look, a wink, something behind her eyes—anything that would give her direction. There was nothing, not even a hint of what she should do or how far she should push.

"Your young friend was disparaging the incentive pay system," Forrester said. "Somehow increased production has become un-American."

"Is that so?" Kathryn said.

Her expectant stare matched Forrester's, and Jenny could only assume she had carte blanche to continue.

Forrester was a charismatic man, Jenny noticed, with piercing eyes that seemed to question one's very existence. He was deceptively jovial, a facade that made her feel that she could spar with him all day, without repercussions, but she was well aware of his reputation. Men had disappeared for less. She decided restraint would be prudent, despite Kathryn's casual posture.

"I'm only saying that increased production should mean

increased pay, without the yoke of performance-driven threats undermining the working environment." Forrester wanted to break the back of the union in favor of cheaper labor and more profit for himself. Despicable in general, but unconscionable during wartime, when production had to move like a well-oiled machine. "That doesn't seem so unreasonable, does it?"

"It's a little more complicated than that," Forrester said with a patronizing grin.

Jenny agreed, especially when the man had planted thugs on the inside, infecting the workforce like Trojan horses designed to destroy the union from within. She held her tongue about his loathsome behavior and accepted the verbal pat on the head gracefully, expecting nothing less. It might have made her angry a few months ago, but she no longer felt it her mission to single-handedly bring this man down. He would get his one day, and with that surety in mind, she affected a pleasant grin and supplied him with some food for thought before dropping the matter.

"Aren't you wary of the War Labor Disputes Act? If this strike goes on much longer, the government will come in and take over your plant for the war effort. How much fiscal sense will your strike make then?"

"You're in trouble now, Marc," Kathryn said with an easy grin, as if she hadn't a care in the world.

"I see that," he said, his eyes never leaving Jenny. "Perhaps, then, we could apply the War Housing Appropriations Act and have the government take over your very large, mostly unoccupied home to house those government workers as they arrive to overtake my plant."

Jenny's grin widened at the comeback, appreciating the dry humor in which it was imparted. "If the government finds it necessary to appropriate my home for the war effort, I will gladly relinquish it."

Forrester smiled. "But until then, I don't see you handing over the keys voluntarily."

Jenny bowed her head under the weight of her guilt, and his point, which was well taken.

Forrester raised his chin triumphantly and then softened to her plight. "We all do what we can, Jenny, what we think is right."

Jenny couldn't disagree, and as she lifted her head, she saw Forrester and Kathryn both staring at her as if they expected something. She could only assume now was the time to grovel. "You're right, Mr. Forrester, I apologize. I've been terribly rude."

"Nonsense." He straightened. "The only thing you need apologize for is calling me Mr. Forrester. Call me Marc, and don't ever apologize for your opinion. People might think you don't mean it."

"Oh, I mean it."

"Of that I have no doubt." He smiled a queer sort of crooked smile and tightened his hold around Kathryn's waist, indicating their departure. "Will you excuse us?"

Jenny stared at their backs as they walked away, her heart pounding in her throat, unsure whether she had just made a mistake.

Kathryn never looked back.

Jenny cursed under her breath and washed it down with a sip of champagne.

"Well, well," Forrester chided, as they moved into the main hall, "she's lively."

"She's not shy," Kathryn said dryly, revealing no hint of sentimentality.

"No doubt how she bewitched you, darling."

"I wouldn't exactly say bewitched, but she does have her charms."

Forrester agreed with a knowing half smile. "I like her. Too bad you are so possessive of her charms."

Kathryn stared straight ahead and refused to acknowledge his remark. He knew their arrangement made her personal life off limits. Forrester quickly gravitated toward a business associate and held out his hand in greeting. "Dr. Anderson."

A distinguished looking gray-haired gentleman, who Kathryn had met on several occasions, extended his hand at the invitation, and it was dutifully shaken. "Marcus." He moved on to Kathryn and leaned in, kissing her cheek. "Kathryn." The man's wife was neither as forward nor as gracious.

"Miss Hammond," she said with a nod, making no attempt to hide her disdain. She turned to Forrester and brought up his wife to drive home her point. "How is Alice, Marc?"

"Alice is well, Beatrice, but I have to inform you that we are divorcing."

Kathryn cut her eyes to Forrester in shock, recovering moments before Dr. Anderson's stunned wife found her tongue.

"So sorry to hear that," the elderly woman said tersely, placing the blame at Kathryn's feet with one flick of her disapproving eyes. "She's a delightful woman."

"Yes," Forrester said. "Very dear to me."

"Come, Bea," her husband said, and then wisely led her away, his eyes relaying his apology. "Cigars in the lounge later, Marc?"

He nodded. "See you then."

Kathryn watched as Forrester's eyes narrowed at the couple's retreating forms.

"Bitter old broad."

"When did this happen, Marc?"

He patted her hand. "My dear, I'm sure she was born that way."

Kathryn glared at him, not amused.

"Just this week," he said. "It was time."

"Why now?"

He looked at her strangely, apparently confused by her concern. "It was always a marriage of convenience. You know that. Does it really matter to you?"

She pretended to think about it. "I didn't think it would ... but it does."

She let the first hint of emotion come from him, unsure how he would react. The smile that split his lips told her what she wanted to know, and she matched it with one of her own, adding a loving squeeze to his arm to sell her contrived delight.

Jenny surveyed the room from the second-floor balcony again. She thought it best to stay out of Forrester's sight for a while. Her stomach was in knots again, wondering if she'd gone too far, wondering if her behavior would endanger Kathryn.

She realized, perhaps for the first time, how serious the repercussions of their love affair could be. Kathryn knew and had tried to warn her, to no avail. Jenny sent a silent apology to Kathryn for her impetuous naiveté and hoped it wasn't too late to tell her she truly understood. Suddenly, Kathryn's trepidation became hers as well, and Jenny knew their affair would never be the relationship she'd hoped for. At best, it would be a few stolen moments here, maybe an entire night there—if they were lucky. It occurred to her that her declaration of *just one night of fun* might actually have been more prophetic than manipulative, sure that she'd failed her first public test miserably and proved what Kathryn had tried to tell her all along.

"Hey, you," Bernie said in her ear from behind, causing her to jump.

"Jimminy, you scared me."

"Sorry, Bug. How'd it go? What did your uncle say? What did Forrester do? How did your girlfriend react?"

"Well, I'm pretty sure she's not going to be my girlfr—"

"I know," Bernie interrupted, as he glanced downstairs, looking for the couple in question. "Did you see how she was hanging all over him? Making with the doe eyes? Nobody's that good."

She didn't hide her disappointment when she cast her eyes to him.

"Sorry," he said.

"That's okay."

They both leaned on the railing and listened to the soothing sound of the orchestra drifting up from the ballroom.

"So, how'd it feel to finally be that close to Forrester?"

"God, it was a disaster, Bernie."

"You didn't lose your temper, did you?"

"Well, no, but in the span of about three minutes, I managed to become quite disagreeable."

"You always was an ornery cuss," Bernie drawled with a nudge.

"And how is Cal?" Jenny joked.

Bernie grinned. "He's Mr. Wonderful, and don't change the subject. You were disagreeable ... not surprising."

"Well, somehow I topped it off by invoking the War Labor Disputes Act."

"You threatened him?"

"No," she shot back. "I was merely pointing out that if he wasn't careful—" The possibility that he had misconstrued her comment as a threat paralyzed her for an instant. Her heart found its way to her throat, and her eyes quickly flashed to Bernie in alarm. "Oh, God." She immediately searched the room, wanting desperately to see Kathryn again, if only to see that she was all right. "I didn't mean it as a threat, Bernie, I swear."

"Of course not. What did your friend do?"

"She was noncommittal, so it was probably okay, right?"

Bernie nodded, but that turned into a shrug. "Of course she *would* be noncommittal."

He responded to her stricken look. "I mean, of course it was okay. She's not going to let you shoot your mouth off if it's going to get you in trouble, right?"

She agreed but wasn't sure Kathryn could have done much to stop her at the time.

Bernie followed her troubled glance around the room. "What are we looking for?"

"I haven't seen Kathryn or Forrester in a while. I'm worried."

"I'm sure she's fine." She didn't respond, so Bernie did what Bernie does—he tried to fix it. "Tell you what. I know one of the waiters, so I'll see if there are any closed-door meetings going on. Okay?"

"Would you? That'd be swell."

"Sure thing, sweetie."

She took his hand as he turned to leave. "Be inconspicuous."

"Oh, Jenny Bug," he said, shaking his head. "What have you gotten yourself into this time?"

She wanted to say *I wish I knew*, but she just smiled the confident smile he expected and sent him on his way.

Jenny's growing unease over both Bernie's and Kathryn's extended absence drew her down to the main floor. She slipped past mingling couples, smiled pleasantly at those she recognized as her father's colleagues, and walked like she had a purpose, to avoid extended bouts of small talk that she was too distracted to conduct.

She spotted Bernie across the room wearing a helpless expression on his face as he pointed to her uncle's back, but there was still no sign of Kathryn. Her uncle was oblivious as he conversed with the mayor and his wife. Bernie motioned to a spot across the room, and Jenny nodded in agreement, hoping he had good news for her.

She furrowed her brow when he approached and threw his hands up in recognition, as if she'd been the one missing, but then she realized he was reacting to something over her shoulder.

Jenny felt a warm hand brush across her back and a welcome voice whisper, "Well done," in her ear. Kathryn squeezed her elbow for emphasis before continuing on her way, as if she hadn't said a word.

Bernie arrived, laughing as he thumbed over his shoulder. "I found her. She was dancing in the courtyard with Forrester." He turned and watched the back of Kathryn's head as she made her way toward the musicians in the corner of the large ballroom. "I guess you were right about her not being your girlfriend. Those two are a couple, and I've got the photos to prove it." He held up his camera. "I thought it would take a crowbar to separate them."

That news would normally upset her, but the relief that Kathryn was fine, and the pride in knowing she'd taken the right tact with Forrester, made her oblivious to her surroundings. She exhaled a relieved breath and took a sip of champagne in celebration. How quickly things changed, and how incredible that a few words and one touch from Kathryn made everything all right.

Bernie nudged her as Forrester walked by, following Kathryn's path to the small orchestra. Jenny drifted forward as if caught in his wake until Bernie's hand on her arm urged discretion. They stopped a respectable distance behind and watched Forrester gently lift Kathryn by her waist until she was perched comfortably atop the grand piano. She thanked him with a dazzling smile and a lingering hold on his trailing hand. The room buzzed at their obvious attraction, and Jenny drained her glass of champagne to bear it.

Forrester stood back, almost blocking Jenny's view, and crossed his arms as if admiring his property. Jenny bristled and moved slightly to the side, treating her annoyance to another glass of champagne from a passing waiter.

"He's getting a divorce, you know," Bernie whispered.

"What?"

"Fresh from the rumor mill."

"Is it reliable?"

"From the man himself."

Over the top of her glass, Jenny studied Kathryn's smiling face. She seemed so relaxed, so genuine. Jenny didn't know how she did it. If not for their brief encounter, she would have serious doubts about her intentions. Instead, she just marveled at a professional in action.

Kathryn turned to the conductor and nodded, touching off an orchestral swell of strings and woodwinds that fashioned itself into "The Nearness of You."

Kathryn's beautiful voice filled the room, and the piano player followed with a delicate interpretation of the melody, a perfect complement to Kathryn's rich, soulful vocals.

Jenny felt Bernie staring at her and knew exactly what he was thinking. She was idealistic and foolish when it came to love. She gave her heart too easily, believing love would conquer all. He knew, because he was the same. He probably wanted to tell her she was playing with fire. That no matter what Kathryn Hammond's intentions were, it wouldn't change the fact that she would always be second fiddle to a powerful, dangerous man like Marcus Forrester. He also knew it would be futile to try to talk her out of pursuing her, so he stood silently beside her like a good best friend, watching Kathryn gaze lovingly into Forrester's eyes as she sang a love song meant for her.

Jenny smiled, her eyes never leaving Kathryn's. Bernie may have thought she'd be upset at such a display, but she shifted slowly to the left, moving out of alignment with Forrester, and Kathryn's focus shifted with her. Bernie's gasp signaled his comprehension: the song was meant for her.

Jenny watched Kathryn's gaze drift as far as she dared without being obvious, and then she closed her eyes, something she never did when she sang at The Grotto. Jenny did the same.

The music was intoxicating and Kathryn's voice seductive. She could almost feel Kathryn's hands on her, the way they had been last night. Her soft kisses, her gentle caresses, her strength, her surrender, and her sounds ... it all came rushing back, the song a soundtrack of remembrance and desire.

"She's making love to you," Bernie whispered in her ear.

"Mm," she said absently.

The song ended far too quickly, but for those few minutes, Kathryn was hers again, and she was in heaven. When the applause started, she opened her eyes and Kathryn did the same a beat later. Forrester was there to fill her vision. He eased her from her perch, and she showed her appreciation by smiling her affection and kissing his cheek as she slid down his body until her feet gracefully found the floor.

"How does she do that?" Bernie asked.

It was a scene Jenny had no desire to see, so she turned away and nursed her glass of champagne. "Are you done with photos?" she asked, changing the subject.

"No, but I do have to go to my bag to get more film. Care to join me? Maybe you can cool off."

"Cool off?"

He eyed her splotchy chest. "Don't look now, but your one-night stand is showing."

She looked down and attempted to cover it with her hand. "Oh, good grief. Here—" She handed him her glass of bubbly. "This is not helping."

"Never a cold shower when you need one," Bernie said with a laugh.

"I'll have to settle for the next best thing. I'll see you later, hon. Thanks for holding my hand tonight."

"Anytime, sweetie."

She walked away and heard him say, "Don't do anything I wouldn't do."

She stopped and turned. "Think about that, Bernie."

"Good point," he said with a grin and finished her champagne.

The spacious ladies' lounge was empty when Jenny entered, and for that she was thankful. She went into the washroom, took one look at her flushed reflection in the mirror and shook her head as she turned on the cold water and let it run across the corner of a hand towel. "Get a hold of yourself, Jenny," she said to herself as she brought the cool, damp towel to her chest and then her rosy cheeks. She held it to the back of her neck and closed her eyes, trying very hard not to give in to her body's vivid memory of the night before. She found closing her eyes did nothing to diminish Kathryn's presence in her mind or the effect she was having on her body. She knew it was a futile attempt to ignore what she really had no desire to forget, so she tossed the towel aside and laughed it off.

She moved into the lounge and sat at the wall-length vanity, gazing into the mirror and smiling at how easily she was undone. She wondered how Kathryn stayed so indifferent. For a moment, she thought perhaps she *was* indifferent, but the song told her otherwise. There was nothing indifferent about that or the sensual energy behind the performance. Desire washed over her again, and she decided she really needed to think about something else. Quickly.

She turned again to Kathryn's cool example. "Indifference, Jenny," she whispered to her determined face in the mirror. "Embrace it." She took a deep breath and smoothed her hand down her abdomen in an attempt to still the burning ache at her core. She exhaled forcefully, convincing herself she'd been successful. "Indifference." The dark lust in her eyes told her she wasn't nearly as victorious as she pretended.

Only one thing could get Kathryn out of her mind at that moment: her uncle and the sting of his harsh words from the afternoon. She must have found some measure of truth in his accusation or it wouldn't have struck such a nerve, but that was the past. She lifted her chin. She was a member of the OSS now. They came to her. She didn't get the job because of her family or as a favor to someone else. They picked her. Little did she know what would become of her application to the Office of War Information. Someone deemed her abilities valuable, and she would not disappoint.

Kathryn was another matter. Kathryn chose her because ... well, she had to admit, she practically dragged the poor woman, kicking and screaming, into their night together, but she had no regrets, and she hoped Kathryn felt the same. She chuckled. So much for thinking about something else. Tonight, all roads led to Kathryn Hammond. In fact, ever since she met her, all roads had led to Kathryn Hammond.

Jenny surrendered to the inevitable and stared into the mirror, where she wore a satisfied grin. Her eyes scanned every nuance of her reflection and found an attractive woman in a black halter column dress sporting the confidence of one blessed with a preternatural ability to know the future and her place in it. Of course, she didn't know the future, and her future, in particular, was never more uncertain, but she wasn't afraid—far from it. The more she pondered her transformation, the more empowered she felt. Indifference, coming right up. Yes, indeed.

The chatter of voices, followed quickly by a group of women entering the lounge, derailed her self-congratulations, and she pretended to arrange her hair until her arousal was under control.

"Honestly, Mother, what makes you say such a thing?" a college-aged strawberry blonde complained as they gathered at the next section of mirror and powdered their faces.

"It's disgraceful. He's a married man."

Jenny had no doubt who they were talking about, and she preened just a little longer so she could eavesdrop on the conversation.

"Soon to be a divorced man, Mother."

"Ha, that's what they all say," the older woman's friend said.

"Oh, you hush, Sylvia," the daughter said. "You're divorced, so there."

"Yes, divorced because of a trollop like that. I have every right."

Jenny's eyes snapped to the woman's reflection at the insult, and she quickly brought them back to her own mirror, trying hard not to let her displeasure show. Indifference repeated in her head like a mantra.

"Didn't that woman kill someone or something?" the mother asked.

"No dear, she was found innocent," Sylvia said erroneously.

Jenny stewed, lamenting the result of only reading the headlines.

"You two really need to spend more time educating yourselves and less time in the beauty parlor," the daughter said, eliciting an eye roll from her elders and a silent nod of agreement from Jenny.

"Your father and I sent you off to be educated, and look what we got in return ... a sass-talking smart aleck who's forgotten how to speak to her mother."

Jenny just barely suppressed a chuckle as she dug in her purse for her lipstick.

"Oh, Mother, you are so terribly dramatic. Where's your sense of romance, your appreciation for the arts, the—"

"World's oldest profession?" Sylvia said under her breath.

The daughter exhaled in frustration. "Ugh, hopeless, the both of you."

Jenny was oblivious to the comings and goings of the other patrons as she kept one ear on the young woman's futile attempt to extract at least an acknowledgment of Kathryn's undeniable vocal talent from her uncooperative audience.

The gossiping group suddenly went silent, and Jenny looked up to see the object of their chatter, and her affection, enter the room. Kathryn took her breath away. The room had filled significantly since Jenny last took notice, and she watched in the mirror as a few women praised Kathryn with offered hands and others ignored her completely until they were behind her back and then began whispering.

It made Jenny furious to think these people had disparaging thoughts about her friend, and it only underscored her awareness that the general public had no idea what it took to keep them safe. The grace with which Kathryn carried her tarnished reputation only added to the list of wonderful attributes and made her a personal hero. Jenny was starting to get that warm and fuzzy feeling again, and she was sure it wasn't going to get any easier to hide as Kathryn spotted her and headed her way.

"Beautiful rendition tonight, Miss Hammond," the college girl said as Kathryn arrived.

"Thank you."

"Yes," the two older women said with false admiration, "beautiful, and what a lovely dress."

Jenny silently cursed the hypocrites as she got up from her seat and held out her hand. "Would you like to sit down, Miss Hammond? I'm through."

"Yes, thank you." Kathryn sat and tucked her long legs under the extended vanity as the two older women eyed her apprehensively.

Jenny ran her hand across her bare shoulders before heading for the exit. "Lovely song."

She knew Kathryn watched her retreating form in the mirror with indifference.

CHAPTER TWELVE

Kathryn gritted her teeth as she offered a hand and a closed-mouth smile to yet another doctor from out of town. It seemed there were a lot of out of towners for such a local charity event, and she kept a keen eye on Forrester for any hint of subversive activity. Medical doctors seemed far afield from his normal shady business, but nothing was too far out of his scope when a profit was involved. On the other hand, he was a major contributor to the foundation being honored, so she supposed his attentive behavior wasn't so out of place after all.

"Big smile, now," the photographer from the *Daily Chronicle* said with a grin as his flashbulb popped. "Thank you."

It was Jenny's best friend, Bernie, and she eyed him critically for any hint of Jenny's mindset this evening. She found none as he extended his hand to her. "Have a great evening."

As she watched him shake hands and exchange niceties with the others in their group, she tucked away the note he pressed into her hand and nonchalantly went on with the business of making Marcus Forrester look good.

She hoped the note was from Jenny, an explanation of her abrupt departure from the ladies' lounge, perhaps. A few more moments and they could have been alone for the first time since their night together, but, she reasoned, maybe that's what Jenny wanted to avoid. The night after might as well be the morning after to her, as far as recreational lovers were concerned. Now, with apparently the same attitude, why wouldn't Jenny? There was nothing more uncomfortable than feigning significance where none existed. The thought annoyed her. Jenny was more than mere recreation to her, and even if she wanted to play at casual bedmates, Kathryn decided that wasn't good enough.

"Isn't that so, darling?" she heard Forrester say. She quickly snapped to the matter at hand and chastised herself for losing track of the conversation. Now was not the time for daydreaming. She safely replied with a generic, "That's right," followed by a smile. Thankfully, her preoccupation had gone unnoticed by her companions, and she quickly caught up with the discussion and participated without missing another beat.

After a few more introductions and meaningless stretches of small talk, Forrester excused himself to the men's smoking lounge with several of the male attendees, a ritual that always precluded her attendance. Alone at last, and with her duty to her assignment momentarily suspended, she looked at the small piece of paper she'd been given. It had a room number on it, nothing else, but she recognized Jenny's slanted script and smiled. She would have about an hour before Forrester would emerge from his den of machismo, so slipping unnoticed from the crowded hall, she sought out the object of her distraction.

Jenny paced the darkened meeting room above the ballroom. It was a relatively small space, empty save for the short bar on the mirrored wall to the left upon entering and a few stacked chairs in the center of the room. She was excited and nervous to see Kathryn alone again but didn't want to show either. She took a deep breath and exhaled it forcefully, shook out her arms, and adjusted the top of her dress.

When she heard the doorknob turn, she quickly took her predetermined place and set her shoulders back, ready to play it cool.

"I was wondering whether you'd come," she said calmly, revealing herself fully from around a corner when Kathryn entered the room.

Kathryn looked startled at the sound of her voice, and then Jenny realized she was confused by the moving reflection in the mirror behind the bar. Jenny had positioned herself so she could see the door in the mirror in case her visitor wasn't who she expected. She wasn't sure what she would have done had it been someone else. She was too rattled by the meeting with Forrester for coherent smooth-talking.

Kathryn's hand slipped into her clutch bag, and Jenny knew very well what was in there.

"Don't shoot," she said to ease the tension, unsure if their meeting was a horrendous breach of protocol. She felt it best to stay put, better to measure Kathryn's attitude and the perfect opportunity to practice her indifference. She put her hands behind her back and leaned against the wall opposite the bar, her body silhouetted against the courtyard lights as they seeped through the tall French doors leading to the balcony.

Kathryn shut the door behind her. Her face was hidden in shadow, but her gown defied the darkness and glowed as the stray light breathed life into translucent glass beads embedded into its length. "Did anyone see you come in here?" she asked.

"No."

"How did you get in?"

"Bernie knows one of the waiters. No one is using this room. We won't be disturbed."

Kathryn reached behind her back and locked the door, pausing briefly before stepping further into the room. Her reticence made Jenny nervous, and she wished she could see her face. When she finally moved closer and into the low light, her cool expression revealed nothing.

"Are you all right?" she asked, her voice matching her indifferent stare.

Jenny was unsure of how to react. She wanted to take Kathryn in her arms and kiss her like crazy, but she didn't seem like *her* Kathryn at the moment, so she answered just as coldly. "Yes."

Her less than enthusiastic response put a crease between Kathryn's brow. She tightened the grip on her purse and scanned the room with a few quick flicks of her eyes, as if questioning their privacy and whether she needed the gun.

"It's okay," Jenny said. "I'm okay."

Kathryn looked at her with concern and tenderly took her hand. "You're sure?"

Jenny smiled and nodded, anticipating an embrace and the return of the kind lover from the night before.

She didn't return. Instead, she dropped her hand, strode to the bar, leaned across and behind it, and straightened with a bottle of scotch in tow. She set it on the counter with a dull thud. "Do you want a drink?" she asked, not turning around or looking in the mirror.

"Don't mind if I do," Jenny said, admiring the subtle play of light and shadow on Kathryn's bare back.

Kathryn slid two glasses from the end of the bar over to the bottle and glanced in the mirror. She caught Jenny raking her eyes up her tall form, and when their eyes met, Jenny felt a chill skitter up her spine.

"See something you like?" Kathryn asked, unmistakably annoyed.

"Sorry."

Kathryn faced her and crossed her arms. "If you're angry with me, I'd rather you just have out with it. I'm sorry for my behavior out there, but I told you this was how it was going to be. I'm sorry if you don't like it, but there it is."

Jenny was shocked that she'd misinterpreted annoyance for insecurity, and she couldn't help but laugh.

Kathryn's arms dropped to her side, her hands balled into fists. "Is something funny?"

Jenny held up her hands in surrender, abandoning her feeble attempt at indifference before Kathryn blew a fuse. "I give."

Kathryn looked utterly lost. "What?"

"You are the most exquisite creature I have ever met in my entire life," Jenny said. "I'm not angry with you, Kat. I am in absolute awe of you. I don't know how you do it." She pushed herself away from the wall, her usual demeanor back where it belonged, and sat on a stool beside Kathryn. "I was a nervous wreck out there. Did you see me babbling on to Forrester? Good grief, please tell me he's not angry with me."

Kathryn blinked the confusion and annoyance away, and Jenny watched her body relax. "He's not angry with you, he—"

"Thank God," Jenny interrupted. "I was so worried. He's deceptively nice, you know." She waved her hand. "Of course you know. I thought I'd throw up when he took my hand, but there you were, cool as a cucumber, and well, if you can do it, I can do it."

Kathryn opened her mouth to speak, but Jenny went on, as the indifference dam crumbled and washed downstream.

"You know, I thought about being polite, but I figured he already knows I don't like him, so hold the line, right? And your song—" Jenny touched Kathryn's arm. "Holy smokes, I thought I was going to faint. And the room thought you were singing to him. Ha!" She raised a fist in the air triumphantly. "That was perfect! You were the talk of the ladies' room, you know."

"I can imagine."

"That young woman found you and Forrester terribly romantic."

"Ah, youth."

"Mm," Jenny said, with a shake of her head.

Kathryn eyed her with interest. "And how do you find it?"

"I think you were brilliant, Kat, obviously. You look stunning, by the way." She looked Kathryn up and down, who appreciated it this time, and finally grinned a more recognizable smile.

"You look stunning yourself."

The soft, kind voice from the evening before returned, and Jenny beamed at the compliment. "Thank you."

"I am sorry about out there," Kathryn said. "To be quite honest, I was a little surprised to see you here, and I'm afraid I didn't handle that very well."

"Are you kidding? You handled it perfectly. You told me the score before we started this thing. For crying out loud, don't apologize for doing your job—flawlessly, I might add. I'm sorry for you having to put up with that pig pawing at you all night." She rubbed Kathryn's arm. "Did I mention you look incredible?"

Kathryn smiled and took her hand. "Welcome back. You had me worried there for a minute. I was afraid tonight had turned you sour on us."

Jenny suppressed the urge to jump up and down at Kathryn's use of the word *us*. "Well, I was going for aloof, but I'm afraid it's not as easy as it looks."

Kathryn chuckled softly, and Jenny welcomed the return of her softer side. She always seemed so perpetually serious, as if the weight of the world was hers and hers alone. For all her poise and beauty, she had a surprising predilection for insecurity. "Did you really think I'd drop you? Just like that? Especially after last night?"

"Well, when you didn't want to speak with me this afternoon, frankly, I didn't know what to think."

"When I didn't—" Jenny racked her brain trying to remember refusing a conversation, then she recalled the phone call at the office. "Oh, Kat. I thought it was Aunt B." She took her hand. "I'm so sorry."

They both had a laugh over the misunderstanding, and after the tension of the night, they both exhaled a sigh of relief. After a few contemplative moments, Jenny directed the conversation toward the newly dubbed *us*.

"Last night was amazing."

Kathryn dissolved at the memory. She'd put up a good front all evening, but with one sentence, Jenny brought back the euphoric abandon of the night before.

"I'll say."

The feeling terrified her, even as she craved it. This was the wrong time. The wrong person. The evening validated her fear and the struggle ahead, but it didn't matter. She couldn't let Jenny go, not after last night.

Seeing her at the benefit had her stomach in knots. She tried unsuccessfully to shield her from Forrester's view, but once he was aware of her presence, nothing would keep him from the woman he thought was her lover. It wasn't a lie when she denied it, but now that it was true, she feared what Forrester might do. What Jenny might do.

She was sure Jenny had accepted that Marcus Forrester had nothing to do with her father's death, but he was a criminal, and once a reporter, always a reporter.

She took slow, measured breaths, trying to conceal her alarm when Forrester approached her, but Jenny was perfect with him—polite, genial, and just aggressive enough to make Forrester respect her without feeling threatened. Kathryn wanted to hug her for her bravery. It made her relax immediately and regain control of herself. She couldn't wait to spend time alone with Jenny again, to thank her, to touch her, to get lost in that place between reality and blissful oblivion.

When she entered the room and Jenny was so cold, she thought someone else was present, causing her strange behavior. When she said she was alone, jealousy over Forrester was the only explanation, and she was sure Jenny would end their relationship before it even started. A flash of fury caught her off guard, and her defenses kicked in. She would end it before Jenny could. When she was alone again, she would fall to her knees and sob over her loss. As her mind moved through this progression, she didn't recognize herself. Jenny had done this to her seemingly overnight. And then, with one simple exchange, Jenny was hers again, and so was the longing.

She took Jenny's face in her hands, peering into eyes glistening with hope, trust, and desire. She looked like Jenny again, young and carefree. She knew she wouldn't be that way forever, but she sent a word of gratitude to whoever watches over such things and captured her lips before she did something silly, like declare her undying lust and devotion.

Stifled moans filled the room as their hands began exploring familiar territory.

Jenny slid her hand down the back of her scandalously low-cut dress, and in return, Kathryn reached behind Jenny's neck and undid the catch on her dress straps.

"Wait," Jenny said as she pulled back, catching her breath and her top. "How long can you be away?"

"Half hour, to be safe."

"That'll do," Jenny said into Kathryn's waiting mouth.

Kathryn agreed with a muffled chuckle, and then stopped, pushed Jenny away, and froze.

"Ka—"

"Shhh," Kathryn said in a clipped hiss, her eyes wide and trained on the door.

A key turned in the lock.

Jenny tugged her behind the bar, where they ducked down in the shadows. Unfortunately, the short length of the structure left Kathryn out of the shadow and exposed in the ambient light of the mirror's reflection. The lower shelf of the bar dug into her back, and Kathryn wondered what she was doing cowering behind a bar. Surely, she could have come up with some reason why she was in the room ... in the dark ... alone with another woman ... partially undressed ... wearing each other's lipstick. Okay, maybe not.

A mature man, by the sound of the voice, let what sounded like a group into the room, and Kathryn lifted her eyes to see her perception confirmed in the mirror, as five men filtered by, single file, none of whom she recognized. Her whole body tensed as she realized if she could see them in the mirror, then they could see her. She cut her eyes to Jenny, hidden in the shadows, and saw that she realized this too. To make matters worse, Kathryn noticed the scotch had been jostled on their swing around the bar and the amber liquid was sloshing frantically from side to side in the tall bottle. She closed her eyes briefly and cursed their situation. It didn't matter who these men were. No good would come of their discovery. Their only chance was to remain perfectly still and hope against hope that no one wanted to see or drink. Chance, by its nature, proved fickle, as someone turned on the light.

"Turn off that light!" a man barked.

Kathryn and Jenny rolled their eyes with a collective *amen, brother*.

"Say, what's the meaning of this, Lawrence?"

"Call it free enterprise."

"I don't like this ..." another man began nervously, "meeting like this. If we are caught—"

"No one is going to catch us," Lawrence, the barking man, assured him.

Kathryn watched the liquor in the bottle teeter like the dying pendulum of a clock left unwound until it was still. She was balled up as tight as her dress would allow, knees almost to her chest, one arm holding them close, the other on the floor like a kickstand to keep her from falling over into the room.

"This is madness, Charles," a voice of reason chimed in.

"Why do we need him?" said someone with more nerve than conviction. "Get rid of him, I say."

"He's got the money and the connections and the muscle," said another.

"We are all wealthy men. If we pooled our resources—"

"Don't be ridiculous. I want no part of this," the reasonable man announced with some finality.

Kathryn heard the rustling of the man's clothes as he stepped to leave and, just as quickly, the movement of Charles Lawrence apparently lunging to stop him.

"Where do you think you're going? You *are* part of this."

"I'll not be party to betrayal," he said. "Not when it could cost me my life. Not when we can just stay the course and everything will be fine."

"Betrayal? It is *he* who betrays *us*! Decades of work, and we will just turn it over to the Germans? For what? For profit? So Marc Forrester can buy another company or three?"

Kathryn remained stone still at the mention of Forrester's name.

The men moved further into the room until she could no longer see them in the mirror. She very slowly disengaged her left arm from her knees and inched her hand cautiously toward her purse. Her eyes never left the mirror, prepared to freeze at the slightest indication the men were coming into view.

"I think not," the irate Lawrence went on.

"We're collaborating, not capitulating," the reasonable man said.

"The Germans don't collaborate. Just ask half of Europe. You're staying right here, and you'll do as I say."

"Are you threatening me?"

"Why, that would be terribly Draconian of me, don't you think?"

"Get out of my way, Charles."

The room was silent as the two men jockeyed for the alpha male position. The top of the disgruntled man's head came into view in the mirror as he began to leave the room.

"Perhaps the university would like to audit their research funding," Lawrence said. The man stopped and turned. Lawrence continued, "Perhaps the police would like to discover the bodies of your test subjects."

There was silence again. Kathryn froze with her hand in her purse and her fingers wrapped around the cool pearl grips of her derringer. She only had two shots if she had to use it, but staring down a double barrel with two waiting .38 special slugs at close range might convince them to keep their distance as they made their escape.

"You're a bastard, Charles."

"Relax, doctor. We all want the same thing. Have a drink."

Worried eyes snapped to the liquor bottle in the mirror. All breathing ceased.

"I don't want a drink," the man said as he disappeared from view and returned to the others.

Kathryn took the momentary reprieve to pull the gun from her purse, ease off the cross-bolt safety, and wrap her arm back around her knees, her legs thanking her as cramped muscles got a well-deserved breather.

"Then you won't mind if I do."

Jenny looked to Kathryn in panic. She wasn't sure what to do. Her mouth was dry, and her heart was beating so loudly in her ears that she was sure everyone in the room could hear. Kathryn was as still as a statue, no trace of breathing, her eyes trained on the floor, as if lifting them would draw her to the man's attention. Jenny couldn't help but look up into the mirror, feeling invisible in the shadows. Lawrence's red hair came into view first, followed by his pockmarked face and tuxedo-clad shoulders as he stood at the bar and removed the cap from the bottle of scotch. His focus was on the men behind him and the matter at hand, so he barely paid attention to what he was doing.

"He can't do any of this without us," Lawrence said, as he poured his drink and quickly turned his back on the bar. "I say we demand a meeting of the contacts and then we take over."

"Take over what?" the reasonable man argued. "We can't move forward in the research unless we find the—"

A knock at the door followed by a muffled voice interrupted him. "Room service."

Jenny watched Kathryn bite off a curse as the man was interrupted, and she realized she hadn't processed anything the man had said. She was too overwhelmed by fear over what might happen if they got caught. She had a lot to learn about this spy business.

The men stood in tense silence. Lawrence left the bar and, from the sound of it, opened the door a crack.

"I didn't order room service."

"Says right here, sir." He paused. "It's paid for." Jenny imagined him holding up the receipt.

"Just leave it there," Lawrence said, annoyed. The boy evidently didn't leave. Jenny heard coins jingling. "Here." Another moment of silence and the door clicked closed.

As soon as the door was shut, the nervous man broke down, "It's from him. He knows!"

"Quiet, you fool!"

"It's not safe here," another man said. "We should disband."

Jenny silently seconded that.

The room was still. "No one breathes a word of this," Lawrence finally said. "I'll contact you soon."

The men filed out the same way they filed in, with Lawrence bringing up the rear. The door shut, but Kathryn immediately held up her hand, stilling her. Someone exhaled, presumably Lawrence, as he gathered himself before returning to the crowd.

Soon the room was left in silence, the door shut and locked. Jenny didn't dare move until Kathryn untangled her long legs and struggled to her feet with a groan. She offered her hand, which was gratefully taken.

She casually slipped the gun back into her purse and then brushed off her dress. "Well, that was fun," she said with a grin.

Jenny didn't know if Kathryn was being brave for her benefit or was really that unaffected by what had just happened. In any case, she was still just this side of petrified and couldn't yet manage a response.

"Are you all right?" Kathryn put a gentle hand on her shoulder.

Kathryn's touch, her silky voice, and confident smile brought comfort instantly, and Jenny knew all would be fine. "Better now," she said, nodding, gaining confidence. "I'm so glad you got here before they did."

Kathryn reached behind her neck and did a proper job of securing her dress, which had been haphazardly clasped in their flight behind the bar. "Me too." She cupped her face. "You okay?"

"Fine. Honest."

"You did really well tonight, Jenny. Really well."

Jenny didn't feel like she did really well, but she took the compliment with a smile and watched Kathryn touch up her smeared lipstick in the mirrored wall. Their kiss seemed like hours ago, their lovemaking an eternity. She wondered when she would see her again, could be alone again, but that was but a fleeting thought in the wake of what had just happened. "Do you know those men, Kat?"

"No, but it's imperative I find out who they are. Come on."

Jenny stood in an inconspicuous spot across the hallway from which she'd emerged ten minutes earlier. She knew Kathryn could take care of herself, but when she sent her on ahead to avoid suspicion, she couldn't help but feel a sense of loss. Jenny never considered herself a codependent sort, but Kathryn had a way of grounding her, of giving her purpose, and she didn't mind the influence one bit.

Kathryn suddenly emerged, head held high, nonchalant as you please, and Jenny smiled, vowing to learn to be just as professional. Almost immediately, a server came up to Kathryn and directed her to Forrester's driver, who was milling about aimlessly, looking bored with the whole affair. The server held up a note between them but appeared to just convey the contents, which sent the pair toward the back entrance with separate nods of their heads. This time, Kathryn did turn around. She appeared to be searching for something, someone, and Jenny raised her chin and stared intently enough to draw a lingering glance. Something was wrong. Kathryn was leaving abruptly, and Forrester was nowhere to be seen. Her parting look indicated regret, not danger, and Jenny assumed it was because she hadn't the chance to uncover more about their surprise guests.

Jenny decided it was her turn to prove her worth, and she began searching the room for her targets.

CHAPTER THIRTEEN

Kathryn stood alone on the landing of the back alley entrance to the hall while the driver retrieved the car. It was unusual for Forrester to send her away in such a covert manner, and it had her on high alert. Her instincts had never let her down.

"Walk," came the command, as the cold kiss of a gun barrel pressed into her back.

She knew that voice.

"Now."

Charles Lawrence.

She raised her hands slightly, as is the custom when one has a gun at the back, and moved slowly forward. She thought it only fair to warn him he was making a mistake. "Don't be stupid."

"It is you who are stupid," he said, as he jabbed the gun barrel deeper into her ribs. "Did you think I didn't see you? Hiding there like a snitch with your little toy gun?" He snatched her small clutch from her hand and stuffed it into his jacket pocket.

He moved closer until his warm breath on her neck made her shiver. "A beautiful snitch, though."

The alley was dark except for the dome of light surrounding

them, and it smelled of cat piss and garbage. She peered into the darkness in vain. Where was her protection? Where were Forrester's men, who she swore followed her night and day? This was a bad time to realize her paranoia was all in her head. She was on her own. Lawrence hadn't mentioned Jenny, but she had to bide her time until she was sure she had gone unnoticed. "Please don't hurt me," she said as pathetically as her restrained anger would allow.

"I'm sorry, my dear, but I'm afraid I have to. You see, I can't have you running to your boyfriend and telling him what you know. It may be hazardous to my health."

Adrenaline coursed through her, as it appeared he saw no one else, and she prepared to break from his grasp and relieve him of his weapon. "I won't say anything, I swear it."

"That's right, you won't. Your driver will pull up here in a moment and we'll get in, calm as can be, you understand?" He poked the gun further into her back for emphasis. "We will drive to the estate, where a murder-suicide will occur. It seems you were having an affair with your handsome driver and it went tragically awry. Perhaps he was jealous ... who knows. It's not so far-fetched for a woman of your reputation."

Kathryn knew most criminals couldn't resist the urge to brag about their crimes, especially right before they triumphantly snuffed out their rival. Charles Lawrence seemed like the arrogant type, and should she botch her escape, at least she would know what she died for. "You'll never get away with this. Whatever you're doing, it can't be worth murder."

He laughed off her warning and didn't take the bait. "It really is a shame," he went on as he shoved her forward into the alley while keeping close behind. "He'll find you dead in his bed when he returns home." He played with her hair, pulling long strands from her perfectly coiffed up-do and running them through his fingers. "Perhaps I'll have my way with you beforehand," he said into her ear. "Payment for all my trouble."

A tin can tumbled into the alley, startling him, and he took a defensive stance, wrapping his arm around her neck and throwing her in front of his body as he turned in every direction.

"Who's there!" he said, his revolver pointing blindly into the dark alley. He thought better of that position and quickly brought the gun to her head. "Come out or I plug her!" On cue, a cat scampered across the alley and Lawrence laughed as he loosened his grip.

"You're a dead man," Kathryn said with a wicked smile.

"Forrester will never know who did this, and you're never going to get the chance to tell him."

Kathryn's eyes focused on a welcome sight. "Forrester is the least of your worries."

"Let her go," Smitty said, gun drawn, his voice echoing in the deserted alley.

Lawrence whirled around and tightened his hold on Kathryn's neck until she couldn't breathe. He was disoriented, Smitty's voice coming from everywhere and nowhere. He backed up against the wall, the gun darting wildly, unable to find his foe. He put it back to her temple. "I warn you … she'll be dead before you can even—"

Smitty's shot rang out from the left, and Lawrence never finished his sentence.

Kathryn closed her mind against the sickeningly familiar sound of a bullet exploding flesh and bone and welcomed the ensuing silence as Charles Lawrence's last words died in his throat with an incomprehensible whimper. She felt the man slump to the ground behind her, the warmth of his life coating the side of her face and neck. She gasped for air as her throat was released, and she fell into the space vacated by her attacker at the wall. The sharp brick dug into her barely covered shoulder blades as she slid against it.

"Son of a bitch," she said as soon as she caught her breath. She purposely avoided looking at the body crumpled at her feet.

Smitty hurried to her side with an outstretched hand to help her up. "Are you all right?"

She took his hand. "Nice timing. Thank you."

Smitty couldn't hide his panic at the sight of her face covered in blood. "Are you hurt, Kat?"

"I'm fine, Smitty."

The black limo came to a screeching halt at their feet, and Smitty trained his gun at the driver. "Get out of the car. *Now!*"

The driver complied immediately, hands in the air.

Two men burst out of the back door of the hall, guns drawn. Smitty pulled another gun from under his coat and held all the men at bay with arms held out at a right angle, like a signpost on a very anxious street corner.

"No!" Kathryn shouted, pushing herself away from the wall and nearly tripping over Lawrence's corpse. "No!" She positioned herself between Smitty and Forrester's bodyguards. "It's all right. It's over."

"Kathryn!" Forrester yelled as he appeared in the doorway.

One of the bodyguards untrained his gun from Smitty and restrained his boss. "No, sir! Back inside. It's not safe."

"Get off me!" Forrester shoved him aside. "Put away those guns."

Smitty didn't move until Kathryn assured him it was all right to stand down. He holstered his Colts, one under each arm, and snapped his long overcoat sharply over his hips.

Forrester rushed to Kathryn's side, searching her face as he wiped the blood away with his handkerchief. "Are you hurt?"

She shook her head, pretending to be too stunned to speak.

He took her elbow. "Come, get in the car. Quickly." He turned to Smitty. "You too." He helped Kathryn into the car and stuck his head over the door, addressing his two bodyguards, "Clean up that mess. I'll deal with it later." He slammed the door after Smitty ducked in. "Go!"

Smitty sat facing backward with his arm resting over the back of the small jump seat opposite Kathryn and Forrester as the limousine sped through the city streets. Forrester had his arm draped protectively over Kathryn's shoulder while Smitty sat ready to be whatever he needed to be under the unusual circumstances.

He watched Kathryn carefully for any sign of a breakdown. She was staring at her hands, seemingly oblivious to those around her. He lay her purse in her lap, having retrieved it from the dead man's pocket, and got no response. He couldn't tell if she was playacting for Forrester's benefit or if she was really in trouble. He watched her lift a hand to her forehead and saw the telltale tremor. She was in trouble. She wiped her brow, staining her fingers with the dead man's blood, and brought her shaking hand to rest on top of the purse in her lap. He wasn't sure she even saw the blood. Her eyes were vacant, her lips unconsciously parted. She was anywhere but where she needed to be—present and on guard.

"Are you all right, darling?" Forrester asked.

When Kathryn didn't answer, Smitty took her bloody hand and began to clean it with a handkerchief from his pocket. "Don't look at it, honey." He looked at Forrester. "Blood makes her swoon. She'll be all right in a minute." He looked at Kathryn. "Won't you." She still didn't respond, so he squeezed her hand hard—hard enough to hurt, hard enough to bring her back to him. He saw her flinch in pain and she blinked, momentarily disoriented, before focusing on his face, and he knew she was back. "Won't you," he repeated.

"I'm okay."

Forrester heard her words, but he looked to Smitty for confirmation. Clearly, women in distress were not his forte.

"That's my girl," Smitty said with a smile, which made Forrester physically relax.

"Thank you." Kathryn returned the squeeze to let him know everything was under control.

"Yes, thank you," Forrester added, offering his hand.

"I'm sorry," Kathryn said, coming out of her daze, "Marcus, this is—"

"John Smith," he interrupted, "your ever-present shadow. I know."

She didn't know why it surprised her that he knew, but she couldn't have him thinking anything was between them. "He's just—"

"Like a brother to you. I know that too. I am eternally grateful, Mr. Smith."

"Glad I could help."

Forrester turned to her. "What happened?"

She lifted a hand to her brow again, and this time it was steady, supportive. She told of how she overheard the men, imparting the gist of the conversation, but not the details, little though they were. He didn't ask where she was or how she came to overhear the men, and she felt no need to elaborate. Forrester seemed satisfied with her explanation, and they spent the rest of the drive in relative silence. She pretended to take comfort from his offered shoulder, and he tightened his hold on her.

Once at the estate, Forrester insisted on a doctor, to give her something for her nerves, as he put it, but she refused, convincing him all she needed was a shower and a good night's sleep. She left Smitty and Forrester to play out their own drama, sure her partner could handle the situation.

She closed the door to her bathroom and shed her gown, letting it fall around her feet like a heavy theater curtain cut loose from its rafters. She didn't turn on the light, not anxious to see her bloody reflection. Instead, she immediately turned on the water and stepped into the steaming shower to wash every trace of Charles Lawrence from her mind and body.

"Would you like a drink, Mr. Smith?" Forrester asked as they entered the study.

"No, thanks."

"I'm afraid I need one," Forrester said pleasantly. He made himself a drink and swirled the ice in the glass as he turned around. "You don't like me very much, do you?"

"I don't know you, Mr. Forrester," Smitty said impatiently. "Ordinarily, I wouldn't give a shit what you do, but I do care about Kathryn. She thinks something of you and I respect that, but being in your presence is dangerous for her, and I don't like it, so yeah, I guess you could say you're not exactly my favorite person—especially after tonight."

"Her safety is very important to me. I want you to know that."

"Yeah, I can see just how important. If I hadn't been there—"

"Precisely why I asked you out here," Forrester interrupted as he made his way behind his ornate Louis XV-style mahogany desk and sat down. "It has become painfully obvious to me that I cannot protect her." It clearly shamed him, and he stared at the drink in his hand before lifting the glass and swallowing his failure. "I think you can."

"I'm inclined to agree with you."

"I thought you might." He reached into his desk and pulled out a large ledger book of checks. "You're a private detective, right?"

Smitty nodded, confirming his cover.

"I want to hire you. Whatever else you're working on, drop it."

"You don't have to pay me to keep her safe."

Forrester ignored him and began writing. "This should cover any expenses you have." He folded the check at the perforation and tore it from the book with a confident stroke that said it would not be refused.

"Listen, I told you—" Smitty looked at the check and did a little selling. "Well," he drew out, not sure he'd ever seen such a large amount in one check.

"I trust that will be satisfactory."

"That would be a well-placed trust."

Forrester closed the book with an arrogant grin and put it back in its drawer. "If something happens to her, it will cost you your life—you realize that."

Smitty's response was immediate and to the point. "If something happens to her, it will be over my dead body, so your threat is moot. I dislike threats, Mr. Forrester, but while we're on the subject, I'll kill anyone who hurts her." He paused, measuring the man in front of him. "And that includes you." He held up the check. "And this doesn't mean I'm your lapdog."

Forrester smiled as he leaned back in his chair and crossed his arms, unfazed. "You are *her* lapdog, Mr. Smith, and that will do."

Kathryn sat at the vanity in her room at the estate and mindlessly pulled her wet hair through a towel. The mirror dutifully reflected her movements, but its unfaltering precision was lost on its subject, her mind far away. She'd almost gone over the edge. She could feel her demons pulling at her, replaying the past in startling clarity over and over—the sounds, the smell, the taste of fear and death. She was lost in a dissolving dream, trapped between sleep and waking, helpless, while the darkness drowned the light. Her fragile hold on reality made her angry. She was stronger than that. She had to be. *Breathe*, she told herself, *just breathe*. If she controlled her breathing, the mind would follow.

In Forrester's presence was no place to falter. She knew better than that. It was unacceptable, and she shook her head. She refused to believe she couldn't handle any situation at any time. Tonight was a momentary lapse, that's all. She would have pulled herself together even if Smitty hadn't been there. Of course she would have—there was no other choice.

She finally recognized her face in the mirror and stopped toweling her hair. She remembered a time when Smitty wasn't enough to bring her back, when nothing short of chemically-induced unconsciousness could bring her peace. Those days were gone forever, she hoped. To put her mind at ease, she reminded herself she recovered quickly this time. She heard Smitty's voice, even if she couldn't comprehend his words, and she followed it like a beacon until she could see again.

"Kathryn?"

She blinked the reflection of the doorway in the mirror into focus at the sound of another familiar voice producing an unfamiliar word —her name.

"Kathryn?" Forrester repeated apprehensively.

He rarely used her name. She was always some indistinct term of endearment like darling, sweetheart, angel, or dear. She supposed using her name was too personal for him, a last defense against making her more than just the other woman in a long line of other women. Becoming personally involved was the last thing he wanted. She, on the other hand, would make sure it was the only thing he wanted.

"How are you?" he asked, as he lingered in the doorway.

"I'm fine." She held out her hand and watched him in the mirror.

He crossed the room to her side and stood awkwardly with his hands behind his back.

"Are *you* all right?" she asked, confused by his trepidation.

"I'm glad you're all right."

"Yes—" She turned from the mirror to face him directly. "I think we've established that we're all glad I'm all right." She paused, searching his eyes for the reason behind his odd behavior. "What is it?"

"I just want to make sure you're all right."

"Marc," she drew out as a warning.

He put his hand under her chin as he leaned over and kissed her forehead. "I have to leave first thing in the morning."

She took his hand as he tried to pull it away. "You just got here."

He disengaged her fingers like she was an unwanted needy child, and his casual tone turned to irritation. "I'm a businessman. I've got things to take care of."

Negotiating the shifting sands of Marcus Forrester's sizable ego had never been particularly difficult, but Kathryn knew she had to be careful. She was losing him. He despised weakness but craved dependence. His mood could change at any moment, and the key to maintaining control was where to apply the pressure and how. "Running away from me will not protect me, Marcus."

Her honesty confounded him, but then he smiled. "I'm not in the habit of running away from beautiful women."

Kathryn pinned him with serious blue eyes and prepared to reel him in. "Then don't."

He sobered under her chastising glare and didn't move when she stood up and slowly, purposefully, pressed her body against his.

"Don't," she repeated, as she ran her fingers through the graying hair at his temple. She made sure her request was insistent but not desperate. "Please don't."

He swallowed, and his features hardened. His focus fell away, and his true emotions rose to the surface. "These men will not get away with this." He looked at her with angry, determined eyes. "They can't do this to me."

Despite his relatively calm exterior, she could tell he was shaken by the night's events, not so much the threat to her life, she supposed, or the fact that it nearly succeeded, but the fact that someone was brazen enough to attempt it.

To her surprise, his eyes softened for a moment and he stroked her face. "They can't do this to you."

She blinked in disbelief, and it took a moment to comprehend his concern. Once past the initial shock, she knew she had him. "What are you going to do?"

"I'm going to remind them who they're dealing with."

"Do you know who those men are?"

"Yes, I do," he said with a faraway look in his eyes, as if the plan for their demise was written just past her shoulder.

That didn't bode well for the four men *or* the investigation. They needed live men to interrogate, not dead examples of Marc Forrester's wounded pride. "If it makes any difference, the others didn't seem very interested in Mr. Lawrence's mutiny."

He searched her face while he considered her statement and finally responded with a simple "Thank you."

She hated when he did that. His eyes would flash with conflicting emotions, and she couldn't tell which one he finally settled on, making it difficult to choose a direction. It didn't matter this time, though, as he changed the subject.

"Mr. Smith is waiting downstairs to say good night. Shall I send him up?"

"Yes, please."

He nodded in a shy sort of way and took her hand. "I'll say good night then."

He awkwardly kissed her on the cheek, and for a moment, she swore he meant to taste her lips. Instead, he pulled back and admired her face, as if he were seeing it for the last time.

"I probably won't see you in the morning." He attempted a smile and abruptly turned to leave, but she held fast to his hand.

"Marc?"

"Yes, Kathryn?"

She paused, as if she wasn't sure she was saying the right thing, but she knew he wouldn't deny her. "Stay with me tonight."

He followed the tug on his hand into her open arms, and he tentatively wrapped his arms around her waist. She knew he could do better than that, so she held him tighter, an unspoken invitation, which he gradually accepted and eventually fell into as he buried his face in her robe-clad shoulder and held her like he wished tomorrow would never come.

CHAPTER FOURTEEN

As Jenny watched the men of the OSS and SOE organize their paperwork and sift through briefcases and folios at headquarters, she wondered what secrets they possessed. She eyed them with envy, wondering if she would ever rate such trust. The scene reminded her of her first day, with the same men, and for her, the same excitement, but this time she was more than just the new kid on the block. She was important, and she'd procured something vital to their cause. The sense of accomplishment and worth was intoxicating.

"Thank you, Miss Ryan, you've done an excellent job for us," Colonel Holmes said.

"Thank you, sir. I look forward to the challenges ahead and hope I can meet them all with as much success."

The men around the table smiled and murmured in agreement. There was a knock at the door and the secretary stuck her head in. "Miss Hammond and Mr. Smith."

"Excellent, send them in," Colonel Holmes said.

Jenny beamed at the mere mention of Kathryn's name but quickly caught herself and dusted off her indifference, owing the present company.

Kathryn did a nearly imperceptible double take when she saw her, and Jenny imagined she'd never get used to seeing her in one of these meetings. She got over it quickly and smiled at her in return as she stopped at the empty place across from her.

Greetings rumbled around the room as Kathryn and Smitty took their seats.

"You look well, Miss Hammond ... considering," Holmes said. "Glad you're still with us."

That was an odd thing to say, Jenny thought. Even odder was Colonel Forsythe's seconding of that notion. She searched Kathryn's face for an explanation, but like at the benefit, she wore her professional mask to perfection.

"Glad to be here."

Holmes cleared his throat as he opened a file and addressed Kathryn. "These men ..."

"I'm sorry I couldn't get more information on—"

"Quite all right," Holmes interrupted, as he began sliding photos with names and short biographies attached with paper clips across the table, one by one. "Are these the men you saw?"

Kathryn scooped up the photos as they slid before her. The last photo, Charles Lawrence's, arrived with a large red stamp across his face that read *Deceased*.

"Deceased?" Jenny asked in surprise. "He was alive just last night."

The colonels looked at each other briefly, and Colonel Forsythe explained, "I'm afraid Mr. Lawrence had an idea to take Kathryn hostage last night, intent on elimination. John was forced to take action. Mr. Lawrence was killed."

Jenny sat wide-eyed and stunned for a moment, her eyes shifting from Smitty's matter-of-fact expression to Kathryn, who was oblivious to the conversation, as she concentrated on the mini biographies before her. "Well," Jenny said as she shifted, aware that all eyes but Kathryn's were upon her, "see if I ever leave a party early again."

The men seemed to appreciate her sense of humor about such a dire matter, and she chuckled with them to sell her composure, but she felt no humor. Kathryn finally lifted her eyes at the sound of the laughter, and Jenny was struck with a severe case of what if. What if she could never look into those eyes again? How close had Lawrence come to taking her life? Her breath caught in her throat, and it was all she could do to remain calm. She repeated *She's fine, she's fine, she's fine* in her head, hoping no one could sense her internal anguish at what might have happened.

Kathryn wasn't fooled. She saw right through her and offered an ever so subtle tilt of the head and a smile to give her whatever reassurance she could.

Jenny acknowledged the effort with a smile that didn't reach her eyes. In truth, it only upset her more. Even looking at Kathryn threatened to undo her, so she concentrated on what Colonel Holmes was saying and was surprised to find him addressing her.

"But that is for another time," he was saying. "For now, this will do. Thank you again, and good day, Miss Ryan."

It took her a beat to comprehend her dismissal, and while she was disappointed, she recognized that she had served her purpose and gracefully took her leave. Trust is earned, she reminded herself, not given just because you were in the right place at the right time.

Kathryn held up one of the photos and looked to Colonel Forsythe. "Where did we get these?"

"Our young Miss Ryan enlisted the help of her photographer friend," Holmes said, with a lilt of pride she'd never extracted from him. "Not only did she get the photos, she chatted them up and got names and basic background too. R&A did the rest in the wee hours of this morning, and we are leaps and bounds ahead of where we were yesterday."

Kathryn shook her head and exhaled, part disapproval, part worry. "That was dangerous."

"Actually, she was quite careful about the whole thing," Forsythe said. "She made sure each man was photographed in a group, none in the same group, and she talked to everyone in the photos to avoid suspicion."

Kathryn still didn't like Jenny that close to potential danger, but she couldn't fault her method and knew she had the personality to pull it off. She was impressed. "That's good work."

"Yes," Holmes said a little too enthusiastically. "In one evening, Miss Ryan has managed what you could not in all the months of being in the man's inner circle."

Kathryn snapped her head in Holmes's direction, as did Smitty, and they both spoke at once. "Now, see here," Smitty barked, almost drowning out Kathryn's "You have something to say to me, Holmes?"

"Settle down," Forsythe's low voice said as a warning. "Care to explain that comment, Holmes?"

Forsythe was not the confrontational sort, but disparage his people and you'd better be ready to explain yourself. The colonels locked eyes briefly, as their aides sat spellbound, waiting for the fireworks.

Holmes backed off his remark, replacing it with an easy smile and a load of bull. "Just pointing out how happy I am with Miss Ryan's contribution, Walter." He turned to Kathryn. "Taking nothing away from you, or your tireless work, Miss Hammond. She just got lucky." He regarded the group. "We all got lucky."

The room was silent for several uncomfortable moments while tempers dispersed and good fortunes were tallied. Holmes looked over Kathryn's report with a somewhat dubious expression. "So, you warned him his life was in danger."

Kathryn stared at him, her dislike growing exponentially every time he opened his mouth. "I could hardly avoid it after what happened."

"Mm," Holmes said, closing the report and moving on to the next folder. "See that you are not becoming too fond of Mr. Forrester."

"Don't be disgusting," Kathryn said.

"Relax, Miss Hammond. You would not be the first agent to get attached to an assignment. In fact," he said, as he began to dig deep into her folder, "it wouldn't be the first time you—"

"That's enough, Holmes," Forsythe said, losing his considerable patience. "Can we move on, please?"

"Certainly," Holmes said with a disingenuous grin. "Miss Hammond," he began pleasantly, "did Mr. Forrester mention anything about these men?"

"As I indicated in my report," she began, annoyed at his condescending tone, "only that he knew who they were and that he was going to take care of them. I think I convinced him the remaining four were loyal, but he still left town this morning for an undisclosed location and unspecified duration."

"I see. And he left you this note?"

"Yes."

Holmes unfolded the expensive linen stationary and began to read. "Dear darling—" He looked up with a smirk. "I feel compelled to bestow upon you my sincerest gratitude for your devotion in these trying times." He looked up again with what appeared to be a genuine appreciation of Kathryn's spell over the man. "I regret my brief stay in *our* home—" He emphasized the word with a raised eyebrow. "But until we are together again, I know you are in good hands. Ever, Marc." Holmes looked to Smitty. "And these would be your capable hands, Mr. Smith?"

"Yes."

Holmes nodded and turned again to Kathryn. "And you have no idea what he has planned for these men?"

"Not specifically. He seemed determined to make an example of them, but by the end, he seemed to think better of it. They may be too important to dispose of. Lawrence seemed to think Forrester couldn't go on without them. The men themselves seemed to think they couldn't go on without Forrester. Something about research and something neither side has yet."

"Yes," Holmes agreed, as if he were well aware of the situation. He closed Forrester's file and began searching for another.

"You may have saved those men's lives," Colonel Forsythe interjected into the break in the conversation.

"I'm not sure if that's good or bad," she said.

"Neither are we," Holmes agreed, much to Walter's obvious chagrin. He slid a file marked *Daniel Ryan* under Kathryn's hand.

Kathryn's heartbeat quickened as the brown folder burned beneath her fingers. She didn't want to know anymore. Whatever Jenny's father was into, it didn't appear to be good. The German's wanted it, and men were willing to kill for it, and most of all, more disclosure meant more to hide from Jenny.

Smitty got a copy of the same file and didn't hesitate to devour its contents. "Woo," he exclaimed, "a real family affair."

Kathryn could no longer put off the inevitable. She cracked the file and was met with Daniel Ryan's photo. His strong jaw and gentle eyes were stained with the red stamp of his fate: *Deceased*. She glanced through his record, tracing his conspicuously vague scientific and medical career straight into the subfolder of his parents. Jenny's grandmother was an artist, her grandfather a chemist and botanist, just as Jenny had said, but her grandfather's hobby wasn't all about the wonder and beauty of the natural world. He was a research scientist. His work, destruction and disease. Biological warfare.

"My God," she said under her breath.

The grandfather's record led to Austria, where he studied and worked early in his career before returning stateside to carry on with his research. His history showed there were always trips abroad, the durations longer and longer, leading up to the outbreak of the First World War and ceasing just before the fall of Germany, never to resume again. The report was incomplete—his wife's role was unclear—but its inference was clear and it was complete enough to illustrate the Ryan family tree was steeped in deception and possibly treason.

Kathryn swallowed the rising bile in her throat. It would kill Jenny if she found out. She quietly closed the folder. "What next?"

"Our focus is what it always has been," Holmes assured her. "Find what they are looking for before they do, and foil whatever plan is in place."

"What about this?" She tapped the Ryan folder.

"Unfortunately, dead men tell no tales," he said.

"And his daughter knows nothing," Kathryn said as a reminder, in case he forgot.

"So, we are back to sit and listen," Smitty said.

"Not exactly." Forsythe shifted as he leaned in. "For the past year, this group—" he said, tapping on the stack of photos, "has been receiving information. Information we assumed was coming from Daniel Ryan." He paused as his agents reached their impossible conclusions. "Except, of course, Daniel Ryan has been dead for the past year."

"And the daughter has been cleared," Smitty said.

Kathryn knew his comment was to keep her from reiterating Jenny's innocence, thus revealing her obvious interest.

"So," Holmes drew out as he clasped his hands across his paperwork, "who is left?"

"Paul," Kathryn said.

"We suspect," Forsythe agreed, "but there is no opportunity. He has been watched extensively. If it is him, we are baffled as to how the information is being exchanged."

Kathryn tilted her head and raised her brow. "Well, he wants like hell to keep Jenny away from Forrester."

Holmes eyed her curiously. "Any chance you could get close to Paul?"

"None whatsoever," Kathryn and Smitty chimed in unison.

Smitty continued, taking the desperation out of their protest. "He despises her."

"I see," Holmes said, as if he could completely understand.

"So, where does this leave us?" Kathryn asked.

Holmes began gathering his papers. "This leaves you right where you are." He looked up, fake smile firmly in place. "Doing a fine job." He turned to Smitty. "Mr. Smith, see how close you can get to Mr. Forrester when he returns. Gain his confidence ... drinking buddies ... you know. Perhaps he will tell you things he wouldn't tell a woman."

He paused, and Kathryn knew her icy glare, backed by the equally frigid stare of Colonel Forsythe, had its intended effect.

"Business things," Holmes clarified. "Man to man. You understand, right, Miss Hammond?"

"Completely."

"Good. I believe we're through here."

"Not quite," Forsythe said as he stood, stilling the fellow officer with a warning look. He softened his demeanor and turned to his agents. "John, thank you. I don't need to tell you—"

"No sir." He shook the older man's extended hand.

"Kathryn—" He pulled her chair out for her as she stood. "Good work, as always."

They filed out with mumbles of farewell to the mute aides and only a cursory nod to Holmes, who sat like a scolded child awaiting his punishment.

"Get out the earplugs, Sal," Kathryn said to the secretary as she passed through the outer office. It wasn't often that Colonel Forsythe lost his temper. She'd only seen it twice, but when he did ... brother, look out. As she and Smitty traveled the hallway, the sound of raised voices seeped under the closed doors behind them like an early morning fog.

"This is ridiculous," Jenny complained to the mirror in the ladies' room as she wiped away her tears. But she knew it wasn't ridiculous. Her fear was well-founded. Kathryn could have been killed. She knew Forrester was dangerous and knew the men around him were dangerous, but Kathryn seemed untouchable surrounded by his power. Who would dare? She barely held herself together as she walked through the outer office, offering a wave over her shoulder to the secretary, knowing no sound would make it past her tight throat.

Once in the ladies' room, she lost it entirely and wondered when Kathryn had taken her over so completely. Just the possibility of Kathryn's loss overwhelmed her. Was it love, instability, or lingering fallout from the loss of her father? She didn't know, but she knew she had to conquer it quickly. She couldn't fall apart every time she saw her.

The majority of her tears shed, she blew her nose and looked at the familiar sight of her weeping reflection. When would it stop? She never used to be this way. "Pull yourself together," she said, raising her chin. "Danger is part of her job." She paused. "It's part of *our* job. Grow up, Jenny."

She plucked a tissue from the dispenser on the counter and dried her eyes. "That starts today." She spent a few more minutes securing her emotions and confidently strode out of the ladies' room only to literally run into Kathryn and Smitty in the hallway.

"Oh, hey," Kathryn said with a grin as she grabbed her shoulders. Then, "Hey," again, this time filled with concern. "What is it?"

Jenny tried to hide her face, looking anywhere but at Kathryn and more than a little self-consciously at Smitty. "It's nothing. Really, I'm—"

"C'mere." Kathryn led her back into the ladies' room, glancing around the small room once inside.

"It's empty," Jenny said quietly, disappointed that she'd been found an emotional wreck, again. "I'm sorry, Kat. It's nothing."

Kathryn reached back and locked the door before coming to her and cupping her face in her hands. "Why are you apologizing to me?"

"Because I'm such a baby." She looked down in shame. "I try to be strong, I really do, but sometimes it just hits me and I can't help it."

"Okay, first of all, what's all this about?"

Jenny looked up into Kathryn's gentle eyes and had to turn away or risk falling apart again. She couldn't reveal what upset her. Kathryn didn't need a weak-minded lover who couldn't handle the rigors of life let alone their relationship. She offered instead the first thing that came to mind. "I saw a fellow in the hallway who reminded me of my dad."

"Oh."

"It's stupid, I know."

Kathryn relaxed and embraced her. "Nonsense."

Jenny melted into the protection of her strong arms, but when an overwhelming urge to bare her soul washed over her, she quickly pushed away, claiming foolishness, and left Kathryn confused, holding nothing but the air.

She turned to the mirror to escape the rising emotional tide, and Kathryn reached out to place a hand on her shoulder. Jenny stopped her with a quick squeeze of her hand before dropping it and returning to the task of wiping running mascara from under her eyes.

"I'm okay. Honestly. Don't fuss."

She saw Kathryn's confusion in the mirror and then her confident resolve as she stepped forward and wrapped her arms around her waist from behind. "But I like fussing over you," she said and kissed the side of her head.

Jenny tensed as a sob nearly escaped. She stepped to the side, out of Kathryn's grasp. "Kat, please. You're not helping."

Kathryn held up her hands. "Sorry."

She looked like she'd been slapped in the face, and Jenny's heart clenched because she'd put that look there. Kathryn's expression hardened and the confident resolve turned to grim resolve.

She turned for the door. "I'll leave you be then." She paused and half turned, her eyes trained on the floor. "Nice work last night."

"Kat, wait, I didn't—"

Kathryn held up a hand and didn't turn around. "It's all right if you don't want to do this, Jenny. In fact, I'd just as soon end it now."

Jenny rushed to her side. "What are you talking about?"

Kathryn faced her. "Look, I understand, I really do."

Jenny certainly didn't, and she didn't understand why Kathryn was always so eager to call the whole thing off—they'd barely gotten started. Was she seriously that insecure? Or perhaps she was taking that casual sex line far too seriously. "You're angry."

"I promise you, I'm not angry. It's obvious you'd rather be alone."

"Please," Jenny said, grasping Kathryn's wrist. "You're wrong. I—" She felt like she would cry again and struggled against it by turning her face downward. "I just don't want you to see me this way anymore." Finally, a kernel of truth.

Kathryn's warm hand tilted her chin up. "What way?"

Jenny couldn't meet her eyes. "Like an overemotional child." She angrily swiped at her tears. "I want to be strong." She still didn't dare make eye contact. "Like you."

"Look at me."

Jenny lifted her eyes. The empathy she found staring back at her showed Kathryn understood the desire to control emotions that had no regard for time and place or logic and reason.

"If I'm strong, it's because I have friends I can lean on when I need to. Like Smitty—" She cupped her face in her hands. "Like you."

Kathryn's face blurred as tears filled her vision.

"Would you be there for me, Jenny?"

"In a heartbeat."

"Then let me be here for you."

That was all Jenny needed to give in to her emotions. She melted into Kathryn's embrace and felt transparent. How could Kathryn not know the tears were about her? She felt the need to reinforce her charade. "I miss him so," she said through a sob into the dark blue gabardine of Kathryn's suit jacket.

"I know, honey."

Kathryn whispered words of comfort until the tears abated and Jenny loosened her grip, signaling her recovery.

"Don't you dare apologize," Kathryn said as she retrieved a tissue and handed it over.

Jenny chuckled through sniffles. "I won't." She could finally look her in the eyes without wanting to break down. "Thank you."

"Better now?"

"Yes, much." She blotted her eyes.

Kathryn cupped her cheek. "Please don't ever feel you have to hide who you are. Not to me. Not ever."

"I don't want you to get sick of it. *Sick of me*. Because I don't know when it will stop."

"Jenny, your emotional honesty is one of the things I—" Kathryn seemed to stumble on the next word and tried again. "One of the things that's so special about you."

Jenny turned away with a dismissive shake of her head and stared at her distraught reflection. "I don't feel very special right now."

Kathryn wrapped her arms around her from behind again, and this time she let her. She held her close and rocked her gently. "How 'bout now?"

Jenny melted into the embrace, glad her emotional upheaval was over. "Do you know how much I love your arms around me?"

"No, but if you hum a few bars, I bet I could make it worth your while."

Jenny turned in Kathryn's arms and got lost in the grace of her complete acceptance. Gone was the urge to burst into tears, replaced by a sense of destiny that extended beyond what the world could throw at them. She was safe, here and now, and if she'd learned anything, it was that the only sure thing was this moment, and she wasn't going to waste another. She captured Kathryn's lips without a thought to what came before or what would come after. She quickly found her body pressed impossibly close to Kathryn's thigh by a strong hand on the small of her back, and she cursed her tight skirt for coming between her and unbridled pleasure.

She vaguely became aware of voices in the hall as Smitty repeatedly announced, "Sorry, out of order."

"Good boy," Kathryn mumbled between passionate kisses.

A loud knock finally got their complete attention.

"Uh, ladies? The natives are getting restless."

Kathryn groaned to the ceiling. "Bad boy."

Jenny chuckled and laid her head on Kathryn's warm chest, where she felt her heart beating wildly. "When will I see you again?"

"How about tonight?"

Her head snapped up in disbelief. "On the level? What about Forrester?"

"Out of town."

"My God, why didn't you say so? Yes! Oh—" She put her hand to her forehead. "I promised Bernie and Cal we'd go out. It's been ages."

"Maybe another night."

"No. I'll reschedule with the boys. I want to see you. Soon."

"Rehearsal is over at four, and then I have a few hours to kill before I have to get ready for tonight's show. Maybe we could get a bite to eat—"

"Or," Jenny interrupted as she reached for Kathryn, undid a button mid-torso, and slipped her hand inside her blouse, "maybe we could find something a little more interesting to do with our precious few hours. Hm?"

Kathryn moved closer with a big grin. "Or we could do that."

"Sorry, out of order!" Smitty bellowed in a none too subtle crescendo, indicating they'd better make themselves presentable in a hurry.

They parted with a chuckle and checked themselves in the mirror.

"Where are you headed?" Jenny asked as she reapplied her lipstick.

Kathryn took out her own lipstick and leaned into the mirror. "I thought I'd go directly to the club." She cut her eyes to Jenny with a mischievous grin. "Maybe I'll finish that rehearsal early."

"Mm." Jenny hummed approvingly. "I'll be up that way shortly, so that will be perfect."

"Want a ride? Smitty's got the car today. Forrester has made him my bodyguard, so we can give you a lift."

"Maybe next time. I'm meeting Bernie and have to make a stop at the store first."

"Bring him along. Smitty will be thrilled."

Jenny chuckled. "Well, anything that thrills Smitty …"

Kathryn broke into a broad-faced grin.

They exited the ladies' room, and the trio began to strut, three abreast, down the hallway.

"Blouse," Smitty commented nonchalantly.

Kathryn one-handed the wayward button. "Thank you."

Jenny blushed as Smitty looked her way and identified her as the guilty party.

"How you doin', kid?"

"Just swell, Johnny, yourself?"

He cut his eyes to Kathryn, who just chuckled.

Bernie waited until Smitty left the car to smoke and Jenny disappeared into the grocery store before leaning on the back of the front seat and settling his chin on his crossed arms. "So, did you like the champagne?" he asked Kathryn, sitting in the front passenger seat. He could tell by the confused look on her face she hadn't a clue what he was referring to. "Last night. I sent it to *the room*." He made quotation marks in the air.

"Ah," Kathryn drew out. "It was a real lifesaver. Thank you."

"You're welcome. I have a friend who—" Something caught his eye just over Kathryn's shoulder, and he cursed under his breath.

Kathryn turned in her seat. "What is it?"

"Trouble." He pointed out the car window, and with his finger, traced the path of a tall redheaded woman as she entered the store.

"Who is that?"

"Satan."

Kathryn gave him a no-nonsense look, and he knew he'd better start talking, and fast. "That's Marcella, Jenny's ex-gir*lfiend*."

Kathryn stared at the door as if she could still see a glimpse of the woman.

"Jenny caught her screwing the doorman of their apartment building. In *their* apartment, in their own bed. And what's worse, it was her birthday, the same night Jenny lost her dad." He shook his head. "Poor thing. She comes back from the morgue only to find that noise going on. Bitch. Jenny walked out of that apartment and never looked back. And I mean that." Bernie tapped her on the shoulder to make sure she knew Jenny was unforgiving of betrayal. "She wouldn't even go back there for her things. I had to go in there and pack up her belongings. I don't think she's seen Marcy since."

He'd barely finished his sentence before Kathryn unfolded herself from the car and tucked her purse under her arm as she strode toward the grocery store.

"Hoo," Bernie drew out with glee as he leaned out the open window. "This is gonna be good."

Once inside, Kathryn easily found the ex. She was a stunning woman with porcelain-like skin and a confident grace that made it easy to understand how Jenny would be drawn to her. Kathryn was surprised to feel a tendril of jealousy straighten her spine, but it was quickly displaced by anger for what she'd done to Jenny.

Marcella had a look of sinister mischief creasing the corners of her perfectly painted mouth. Kathryn followed her eyes to Jenny, arriving at the checkout line. The she-devil picked up an obviously random item from a shelf and quickly made sure she was next in line.

Kathryn picked up her own random item and made for the front register.

She watched the redhead lean into Jenny's ear from behind and saw the life drain from her face.

Kathryn was close enough to hear Jenny say, "Don't speak to me, Marcy." Her words were as cold as her expression.

"Oh, now, sugar," Marcella said. "Don't be that way."

Jenny slammed her detergent on the counter. Kathryn anticipated a tirade that would make a sailor blush, so she quickly excused her way to the front of the line, a bag of coffee held high, and caught Jenny's attention, silencing her.

"Sorry, excuse me, sorry," she said as she brushed past the ex with a not so accidental jostle.

"Say, sister," Marcella said in irritation.

Kathryn turned and offered a sweet smile. "I'm terribly sorry."

"Say," the redhead repeated seductively, as if she had a chance in hell. "Be my guest."

"Thank you."

Kathryn took her place beside an astonished but grateful Jenny. "Okay, honey, here's the coffee. Are you sure we don't need anything else?"

"Uh, no ... sweetie," Jenny said, catching on quickly. "That's it."

The look on Marcella's face was priceless. Stuck in a place between shock and envy, her expression was very much like the ridiculous look on a Kewpie doll, the kind one wins at the amusement park for a nickel a try.

"Ration coupon for the coffee, hon?" The cashier held out her hand.

"Oh—" Jenny blinked. She reached into her purse and pulled out her ration booklet. She was out of coffee stamps for the month. "I uh—"

"It's my turn," Kathryn spoke up as she plunked the appropriate stamp into the cashier's hand and showed her ID.

She saw Jenny staring at her like she could kiss her right there in the line at the A&P for castrating her ex-lover, and Kathryn had to admit, she got a thrill out of it.

She paid and took her change and watched Jenny calmly head for the door without a backward glance to her painful past.

"Say," the redhead tugged on Kathryn's elbow before she could follow.

Kathryn turned and found a card with a phone number thrust into her face.

"When you get tired of kindergarten recess, why don't you graduate to a real woman?" Marcella whispered.

Kathryn cut the suggestion down with a warning look that saw the woman physically wither. She awkwardly put the card away, as the people in line behind her made their impatience known.

Kathryn hurried out the door and caught up to Jenny, placing a protective hand on her back for the short walk to the car.

Bernie watched the women approach with broad smiles on their faces and saw Satan appear over their shoulders as she emerged from the store and stared at them with her hands on her hips. Smitty started the car and pulled into the street as Bernie gleefully shot Marcella double birds out the back window.

CHAPTER FIFTEEN

It was late afternoon, and rehearsal was over when a timid middle-aged woman stepped into the mostly empty club. She looked overwhelmed by the fancy surroundings, but Bobby greeted her warmly, and she seemed more comfortable by the time he directed her to the end of the bar, where Jenny and Kathryn were having a drink with Smitty before making the most of their abbreviated date night.

"A Mrs. Grayson to see you, Kat."

Not recognizing the name or the face, Kathryn motioned her over. The woman held her purse tightly to her chest with both hands as she approached, but as she got closer, she shifted her gloves and purse into one hand and offered the other.

"Miss Hammond?"

Kathryn automatically extended her own hand, and they exchanged a polite handshake. "Yes?"

"My name is Marian Grayson."

The woman had a soft accent, decidedly Midwestern. She smiled pleasantly as she spoke, and her eyes twinkled with appreciation upon meeting, though for the life of her, Kathryn couldn't imagine why.

"Joshua Grayson was my boy."

That name Kathryn knew. She froze, with their hands still clasped. Her rib cage seized and she couldn't inhale. She raised her chin, as if the motion would force much needed air into her lungs. Breathe. She needed to breathe.

Mrs. Grayson nervously eyed the strangers still sitting at the bar and tentatively began. "He was—"

"I know who he was," Kathryn interrupted gently, placing a hand on the woman's elbow and moving her a few comfortable steps away, with their hands still joined. "He was a handsome red-haired young man, with a scar right here—" she said, as she drew a line under her chin, "where he fell off his daddy's tractor when he was thirteen."

Mrs. Grayson's face lit up with a proud grin as she released Kathryn's hand and relaxed her death grip on her purse. "He wondered if you really recognized him every time you saw him. Thought maybe you were just bein' polite, 'cause that's the kinda lady you are." She looked Kathryn up and down affectionately and grinned as she opened her purse and began digging. "Glory be, you sure are everything he said you'd be."

Kathryn wasn't quite sure what that meant, but she was upset she hadn't placed the Grayson name sooner. Had her life moved that far out of context? She should have taken it as a sign of healing, a healthy side effect of moving on, but, instead, she reprimanded herself for her momentary lapse in guilt. Mrs. Grayson had gotten over her initial shyness, but Kathryn was too distracted to comprehend the woman going on in rapid oratory about a great aunt's funeral and how she located her at The Grotto.

"And I just knew it had to be you," she was explaining. "So I said to Edgar ... that's my husband ... since we're going through that big city, I'm going to make it a point to find that woman, and here you are." By this time, she'd fished a piece of worn paper from her purse and held it out.

"It meant so much to him, what you done, how you treated him."

Kathryn took it and carefully unfolded the paper to reveal a letter scratched in a hurried scrawl in blue ink.

"He said one day you pulled him up on that stage and made him feel like the only man in the world." The woman pointed out the passage. "The other boys treated him right special after that. Do you remember?"

He was one of a hundred boys she'd given that treatment to, and she didn't know whether she really remembered Joshua in her arms on stage or whether she'd just imagined it after the fact, his face now one she would never forget.

"Yes," Kathryn said quietly.

"He thought the world of you, Miss Hammond. You don't know how much that meant to me and Daddy, knowing he had someone lifting his spirits in that awful place over there."

Guilt found its way home, and Kathryn could only muster a weak smile.

"I just wanted you to know that you made a difference, and I—" her voice cracked with emotion, "why, I'm right grateful, is all."

Kathryn didn't know what to say. She smiled again and nodded in understanding as she offered the letter back.

"No, no," Mrs. Grayson insisted as she patted Kathryn's arm. "You keep that." She leaned in close and made sure Kathryn had her undivided attention. "Don't you ever forget what you done for those boys." She turned before the tears welling in her eyes could fall and left as quickly as she came.

Kathryn stared at the letter in her hand, her eyes drawn to the date. One week before Joshua Grayson's death. "No," she said grimly, her voice barely a whisper, "I won't ever forget what I did to them." She stared at the words and numbers until they became a blur. A gentle hand on her back brought the world back into focus.

"Are you all right?"

She looked into concerned green eyes and made a poor attempt at a smile. "Yeah."

Jenny looked at the letter. "Who's Joshua Grayson?"

Kathryn looked up at Smitty. "Someone I killed."

Disapproval frowned behind his eyes but his face remained focused and neutral. Her hand began to shake as she carefully folded up the note. Everything around her dimmed, and she was vaguely aware of Smitty sliding off his stool.

"I ... uh ..." She thumbed toward her dressing room. "I'm going to get my coat. I'll be right back." She mindlessly patted Jenny on the shoulder and then turned and headed across the club.

Jenny looked to Smitty for an explanation. "What does she mean?" He ignored the question entirely as he rushed after Kathryn, who was taking the stairs to her dressing room two at a time.

The sounds were getting louder, and even with her hands over her ears, Kathryn couldn't drown out the desperate screams. The begging, the pleading! Why wouldn't they listen!

"I don't know anything!" the hoarse voice croaked over and over.

Gunshots and crumpled bodies. One after another fell until it was silent, but it wasn't silent. The screaming had become background noise, like a train whistle that melts into one's consciousness from living too long within earshot of the tracks. The pleading went on until the "I don't know anything" was a meaningless whimper merely repeated for the sake of one's own sanity. More gunshots followed by angry shouting instead of pleading, strong arms pulling instead of pushing, words of assurance instead of threats.

"I don't know anything," became a wordless sob into a stranger's scratchy wool uniform. Only then did it truly become silent and she realized the screaming and pleading had been hers.

Her ears were ringing. She couldn't get enough air. She felt light-headed, sick. She couldn't see, or, more accurately, what she could see she didn't want to see: dead eyes, dead bodies, lives ended in slow-motion clouds of exploding red mist. Her eyes were tightly closed, but still the vision played on mercilessly.

"Look at me," she thought she heard.

"I can't," she cried, just in case it was real.

"I'm right here."

Her eyes were open now but she still couldn't see. She couldn't breathe. The sounds were coming again. Demons were dancing. She had to get out of her own skin. Something was holding her down, holding her in. Someone was pleading, but this time it wasn't her. Her body felt like a live wire, her heart beating impossibly hard until she thought it might burst. Pins and needles were bombarding her skin until she could no longer sense her limbs. She couldn't stand it anymore. She had to get out!

"Here," the voice said.

"Let me go!" she pleaded, her useless extremities refusing to help themselves.

"Look at me, Kat!"

She was trying, but she was lost. The voice was familiar, and she knew it would lead her home, but she couldn't find the way. "I can't!" she cried.

"Breathe, and look at me."

She knew that voice. Trust came with it, and safety too. She blindly reached out. "Don't let go."

"Right here."

She recognized warm hands on each side of her face, and she lifted her numb fingers to encircle the wrists.

"That's it. Right here, honey."

Her focus found Smitty's eyes, mere inches from her own, before they blurred into an opaque pane of tears and she broke down into his arms.

Smitty could only hope that Kathryn just needed to gather herself—she'd been fine for so long—but as his bum knee complained with every hurdled step up the stairs, he knew Mrs. Grayson's visit, combined with the previous night's dramatics, could spell trouble.

He burst into her dressing room and found her curled in the corner, holding her head, with Joshua Grayson's note abandoned at her feet. She was gone, but how far gone?

Broken sobs and pain-wracked pleading filled the small room, as his questions went unanswered and demands ignored. He took her rigid shoulders in both hands and tried to shake her back to reality. He would have slapped her face had he not known it futile. It was an all too familiar scene, and he knew she would either fight to find her way out or two pills to oblivion would have to do it for her. He couldn't bear to see her suffer, so he dumped the contents of her purse, looking for the pills, and rifled through drawers as he rhetorically asked for her help, knowing he'd get none in return.

Jenny knew something was terribly wrong. Smitty wasn't fond of her, but he'd never been downright rude. His concern bordered on frantic, and as she watched him bound up the stairs, she decided one good turn deserved another, and she was going to be there for Kathryn, whatever the problem, just like she said she would.

When she reached the top of the stairs, determination turned to confusion, then to unease, as the muted sounds of someone in terrible pain assailed her ears. She listened, not able to comprehend what she was hearing. It almost didn't sound human, and it certainly couldn't be Kathryn. Jenny's heartbeat quickened, and dread seized her when she realized it could be no one else. She rushed to the partially open door of her dressing room and stopped abruptly, unprepared for the scene that greeted her.

"Where are your pills, Kat—dammit!" she heard Smitty bark as he came into view, his hands waving in utter frustration. He continued to ransack the room, and just past him, Jenny saw a sight that froze her to her spot. Her strong, confident lover was crumpled in the corner like a frightened child, and the agonizing cries were indeed coming from her.

For a few abstract moments, as Smitty frantically searched the room, it appeared as if he had attacked her, but Jenny knew that certainly wasn't the case. Whoever Kathryn was fending off with her sporadic, half-hearted flailing was in her mind. Jenny barely had time to register the poor soul as Kathryn when, suddenly, Smitty was standing before her, about to close the door in her face.

"Not now," he said.

She put out her foot, blocking the door. He was not shutting her out, not when Kathryn was in such pain. "Smitty—" She didn't know what to say. Obviously, *is she all right?* would sound ludicrous. "What can I do?"

"Leave us alone." He pushed hard on the door, overpowering her foot.

"Smitty!" she said, pushing back.

"Please," he said, "you can't help her right now!"

She could tell by the desperation in his voice and the worry in his eyes that it had nothing to do with her or any dislike between them, and truth be told, she had no clue what to do for Kathryn, so she let the door close, entrusting her to the only other person she knew cared as much as she did.

She stepped back, still trying to process what was happening, and found herself torn between an overwhelming urge to barge in and an undeniable instinct to turn away, as if turning her back would render it all just a bad dream. But it wasn't a bad dream, it was a nightmare, Kathryn's nightmare, and she wasn't about to go anywhere until it was over. She decided if she couldn't be there physically, she could at least be there in spirit, so she hovered just outside the room with her hand and ear to the door and offered her strength in a silent prayer.

She could hear Smitty's voice, at times both hard and gentle, begging Kathryn to come back to him.

"Look at me!" she heard him command.

Kathryn made nothing but incomprehensible sounds of desperation, and every one of them cut Jenny to the core. The broken person in the next room was so far removed from the vital woman she'd come to know and admire that she'd almost forgotten her history at the hands of the enemy. She could only imagine, yet loathed to do it, the horrors she'd endured and the waking nightmares that obviously plagued her still.

Eventually, the desperate cries ceased and Smitty's voice became calmer, his urgings more productive, until finally she heard Kathryn's voice. It was barely recognizable, weak and upset, but she was responding, and that was something. For a moment, Jenny was relieved, but it was short-lived, as a low, despondent sobbing began. The sounds weren't the abstract torture of a mind adrift like before. This time they came from a conscious place, the mournful expressions of grief reverberating from an oft sampled well residing deep within. This unfathomable sorrow she recognized as Kathryn's constant anguish, present and bleeding still.

Jenny didn't know who Joshua Grayson was or, from Smitty's reaction, how responsible Kathryn actually was for his death, but she knew the heavy burden of feeling responsible, and her heart went out to a kindred spirit.

Smitty cradled Kathryn in his arms, rocking her gently while she cried, until exhaustion took her mercifully away from the cruelty of her conscious mind. He picked her up and gently placed her on the bed and brought the throw to her chin. He kissed her forehead as a tear escaped the corner of her eye and followed the moistened path down her cheek like so many others before it.

He fought back tears of his own and carefully guided a wayward lock of hair from her face, wishing her torment as easily tamed. There was no more he could do for her now, so with a soft exhale, he turned off the light and quietly slipped from the room.

The door responded with a dull click as he slowly pulled it closed, and he turned to see Jenny struggling to her feet from her place against the wall.

"Is she all right?" she whispered. "Can I see her?"

Smitty took her by the elbow and led her silently away from the room and toward the stairs. He knew she'd have a million questions, questions he wasn't prepared to answer. Once at the stairs, he motioned her to go first, which she did. He didn't follow her. "She's fine. Go home."

He didn't expect her to leave without objection, but he didn't expect the intensity of her protest.

"Bullshit, go home," she said, as she marched back up the stairs to face him.

"Listen, kid," he said, holding up his hands to defend himself, "she's got a migraine, that's all. She'll be fine." He could see the fire in her eyes as she closed the gap between them, and he stepped back to avoid a very outraged finger thrust in his face.

"Don't fuck with me, John," she said, the anger in her voice quickly consumed by emotional concern. "Not about this … please. Not about her."

He saw tears welling in her eyes, but she blinked them away before they fell. She couldn't know the truth, but he had to tell her something or she'd never leave. He nodded and led her to just outside Dominic's office.

"Wait here."

Jenny watched Smitty through the blinds as he explained the situation to Kathryn's boss, who was obviously concerned and immediately on his feet, but Jenny could also tell from his body language that this wasn't the first time it had happened. He picked up the phone to make alternative arrangements for the evening's performance, she assumed, and Smitty nodded and left the office.

"Walk with me."

Jenny looked toward the dressing room. "But …"

"She'll sleep now."

Smitty led her outside to his car, where he opened the passenger side door and closed it after she got in. He circled the car and slid into the driver's side, putting both hands on the wheel. He made no effort to put the key in the ignition, so Jenny knew they weren't going anywhere. He obviously chose the car for its privacy, and she hoped he was going to tell her what was going on, but the heavy silence told her she would have to start.

"What happened in there, Smitty?"

The corner of his mouth twitched, and he worked his jaw before answering. "It's really not my place to say."

Jenny exhaled her frustration, though she really didn't think answers would come that easily. Delicate matters required a delicate approach, and she would have to convince him it would be in Kathryn's best interest for him to confide in her. "Do you think she'd tell me if I asked her?"

Smitty looked at her as if she'd read his mind, and he was struggling with the answer. "She might," he said.

That was a start, Jenny reasoned. "But if I asked her, it would probably be very painful, right?"

"Right."

"So," she drew out, "if she might tell me anyway …" She sought out his guarded eyes. "Why don't you tell me instead, and we can both save her from that particular pain?"

Smitty cut wary eyes in her direction. "I said she *might* tell you. That's not a ringing endorsement to betray a personal trust."

"Smitty," Jenny said, as she turned to face him in all seriousness, "no matter what you think of me, I care about Kathryn very much."

He looked down and nodded. "I know you do."

She was both surprised and encouraged by his response. "I'd never do anything to hurt her. I need you to know that."

"I do."

She raised her brow. He was being awfully agreeable, considering their history, so she pressed on while the pressing was good. "I want to help her. I want to be there for her if I can. I can't do that if I don't know what's wrong." He didn't respond, and she could only assume he agreed. "Who was Joshua Grayson, and how did he die?"

Smitty exhaled with an undecided shake of his head. She could tell he was torn between Kathryn's penchant for privacy and her need to heal.

Before he could verbally refuse to answer, Jenny made sure he knew she wasn't totally ignorant of Kathryn's past. "If it makes a difference, I know she was overseas, and I know she was captured."

He turned to her in surprise, then faced forward again with a crease in his brow. His contemplative expression told her it did make a difference. She gave him all the time he needed and waited patiently for the answer she hoped would come.

He set his jaw and began. He skipped right to Kathryn's confinement after capture. He said the hows and whys of the mission gone bad were merely a tragic backdrop painted by unexpected betrayal.

An ill-conceived rescue was attempted—unauthorized, of course, and strictly against protocol—by a group of undertrained, oversexed boys bent on being heroes, Joshua Grayson among them. Things went from bad to worse, as the men were either killed or captured themselves.

Kathryn, for her part, withstood the physical abuse typical of interrogation and kept her secrets to herself. The Nazis, with growing frustration, turned to the newly acquired prisoners as a way of extracting much-needed information from their reticent star.

The men were lined up and Kathryn told to choose one. This was the man they would kill if she didn't give them the information they sought. If she refused to talk and refused to choose, they would choose for her, but they would choose three instead of one, and so it would go every time she didn't give them an answer.

Jenny hung her head and uttered a curse under her breath. She felt sick.

"You okay?"

She nodded.

"There was no way she could choose," he said. "She knew those guys. She couldn't tell the bastards what they wanted to know, and she couldn't choose." He looked away and pressed the back of his balled-up fist to his lips. "Tore her up inside." He paused a beat and put his hand back on the steering wheel. "That's where Josh comes in. He spoke up, said he wasn't afraid to die, and it would be all right if she picked him first."

Jenny exhaled and looked to the sky, giving the young man respect for his futile gallantry. "Did she?"

"No." Smitty stared blankly out the windshield, his words

measured, devoid of emotion. "She couldn't. They shot the kid in the head, and did two more, as promised."

Jenny swallowed the bile rising in her throat. "My God."

"They left her with the bodies to think about it and assured her they'd come back every hour and try again, which they did."

Jenny could hardly conceive of such a scene. The wholesale execution of anyone, let alone friends, was an impossible choice. Just the abstract notion of having to make such a choice between Bernie or Kathryn, or even Smitty, had her trembling. She had to stop imagining. She was on the verge of breaking down herself, and that wouldn't do. She had to be strong now. Kathryn needed her. She pushed the overwhelming thoughts out of her head and focused on Smitty's deliberate recollection.

"When they came back, she did as they asked. She chose one."

Jenny turned in disbelief, and it set Smitty on the defensive.

"She did it to save what lives she could!" he said. "Three at a time!"

Jenny held her hands up immediately. "No, Smitty," she said, hoping he understood there was no judgment in her reaction. "It's … it's just so horrible."

He stared at her and then finally nodded, letting his defensive anger dissipate. "Yes, it was." He gathered himself. "Sorry."

His knowledge of the event seemed more than just hearsay. "Were you one of those boys, Smitty?"

He took a moment to respond. "Yes, I was." He worked his jaw in disgust. "And I couldn't do a damn thing to help her. Just stood there, mute, while a nineteen-year-old kid did what we all wished we had the nerve to do."

"You couldn't have done anything."

Smitty snapped his head in her direction. "You don't know what it's like to be so helpless!"

Jenny flinched at his bark.

He softened his glare and tilted his head in silent apology before turning to stare vacantly out the windshield. "I pray you never do."

Jenny bowed her head and softly exhaled as she said a silent amen to his prayer and warned herself to step lightly around the emotional minefield.

"I could have spoken up," Smitty went on, "told her it wasn't her fault and it was okay. We all could have. It would have saved her the agony of choosing man after pleading man until she was so distraught she was out of her mind." He quickly pinched tears from his eyes with an impatient hand. "Goddamn it."

"I'm sorry," Jenny whispered. Had she known he was so personally involved with the tragedy, she wouldn't have pushed him for details, but now that she had, she hoped she could at least say something useful. "Joshua Grayson's sacrifice was short-lived, Smitty. He didn't save anyone, and neither could you. In fact, had they known you and Kat were close, it would have been worse for the both of you." She sought his eyes and gently chastised him. "I think you know that."

He worked his jaw and closed his eyes in begrudging agreement.

"You can't blame yourself for her pain any more than she can blame herself for their deaths."

Smitty snorted and shook his head.

Jenny knit her brow in confusion. "She really doesn't blame herself for their deaths, does she? It wasn't her fault."

"No." He looked to the sky. "It was mine."

She waited in silence for his explanation.

"It was my idea to go after her," he said hesitantly. "I convinced them to follow me in there."

Things were finally getting a little clearer, and Jenny was not going to let Smitty take responsibility for everyone else's actions. Hell, she would have gone in herself without a second thought. "Was it a hard sell?"

Smitty looked at her as if her question was a sacrilege to his finely-honed guilt, but then he looked away.

Jenny sensed the truth tempered his indignation and that it wasn't a hard sell at all.

"You did what you had to do."

"It cost those men their lives. And Kat ..."

Jenny recognized a man swallowing his guilt.

"It destroyed her. She'll never be the same."

"Smitty—" Jenny leaned forward to make sure he could see her face. "You wouldn't have been able to live with yourself had you done nothing." She knew she couldn't have. "So you did the only thing you could do. You had to try. You knew the risks and so did those men. You said it yourself. They *followed* you in there. You had no choice, really." She raised her brow and leaned in, waiting for his response. "Did you?"

He turned to face her, and she watched the tension in his face ease into a gentle shake of his head.

"I think everyone needs to stop blaming themselves for something they had no control over," Jenny said.

Smitty's humorless exhale said *Good advice, spoken with the innocence of a true neophyte*. But evidently, he forgave her naiveté by virtue of her noble intent. "I can see why Kat likes you so much."

Jenny couldn't contain her full-faced grin. "Does she now?"

Smitty returned the smile. "God help her, she does."

"Good," Jenny said, because she realized Kathryn meant more to her than she previously imagined.

Sitting in the hallway of The Grotto listening to Smitty comforting Kathryn in her moment of anguish physically hurt. She wanted to be the one holding her and promising that it would be okay. She wanted to be the one Kathryn trusted, the one with whom she sought refuge, her constant relief from a tumultuous past that Jenny was only now beginning to grasp. In time, that would come, she decided. Whatever it took, she was going to make sure of it. For now, Kathryn had Smitty, and Jenny was glad. She was sorry for his experience but glad he was there and Kathryn wasn't alone, then or now. She looked at the man in the driver's seat, his square jaw set in contemplation. John Smith was a good man, the best, she'd decided, and his candor and his faith in her told her all she needed to know about how he felt about her and her relationship with Kathryn. She slowly reached out and touched his hand. "Thank you, Smitty. I know that was hard for you."

He paused for a moment before responding. "You make her happy, Jenny. Happier than I've seen her in ages."

It was the first time he'd used her proper name, and that, along with the sentiment, almost made her cry. She caught Smitty enjoying her reaction, and the two exchanged smirks as they considered the new bond they'd just forged.

"What now?" Jenny asked.

Smitty relaxed into his seat. "I'll take her home in a bit. She'll feel a little hung over in the morning, but she'll be fine."

Jenny nodded, satisfied Kathryn was in good hands. Smitty and Kathryn were forever linked by tragedy, and she, in turn, was woven into their tapestry by way of Smitty's trust in her. She couldn't conceive of the horrors they'd experienced, and she really couldn't afford to if she was going to be strong. Kathryn had no choice, and how she managed to pull herself together and fashion any sort of life at all was nothing short of a miracle. "She's an incredible woman."

She knew she'd get no argument from the man next to her, and his soft snort of agreement proved her right.

He smiled wistfully. "I wish you could have known her before."

Jenny just barely managed a grin. His comment was a futile regret that hurt too much to contemplate. She patted his hand. "Don't worry, Smitty, we'll take good care of her."

An easy smile split his lips. "You're all right, kid."

Jenny returned the smile and squeezed his hand. "You're all right yourself, Johnny."

CHAPTER SIXTEEN

Kathryn rolled over to the smell of coffee. It took her a few moments to clear her head as she blinked in her surroundings. She was in her room, in her bed, but for the life of her, she didn't remember leaving the club the night before. She sat up with a groan, her neck and shoulders stiff, and smiled when she saw she was still in her slip. *Smitty.* She momentarily entertained the idea that Jenny was in her kitchen, lording over the coffee, but had she been the one to tuck her in last night, she certainly wouldn't have left her half-dressed. Not Jenny.

She slipped on her robe and wandered into the kitchen, where she greeted Smitty, who was leaning on the counter, reading the sports section, in his trousers and undershirt, his suspenders hanging limply from his waistband.

"Oh, pretty," he said as he looked up.

Kathryn pushed her disheveled hair from her face. "Thanks." She kissed him on the cheek on her way to a desperately needed cup of coffee.

Smitty tucked the paper under his arm as he turned to face her. "How are you?"

"Better, thanks," she said as she poured her cup.

He watched and waited. No words needed to pass between them about the night before, but it had been so long between episodes that she knew he just wanted to make sure. She picked up her cup and smiled as she playfully snapped his suspenders against his hip on her way to the table.

"I'm fine."

He smiled, sliding the rest of the paper from the counter before joining her.

"Want the front page?" he asked as he settled into his chair.

"Is the war over?"

"No."

"No thanks, then. How about the funnies?" She didn't know why, as she rarely found them funny. She took the offered comics section and smiled as she fondly regarded him. He looked particularly handsome this morning, in a rugged sort of way, his unshaven face accentuating the bottomless dimples in the hollows of his cheeks. It was times like this she wished him married, or with a sweetheart, at least, someone who could truly appreciate everything he had to offer. Instead, his life was chained to hers, walking the same tortured path, with no hope of escape. Even worse, he didn't seem to mind.

"You didn't have to stay here last night."

"I love your couch, Kat," he said with a grin, as he pretended to stretch a kink out of his back and then turned the page.

"You've seen it enough." She rubbed her face. "I don't even remember getting home last night. Did you carry me out of the club?"

"Out of the club, to the car, out of the car, up your steps, into bed …"

"That had to hurt." She pointed at his knee.

"Aw, twern't nuthin', ma'am," he drawled.

"Uh-huh," she said with a smirk, knowing the truth. She scanned the comics without really seeing them. "What about Jenny?"

He turned the page of the sports section. "I told her you had a migraine and sent her home. Said you'd call her this morning, so don't forget."

Kathryn grinned. As if she could forget. "I won't." She eyed him sincerely. "Thank you."

"She was pretty worried about you. I practically had to kick her out of the club to get her to go home."

Kathryn chuckled, appreciating Jenny's devotion, and settled her attention on one of the silly brainteasers at the bottom of the page.

Smitty was staring at her, and she knew he had something to say about the night before. "What did you do with your pills, Kat?"

She pretended to ignore him as she turned the page upside down, looking for the answer to the number puzzle. "You know, sometimes these things just make no sense. It's all logic and mathematics, yet—"

"Kat," Smitty drew out.

She righted the paper and nonchalantly reached for her cup of coffee.

"I threw them out."

Smitty didn't say anything, but she knew he wanted to, so she took a sip and swallowed, lifting unrepentant eyes. "And I'm not replacing them."

Smitty raised his brow in guarded acceptance, as her decision settled around them like specks of dust in the light of an unadorned window. He cleared his throat and went back to his paper. "Spud Chandler is pitching today. Want to go?"

"Can't. I think I have a date to arrange."

Smitty stared at her in mock disbelief. "I can't believe you're choosing sex over baseball."

She chuckled and watched him shake his head as he disappeared behind the sports page. She returned to her section of paper and laughed out loud at the sight of Dagwood Bumstead bowling over the mailman for the umpteenth time, letters flying.

CHAPTER SEVENTEEN

Jenny couldn't stop grinning as she took in the casual elegance of Kathryn seated opposite her in the charming French restaurant. Atmospheric music played softly in the background, and a flickering candle between them reflected mesmerizing highlights onto Kathryn's eyes. Jenny was glad to see her back to herself after the horrible evening the night before.

She was glad she took Smitty's advice and let Kathryn come to her in her own time rather than pushing, which would have been her first instinct. It didn't take long. Kathryn rang her in the early afternoon to plan a date for dinner.

The scene was perfect, and Jenny's heart was full. She felt connected to Kathryn like never before. The knowledge of her tragic past wrapped itself around her mind and soul until she felt the heartbreak form a bridge between them, with only time and opportunity keeping them apart. It was Smitty who gave her this gift, however, not Kathryn, so the bond came with a caveat. Still, knowing the truth only accentuated everything she already admired about her, drawing her deeper into Kathryn's enigmatic aura and sending her inexorably on a path of no return.

Kathryn was everything she could ever want in a woman. Anyone could admire her beauty, but very few would ever know the complex woman inside. Jenny was one step closer to that. One step closer to Kathryn letting her in completely. She didn't know if Kathryn was ready for that yet, but a few more nights like the one they spent together and Jenny sensed she would be.

She seemed so carefree and relaxed tonight. The sophisticated sweep of her dark hair complemented the graceful arch of her brow when she had occasion to smile, which, as the evening went on, became more and more often. Jenny loved how her lips subtly revealed emotions that her eyes tried to hide when she'd suppress a smile and look away.

When she looked away, Jenny studied her more intently. She couldn't help but admire her confident body language, perfect posture, and the precise, delicate grace of her hands as she handled her silverware. Those hands were anything but precise and delicate when they were on her body. They were strong, insistent, and surprisingly possessive during their first passionate hours together. Only later, after they were both sated, did the heavenly, precise, delicate exploration of her most intimate places occur.

Jenny clutched the napkin in her lap as a wave of arousal engulfed her.

Kathryn caught her staring, and with a grin that said she probably knew exactly what she was thinking, said, "Are you all right?"

Jenny cleared her throat and took a sip of wine as a stall tactic while she thought of a response. She glanced at the silverware in Kathryn's hands again and noticed she'd employed the fashion abroad by using both hands—one to cut, the other to eat—instead of the American habit of cutting and switching the fork to the knife hand, which she employed at their last dinner at the very American Blue Note Lounge. It seemed like a viable excuse.

"I was just admiring your international table manners."

"When in Rome," Kathryn said with a smile.

Jenny supposed her OSS training instilled ways to remain inconspicuous in foreign countries by adopting their customs, and now it was second nature. She wondered if she would get the same training one day.

She must have had amorous intentions written all over her face, because Kathryn suppressed a smile and offered a covert glance around the crowded restaurant.

"You know," she said, "if you're not careful, everyone in this place will know what you're thinking."

Jenny arched a brow. "What a treat for them."

Kathryn broke into a full-faced grin and made a sound that was part exhale, part laugh. She'd made the same sound during their night together when Jenny had stroked a particularly sensitive spot, and another wave of arousal sent her entire body thrumming with desire.

She didn't hide it very well, because Kathryn's eyes darkened in response. Jenny was about to signal for the check when Kathryn's gaze drifted past her shoulder.

A man approached, and she raised her chin with a welcoming smile. "Ah, Henri!"

After the traditional *faire la bise* greeting, Jenny listened to them exchange pleasantries in impeccable French before Kathryn turned to her and introduced her in English.

"Henri, this is Jenny Ryan. Jenny, Henri is the owner of this fine establishment."

He took her offered hand in his. "A pleasure, mademoiselle."

Jenny responded to him in equally impeccable French.

Henri turned to Kathryn in impressed surprise, which Kathryn returned. After a few more pleasantries, the gregarious man departed. An uncomfortable silence fell as Kathryn suddenly found rearranging the silverware more important than meeting her eyes.

Jenny let it go on for a few seconds, not wanting to derail the progress they'd made. The man was obviously from France, and she wondered if he was connected to the horrific overseas experience or, perhaps, a reminder of its occurrence.

"Are you all right?"

Kathryn looked up and smiled. "Sure." She glanced at the owner across the room. "He's a lovely man."

Something had changed, and Jenny tilted her head with a furrowed brow, hoping Kathryn would fill her in. Kathryn's version of filling her in was a forced smile followed by, "You speak French very well."

"I thought you knew I spoke French."

"I don't recall you mentioning it."

Jenny leaned in to make sure they weren't overheard. "I just assumed you'd read my file."

Kathryn shifted uncomfortably. "I confess," she said. "I did. I'm sorry."

"You look embarrassed."

"I just … well, some might see that as an invasion of privacy."

"It's not like you've done anything wrong, Kat. I mean, you have clearance." She smiled. "And my permission, if that makes you feel better." She watched Kathryn relax as she accepted the permission with a downward glance and a relieved nod of the head. Jenny was glad, because the last thing Kathryn needed was something else to feel guilty about.

"I don't have any secrets, and I'd be more than happy to tell you anything you want to know about me."

Kathryn stared at her with what Jenny swore was admiration. Considering the secrets she must keep, maybe she longed to be that free. She shrugged. "Still, it makes me feel like I should apologize, so again, I'm sorry."

"Nonsense," Jenny assured her, as she cut up the last string bean on her plate, resisting the urge to switch hands to eat it. She speared all three sections and smiled, hoping to charm Kathryn out of her regret. "Besides, I bet you couldn't wait to crack open that file to find out everything about me."

Kathryn finally grinned. "I confess to that as well. Actually, I'm glad you know I've seen it."

Jenny nodded as she swallowed and placed her silverware across her empty plate in the same pattern that Kathryn had. "Confession is good for the soul, isn't it?"

Kathryn produced another forced smile as the waiter cleared their table of dinner plates. She still seemed uncomfortable about something. When she closed her eyes and briefly rubbed her forehead, Jenny got worried.

"Are you all right?" she asked after the waiter cleared out. "Do you have a headache?"

"No, no," Kathryn said, "I'm fine."

"Good." Jenny breathed a sigh of relief. Kathryn had reiterated Smitty's lie about a migraine derailing their previous evening, and she wondered if there was any truth in the excuse.

"Do you get migraines often?"

"No," Kathryn said, as she picked up her wineglass. "Not so often, thank goodness."

Jenny nodded. She hated that Kathryn had to lie about the night before, but, at the same time, she was amazed at her ability to carry it off so convincingly. She supposed lying was a big part of her job, but that didn't make it any easier when the skill was employed on her, especially when the truth could bring them so much closer.

"I have a confession," Jenny began carefully.

"Oh?" Kathryn said with a smile, "I hear it's good for the soul."

Jenny would have smiled too, but she wanted Kathryn to know she was serious. "In the ladies' room yesterday, when I was crying? It wasn't because someone reminded me of my dad. I was frightened."

Kathryn tilted her head. "Of?"

"I was frightened by what Lawrence did to you—I mean tried to do to you."

Kathryn leaned in. "Nothing's going to happen to me."

"He could have killed you."

"With Smitty around? Not a chance."

Jenny swallowed, the emotion of her next statement almost getting the better of her. "He can't always be there. One day he won't."

"Well, he's here for me now, so no more of this, okay?"

Jenny bowed her head.

"Hey—" Kathryn leaned a little closer. "Nothing's going to happen to me."

Jenny looked into Kathryn's eyes and nodded. "Okay. I mean, I know. Sorry."

"Don't be." Kathryn straightened and picked up her wine glass. "Thank you for telling me that. I appreciate your honesty."

"Confession's good for the soul," Jenny said, then smiled, though she didn't feel it.

I appreciate your honesty rolled around in her head as she looked into Kathryn's very open face. They were so close to really connecting, she could almost reach out and touch it but for this one thing standing between them. She was sure that once that barrier was breached, there would be nothing to stand in their way. No more lies, no more misunderstandings. *I appreciate your honesty.*

"I have another confession to make," Jenny said tentatively. "I saw you last night."

Kathryn's eyes widened ever so slightly as she slowly raised her chin and set down her glass. "I'm not sure I know what you mean."

"In your dressing room. Your breakdown."

Kathryn held Jenny's gaze for a few moments and then quickly scanned the room as if every single person there knew what had happened. Her gaze dropped to the table. "Jenny, that's ..." She raised an uneasy hand to her forehead. "That's something—"

"It's okay, Kat." Jenny reached out. "I know."

Kathryn looked up. "You know what?"

"Overseas. The boys. Everything. Smitty told me."

"That's a lie," Kathryn said in a clipped whisper. "He would never do that!"

Jenny pulled back her hand and straightened in her chair, not sure she liked being called a liar. "I'm sorry, but he did."

Kathryn's jaw visibly tensed. She closed her eyes and pinched the bridge of her nose. Jenny sensed Smitty was going to get an earful when next they met.

"Please don't be angry with him. It's my fault. I dragged it out of him."

Controlled irritation rolled off Kathryn, and Jenny reached out again to touch her hand, which had worked itself into a fist. "Kat—"

Ferocious blue eyes flashed, and Jenny withdrew immediately.

"He had no right to say *anything*!" Kathryn said through gritted teeth, conscious of her volume and the people around them.

"It was my fault," Jenny reiterated, hoping to at least save Smitty from Kathryn's wrath.

"You—" Kathryn started and then stopped, quickly glancing around the room before leaning in to speak. "One roll in the sack does not give you an all-access pass to my personal life! Do you understand? You want to know something about me, you ask *me*!"

"I'm sorry, Kat. You're right," Jenny said feebly, wishing like hell she could start over. "I just wanted to help ... to be closer."

"Going behind my back and snooping into my personal life is not going to bring us closer!"

"I didn't—" Jenny realized trying to explain at that moment wouldn't do any good, so she issued another apology and hoped it was enough. "I'm sorry. I realize that. It won't happen again."

"You've got that right." Kathryn threw her napkin on the table and stormed off toward the ladies' room.

Jenny watched her go and then exhaled to the ceiling at her stupidity.

Kathryn paced the small ladies' room, trying to make sense of the last few minutes. She knew Smitty didn't like Jenny, but to deliberately sabotage their relationship? And then to lie to her at breakfast? She didn't know what angered her more, his betrayal or the corruption of her relationship because of it. Jenny knew now, and how casual she was about it! It ruined *everything*. Didn't she realize?

When Jenny met her for dinner, she sensed something had changed. She just didn't know why. Now it made perfect sense. What she thought was adoration, maybe even lust, was clearly pity brought on by the information Smitty had given her.

Everything was going so well. She even tamped down the brief panic brought on by the jarring reminder of Jenny's language skills and the implications for her future at the OSS.

How could she have been so stupid to believe herself worthy or capable of a relationship without the long arm of her past dropping a live grenade in the middle of it? Dropped by Smitty, no less!

Between the two of them, she didn't know where to start. Anger, loss, embarrassment, and frustration swirled in her head until the room was spinning, but she knew it was only her life swirling down a familiar dark hole.

Jenny stood outside the ladies' room for what seemed an eternity. Her hand had been on the doorknob more than once, but she was in no hurry to greet what was waiting on the other side. How many times would she have to tell herself to think things through? What did she think Kathryn was going to do, welcome the news?

It wasn't going to get settled standing on the wrong side of the door, so she took a deep breath and reached for the knob. She grasped empty air as the door flung open and Kathryn, in all her rage, was on her way out.

Jenny instinctively stepped aside, quite sure that, at that moment, Kathryn would have no qualms about bowling her over. Kathryn stopped in her tracks but only long enough to issue an annoyed sneer as she brushed past her and headed toward the telephone cabinet at the end of the hall.

"Kat—"

As expected, she was ignored, so she dutifully followed, preparing for the worst. Kathryn entered the phone cabinet, and fortunately for Jenny, it had no door. She leaned on the frame and said, "Kathryn, please. You can't just ignore me."

Kathryn did just that and put her nickel in the slot and dialed. "I'd like a taxi, please."

Jenny reached in, brushing Kathryn aside, and depressed the receiver cradle. "We're not leaving things like this."

She realized that was probably not a good idea when Kathryn

slammed the receiver against the wall and let her temper fly, all the while keeping her volume for Jenny's ears only.

"Damn it, Jenny! You don't seem to understand that I don't even want to see you right now, let alone have a conversation with you!"

"Well, that's too bad, Kathryn, because there's been a huge misunderstanding, and I'm not letting you walk out on me without getting a chance to explain."

"I don't want to hear it." She slammed the handset on its receiver, barely missing Jenny's retreating fingers, before digging in her purse for another nickel.

"Keeping everything bottled up is no way to have a relationship. You have to talk to me."

Kathryn let loose a humorless chuckle as she continued digging in her purse. "We were having sex, not a relationship, and now we're having neither."

"That's not true, Kathryn!"

She ignored her.

Jenny grabbed the purse, ensuring Kathryn's complete attention, and, most assuredly, her wrath, but she didn't care. "That's not true, Kathryn, and you know it."

"You know what I know, Jenny?" Kathryn began conversationally as she snatched her purse back and leaned menacingly forward. "I know that the man I trusted the most in this world stabbed me in the back, and you know why? Because he didn't like who I was seeing. And *you*? I haven't figured out your game yet, but all the angling you did with Smitty for the upper hand was wasted."

"What?"

"Wasted," Kathryn reiterated. "I am not going to be manipulated by you or Smitty or anyone else."

Jenny was astounded. "Manipulated?" Misunderstanding had been an understatement. What kind of relationships had this woman had? "Kathryn, no."

"It's over, Jenny. You had your one night of fun, so I hope you enjoyed it."

Kathryn attempted to brush past, but Jenny held fast to her arm, eliciting another warning glare. Jenny ignored it. "You're so wrong, Kat."

"Let go of me."

"Not until you listen to me. You're wrong, Kathryn. Please."

Kathryn could have broken away in an instant, Jenny knew, but evidently something still burned within, because she leaned back into the cabinet and crossed her arms. Jenny paced in a small circle, wondering where to begin. The truth seemed like a good place to start—ironic, since that's what got her into trouble in the first place—so she took a deep breath and methodically began. She told Kathryn how she went to her dressing room because Smitty was so concerned about her and how she convinced him to tell her what was wrong. Kathryn remained silent throughout, finally uncrossing her arms to unnecessarily arrange her hair.

"I know you're angry, Kat, but please, don't blame Smitty. He loves you. You know he'd never do anything to hurt you." She paused. "And neither would I."

Kathryn tucked her purse under her arm. "Are you through?"

"Are you still angry?"

Kathryn considered the question but didn't answer it. "Ring us a taxi. You wasted my last nickel."

That beat a poke in the eye, Jenny supposed.

Kathryn stared vaguely ahead from the back seat of the shared taxi as dimmed streetlight after dimmed streetlight droned by. Jenny refused to send her home alone and climbed into the cab after her. They weren't far from her apartment, and neither had spoken. She didn't know what to say, where to start. Jenny's explanation made perfect sense, and she had overreacted. She had no anger now, only regret. Jenny was trying to help. She didn't deserve the things she'd said to her, and oh, the things she'd said. How could an apology possibly be enough after reducing their beautiful night together to a vulgar roll in the sack. She exhaled and rubbed her forehead.

"Are you all right," Jenny asked softly.

Kathryn crossed her arms and nodded. She would be home soon and would get out of the taxi, burdened with too many things said and too many things left unsaid. How could she explain what she was feeling and why she had reacted so badly? How does one explain, after a lifetime of fighting for normalcy, how it feels to finally come so close only to have it taken away?

Shock and disappointment led to irrational anger, and Jenny unfairly bore the brunt of it. In reality, it had very little to do with her. The anger was for the past, from the past, for what she did, for what they made her do. She hated that it still poisoned her life, her thoughts, her actions. She felt guilt, wounded pride, and shame for being so weak. It was too hard to explain, just too hard. Jenny could never understand. Why would she want to? Kathryn was pretty sure she'd shown enough of her true nature to destroy any hope of yet another chance with her, and sensing this was goodbye, she supposed she could at least attempt to say she was sorry.

The word rolled around in her head as they reached her block, but the more she thought about it, the more inadequate it seemed. What was the point? What was Jenny supposed to say? *Gee, I forgive you for being an asshole? I can't wait for you to tell me how little I mean to you again?* No. Let it go. Let her go. Let her find someone who can make her happy.

The taxi came to a halt at the curb in front of her apartment, and she continued to stare straight ahead. She felt Jenny's expectant eyes boring into her cheek, and the heavy silence taunted her in its deafening recrimination. She'd been horrid to Jenny, and she just took it. No one should put up with that.

The cabby turned around. "Ain't got all night, ladies. This the place or what?"

Kathryn reached into her purse and gave him triple what it should cost to get Jenny home. "Take her wherever she needs to go." *Sorry* never did pass her lips as she got out of the taxi without a backward glance. She wasn't surprised to hear Jenny say, "Wait a moment," to the driver and slam the door as she followed her to the curb.

Jenny should be long gone, not trying to fix things after how she'd spoken to her. Kathryn exhaled and turned around. "Jenny—"

"This is how it ends? After what we shared, this is how it ends?"

She shouldn't have looked Jenny in the eyes. She was hurt but determined. And so damned beautiful. The woman was like a drug, so help her. She looked at the sidewalk and said what she needed to say before they parted.

"You shouldn't let anyone push you around."

"You're not pushing me around, Kat. You're punishing yourself, and that's got nothing to do with me."

Jenny was silent until Kathryn met her eyes again.

"We either move on from here or we don't. It's up to you. When you decide to forgive me for caring and yourself for being a jerk because of it, call me."

Kathryn was speechless.

"Good night," Jenny said curtly, and yanked the taxi door open.

"Drive." Kathryn heard her say as she climbed in and slammed the door shut.

She stared at the taxi's small red taillights until they faded into the darkness and the sound of shifting gears blended into the nondescript hum of the night.

She exhaled and looked to the sky. It was up to her. She left her ruined evening on the empty street and slowly entered the stairway door to her apartment. Her evening ended as it began: dreaming of a future she once only imagined and not surprised to find that what she imagined was only a dream.

The taxi left Kathryn on the curb, and Jenny struggled against looking back. Seeing Kathryn standing alone in the street would break her heart. She barely resisted telling the driver to turn around. She wanted to take Kathryn in her arms and hold her until all her fears and insecurities surrendered their piece of her.

Be patient, Smitty had said. *Give her time to decide what she really wants. She'll come to you or she won't.* Jenny cringed. This is what she was counting on? She didn't look back, but in her mind's eye, she could see Kathryn's lonesome silhouette, and she wondered if that was the last memory she would have of her. It seemed to typify Kathryn's life, and, in the most distressing way, was only fitting.

Jenny arrived home and numbly went through her nighttime routine, unable to think of anything but her disastrous evening. She was initially shocked by Kathryn's backlash, the harsh words like a slap in the face, but any fool could see they were out of fear and pain, not hatred, and certainly not personal.

She rolled over in bed and looked at the mute phone, her only link to the woman who had come to mean so much to her. What would she do if she didn't call? She pulled the phone closer and rolled onto her back. "Please, Kat. Don't give up on us."

Kathryn nervously clutched the telephone receiver as she listened to the tinny ring grinding out its pattern on the other end of the line. She would let it ring this time. She'd picked up the handset and replaced it five times in the last hour before finally gathering the nerve to actually dial Jenny's number. It was late, and she wasn't sure what to expect, but Jenny did say it was up to her, and she never did give her that apology. For once, she would not run away. She would face the consequences of her actions head on, come what may.

An odd array of noises came from the other end of the line when it was picked up, accentuated by a string of curses and finally a grumpy, "Yes! Hello?"

Kathryn winced. This was bad already.

"Hello?" Jenny impatiently repeated.

Kathryn thought about hanging up.

"Kat?"

But she couldn't. She was determined to settle this one way or the other tonight. "I'm sorry, it's late," she said. "Please don't hang up on me, okay?" Her eyes flicked around the room, anxiously awaiting Jenny's reply.

"I won't hang up on you."

She was relieved when she was met with more sympathy than she felt she deserved. "Okay. Thank you."

Jenny tilted her head at Kathryn's tremulous voice, an unfamiliar sound coming from her usually self-assured friend. She was startled from a dead sleep by the ringing phone and played hot potato with the handset until she dropped it on her forehead. A rude awakening to be sure, but well worth the lump. She didn't really expect Kathryn to call so soon, and the fact that she did gave Jenny hope that it was good news rather than bad. She slid down on her pillow and waited for whatever Kathryn had to say, which, at first, wasn't much.

She heard a quivering exhale.

"I, uh ..."

Silence. Another exhale.

Jenny bit her tongue, dying to tell her it was all right. Everything would be fine. But it wasn't up to her to decide what was fine. This was Kathryn's burden, a wall she needed to tear down for her own sake. So Jenny waited, cradling the handset with all the tenderness she wished to impart to the woman on the other end of the line.

Kathryn closed her eyes and balled up a fist on her forehead for strength. She sat slumped on the edge of her bed and just had out with it.

"I'm sorry, Jenny, and I know that's not enough. I know that doesn't make up for the things I said or how I behaved, but I'm afraid I don't know where to start or what else to say."

Jenny was silent for too long, and Kathryn swore her heart stopped beating, waiting for her response.

"I thought I told you to call me when you had forgiven yourself."

Kathryn opened her eyes and stared at the numbers on the phone dial as she decided very carefully what to say next. "I can't forgive myself unless I know you forgive me, because I've made a terrible mess of things, and whether or not we're ever lovers again pales to whether or not we're ever friends again." She paused, on the verge of tears. "You were my friend, Jenny. Whatever happens, I don't want to lose that."

Ten heartbeats passed before Jenny answered. Kathryn knew the number because she counted each one thudding loudly in her ears. "That's really up to you, Kathryn."

She had thought long and hard on that before deciding to call. Was the fact that Jenny now knew about her past worse than not having her in her life at all? No, she decided.

"I don't want to lose that," she reiterated softly. "The things I said —" She covered her eyes with her hand. "Please know I didn't mean it. I was—" She grimaced and put her fist to her forehead again. There was no excuse. "Please forgive me, I didn't mean it."

Silence.

"Jenny?"

"I forgive you."

Her voice was a caress, her words absolution, and Kathryn wiped a tear from her cheek. "Thank you."

She didn't know when Jenny's presence in her life had become so indispensable, but she was grateful for her forgiveness and her patience. "I'm so very sorry, Jenny."

"I'm sorry too. I didn't mean to upset you. I wasn't thinking about how it would affect you. I just wanted to be there for you like you have been for me."

"I know. I was a fool. I ... it's hard to explain. I just ... I didn't want you to know." She sensed Jenny opening her mouth to protest, so she held up her hand as if Jenny could see it through the line and cut her off before she could speak. "I mean, I did. Maybe. One day. Eventually. I don't know. I—" She threw her hand in the air. "I just wanted one part of my life to be untouched by that. You were it."

"If it touches you, Kat, it touches me. I want to help if you'll let me."

Jenny was nothing if not persistent. She had no idea what she was getting into or any sense of the loss her mining of the past had wrought. "Our relationship is different now, Jenny. Before it was—" She paused, trying to find the right word. "Unspoiled. And now—"

"And now?"

"And now you know."

"And?"

Yes, and? What exactly had changed? Was Jenny walking on eggshells? Treating her differently? No. So far, all her fears were unfounded. The only thing poisoning their relationship was her insecurities.

"And," she drew out, embracing her epiphany, "I'm an idiot."

Jenny chuckled through the line. "Are you still angry?"

"No. I'm not angry."

"You sure?"

"Yes."

"Smitty off the hook?"

Kathryn smiled. "Off the hook."

"Good. Now ... what's this *whether or not we're ever lovers again* business?"

CHAPTER EIGHTEEN

Kathryn lit the last candle and stood back to admire her handiwork. Her apartment was bathed in the inviting glow of a dozen candles strategically placed in a romantic halo, the last two on the small kitchen table now residing in the middle of her living room.

She looked at the clock. It was five until seven. Perfect timing. Jenny would probably be on her block by now, or, perhaps, in unbridled anticipation, uncharacteristically early.

Kathryn rubbed her hands together and looked around, hoping she hadn't forgotten anything. Dinner was warming, the wine was chilling, table made, fresh flowers, soft music, clean sheets, candles burning. Now all she needed was a certain wonderful someone to knock on her door and make the evening perfect.

She deposited the box of matches in a drawer and closed it with a quick swat of her hip before treading expectantly to the front window to see if she could get a glimpse of Jenny coming down the street. She wondered if she was as nervous as she was. *Nervous*, she chuckled to herself as she parted the wooden blinds ever so slightly. What the hell did she have to be nervous about?

Jenny made everything easy, so terribly easy. Even their phone call the night before, the one she was convinced would end badly, had quickly become a cathartic lesson in the power of forgiveness, an unexpected reward for letting go of expectations and fear. She couldn't remember allowing herself to be so vulnerable, yet she felt perfectly safe in the intimate isolation of Jenny's disembodied voice at the end of the phone line. How safe she would feel face to face remained to be seen, but trying very hard to remember her new lesson, she pushed the insecurity out of her head.

She leaned back from the window, letting the blinds flap into place. No Jenny. She glanced at the clock. Seven on the dot. Well, Jenny wasn't known for her punctuality. She rolled up the sleeves on her crimson colored blouse and tried to busy herself. She checked on dinner, rearranged the flowers, unboxed the pie she'd rushed out and bought at the last minute, having completely forgotten about dessert, and before she knew it, it was seven thirty. She found herself at the window again, hand on hip, and this time there was nothing slight about the parting of the blinds, her fingers prying the wooden slats into unnatural curves.

She was more concerned than angry. A few minutes late was typical, but a half hour was worrisome, especially knowing how much Jenny was looking forward to their date, or so she had said. Kathryn set free the blinds and shook her head. She was not going down that road. She had not been stood up. There was another explanation. Jenny would call at any minute. She looked at the ominously silent phone. Why hadn't she called already? Possibilities took turns tormenting her. Did she miss the call while getting dessert? Not likely. Surely, she would have called back. Train behind schedule? Accident? Her heartbeat quickened. She spared one more futile look up and down the street, not wanting to consider the option, and disregarded it. Fate had already played that card. She paused and dialed the hospitals anyway. Thankfully, she came up empty.

As the minutes dragged on, she paced her small apartment and tried to keep sinister thoughts from her mind. Jenny wasn't exactly a shrinking violet. She'd antagonized Forrester, the strikers at the plant, and Lord knows what her Uncle Paul might be into that could come back on her. She cleared her head of such thoughts and passed them off as a reflection of her own paranoia. She found herself leaning on the kitchen counter, staring at the dinner plates she'd taken out of the oven. The domestic normalcy of the oven mitts on her hands was an absurd contrast to the conspiracy theories fighting for supremacy in her head.

A shrill ring quickly erased it all, and she bolted for the phone, taking note of the time—seven forty-five.

"*Please be you,*" she whispered before she picked up the handset. "Yes?"

Jenny impatiently grabbed her coat from the hall tree. For once, she wasn't late, just excited. She looked at her watch. Six thirty. She would get there with ten minutes to spare if everything was running on time. She checked her reflection in the hall mirror and grinned at the thought she might catch Kathryn dressing.

She gathered her purse and keys from the foyer table and headed out the door. She no sooner got outside when a taxi pulled up in front of her house and Bernie emerged. She could tell by his body language that something was wrong. Very wrong. She hurried across the lawn to meet him and, she could see he'd been crying. He wiped his nose with his sleeve.

Jenny reached out for his hand. "What is it?"

He cleared his throat and sniffled. "Cal's shipping out."

"Oh, Bernie."

"We had a fight. I told him if he came back, I didn't want to see him again."

"Oh, Bernie," she repeated, trying not to sound incredulous but failing badly. "You didn't."

He nodded regretfully and wiped his nose with his sleeve again. That didn't sound like him. "That must have been some fight."

"He's known for weeks, Jenny, and he didn't tell me."

"Well, Bernie maybe—"

"I know, I know. I'm sure he had a very good reason, but it just made me so darn mad. I could have spent more time with him, or cherished the moments more, or something! He didn't give me the chance."

"Did you mean it?"

"Of course not." He looked to the setting sun and then to his feet. "I think I love him."

That's all Jenny needed to hear. "Okay. You've got to straighten this out before he leaves."

"Can't."

"Bull. There's nothing you can't fix."

"He's leaving tonight. He's at the station now."

"Penn?"

Bernie nodded.

"When does his train leave?"

"Seven forty-five."

Jenny looked at her watch and grabbed his arm, dragging him toward her father's Cord. "Come on, we can still make it."

"Bug, I can't," he said as he resisted. "The things I said."

Jenny wanted to say, *Yeah, that's going around.* "Bernie—" She stopped short and faced him. "Can you live with yourself if something happens to him and you don't have the chance to set this right?"

He hesitated, and she answered for him. "I'm here to tell you that's one burden you don't want to bear. Now come on. You've got plenty of time to learn to eat crow. I hear it tastes pretty good with a little humility on top." She pulled him toward the car and then stopped. *Kathryn.* She looked at her watch. "Get in the car, I'll be right back."

"Say, does this thing even run?"

"I sure hope so," she said as she hurried to the house. With gas rationing and the rubber shortage, it mostly just sat in the driveway, but she drove it once a month just to keep the temperamental thing running.

She dialed Kathryn's number but got no answer. "Damn." She looked at her watch again. By the time she got to another phone, she would be fifteen minutes late for her date. Time was wasting, and allowing a half hour to actually find Cal in the madness of Penn Station meant she didn't have a moment to spare. She decided she'd just have to drive a little faster, in hopes of calling Kathryn sooner, and trust that after their phone conversation the night before, she would understand.

Two traffic jams and one construction detour later, they were standing in a maelstrom of humanity with only fifteen minutes to find a needle in a haystack. Jenny sent Bernie to the concourse and she headed to the phone bank. Luckily, someone was just hanging up as she arrived, and she managed to convince the next fellow in line that her call was a minor emergency, thus avoiding the lines of primarily soldiers and businessmen. It was seven thirty by her watch, and she was prepared to grovel. She was not prepared for a busy signal. She looked at the handset like it was insane and thought about dialing again, but she caught sight of Bernie pointing down at the trains and arguing with a porter at the top of the platform stairs. She relinquished the phone and made a mad dash for her friend, feeling like a steel ball in a pinball game, as she curtly excused her way through the bustling crowd.

The porter wouldn't let Bernie down to the platform without a ticket, and one look at the ticket window line told Jenny there was no way they would get through in time. She reached into her purse and pulled out a letter she hadn't mailed and waved it in the porter's face with a sob story about a dying mother writing down her last words to her son before he ships out.

"He's right there," Jenny lied, pointing vaguely at the crowd of boarding soldiers below.

Shouts of "For crying out loud, brother, have a heart! The kid's mom is dyin'!" floated above the impatient crowd. Reluctantly, the man let them pass, and by some sheer stroke of luck, or fate, or serendipitous coincidence, there was Cal, just ahead, with his stuffed duffle bag hanging low from his shoulder, his hat perched lackadaisically at an angle atop his red hair, and an unlit cigarette tucked behind his ear.

Bernie suddenly got a case of the nerves, but Jenny marched right up to the soldier, yanked him out of line, and dragged them both to a dark corner beside a large electrical conduit box under the stairs.

"Cal, Bernie has something he needs to tell you." She turned to her friend. "And if you don't tell him, I will."

He knew she was serious.

"You have eight minutes. Go." She shoved them into the corner and stood guard with her back turned, shielding them from the mass of humanity swirling around them.

The final call for boarding rang out, and the two men emerged. Jenny could tell by their appreciative smiles that the trip had not been in vain. She hugged Cal and finally allowed her emotions to register that he was shipping out.

"Please be careful," she whispered into his ear as his long arms engulfed her.

"I will, Jenny. Thank you." He looked at Bernie, who was doing his best to hold back his tears. "You take care of him," he drawled with an easy grin as he released her and stood up straight.

"Don't you worry." She smiled bravely. "You just come back to us."

"Do I have a choice?"

"No!" Bernie and Jenny said in unison.

Cal and Bernie exchanged a brotherly hug, and Jenny turned away again, trying to make their last moments as private as one can on a crowded train platform.

When Cal was safely on board, they climbed the stairs to the concourse. Jenny tipped a hand of thanks to the porter as she passed him and headed toward the phones again. Bernie stayed at the top of the platform and watched the train pull away.

The telephone bank cleared, thanks to the departing train, so Jenny stepped right up, and this time when she called, she got an answer.

"Yes?"

Kathryn didn't sound angry, but to cover all the bases, she immediately said, "I'm sorry. I couldn't get away to call. I—"

"Jenny! Thank—" A pause "What do you mean *get away?*" Kathryn sounded a little frazzled. "Are you all right? Did someone—"

"Kat, I'm fine. I'm okay." Jenny went on to tell her story, apologizing over and over for missing their date. Kathryn's lack of comment concerned her. "Are you angry?"

"Of course not." Kathryn's voice became softer, more intimate. "I'm just glad you're all right, and I'm glad Bernie got to see Cal before he shipped out."

"I'm so sorry about dinner, Kat." She looked at her watch. "Listen, I want to take Bernie home and make sure he's okay, but I'll head right over after that."

There was a pause on the other end of the line. "That's okay, Jenny. We can get together some other night. I'm sure you're exhausted, and I've got an early day tomorrow."

Jenny bit her lip, wondering if Kathryn was a little more upset than she was letting on. "Are you mad?"

"No, honey, I promise. Just disappointed."

Kathryn's term of endearment and the tone in which she breathed it hit Jenny in all the right places, finally settling in her weakening knees. "Me too."

They heard a click on the line and the operator broke in. "Please limit your call to five minutes. Others are waiting."

The curfew on nonessential calls meant theirs was over.

"Be careful driving home. I'll talk to you tomorrow."

"Okay. I'm sorry, Kat. I was so looking forward to tonight."

"I'll talk to you tomorrow."

Kathryn replaced the handset and paused for a few moments with her hand on the phone. She was disappointed but thankful Jenny was safe. Her evening over, she sat at the candlelit table, reached into the now-melted bucket of ice, removed the wine bottle, and poured herself a glass.

"Expectations," she said with a weary grin, finding them a hard habit to break. She gave them one more thought, then bid them farewell, like the candle flame she extinguished between her two moistened fingertips.

Jenny propped her head up on her fist and exhaled for the umpteenth time, trying to pretend it was the snarled traffic responsible for her foul mood, but Bernie knew better.

"I'm sorry about your date, Bug. You should have said something."

She shrugged and smiled amiably. "Don't worry about it, Bernie." She glanced in the rearview mirror in an attempt to sell her deflected annoyance and waved her hand at the beeping frustrated jumble of taxis, cars, buses, and delivery trucks before them. "Look at this mess." She laid on her horn for effect. Getting Bernie to the station to set things right with his guy was more important than her date, in the big scheme of things, but having accomplished that task, her lost evening was beginning to demand payment for its neglect. She didn't want Bernie to feel any worse than he already did about it, but she could tell from his expression and the way he absently scratched his cheek at her performance that she wasn't doing a very good job of masking the extent of her disappointment.

After a few moments of guilty contemplation he asked, "So how's it going with her?"

Jenny eased into the adjacent lane of traffic, its turn to crawl, and used the distraction to arrange her thoughts. Knowing most of the details were not only personal but out of Bernie's scope of allowable knowledge, she decided on a positive, but generic, "It's going well."

Bernie looked at her sideways. "Well? Not terrific, fantastic, the best sex ever?"

Jenny had to admit that the slow progress of their relationship was frustrating, but if their one night together was any indication, there would be many more nights to compete for the title of the best sex ever. In fact, if only they could get on the same page, she was sure their relationship would be terrific and fantastic as well. "It's complicated. You know that."

"Well, there's complicated and then there's not worth it."

She turned to him with a look that was almost a warning, his casual comment betraying his lack of comprehension. "It's worth it to me."

Bernie paused, and she knew he recognized the same fierceness in which she defended her last disaster, Marcella.

"I just don't want you to get hurt, Jenny."

The use of her first name accentuated his concern, which she appreciated, but he needed to understand. "She's nothing like *her*, Bernie," she said, unable to speak her ex's name in comparison.

"What do you really know about this woman?"

Jenny debated about what to say. She couldn't very well avoid the subject, and keeping in mind what was public knowledge and what was private or OSS business, she covered the basics as she knew them: schooling, singing, a stint in Paris, and what she imagined would be the typical life of a nightclub singer, with the added adventure of being a mobster's mistress. Having heard herself tell the story, and suffering through Bernie's deafening silence after, she could understand his trepidation and felt the need to instill upon him just how important Kathryn had become. "She's an incredible woman, Bernie, unlike anyone I've ever met."

"You're in love."

"Is it that obvious?"

He tilted his head, incredulous. "Hello?" He scolded her for even asking and then softened his demeanor. "Does she know?"

"I hope not," Jenny said into the driver's side window as she negotiated another lane change.

"What does that mean?"

"I'm afraid she'll run if she finds out."

Bernie shook his head and proffered a look, expressing both warning and concern. "Jenny—"

"She's special, Bernie," she said before Bernie could articulate everything she already knew was against them. "I can't explain it. You're just going to have to trust me."

He was quiet for a few moments, and Jenny knew he was

cautiously accepting her devotion while turning it over in his romantic head.

"Life's too short, Jenny. If you love her, tell her."

Kathryn turned off the music and circled her apartment, blowing out candles. Worry and relief had grounded her uncharacteristic flight into romantic giddiness, and the dousing of the flames was merely ceremonial, signaling the end of a pleasant distraction. It was an odd feeling, returning to herself. Odd in that she hadn't purposely tried to become someone else. But there she was, a happy girl, anxiously awaiting her date. How often had she pretended to be such a thing, using her performance to ensnare this person or that, flawless and irresistible in her portrayal? Whether acting for personal gain or under government directive, it was never *her*, never genuine. Feelings weren't something she reserved for herself. They were for assignments, playacting, a means to an end. But suddenly, there they were, and unbidden.

It had been so long since she'd looked forward to something—to someone. She wondered seriously if she ever had before. Could one person, much less one she hardly knew, change a lifetime of opportunistic make-believe? She took a full swallow from her glass of wine and shook her head, as if she'd imagined the whole thing.

Her unusual foray into the sophomoric world of raging hormones was over now, and she reminded herself that personal sentiment was something she'd banished for a reason. Emotions only complicated a life that had no room for them. They could only bring disaster, or, worse, ignite experiences she had no desire to relive. This is who she was, who she had to be. She finished her glass of wine and poured another to celebrate her return to form.

She raised a toast to herself. "Here's to you, Kat Hammond—" Then the first glass of wine hit her, and she couldn't think of anything to celebrate. Certainly not a return to self.

She meandered toward the bedroom, her second glass now half

empty, and she leaned on the doorjamb, smiling at the single yellow rose she'd placed in the middle of the bed. She caught a glimpse of that happy girl again, but she was just a ghost, a gentle smile and a lift of the spirit, and then she was gone. *Another time,* she lamented, as she took another drink, *another lifetime, maybe.*

Her muddled pragmatic mind struggled to convince her alcohol-induced optimistic mind that she didn't deserve Jenny or happiness, but she was tired, so very tired of the darkness, of herself. She sat on the bed and twirled the rose between her fingers. She brought it to her face and reverently buried her nose in its fragrant petals, vowing from this day forward, the flower would remind her of the happy girl, however fleeting she might be. She placed it on what would have been Jenny's pillow and smiled. Jenny made it all bearable. Until just then, she hadn't realized how unbearable it had become. She exhaled the heaviness and rubbed her eyes, finally blinking at the wineglass in her hand.

"You know you can't drink wine," she scolded her sentimental self. She put the glass on the nightstand and lay back, staring at the dancing shadows on the ceiling as the remaining candle cast its glow past the motionless ceiling fan blades.

She didn't jump when the phone rang. She merely rolled to the side and dragged the whole unit with her as she returned to her back again, far too relaxed to even venture a guess as to who it might be.

"Hello?"

"Are you sleeping?"

"No," Kathryn said with a grin into the receiver, "I'm not sleeping."

"I can't stop thinking about you. I had to call."

She curled onto her side. "I've been thinking about you too."

Marcus Forrester's grin crackled through the phone line, and Kathryn rolled her eyes.

She babysat his uncharacteristic longing for her and played the part of the lonely mistress on cue, slipping into the role with little effort or thought.

When their conversation ended, she dropped her cheerful

persona and frowned as she hung up the phone. She sat up and finished her wine with one annoyed gulp before stalking into the living room and depositing the empty glass on the dinner table with a thunk. How effortlessly she could pretend to care, and poor Jenny, for whom pretending had long since ceased, had to settle for sporadic bouts of *does she or doesn't she*, brought on by inadequate attempts to express emotions she barely remembered, let alone understood. Why was it so hard to surrender to something, to someone, she wanted so badly? But then she realized that she *had* surrendered. Jenny was more than a want now. She was a need—a need that threatened to upset the delicate balance between her ingrained indifference and her desire to love and be loved.

In a strange moment of panic, Kathryn recalled her automatic surrender to Forrester and found herself unsure, confused, and wondering if she really knew how to care about Jenny or if she was just going through the motions, like with Forrester. Had she become so adept at pretending that she'd begun to think they were real feelings? Had she just adopted another guise? Would Jenny see through it and realize she was dealing with an emotional fraud?

She'd already told Jenny she couldn't express real emotions. If suddenly she could, would Jenny believe her? Or would she think it was a performance, one she'd seen enacted on many occasions with Forrester?

Kathryn's quickened heartbeat gave life to her fear. She looked at the half empty wine bottle and exhaled a relieved chuckle. She shook her head and scrubbed her face in her palms. "You really need to swear off wine."

Jenny picked up her pace as she crossed the street to Kathryn's apartment. The traffic and settling Bernie into his place took longer than she intended, but he had said *Tell her you love her*, and she decided that life was indeed too short not to.

She could see a light on in the living room, so her first fear was alleviated. Kathryn was still up. Her second fear was proclaiming her love and Kathryn's reaction. She was at home, so there was nowhere to run, and Jenny couldn't quite see her removing her bodily from her apartment, so she reasoned now was as good a time as any to confess.

"Tell her when you first walk in," she said under her breath as she reached for the outer doorknob, hoping Kathryn hadn't locked it when their date was called off. It was unlocked, so she started up the steps to the second floor and then stopped. "No, after sex." She nodded and continued to the landing, where she stopped again. "No, before sex." She thought again and shook her head. "No, after. There might not be any sex if you tell her before." Satisfied with the game plan, she proceeded to the door, where she heard music. She put her ear to the door and at first thought it was the radio, but then she realized it was Kathryn playing the piano. Jenny smiled as "Clair De Lune" filled the space.

She closed her eyes and relaxed into the door, enjoying the moment, as she imagined Kathryn's long, graceful fingers dancing effortlessly over the keys. The music stopped abruptly, and Jenny worried that Kathryn might turn in before she got a chance to speak her peace. The worry dissipated when she heard the same note struck repeatedly, followed by a few quick scales through the note and then the note again, Kathryn apparently questioning the tuning of that particular key. Jenny decided that while there was a break in the music, she would take her shot. She took a deep breath, straightened her coat, and knocked confidently on the door.

The door opened a few inches, and Kathryn apprehensively appeared behind it.

"Jenny. What are you doing here?"

Jenny raked her eyes down the pleasantly disheveled woman before her and smiled. Kathryn's hair was haphazardly down, loose ringlets falling over her reticent face as she tucked in her shirt. Jenny thought *God, you look sexy* would have been an appropriate opening line, but by Kathryn's demeanor, she didn't think it was a good idea. "Is this a bad time?"

"No," Kathryn said, as she guided her hair behind her ears and glanced around guiltily.

It occurred to Jenny for a panicked second that Kathryn wasn't alone and that she was interrupting something. "May I come in?"

Kathryn gave way. "Of course. Sorry."

Jenny entered and didn't need to see the half-empty bottle of wine on the table, or the uncomfortable expression on Kathryn's face, to get the picture. She had been drinking, and she was obviously embarrassed about it. She was alone, and judging from her disposition, the company had not been pleasant.

Kathryn didn't move forward to greet her in any way, so Jenny followed her lead and didn't attempt to either. "Sorry I'm late."

Kathryn shut the door. "That's okay." She absently rubbed her hands on her pants and looked lost in her own living room.

Jenny quickly looked around, searching for some way to diffuse Kathryn's discomfort. "Ah, wine. Thank God. What a night." She shrugged off her coat, handed it to Kathryn, and headed for the table. "Do you mind?"

"Be my guest," Kathryn said, laying the coat neatly over the back of the wing-backed chair.

Before pouring, Jenny raised the bottle at Kathryn's empty glass on the table next to hers, wondering if she would accept.

She smiled and shook her head no, so Jenny filled her glass and approached Kathryn until they were toe to toe—someone had to get this evening started. "Hi," she said.

"Hi," Kathryn said politely, as if they were mere acquaintances.

Undaunted, Jenny moved even closer and put her arm around Kathryn's waist as she pressed her pelvis to her thigh, reminding her of the progress they'd made after the falling out on their last date. "Hi," she whispered intimately as she raised her chin, mouth hopeful.

That finally elicited an easy grin from Kathryn, and Jenny was rewarded with a tentative kiss for her efforts. Tentative wasn't in her plan, however, and she made sure Kathryn knew it, as she purposefully, sensually, kissed her top lip, then her bottom lip, until Kathryn finally surrendered to the invitation. She parted her lips and accepted her tongue with a pleasurable moan.

Jenny felt Kathryn relax into her arms, and if there was any question from the night before about whether they would still be lovers, it was answered in the intense desire swimming in the half-lidded blue eyes staring back at her when they finally parted.

Jenny backed off slowly to get a better look and grinned. "That's better."

"Sorry."

Jenny cupped her face. "Are you all right?"

"Wine on an empty stomach," she said. "Not good."

"You haven't eaten?"

"Not yet, I ... I got distracted."

"I haven't eaten yet either. Dinner in the fridge?"

"Yeah, I'll—"

"Never mind," she said, as she put her hand on Kathryn's warm chest, "it's my fault we're starving. I'll take care of dinner, you stay here and," she looked around, settling on the piano, "play me something."

"Probably safer that way," Kathryn said.

Jenny laughed and headed toward the kitchen.

Kathryn sat down at the piano and put her head in her hands, begging it to clear. She wasn't drunk exactly, but she was out of sorts enough to make her uncomfortable, especially around Jenny. The last thing she needed to do was blurt something out about her assignment, or, God forbid, admit her feelings. Her elbow slipped from its resting place on the music stand and landed on the keys in a cacophony of sour notes.

"Oh, hey," Jenny called from the kitchen, "I once had a cat that could play that tune."

Kathryn laughed. "Oops." Despite her unease, it was hard not to feel comfortable around Jenny. "What do you want to hear?"

"'Clair De Lune' was pretty."

"Mm," Kathryn said, more to herself than to be heard. She began to play, and immediately the music filled her with a familiar peace. Muddled mind or not, her hands needed no direction, as her heart led the way. She got lost in the depths of the bass and the hollows of the sustain, accenting both with the sweetness of the melodious treble line. She didn't hear Jenny come to her side, noticing only when she leaned on the piano in quiet wonder.

Jenny watched Kathryn's hands in fascination. The music flowed from them in equal parts grace and aggression. Some notes were attacked while others seemed merely an afterthought on the way to the next and the next. Kathryn spared her a smile before launching into a flowing rush of frenzied but precise finger movements and sweeping arcs, hand over hand, creating such a seamless, fluid stream of sound that if Jenny hadn't seen it with her own eyes, she would hardly believe ten fingers could create such an effect. The symphony of notes rolled in the air like waves on an open sea until they finally reached safe harbor, the musical passage serene again and thoughtful, like waves melting into the sand as they're welcomed back to shore.

Kathryn closed her eyes as the last notes played, and the faint smile on her lips made her face glow with contentment, as if she'd just received an answer to a prayer.

"That was beautiful," Jenny said with the reverence she felt the moment deserved.

Kathryn let the final chord resonate on the sustain pedal as she brought her hands to her lap and didn't release it until she raised her eyes and smiled a thanks.

"I always play the middle part too fast."

"Well, I certainly didn't notice. That was amazing."

Kathryn leaned back on the bench, letting her posture relax as she ignored the praise. "I played it too fast when I was a child, and I guess I never got out of the bad habit."

"You could play that when you were a child?" Jenny asked in disbelief.

"A simplified version, yes. It was my mother's favorite. She used to serenade us to sleep with it, and I insisted she teach it to me." She chuckled and shook her head. "The sheet music said presto, so I would play it fast. My mother would say, 'It says presto, not fire in the barn. Give the notes some room to breathe—slow down, Kathryn.' But my fingers just had a mind of their own, and soon it was a game. It became like a lyric to the song. The arpeggios start, and then … *slow down, Kathryn*' would come like clockwork at the start of the next measure."

She smiled, and Jenny imagined her remembering her mother's voice.

"I hear her say that even to this day. So, when I'm missing her, I play it."

"I was wondering what you were thinking."

Kathryn smiled wistfully. "I'm thinking of her. Remembering her. Sometimes I can't remember her face, but when I play, she's with me again." She looked past Jenny to a small painting on the wall, where a child's hand reached for a seashell offered from a woman's open palm. "I may not remember what she looked like, but I remember what she felt like. She was warm and safe, and she'll always be that way." She looked at the keyboard reflectively. "Eternally young and beautiful."

"You're missing her today."

"Today is her birthday."

Jenny allowed the significance of the day to sink in and slid onto the bench. She ran a comforting hand down her arm and then entwined their fingers.

Kathryn acknowledged the gesture with a smile and an appreciative shrug of shared understanding. "I used to go out to the cemetery on her birthday. Just to be with her, to let her know she's not forgotten and that I love her. But I've decided to celebrate her life, not her death. This is where she is—" She caressed the ivory keys. "In the music. In my heart."

Jenny squeezed her hand. There was nothing to say.

Kathryn closed her eyes and pressed her lips into a thin line. Jenny expected a tear to escape at any moment, but Kathryn merely inhaled and opened her eyes, a brighter expression on her face.

"So, what happened to that dinner?"

Kathryn's head was considerably clearer after dinner, and the coffee didn't hurt either. She didn't know what had come over her earlier, revealing something so personal. It went against everything her life had become. Years of losing her identity, forgetting her past—first out of necessity, then part of her training—it was all gone in an instant, ancient walls demolished by a young woman too enamored to see the difficulties or too self-absorbed to care.

She didn't honestly think either was true, but she was hard-pressed to explain Jenny's devotion or her effect on her. It should have made her uneasy, but, instead, it gave her comfort. Maybe it was the wine, or maybe it was the desire to be alive, if only for stolen moments, to love and be loved for who she was, not for someone she pretended to be. Jenny was oblivious to her many faces, or maybe she just saw through them all, blessed like an oracle with the gift to know the truth in one's heart.

Kathryn realized she wasn't an emotional fraud. Her feelings for Jenny were like none she had ever known. She wanted Jenny to know her, to understand her past, so that perhaps their future had a chance. Just seeing her again filled her heart and lifted her spirits. She knew, without a doubt, she'd fallen in love. Even she wasn't good enough to pretend that.

"Kat?"

"Yes?" she said, blinking Jenny into focus. Jenny had carried the whole conversation through dinner, regaling her with her day and Bernie's woes, and somewhere along the way, Kathryn got lost in her thoughts.

"You mentioned *us* when you spoke of your mom. I asked if you have siblings."

"Oh, yes, sorry. I have an older brother."

Jenny settled in for the rest of the story that Kathryn had no intention of telling, and then Jenny did what Jenny does. "Tell me about him. Is he in the service?"

"Not that I'm aware of. Clay's a banker, lives just outside the city with his wife, I think."

"You think?"

Unfortunately, this new openness required her to field questions about her family, which also required her to admit she rarely had contact with her brother.

"What about your father, where does he live?"

Kathryn shifted in her chair. She really didn't want to talk about her family anymore. "I'm afraid I've lost track of my father."

"And you haven't been able to locate him?"

Kathryn was sure it was inconceivable to Jenny that one could misplace a father on purpose, but she had, and it would stay that way.

"Well, it's—"

"I'm sure you've tried the police, but I'm sure the OSS has resources that—"

"I think the OSS has more important things to do than find my father."

"Well, your brother must—"

"Jenny," Kathryn said sharply, and then smiled curtly, trying to reign in her irritation, "I have nothing whatsoever to do with my family, and I have no interest in changing that."

Jenny was speechless for a beat. "I'm sorry. I didn't mean to pry."

Kathryn shook her head and raised a hand, turning the apology around. "No, I'm sorry. I didn't mean to snap at you, it's just ... well, there's nothing to be done about it."

"I understand."

But Kathryn knew she couldn't possibly understand. She berated herself for being unable or unwilling to explain it. So much for her newfound openness and trust. Maybe it could only be found in the bottom of an empty wineglass after all. The thought was unsettling and did nothing to promote her chances for a healthy relationship. She'd hurt Jenny's feelings. She wanted to blame the wine, but she knew its effects had long since worn off, and she was left with her dour self and typical results.

Jenny sipped her coffee, now gone cold like the conversation, and flagged another mine in the Kathryn Hammond minefield. "Maybe we should have finished that bottle of wine instead," she said with a smile, trying to blame the caffeine for the aggressive behavior.

"Maybe so," Kathryn said

"*In vino veritas*," Jenny said with a grin.

Kathryn's humorless eyes snapped to hers, and she knew she'd just stepped on another mine.

"Are you insinuating that I can only tell the truth when I'm drunk?"

Jenny clanked her coffee cup onto its saucer in frustration. "No, I'm trying to impress you with my conversational Latin and get this evening back on track. Honestly, Kathryn, I don't understand you." She threw her napkin on the table.

It could be good between them. She knew it could, she'd seen glimpses of it, but as soon as she tried to pursue that avenue, she'd find a dead end and more frustration. While she was not ready to give up, she was not willing to put up either.

"Back and forth, back and forth, Kat," she said, hands demonstrating the pattern. "Most of the time I don't know what you're thinking, what you're feeling, where to step, what to say … I've tried, I've really tried, but if we're going to make this work, something's got to change."

Kathryn closed her eyes. "I'm sorry, Jenny."

"Don't be sorry, just—" She stopped when she realized she was yelling and reduced her volume to something more sympathetic. "Just let me in."

"It's not that simple."

"Have you tried?"

Kathryn bit down on her response, and Jenny could see a blanket of weariness settle over her bowed head.

"I don't want to fight with you, Kathryn. It shouldn't be a fight."

"I know it," Kathryn said as she stared at her hands. "I'm just no good at this."

"At what?"

"I know how to have sex, Jenny. I don't know how to have a relationship."

Jenny wondered if it was as painful to admit as it was to hear. She didn't know how to respond without crying or stepping on another mine. She stared for a moment, holding in her emotions, and then nodded without comment as she reached over and squeezed Kathryn's hand before getting up and gathering their finished dessert plates and silverware and heading into the kitchen.

Kathryn stared at Jenny's empty chair and wondered what she was thinking. It scared her when she was quiet. If she needed any proof that what she felt for Jenny was real and not a performance, like with Forrester, the fear of losing her confirmed it. *Let me in*, Jenny had said. Maybe it was that simple, but it scared the hell out of her.

She approached her from behind and longed to encircle her waist, bury her head in the soft blond hair falling over her shoulders, and beg for forgiveness. That would lead to soft kisses trailing down her neck and wandering hands as Jenny leaned into her body, and she would be hers, unable to resist—no one ever resisted. It would be so easy, so typical, and so wrong. Instead, she stood to the side, where Jenny barely acknowledged her arrival.

"I'll do that," she said, taking the soapy dish and dishrag from her hands.

Jenny let her take it and moved over, rinsing her hands and then drying them on the towel casually flung over her shoulder. She stood expectantly with her hand on her hip, but didn't say a word.

Kathryn pretended to care about removing a stubborn bit of

baking from the dish in her hands but soon let it fall into the suds-filled sink and turned off the water. She stared out the kitchen window into the blackness of the night and took a deep breath before she began.

"Do you remember when I told you my mother was killed by a drunk driver?"

Jenny softened her stance. "Yes."

"My father was the drunk driver."

After a beat of silence, Jenny's hand settled on her arm.

"Oh, Kat, I'm so sorry."

Kathryn didn't want her sympathy. She just wanted to get the story out before she felt the full impact of the event she was retelling.

"They were on their way home from a party. My father was drunk and drove the car into a tree. My mother was killed instantly when she went through the windshield. He walked away without a scratch."

The hand on her arm tightened, but Jenny didn't say anything. Just as well.

Kathryn returned to her task and braced for whatever letting someone in brings.

Jenny moved closer, her hand dropping from her arm to her hip, inviting her to face her. "I'm sorry," she said again. "About them and about tonight."

Kathryn dried her hands, accepting the invitation. "You don't have to be sorry. I just want you to understand." She stroked Jenny's face, trying to ease her stricken look. "I don't want you to stop trying. I don't want you to think that I'm not trying. I want to give us a chance, I do, but—"

Jenny silenced her with a hug. "No, buts. You want to try. That's enough."

Kathryn tightened her embrace, wondering how on earth she'd found someone so patient and forgiving. "I do. Of course I do."

Jenny gave her an extra squeeze and released her. "You won't regret it."

"Regret never entered my mind."

The lie didn't fool Jenny, who laughed and picked up the next plate.

As they went about finishing the dishes, Kathryn noticed that she was suspiciously quiet.

"What is it?"

"Nothing," she said as she dried the silverware.

Knowing Jenny as she did, Kathryn imagined she had dozens of questions running through her head.

"Go ahead and ask."

"Ask what?"

Kathryn smiled, and Jenny gave in with a sheepish grin. "Feel free to tell me to mind my own business."

"Ask."

"What kind of sentence did your father get?"

Kathryn exhaled a humorless chuckle. "He didn't get any sentence. You see, my father was a high-ranking police officer with political aspirations. The accident report stated he was run off the road by a truck that then fled the scene. But it was a lie. There was no truck, and the beat cop who took the report got a promotion shortly after."

"They covered it up," Jenny said in disbelief.

Kathryn nodded and continued putting away the silverware.

"How did your brother take that?"

"He doesn't know."

"How can he not know?"

Kathryn stopped what she was doing. No one knew her personal story except Smitty, and even he didn't know all of it. She wanted Jenny to know everything. She deserved to know, and soon, before they went much further, so she could choose to stay or go, but not tonight. Tonight, she would share the beginning, not where it led.

She explained that a few months after the accident, she heard her father on the phone late at night, apparently in an alcohol-induced state of guilt, crying and begging the officer involved to arrest him for manslaughter. *I killed her*, he kept crying, *I killed her!*

"I confronted my father the next day, and he didn't deny it. He found it hard to face me after that, and, frankly, I couldn't bear to be in the same room with him, so I ran away."

She continued putting away the rest of the silverware. "They would bring me back, and I'd run away again. This went on and on until, finally, the authorities got the hint that I wasn't going to stay. My brother was away at college, so I was put into another family's care until I graduated high school." She smiled. "Smitty's parents took me in. They were wonderful." She closed the silverware drawer, wishing her past as easily put in its place. The Smiths were good people—she couldn't have wished for any better—but nothing could replace the family she'd lost, and the look on her face must have shown it.

"Did you never try to talk to your brother about it?"

Kathryn shrugged and mindlessly rearranged the spice jars on the counter. "He's always had a good relationship with my father. I see no need to change that. Telling him won't bring Mom back."

"Is that why you don't speak?"

"He couldn't understand why I behaved the way I did. He said I broke my father's heart, and I couldn't tell him how the man had broken mine."

Jenny was silent again, and Kathryn could see her struggling with her emotions.

"It's okay, honey," she said, gently lifting Jenny's crestfallen chin, "he's got his life now, and I've got mine."

"But it's just so unfair to you, and now you're alone."

Kathryn smiled. "I've got Smitty and his mom." She paused and softened. "And I've got you, if you'll put up with me."

An armful of agreeable blonde was her answer.

Standing in the kitchen had worn out its welcome, so they moved to the living room and began dismantling their little romantic set, starting with the table in the middle of the room. The silence was decidedly easier this time, and Kathryn marveled at how safe Jenny made her feel in sharing something so personal.

She cleared the candles from the table while Jenny folded the tablecloth and then stopped abruptly.

"Do you wish you'd never found out?"

It took a moment to register the question. "About the truth?"

Jenny nodded.

Kathryn had never really thought about it. She tried to imagine how her life would have been different. She had lost her mother and, shortly after, her father. Only pity could explain why she distanced herself from her beloved brother. She was unwilling to expose the truth and leave her mourning father childless. She'd long forgotten the close bond she'd formed with her father immediately after the accident, how her brother had rushed home, putting off school to be by her side. In the midst of tragedy, she'd never been so loved. No doubt her life would have been completely different.

She pursed her lips regretfully as she attempted to wipe the vision of what might have been from her mind. "Yes," she said, "I wish I'd never found out."

Jenny had spent the last ten minutes sitting in her car, wondering why she was leaving. She knew in her head it was the right thing to do. Kathryn was emotionally exhausted and just barely managing to focus on their relatively, thankfully, mundane conversations. But in her heart, Jenny was still with her. She wanted to absorb the tragedy and heartbreak of her childhood and the horrific events of her recent past and offer her sanctuary in loving arms. She knew Kathryn would surely perceive it as pity and would never surrender to such an idealistic panacea, but how much could one person bear with no respite from the pain? To lose so much at such a young age … and that was not the end of her suffering. She wondered how Kathryn survived. She supposed those survival skills were the same that allowed her to endure her war experience and perform her OSS job so admirably, but at what price? Kathryn stood alone, surrounded by a carefully crafted shield, propped up by a staunch denial of emotions that, if considered, would bring her to her knees. Her survival was a testament to her strength, and Jenny could not fault her inability to let someone in.

Watching Kathryn relive her mother's memory in her music

showed her a glimpse into the beauty and depth of her soul, something she was afraid Kathryn had forgotten existed. How could she tell her she loved her? How could she breach defenses that enabled her very existence? She couldn't. Not tonight. Maybe not ever. Kathryn suddenly seemed precariously positioned atop a house of cards, her strength merely a shell surrounding the fragile remains of a fourteen-year-old girl who never had a chance to live.

When Jenny stepped out onto the sidewalk, she heard the strains of "Clair De Lune" floating down from the apartment above. Kathryn was alone again with her mother, perhaps the only person with whom she would allow herself peace. At least she had that.

Jenny slid over into the passenger seat of her car, hoping to get a final glimpse of Kathryn. She lifted her eyes to the second-floor apartment, watching as the living room window went dark and then, shortly after, the bedroom. She put her hand on the glass and closed her eyes.

"I love you."

"You're awfully quiet this morning," Smitty said as they drove to the training center.

Kathryn hadn't noticed. So many things were going through her head, and all of them involved Jenny.

"Didn't you have a date last night?"

"I did."

He waited for details, which were not forthcoming.

"That bad?"

"It was good, actually." She paused, considering whether she should elaborate. "I told her about Dad ... the truth."

Smitty looked over in disbelief. Kathryn wasn't surprised by his reaction, as he knew he was the only person she'd ever told.

"What brought that on?"

She wanted to say she was tired of being alone, but she was afraid it would hurt his feelings, so she offered a noncommittal shrug and said, "I just wanted her to know."

Smitty nodded. "What did she say?"

"She didn't say anything."

He chuckled. "That's a neat trick."

"What's there to say?"

"True."

Kathryn thought long and hard about how to approach the next subject. She didn't like testing Smitty's loyalty, but things of late had been anything but routine in her life.

"She knows about overseas."

Smitty was silent for a beat. "How did that happen?"

There was no hint of his dishonesty. She didn't think there would be if he chose to lie about it—he was too good for that—but she had hoped he would choose to tell her the truth. "Gossip at HQ, I guess." She rubbed her forehead as if she were exasperated by the intrusion into her personal life. "You know Jenny, always making with the questions. She's hard to resist once she sets her mind to something."

"Mm," was the extent of his reply.

Kathryn was sure he'd take the opening to come clean, but he didn't, and disappointment deflated her confidence in her longtime friend. Their bond took another blow, as, once again, trust proved to be an elusive commodity. She let his deception hang in the air, hoping its weight would make him think better of it, but apparently it settled comfortably on his shoulders, because he bore it in silence. Kathryn noted his decision and moved on.

"Forrester called me last night."

"At home?"

"Mm, he misses me."

"And?"

"That was it. He just wanted to tell me he misses me."

"Next thing you know, he'll be asking you to marry him."

"Wouldn't that be fun," she said sarcastically.

"Would you?"

She looked at him, surprised he would ask. "Whatever it takes,

Smitty. Nothing's going to change that." Not even Jenny, she reminded herself, just in case her subconscious had any notions to the contrary.

Smitty appeared eager to change the subject.

"Did you hear what Forrester did to your boy Lawrence?"

Kathryn raised an interested brow.

"Cut him up into pieces and sent him to his *compadres* as a warning."

"Charming."

"Head to Phoenix, unmentionables to Chicago—"

"I get the picture, Smitty, thank you."

"He's a real piece of work, that guy."

"He feels threatened."

Smitty glanced her way.

"Threatened people do desperate things," she explained, as if she were turning her assignment to the monster over in her head. In fact, Jenny was in her head. What would she do if Forrester asked her to marry him? Could she live such a life? The question wasn't would she do it but how would she juggle her relationship with Jenny? Could Jenny accept such an arrangement? Such questions were ridiculous. She didn't have the luxury of asking questions. Since when did *her* wants shape what she would or wouldn't do to get the job done?

As if he could read her mind, Smitty asked, "So, when do you see her again?"

He may have lied to her, but no one knew her better, and with everything else in her world seeming less and less certain, she found comfort in that. She smiled. "Tonight."

"I thought you had that gig with Tommy Wallace tonight?"

"Oh, nuts! I forgot."

"That's not like you."

A lot about her was off lately, and it was disconcerting and exciting all at the same time. This, however, was an oversight she could do something about. She would just meet Jenny in the city, go to the gig together, and take their date from there. It would be spontaneous and, dare she say, fun.

Kathryn organized papers on her desk in the small wooden outbuilding she used as a classroom at the training center at the Long Island estate on loan to the OSS for the duration. The day went by quickly as she got ready for the monthly class of new recruits and brushed up on procedures, just in case Colonel Forsythe accepted her application for mission training. Her mind kept going back to Smitty and his duplicity, though, and the more she thought about it, the more it ate at her. She knew it wasn't done out of malice. It was just his way of protecting her, but trust was a fragile thing, and lies had a way of burgeoning into bigger lies if gone unchecked. It was the principle of the thing, and he had to know he wouldn't get away with deceiving her.

They rode home in relative silence, with only a few exchanges about procedural updates dominating their sparse conversation. Smitty stopped the car in front of her door, and she kissed him on the cheek, as usual, and thanked him for the lift. He watched her unfold her long legs as she got out of the car and slammed the door. Instead of walking directly to her apartment, she stood at the open window, her fingers impatiently tapping on the top of the doorframe. Smitty leaned over to get a glimpse of her face, but she made that unnecessary, as she bent down and leaned into his field of vision.

"I asked you not to lie to me ever, Smitty," she began in deceptive calm.

"Okay," he drew out. "I'm not sure what this—"

She held up her hand. "Smitty, don't say anything. Please don't say anything."

He reluctantly complied.

"I know you told Jenny about overseas."

"Kathryn—"

"That's one issue," she interrupted with a raised finger, "then you lied to me about telling her."

"You have to listen—"

"No, I don't have to listen to you. In fact, right now, I don't really care why you did it. It irks me to no end that you continually try to deceive me."

"Continually?"

"Yes. Doing *this* for my own good and *that* for my own good. I'm not a child."

"I know that."

"Then stop treating me like one." She straightened and abruptly turned, walking purposefully toward her door.

"Kat!"

She ignored his plea, throwing a cool "See you tomorrow" over her shoulder.

"Ka—" Smitty knew explanations at that moment were futile, so he let her name die on his lips and let her go, slamming his palms into the steering wheel as he slumped back into his seat. "That damned kid!"

CHAPTER NINETEEN

Jenny turned up the half collar on her shirt and jacket, trying to at least look sophisticated as she entered the theater on West 45th Street. She didn't mind the change in plans, but she wished she could have gone home to change first. As it was, she felt out of place in her modest tailored business suit among the classical music set, with their long gowns and pretentious jewels.

She smiled politely to the judgmental stares that followed her every move as she passed through the lobby on her way into the auditorium and then backstage. She shook her head at the righteous indignation that blinded them to the fact that, for years, she had been one of them—decked out in her finest, appearing on her father's arm at this important function or that. Clothes may make the man, but more times than not, they just made him blind.

The concert hall was small, but the cavernous ceilings made it seem spacious. Yards of mulberry colored velvet swooped majestically from the upper boxes, and the glow of the footlights highlighted the ornate Italian renaissance woodwork. The old-world charm of the place spoke of an age gone by, and it matched the old-world attitude of its patrons. The mood of the room was subdued and reverent, like an audience filing into church for Sunday Mass.

Backstage was another matter, however. It was a cacophony of bustling black-tied musicians pacing nervously with instruments in hand or huddled in the corners, pantomiming their routine in intense concentration as they prepared for their performance.

In stark contrast was a small group of men, quite relaxed, sitting around a table, playing cards and laughing. Jenny recognized Tommy Wallace right away. A cigarette dangled from his mouth, and his hat was pushed way back on his head. There was no sign of Kathryn. She imagined her off somewhere, warming up, taking time to gather herself as she focused on whatever piece of music they'd chosen.

Suddenly a roar went up from the table. Tommy shouted, "You wench! You had nothing!" Obviously, poker was the game, and Jenny smiled as a familiar voice teased, "Read 'em and weep, ya sap."

Jenny craned her head around some standing spectators to see her date reach across the table and scoop up her winnings. She was devastatingly beautiful, as always, with her hair up in a sophisticated sweep befitting the venue and her makeup heavy for the stage. It was good to see her smile, and Jenny matched it with one of her own as she approached.

"Hi."

Kathryn greeted her with an embrace before she even got the word out.

"Sorry about the change in plans," she whispered in her ear. "Won't be long here."

"That's okay," Jenny said, backing off. "You look fantastic."

As usual, the compliment was ignored.

"Come on, meet the boys."

Kathryn's dress was a simple black high-neck column dress, deceptively prudish from the front, but as she walked away, her back was revealed in a large hourglass shape, stretching from her shoulder blades to the small of her back. She reminded Jenny of a cello, and it made her smile. Such an aesthetically pleasing way to ration material.

Tommy recognized her from the Blue Note Lounge, and before she knew it, she was dealing the next hand at the table. The scene was odd, with everyone but their group taking matters very seriously.

"It's kind of tense back here," she said, as she expertly flicked the cards around the table.

"It's those sticks up their asses," Tommy said absently as he studied his cards. He lifted his eyes to Jenny in apology. "Oh, I'm sorry. I mean their *behinds*."

"This is a very important night," Kathryn explained. "It's an audition for a lot of them. A way for new musicians to break into the rotation and get their names out there."

"It's a dog and pony show," Tommy said.

"And which are you?" Jenny asked with a grin as she gathered her cards.

He laughed and turned to Kathryn. "Say, I like this girl."

Kathryn winked at her and threw two cards on the table. Jenny, in turn, dealt her two more and was rewarded with the odd tale of Tommy Wallace's mission.

Apparently, his younger brother had been treated shabbily at the last such event and he had a plan to get even.

"How many songs are you playing?"

Tommy grinned. "Oh, we'll only get the chance to play one."

Jenny looked at the bongos and flamenco guitars and asked what they were playing.

"Carmen," Kathryn said.

Jenny did a double take at the instruments. "Miranda?"

Kathryn smiled and shook her head. "You'll see."

It seemed innocent enough. Musicians would go out on stage, either in groups or solo, and perform for an appreciative crowd. Then Jenny imagined some scout in the audience would write down the act and pass it along to the proper channels, thus ensuring the musician would be on his way. Once the music started, she was shocked to find it was nothing like that. Should the musician falter, or fail to please, the sophisticated, reserved crowd would suddenly transform into something more akin to a mob at the coliseum. In lieu of the thumbs up, thumbs down to determine the performer's fate, boos or an equally effective silence would rain down on the stage, as humiliated musicians slinked off into oblivion. Jenny had never seen anything like it.

She knew Tommy was a fine musician, as was his group, she was sure, and Kathryn was a consummate professional, so for the life of her, she couldn't see how their performance could draw the ire of this crowd, or the fury of the event's organizer, who was in the center box seat. Considering Tommy was a jazz musician and Kathryn sang swing in a nightclub, perhaps it shouldn't have been such a leap, but she didn't think they'd purposefully cause trouble. Would they? From the wings, Jenny eyed her friends, who were filing onto the stage. She tilted her head in appreciation of the view and decided the cello was a very sexy instrument. They all took their places and stood in darkness, waiting for the curtain to rise.

Besides Kathryn, there were two guitarists, a quartet of strings, two percussionists on bongos and kettle drums, four backup singers, one with a tambourine, and Tommy, forgoing his horn for, of all things, a pair of maracas. Jenny shook her head, impressed. He was going all out for his revenge.

The curtain rose, and Kathryn stood motionless, her head bowed, hands clasped at her diaphragm, elbows out—a statue in the sterile spotlight. Jenny's heartbeat quickened as she waited for whatever evil scheme Tommy had dreamed up for the event.

Kathryn raised her head, her face bleached from the blinding white spotlight. She swept her eyes slowly from side to side, and Jenny could feel the audience's anticipation slowly turn to discomfort and uncertainty at her silence. The tension built until it became an audible rustle, as bodies shifted and whispers began to drift to the stage.

Kathryn turned her head toward her and stared stone-faced until she winked with a half-smile and then dropped her chin in a nod.

Her curt movement set off the flamenco guitarist, who took his cue and began to pluck the simple strains of "Habanera," from the first act of *Carmen*. The cellist added his part, but the hum of the instrument's delicate bass line was all but lost under the bright finger work of the guitarist. Kathryn faced the crowd and began singing. Her voice floated effortlessly from her throat in an upper register Jenny had never heard from her before. She stood transfixed. There was nothing evil about this performance. Kathryn's vocals were positively angelic, soaring over the strings and filling the hall with the French libretto of the gypsy's song. The percussionists introduced their Latin rhythm, and the background vocalists lent their delicate harmony to the chorus as they completed, what seemed to Jenny, a slightly pared down, but otherwise traditional, treatment of the operatic favorite.

In a performance worthy of the theatrical opera, Kathryn embraced the sultry role of Carmen, but in the absence of a Don Jose to seduce, she turned her charms on the audience, to mixed reviews. Most stared skeptically, waiting for the performance to go off the rails, but quite a few surrendered to the moment and looked like they were enjoying themselves.

Jenny was disappointed in the lack of fireworks, but the calm wouldn't last long, as tradition suddenly turned aggressive and Kathryn's perfectly sustained bridge note was swept away by furiously strummed guitars and overexcited drums. For better or worse, the focus shifted to the band, as their frenzied rhythm and furiously plucked melody took over.

Kathryn stepped aside, and Jenny saw a distinct grin on her face as she surrendered to the infectious energy of the decidedly rebellious composition. Based on the sour faces in the audience, Jenny could tell they were not amused. She ventured a peek at the center box in time to see the event's organizer stand abruptly and storm from view. She cringed, imagining the man wielding Little Bo Peep's staff as he charged the offensive musicians, ready to yank them off stage.

She turned back to the stage, where Kathryn's smooth flowing vocals provided a calm contrast to the manic musicians behind her. It wasn't enough to earn the audience's respect, however, as boos began raining down from the disgruntled crowd. The musicians valiantly continued, ignoring the indignity, as Kathryn's voice only got stronger in response. She engaged the audience, imploring them with the lyrics and her body language to open their minds and let the music move them. It worked to a certain extent. They were allowed to finish at least, but all hell broke loose when they defied the crowd's displeasure and bowed brazenly against the onslaught of disapproval.

The curtain fell, nixing an encore, but that was the last thing on Tommy Wallace's mind, as he helped his fellow musicians hastily pack up their instruments and head for the stage door before the event's organizer could make his way backstage.

"Go, go, go!" he shouted at the bottleneck of bodies and instrument cases trying to squeeze through the back door.

"You!" the booming voice of the event organizer resonated across the room.

"Go!" Tommy gave one final good-natured shove to his mates as they poured into the alley like an uncorked vat of wine.

Kathryn and Jenny grabbed their coats and brought up the rear, too late for a clean getaway. The angry coordinator recognized Kathryn immediately. "I'll have your cabaret card for this!"

Hurried footsteps and laughter echoed off the brick buildings standing guard over the alley as the musicians dispersed into the night, their mission a success.

"I'm sure we made their night," Kathryn said with a chuckle as they exited the alley and slowed to a leisurely stroll down the sidewalk.

"What snobs," Jenny said.

Kathryn shrugged. "They have a point."

Jenny couldn't believe she was defending them. "Such as?"

"Classical music is a very specialized field, with very high standards. The acceptance of mediocrity only diminishes the art form as a whole."

Jenny was astonished. Kathryn was one of *them*. "I didn't know you were a longhair, Kat."

Kathryn smiled. "I merely respect their appreciation of the craft."

"Then why did you do this tonight?"

"Because Tommy's a friend and he was in a jam. And it was a brilliant arrangement and a challenge for me." She smiled. "And because some of those people couldn't care less about artistic purity and are just snobs for snobbery's sake."

Jenny chuckled.

"I'm afraid I took some of Tommy's thunder, though. He meant for the arrangement to be offensive, not the vocalist."

"I hardly think anyone was offended by your vocals."

Kathryn snorted. "Well, if they weren't, they should have been. The piece is written for a mezzo-soprano, at the very least. Tommy did his best transposing the arrangement, but, honestly, I haven't the range for it."

"It sounded fine to me."

"Yes, it was fine if you ignore the pinched coloratura and the straining through the passaggio." She shook her head. "Lily Pons I ain't."

Jenny rolled her eyes. To her, the famous soprano was about as soothing as a whippoorwill outside the window the morning of a hangover. "Lily Pons gives me a headache."

Kathryn clutched her chest. "Sacrilege!"

"Stop. You were great."

"What I lack in talent, I make up for in attitude."

Jenny stopped walking. "Kathryn?"

She turned around. "Yes?"

"Will you just let me give you a compliment?"

Kathryn respectfully put her hands behind her back and smiled. "Go right ahead."

"You were wonderful tonight."

"I'm glad you liked it."

Not exactly acceptance, but Jenny knew it was the best she was going to get. "Fair enough."

A taxi pulled up along the curb with Tommy Wallace hanging out its window. The rest of the band was nowhere to be seen, but the horn player and two of the backup singers had opted for a night on the town to celebrate their triumph.

"Hey! Are you coming?"

Kathryn smiled. "I think we'll pass. I owe Jenny—"

"Hey, sweetheart," Tommy interrupted, pointing his finger, "you owe *me*. You almost blew the gig tonight."

Kathryn held up her hands. "Wait a minute ... blame Claire's sister for going into labor. I told you it wasn't my range."

"What are you talking about?" He opened the door and swung out onto the sidewalk. "You were great, baby ... almost *too* great. They nearly forgave my arrangement." He turned to Jenny. "Did you see them at the end there? A real snake charmer this one."

"You're preaching to the choir, brother. I think she's tremendous."

"Come on, kids." He motioned into the cab. "Whaddaya say ... dinner?"

"Tommy—"

"Gotta eat, right? My treat."

Jenny loved that Kathryn was prepared to fight for their evening alone together, but Tommy was not beyond begging, and Jenny succumbed to his irresistible pleading. They squeezed into the cab and put off their date for just a little while longer.

Dinner was a boisterous affair. Tommy was a charismatic fellow, with boundless energy, which inspired the same in the people around him. The banter between friends began innocently enough, but catching up turned into reminiscing, and Jenny saw Kathryn lean on the table and look sideways at Tommy when she became the topic of conversation. He winked at her, and she just shook her head. Jenny sensed Tommy had an ulterior motive for this spontaneous get together, and it appeared Kathryn was on to him.

Jenny was surprised to learn that Kathryn had been the lead singer with the group once upon a time, and she listened intently to story after story about living in cars and worshiping public restrooms on the road while trying to make a living and a name for themselves.

Kathryn took it all in stride, eventually smiling and laughing, even offering a few tales of her own. Jenny had never seen her so animated and jovial, but it was her laugh that caught her off guard. Of course, she'd heard her laugh before, but not like this, so carefree and, dare she say, spontaneous. Not that Kathryn was rigid or humorless, but she was definitely deliberate and measured in all things. This behavior was a revelation, and she remembered Smitty saying *I wish you could have known her before*. The momentary glimpse of that other woman from that other time left her feeling cheated. The war had stolen so much from so many, and it wasn't done wreaking its havoc. Jenny swallowed the lump in her throat for all that was lost and lifted her chin to enjoy the ghost of that stolen life before it fled, hand in hand, with the mirage of reminiscence.

It soon became apparent that there were limits to Kathryn's good humor, and Tommy seemed to know them. He lifted his hands in surrender when she crossed her arms and tilted her head, indicating her patience was wearing thin. He'd better get to the point of his little trip down memory lane, and quick.

As it turned out, Tommy Wallace had been given a contract, thanks to Kathryn's suggestion to the agent at the Blue Note Lounge, and now he was assembling a band in preparation for a warm-up tour across the states, before their official debut in Los Angeles. Out of gratitude, he offered her the job of his lead vocalist. Heartfelt congratulations were given, but they were served with a cold side of *no thanks*, as Kathryn pointed out that she already had a job. His promises of record deals, sold-out shows, and fame and fortune fell on disinterested ears. She graciously bade them all a good night and wished them all the luck in the world.

Kathryn adjusted her coat on her shoulders as they exited the restaurant. "Sorry about that."

"Next time we have a date, can we just stay in?" Jenny asked with a grin.

"Deal." Kathryn slipped her arm through the crook in Jenny's elbow, thankful no one thought twice about them strolling down the street arm in arm. "I promise, I'm all yours for the rest of the evening."

Jenny settled in closer. "I liked meeting your friends. Did you have a good time?"

"I did. It was good to see some of the gang again."

Jenny laughed. "Those stories!"

Kathryn shook her head. "That was one wild summer."

"All *that* occurred in just one summer?"

"Mm. The summer before I went to Europe. Kids. We were crazy."

Jenny was silent for a long stretch, and Kathryn sensed her imagining what she was like as a happy-go-lucky musician having fun on a daily basis. She was sorry she wasn't that person for Jenny now, but maybe they wouldn't be together if she were. They certainly never would have met.

That notion spurred an unexpected jolt of panic, and she almost didn't hear Jenny's question.

"I know you turned Tommy down, but would you ever do that? Tour, record, you know, all that?"

"I haven't time for that sort of thing."

"Well now, yes, of course. But I mean after the war, after your—" Jenny paused, then chose an innocuous word for their public conversation, "*workload* has eased?"

Kathryn shrugged. "I hadn't thought about it."

Truth be told, she never imagined she would survive the war, and somehow that made her continued existence bearable, allowable. In the end, she knew she would get her comeuppance. It only seemed right, and she accepted it without question. Memories of wild, carefree days gave way to memories of wild, reckless days, not caring whether her next mission was her last. Some called her behavior daring, others called it foolish, most called it insane, but there was no denying it was suicidal, and it eventually got her sent home. The adjustment to the relative safety of assignments like Forrester and the Ryan case was something she tolerated while biding her time until she could convince her superiors she was stable enough to get back to the important work behind enemy lines, work that would inevitably lead to her premature demise. It couldn't be by her own hand—never that—as that would deny the dead their restitution. No, her death would mean something, ensure the completion of some important mission, save someone, many someones, preferably, anything, as long as it served her debt.

Despite such dour thoughts, having Jenny by her side allowed her mind to venture to the future. What if she did survive? What if, by some miracle, Jenny stuck it out and they made a life together? It made her smile. It would be a happy life, she imagined. She immediately dismissed the vision as they passed a brownstone with a gold star flag in the window. A loved one lost. She was assailed with thoughts of mothers without sons, sisters without brothers, wives without husbands. She caused that for someone. Happily ever after wasn't for people like her.

She felt Jenny squeeze her arm, her adoring green eyes questioning. "Penny?"

Kathryn slammed on the mental brakes, throwing her demons to the front of the bus until they dropped one by one from the windshield to the floor in a heap. Not tonight. She would feed them—it was as natural as breathing—but not tonight. She pushed the prophetical guilt of surviving the war out of her mind. This was Jenny's night. This was *her* night. Happy for a little while would just have to be tolerated.

"Just thinking of Tommy," she said. "I'm glad he made it."

Jenny stared at her long enough to show she wasn't buying her lie, but she picked up the conversation. "I guess he's on his way now."

"He'll do well. Sometimes all you need is a break." She looked at Jenny, and some new facet of her mind wondered if she was her break. She breathed in the idea of it and cleared her head of unpleasant thoughts. She looked around, realizing she hadn't been paying attention to their surroundings. "Where are we going?"

Jenny tightened her grip and smiled. "It's a surprise."

Kathryn stopped walking. "I hate surprises."

Jenny pulled her along with a determined grin. "You'll like this one."

Kathryn didn't know how many blocks they'd walked, and she no longer cared. Jenny was leading, she was following, and their easy banter took her mind far away from the war, death, and guilt.

In the middle of a block, Jenny stopped walking and put her hands behind her back. "Here we are."

Kathryn looked past her and tried to keep her expression neutral. *Anywhere but here*, she wanted to say, but it was Jenny's choice, and after taking up half their evening with her business, she didn't have the heart to refuse.

She should have recognized the street, or at least the neighborhood, but Jenny had a way of captivating her attention, and she was oblivious to their surroundings until it was too late. Apparently, a night of dancing was in order, which normally would have thrilled her, but not here. Not with Jenny. It wasn't a bad crowd, or a bad club, just a life she no longer led, and one she had no interest in revisiting. She took a bracing breath as she set her jaw and prepared to follow Jenny into the shark pit, more commonly known as the Mayfly.

"Is this all right?"

"Mm-hm," Kathryn said with a smile as they started up the steps to the restaurant and bar that housed the underground women's club. They made their way through the public outer bar before heading toward the long hallway that led to the club downstairs. A hulking man at the end of the bar eyed them briefly as they passed, no doubt muscle for the mob boss who owned the Mayfly. They turned left at the end of the hallway and nodded to the well-dressed lady at the door who gave them access to the stairs with a smile. Kathryn didn't recognize her and hoped that would bode well for the rest of the evening. It had been a while, after all, and people and places do change.

The dim, smoky interior reeked of alcohol, tobacco, and the sickening combination of too many perfumes in one room. Kathryn ducked as she passed under the low door jamb of the main room, a remnant of the building's Civil War-era construction. Once at the bar, they were met with a gauntlet of hopeful singles and bitter exes eyeing the new arrivals with equal parts hope and disdain. The place hadn't changed after all.

They deposited their coats on the rack along the brick wall, and Jenny didn't waste any time wrapping her arm around her waist. She didn't know whether Jenny was just happy to have a safe place to show her affection in public or whether she wanted everyone to know the score before they even thought about hitting on her woman. A little of both, Kathryn assumed, and she reciprocated with a tight squeeze and a kiss on the head. Jenny led her past the gauntlet toward the dance floor, where female couples were swaying to the sensual slow song of the live band.

Kathryn hoped they could bypass the dance floor and get to a booth in the back before anyone recognized her. No such luck.

"Holy shit," the heavyset bartender said as she put down the glass she was drying. "As I live and breathe … Kat Hammond! Let the party begin!" She flung her arms out in an enthusiastic welcome. "Where the hell have you been hiding, gal?"

The people hadn't changed either. Kathryn winced and squeezed Jenny's shoulder, indicating she was going to have to stop and say hi.

"Hey, Ruby." She backed up and reached across the bar to shake hands. The bartender playfully slapped her hand away. "Bullshit, I'll shake your hand," she said with a grin. "Get your ass back here and give me a damn hug." The bartender met her at the end of the bar and picked her up off her feet in a bear hug and then put her down. "Damn it, too tall, where've you been?"

"Here and there," Kathryn said warily with a glance around, hoping to avoid any more attention.

"Well, safe to say, we aren't between here or there, 'cause I haven't seen you 'round here for what … four years?"

"More like five or six," Kathryn said, hazarding a guess. The past few years were a blur of indeterminate measure to her.

The bartender shook her head. "Five or six. No wonder things have been so dull. Shit, I'm glad to see you. I was afraid you'd turned tail and retreated to the other side of the street, if you know what I mean." She gave her a wink and a nudge.

Kathryn forced a smile, looking toward Jenny for a rescue. Jenny was standing off to the side, appraising the interaction, but she came to her outstretched hand as if drawn to a magnet.

"Ruby Stevenson," Kathryn said, as she positioned Jenny in front of her and put her hands on her shoulders, "this is Jenny Ryan."

"Pleased to meet you," the women said in unison as they shook hands. The bartender stepped back and looked Jenny up and down. "Let's see—"

"Ruby," Kathryn drew out in a warning tone.

"Shut the hell up, Kat," Ruby snapped playfully. "I want to see the flavor of the week."

"She's not an ice cream cone, Ruby, she's my—" Kathryn paused and searched for the appropriate words. She knew from the slight turn of Jenny's head that she was interested in her description as well.

"My date for the evening, and I would appreciate it if you would treat her as such."

Jenny put a hand over the one on her shoulder and raised her chin.

"Aye," Ruby put on a cockney accent and did a mock curtsey. "Right, Mum. And what can I get her highness and her luffley swee'-heart this eve'nin?"

Kathryn tilted her head in annoyance.

"Still have your sense of humor, I see," Ruby said sarcastically, as she dropped the accent and walked back behind the bar. "Vodka rocks, right, Kat?"

"That'll be fine."

Ruby looked at Jenny and smirked. "Glass of milk for you, honey?"

"Cut it out," Kathryn warned.

Jenny patted Kathryn's hand, which was tightening its grip with every exchange. "Scotch. Neat, please," she said politely.

"Oooh—" Ruby stood back. "Got yourself a real man there, Kat."

"Ruby," Kathryn said again, making sure she knew from the tone that it was the last warning.

"Oh, Christ on a cracker, Hammond."

Kathryn stared Ruby down until the bartender blinked and turned to Jenny. "I hope you've got a sense of humor, honey, 'cause Kat here seems to have misplaced hers."

"We're sitting in the back," Kathryn said abruptly. "Drinks when you get around to it, will ya?" With that, she took Jenny by the hand and tried to make a quick path to the back of the club.

"Yeah, I'll get right on that," she heard Ruby say to their backs.

They'd almost made it to a table when from the microphone on stage came, "I see you," drawn out in a sing-song manner.

Kathryn recognized the voice but kept on walking.

"Kat," the woman at the mic drew out playfully, as Jenny slid into the corner booth, "don't you even think of sitting down without coming up here to say hi to us."

The whole room looked their way, but Kathryn didn't turn around. She glanced toward the bar to see Ruby shelving the flashlight she used to get the bandleader's attention. Kathryn turned to Jenny and sighed regretfully.

Jenny pressed her lips into a smile. "Go on."

Kathryn held out her hand. "All right. Let's meet the natives."

Jenny took her hand but declined the invitation. "Go catch up with your friends. I'll meet them later."

"You sure?"

"Mm," she said with a quick nod.

"Sorry. Won't be a minute." She tugged an apology on Jenny's hand and then headed toward the grinning group on the small stage in the corner.

Jenny settled back into the booth and wished she had that drink. Considering the limited number of lesbian clubs in the city, it shouldn't have surprised her that in this place, of all places, she would know people. She just wanted to go dancing. Was that too much to ask?

As Jenny took in the room, she realized half the club was staring at Kathryn and the rest of the club was staring at her, sizing her up. Apparently, she was not as interesting as tall, dark, and sexy, because the attention on her quickly waned and she was left basically twirling her thumbs, awaiting Kathryn's return.

Wilting under the scrutiny, Jenny decided to retrieve the drinks from the bar. At least that would give her something to do.

"Hey, Ruby," she said to the smug bartender as she leaned on the bar top, "how about those drinks."

"Sure thing, short stuff," she replied with a smile.

Jenny couldn't tell whether she was being antagonistic or just kidding, but she would give her the benefit of the doubt for the moment. While she waited for the drinks, she couldn't help overhearing the two women sitting beside her at the bar.

"Wow. What the hell happened to Kat?" one woman said, peering over her shoulder to where Kathryn was standing next to the stage.

"What do you mean?" said the other, turning around.

"She looks ten years older."

"Are you screwy? She looks fantastic."

Ruby overheard the conversation too and, in between pouring drinks, was watching Jenny's face for a reaction. Jenny was trying her best to remain casually disinterested.

"I didn't say she didn't look fantastic," the woman continued, "I said she looked older. She's lost that voluptuous look and exchanged it for the lean, sophisticated look."

"Well, we all have to lose that baby fat sometime," the second woman commented as she turned to face the bar again.

"Yeah? When do you start?"

"Nuts to you, sister. Look in the mirror lately?" She took an annoyed swallow of her drink. "Besides," the woman said, as she looked toward the back of the club to where Jenny had been sitting, "she's wearing her baby fat on her arm these days. Did you get a load of that blonde number she came in with?"

"Yeah," the first woman said, peering into the crowd, trying to get another glimpse. "What's she got that I ain't got?"

"Kat Hammond," Jenny said, as she waited for the bartender to finish her task.

Ruby grinned and winked as she handed over the drinks. Jenny acknowledged the wink and the conversation with a smile. "Thanks." The two conversing women took that opportunity to slither away from the bar with disapproving grunts.

"Congratulations," Ruby said before Jenny could get away.

"For?"

"You must be something pretty special." Ruby lifted her chin toward the stage, where Kathryn's former bandmates flocked around her. "Somehow you're under her skin, and she's a tough nut to crack."

"Really? I hadn't noticed."

She walked back to the table and slid into the booth, disturbed by the exchange. The remarks hit close to home. Was she *that* special? She didn't think so, and as she watched Kathryn reconnect with old friends, insecurity began to rear its ugly head. She took a drink and reprimanded herself. She willed herself to knock it off. She's catching up with old friends, that's all. They arrived together, and they're going to leave together.

Jenny noticed the saxophone player stayed in her seat, wearing a disgusted look on her face. She was an older woman with short curly red hair, and as the other girls fawned, she feigned disinterest and started polishing her instrument.

From Kathryn's body language, Jenny could tell the band members were trying to convince her to sing with them and she was trying to bow out gracefully. The group was not having it, though. She would sing or bust. The saxophone player vehemently complained, which caused a ruckus with the leader of the group. There was a lot of hissing and pointing, which attracted the attention of the patrons and resulted in the saxophone player leaving the stage in a huff.

The leader leaned into the microphone. "Sorry, ladies, no sax tonight." That caused a rimshot from the drummer and a smattering of laughter and groans throughout the club. "But we do have an old friend who we've kidnapped for a song or two." The leader looked at Jenny and lowered her voice. "Don't worry, honey, we'll return her undamaged."

Jenny smiled and nodded her head at Kathryn's apologetic shrug.

It was a nice band, six women in all, including the leader/singer, who surrendered her place at the microphone. Jenny watched the women on stage huddle together like football players deciding on a play. They all broke off and settled into their spots, with the bandleader paying close attention to Kathryn, touching her in a way that Jenny could only describe as very familiar—as in ex-girlfriend familiar. She took solace in Kathryn's uncomfortable reaction to the physical intrusion.

The bandleader slid her arm around Kathryn's waist. "Say, Kat, after this number, whaddaya say we grab a bottle and head upstairs for some recreational fucking?"

Kathryn resisted the urge to look Jenny's way, stifling the instinctual reaction to a crass suggestion that seemed suddenly so out of place. Never mind that it normally would have rated an enthusiastic affirmative.

"I'm here with someone, Lani."

Lani snorted incredulously. "Never stopped you before, woman. Come on. Just like old times, eh?"

This time she did look at Jenny, and the sight of her warmed her heart. "I'm not that person anymore."

Lani followed her gaze, and her look softened. She slowly removed her hand from Kathryn's waist and smiled respectfully.

"Yeah. I can see that."

She had the countenance of a concerned friend, an acknowledgment of the obvious changes, now that she really took the time to look, and the gesture reminded Kathryn of why she liked Lani. She was all gruff and bravado, but she'd do anything for you, and she'd always tell you the truth. They had been on and off bedmates a long time ago and again when she first returned to the city, but nothing Kathryn would consider meaningful. They were never exclusive, and not even particularly nice to each other, an arrangement that suited them both just fine.

Lani smiled and playfully poked her in the shoulder. "You still sing, don't cha?"

"Better than you ever could."

"Bitch."

Kathryn grinned. Just like old times indeed.

"G'wan—" Lani shoved her toward the microphone, laughing. "Slay us."

Jenny imagined her insecurity was showing, because Kathryn tilted her head slightly and frowned regretfully. She turned back to the band to make sure they had the right key, Jenny supposed, and winked as she turned around and adjusted the microphone to account for her height.

"This might sound a little flat without the sax," Kathryn said with a grin, "but I'm sure these ladies will fill in nicely."

And fill in nicely they did. Jenny didn't know much about the technical aspect of making music, but she knew when it sounded good, and she couldn't complain about this group.

Kathryn held her gaze throughout the musical introduction of "Be Careful, It's My Heart," and before she even started singing, Jenny was lost. The room fell away until all that was left was the music and Kathryn's sultry voice, singing a song about, of all things, falling in love. Jenny couldn't believe what she was hearing. Kathryn was offering her heart in front of a room full of people.

The room, however, couldn't possibly know the intricacies of their relationship, and every eye, at one time or another, was eventually cast in her direction, either rejoicing in her good fortune or sneering in derision, jealousy the culprit. Jenny didn't care. She was falling deeper and deeper under Kathryn's spell. She realized by the tilt of Kathryn's head, the expression in her eyes, and the slightly upturned smile as she sang certain lines, that the song wasn't just another song. She picked this one specifically. She meant it. Jenny's heart began to flutter. Kathryn's gaze never wavered, but soon it was obscured by dancing couples. Jenny did the next best thing and closed her eyes, concentrating on the very personal declaration as her heart soared. Kathryn loved her.

A sudden unwelcome cloud of smoke assaulted her senses, and Jenny looked up to see the disgruntled saxophone player standing in front of her with her hands on her hips and a cigarette dangling from the corner of her overpainted red mouth.

"Do you mind?" Jenny said, trying to peer around the obstacle. The redhead was no friend of Kathryn's, and Jenny could tell by her demeanor that she certainly wasn't there to have a pleasant conversation.

"Don't mind if I do," the musician said, sliding into the booth as if they were old friends. She took a drag on her cigarette and exhaled it through her nose like a dragon. "What's your name, sweet thing?"

"Jenny," she answered warily. She was annoyed with the woman's condescending manner and even more annoyed with her intrusion, which was interrupting a dream come true. Jenny looked to the stage, where between dancing bodies, she could see Kathryn continuing the song with a dangerous look on her face. If looks could kill, the saxophone player would be one of those tiny piles of ash her cigarette was leaving on the table.

"Get her," the redhead said, motioning toward the stage, "watching over you like a mama bear watches her cub."

Jenny smiled, letting Kathryn know she felt safe and protected. Not even the acerbic pariah was going to get to her tonight.

"You know why they call this the Mayfly, don't you?" the redhead offered without invitation.

Jenny glared back blankly. She wasn't going to give her the satisfaction of a reaction.

The musician smirked at her resolve and then continued, "Because some species only live a few days, and that's about as long as most relationships last around here." She took a drag on her smoke and smiled a diabolical little smile, as if it were the grandest joke ever told.

Jenny countered with a wicked smile of her own. "And here I thought it was because some species reproduce parthenogenetically."

A crease of annoyed confusion clouded the redhead's brow.

"That means there are no males involved," Jenny said, enjoying the point for her.

The musician recovered quickly, evident from the ever-present smirk finding its way back to her face. "Well, get you. A real brainiac." She became annoyed. "You're no better than the rest of us, sweet thing, and you'll fare no better either."

Jenny did her best to ignore her, looking to the stage instead, wishing she could see more of Kathryn through the throng of dancing women.

"She'll take what she wants," the musician went on, "which ain't your mind, honey, believe me, and she'll leave you flat, with a handful of nothin' to keep you warm at night." She paused to take another drag on her cigarette and then raised her chin and narrowed her eyes on her exhale, looking for any chink in her armor.

"What's she get from you?"

Jenny snapped her eyes to the annoying woman, showing a reaction for the first time, and she regretted it immediately, as the vindictive redhead seemed to feed on it.

"Kat doesn't give it away for free, sweetie," the woman said. "She's getting something, and when she's through—" She looked Jenny up and down, as an idea interrupted her thought. "Say, are you rich?" She looked at Jenny's sensible suit. "Nah. Just lucky."

Jenny's jaw clenched, as she tried not to respond, but it only made matters worse.

"She bats from both sides of the plate, you know. You're the dolly of the week, and next week it'll be some Joe. That's how she got that fancy job of hers, you know … laid the boss's son. Might have even laid the boss. Who knows?" She glanced over her shoulder. "Wouldn't put it past her. Slut."

Jenny focused on the stage, but she couldn't see anything but red.

Rage boiled inside her—lies, all lies. She knew it wasn't true, and she was furious that this woman was saying such things. Restraining her anger made her blood pressure rise until her hearing dimmed, and she was sure her flared nostrils gave her away even as the lies continued.

"She brings all her new playthings here, you know." The redhead flicked her cigarette, and the ashes landed on the table. "Sings 'em that song. Makes 'em feel special." She took a drag and released a condescending exhale.

Jenny tried to remain silent, but the remarks had found their mark, and she'd had enough. She shifted her gaze to her tormentor. "If you must know, *I* brought her to this club. If she had her way, she wouldn't step foot in this place, and, frankly, I don't blame her. Now, I don't want to be rude … I really don't … but I'm trying to enjoy an evening with my girl, and you're a wrench in the works, so beat it."

The redhead smirked, pleased that she'd struck a chord. "Take it easy, sister, I understand. Heck, I'd fight for her too." She offered a glance at the stage. "She's the best lay you'll ever have." She leaned in. "Don't think for one minute she'll let you in, though."

She was punctuating the air with her cigarette hand, and the smoke burned Jenny's eyes and nose.

"And if you know what's good for you, you won't let her in either," the woman went on. She took a drag on her cigarette, exhaling as she spoke, "And if you do, don't ever let on that you're serious. She'll leave you so fast, you'll wonder if she was ever really there at all." She paused dramatically, making sure her poison was seeping in. "She doesn't have a heart, you know, and emotions … tst!" She rolled her eyes dramatically, leaving the remark unfinished.

The words were bitter, and Jenny recognized the relationship-gone-bad venom. She almost felt pity for the woman, but it didn't last long, as the vindictive redhead leaned back with a smug grin.

"That's why she sings, you know. Emotionally constipated." The woman raised a victorious brow, as if revealing a sacred secret. "If she can't sing it, you won't hear it." She flicked an annoyed ash and mumbled, "Lazy fuck."

It was one of the first things Kathryn admitted in a vulnerable moment, and any sympathy Jenny had for the saxophone player quickly vanished when she used the personal information as a weapon.

"You know," Jenny finally said, having heard enough, "I'm sorry you're having such a hard time moving on, but I'm not your damn therapist, and I'm not really interested in anything you have to say regarding Kathryn Hammond."

"I'm just trying to help you out here, sister," the musician remarked casually. "Save you some heartache."

Jenny leaned in. "Listen. You're a vindictive fucking bitch. I'm not your sister, and I'm not your sweet thing, and I'd really appreciate it if you'd take your smelly cigarette and your lying, troublemaking ass elsewhere."

The redhead raised her hands in defeat and slowly slid out of the booth, but not before she added a parting shot. "You'll never keep her, you know. Not her. Mark my words." The woman looked her up and down as if she couldn't imagine what Kathryn saw in her. "She'll take what she wants from you, and she'll leave you as quickly as she came." She took another drag from her cigarette and watched her carnage take effect through the ensuing smoke. "Besides," she said with a smirk, "you're definitely not her type." She looked at Kathryn, who was now glaring at her, and then back to Jenny, who had the same murderous stare. The musician laughed. "Definitely not."

Jenny watched the obnoxious redhead saunter away and disappear into the crowded club. As much as she hated to admit it, the woman had laid out the sum of all her fears. She couldn't imagine what Kathryn Hammond was doing with her. She quickly squelched her doubt, realizing it was precisely the effect the hateful musician had intended. She closed her eyes instead and listened to Kathryn's smooth vocals send the final lines of a very clear message.

"Now leave me alone and play me something I can dance to," Kathryn said over her shoulder to the band as she left the stage. Lani laughed and instructed the ladies to begin the mellow swing lines of "Manhattan Serenade." Kathryn smiled and lifted a hand of thanks without turning around.

Jenny greeted her with a wide smile when she returned to the table, and Kathryn was glad to see the saxophone player's venom hadn't gotten under her skin. She returned the smile and held out her hand. "Dance with me, you."

"Thought you'd never ask," Jenny said, as she slid out of the booth and into her waiting arms.

Kathryn's body hummed as they became one, and she reveled in their embrace before kissing Jenny's hand and assuming a dancing posture. She seemed stiff in her arms.

"I hope you didn't listen to anything she said."

Jenny looked at the floor.

Kathryn ducked her head until she found stormy green eyes trying to deny their rage.

"I know," Jenny said. "She's a jackass. Sour grapes, that's all."

"That's my girl." Kathryn smiled as she held her close and they began to sway to the slow rhythm of the song.

"Exes," Jenny said into her chest, as their feet began to move in time to the music. "What were we thinking, right?"

Kathryn chuckled. "She's not an ex. She got me a job with the band here a very long time ago. Thought that entitled her to something. I disagreed."

"Really sour grapes then."

"Mm, a whole rotten vineyard."

Jenny relaxed into Kathryn's arms, reprimanding herself for letting the bitter musician get to her. She closed her eyes as their bodies pressed together and the rest of the room fell away. Kathryn's bare back burned under her hand, and memories of their one night together came flooding back. Her body warmed with desire, and she fought to keep her hand from wandering. Dancing was the closest thing to making love that you could get away with in public, and she was proud to show this crowd—especially this crowd—that they were in love. She still found it unbelievable. They were in love. That glorious revelation, coupled with the sensuous motion of their dance, would almost guarantee an early exit from the club.

She wondered when exactly Kathryn had fallen. Kathryn loved her. She wanted to say it over and over and hear it over and over. She wondered if she would. Could Kathryn bring herself to say it or only when the proper song presented itself? It shouldn't have mattered. She was sure she got the message right the first time, but love Kathryn Hammond style was still a mystery, and she was curious as to what she could expect.

"Nice song," she said, starting to probe.

A hum of agreement.

"Did you choose that for me?"

"Just for you."

"Did you mean it?"

"Every word."

For Jenny, the conversation held the promise of words not yet spoken, but her heart sank a little at each distracted response. She understood Kathryn had a hard time expressing herself, but she had to be sure of Kathryn's intentions before she confessed her own. She regretted that the redhead's warning played a role in her apprehension. She knew Kathryn was doing the best she could, but her brief answers weren't exactly a declaration of love, so she decided to step off the edge of the cliff and just have out with it.

She bravely lifted her head. "Did you just tell me that you loved me?"

For a moment, Kathryn didn't respond, and Jenny stopped breathing, hoping her pounding heart wouldn't drown out the answer. Kathryn stopped dancing and gently stroked her cheek. "I guess I did."

Jenny was no longer falling. She was floating. She closed her eyes in relief until two hands cupped her face and Kathryn quickly took back her words.

"No." Tender affection suddenly turned serious. "I know I did."

Humble blue eyes looked deeply into hopeful green eyes. "I love you."

Jenny froze. She didn't know whether it was the intensity of the emotion in Kathryn's eyes or the ease with which the exalted words fell from her lips, but it took her by surprise, and she was speechless.

She watched Kathryn's brow begin to knit in concern, and Jenny realized she was blowing her long-awaited moment. "I love you too," she blurted out defensively.

Kathryn's concern turned to amusement and they both laughed. She kissed her on the forehead with as much gratitude as affection and pulled her close.

At that moment, Jenny was glad that she didn't kiss her on the lips, because if she had, she would have started something that couldn't be finished on a dance floor. She held Kathryn tighter, and they began to dance again. "I love you too," she repeated, this time from the heart. She was rewarded with a kiss on the head, which made her smile. "This is my new favorite song."

Kathryn hummed her approval and began singing softly into her ear.

After their declaration of love, and now Kathryn's warm breath caressing her ear, Jenny thought she would pass out. She melted even further into the strong arms holding her and warned, "Keep doing that and I'm going to take you right here, I swear to Howard."

Kathryn grinned and backed off. "And that's supposed to make me stop?"

"Ugh." Jenny buried her head into her chest. "Give me strength."

Kathryn tightened her hold and began to hum the tune.

"Kat," Jenny drew out as a warning.

"I'm not singing, I'm humming."

"Both produce the same result, and we're a long way from home."

Kathryn stopped dancing. "Maybe we'd better get a move on, then."

Jenny smiled and started to dance again. "We just got here, and you owe me a dance."

"You're right." Kathryn held her closer and began to sing into her ear again.

It took exactly one line before Jenny had her by the hand and they were heading toward the exit.

"Wait," Kathryn pleaded in mock distress as she was pulled along, "I haven't introduced you to my friends."

"Hi ya, nice to meet you. Yes, I'm of legal age, must away," Jenny said to the air, not bothering to slow down. They beat a hasty retreat back the way they came, and Jenny didn't wait for Kathryn to negotiate the steps to the sidewalk before she was two steps into the street, hand in the air.

"Taxi!!"

The taxi ride to Kathryn's apartment wasn't long, but it felt like the longest ride of Jenny's life. Her body was thrumming in anticipation of their second night together, and she couldn't suppress her stupid grin. She glanced at Kathryn, expecting the same, but her face was a mask of indifference as she stared vacantly into the distance, her head bobbing loosely with the motion of the cab.

Jenny gently squeezed the hand in hers, which caused Kathryn to look at her and, to Jenny's relief, smile. The enamored look was back, but it was tempered by something else—she swore it was sadness. She tilted her head, questioning the mood, and Kathryn indicated it was nothing with a slight shake of the head and a reassuring smile. Jenny knew that wasn't true, but unable to discuss it openly, the truth would have to wait. Little did she know how long it would have to wait.

As they climbed the steps to Kathryn's apartment, Jenny had a sinking feeling. Something had changed dramatically from the club to this moment. She briefly entertained the notion that the redhead was right: confess your love and Kathryn will bolt. They'd hardly said two words to each other from the club to home, but Kathryn never let go of her hand in the cab. Jenny dusted off her patience and reminded herself to just let Kathryn find her way.

Kathryn uttered a mild curse as she dropped her keys at her doorstep and frowned in annoyance as she held the ring up to the dimmed streetlight to find the one for her front door.

Letting Kathryn find her way was one thing, but letting something eat at her that seemed to be making matters worse was another. She waited until she'd found the proper key and forced it into the lock before voicing her concern.

"Please tell me you're not having second thoughts."

Kathryn turned with a furrowed brow. "I love you, Jenny. That's not going to change." She unlocked the door, proceeded up the stairs, and entered her apartment, with Jenny following closely behind.

"But are you having second thoughts?" Jenny said, a little panicked.

"I don't think I can."

"What does that mean?"

Kathryn gently put down her keys on the bookcase beside the door and stepped further into the room, shedding her coat as she went. "It doesn't matter."

Jenny wasn't going to let a statement like that go. She shut the door and darted in front of Kathryn, taking her arm when she tried to brush past. "What does that mean?"

"That means I love you, and I don't think I could stop if I tried."

Jenny was more confused than ever at the shift in mood but recognized that Kathryn had just left herself open as an easy mark for heartbreak, should one choose to exploit it. She gently took her hand. "Then don't try."

Kathryn looked away.

"Don't try," Jenny said, seeking her downturned eyes. She grabbed her by the shoulders until she faced her. "There's no reason to try."

Kathryn exhaled and sat on the couch. "There's so much you don't know. The things I've done—"

Jenny sat beside her and put her hands on both sides of her face, forcing her to look into her eyes. "I don't care who you were. I don't care what you've done. I know who you are now, and I love you. Please let me."

The weight of Kathryn's past settled between them like an unwelcome chaperone. Jenny was determined to make their relationship seem less daunting.

"One day at a time, Kat," she said. "I don't care what happens tomorrow, or next week, or next year."

It was a lie, but a lie Kathryn seemed willing to accept. Her pained expression turned to consideration.

Jenny pressed on. "We've been blessed with this night." She stroked her warm cheek and smiled. "The night you told me you loved me." She pressed her forehead against Kathryn's. "I love you. The world is hard enough. This doesn't have to be hard. This is our night ... our time together. Let's take it." For a moment, Jenny thought her words were getting through, but Kathryn leaned back and regretfully shook her head.

"Jenny—"

"It doesn't matter," Jenny interrupted, "I don't care."

Frustrated, Kathryn stood abruptly. "Stop saying that."

Jenny stood in frustration as well. "Why?"

"Because I want to believe it!" Kathryn snapped.

They both stared at each other, and the room became painfully silent, as the walls absorbed the terse words. How did they go from I love yous to another argument?

Kathryn closed her eyes and bowed her head, clearly blaming herself. Jenny put a comforting arm around her shoulder and pulled her close. "Believe it," she whispered, "please, believe it." She took her hand and kissed it. "I love you." She kissed the inside of her wrist. "Nothing else matters." Kathryn slowly raised her head and Jenny tenderly kissed her neck. "I love you." Her lips brushed her jawline on the way to her mouth, and she gently kissed her lips before pulling back and looking into her eyes. "I love you."

Kathryn closed her eyes as if she were burning the words into her memory. "I love you too."

"Then—"

"But—" She held up her hand. "There are things you need to know."

"God, Kathryn," Jenny said, as she turned away and put her hand to her forehead.

Kathryn put a hand on her back. "Are you afraid of the truth?"

Jenny turned with tears in her eyes. "I'm afraid you're going to push me away before we even have a chance to get started!"

Kathryn gathered her into her arms. "Please don't cry." She rocked her gently and kissed her head. "Please don't. It's not like that. I'm not trying to push you away."

"I don't understand."

"I know. I'm sorry. Please don't cry."

Jenny wiped her tears and backed off. "I know what I need to know. I don't care about your past."

"I do." Kathryn held out her hand. "Give me your jacket."

She was staying. Jenny reasoned that was progress. She slipped out of her suit jacket and handed it over. Kathryn placed it on the back of the chair and led her by the hand into the kitchen.

Jenny sat at the kitchen table and watched Kathryn move gracefully through the task of making tea. No words were spoken, something Jenny was finding an unfortunate norm, but she could see the wheels turning in Kathryn's head as she plotted the course of her confession. Whatever she was going to tell her loomed larger and larger until she questioned her own ability to accept it. What if it was horrible? What if she *couldn't* accept it? Would she walk away? Could she? The silence, and her imagination, were taking its toll.

"You're scaring me."

Kathryn smiled, though Jenny could tell levity was not the intent. "Sometimes I scare myself."

She poured two cups of tea and presented one to Jenny as she sat across from her at the table. "Stiff drinks for dessert, should it prove necessary," she said with a grin.

It was her first attempt at humor since their evening went terribly awry, and while Jenny appreciated the effort, its effect was lost, thanks to her own growing trepidation.

Kathryn acknowledged her stricken look with a tight-lipped smile but didn't reach out to comfort her. She clasped her hands around her cup and focused on it.

Kathryn chewed her lip for a moment, doubting the wisdom of her next move, but Jenny deserved to know what she was getting into, and there was no moving forward without disclosure. There was no easy way to say it either, no casual "start at the beginning and work your way up to it" sugarcoating that would soften the sordid details. She could only hope that Jenny could get past it or, at the very least, understand and not judge her. In the absence of wisdom, she found courage and cleared her throat.

"As you can imagine," she began, "it was very hard for me after my mother died." She stared into her cup of tea, finding the steaming sienna pool less intimidating than Jenny's questioning eyes. "Then discovering my dad was responsible—" She absently turned the cup. "I couldn't be at home any longer."

"You ran away," Jenny said.

Kathryn lifted her eyes, surprised at the commentary. She'd forgotten that Jenny was an interactive listener. Her gaze returned to her cup, and she suppressed a smile. "Right. I ran away. I had to get away from the lies, away from the pain. I had no money of my own, so I stole some from my dad and I came here to the city. He would never find me, and no one would know who I was or what I'd been through. I could just melt into the city and start over." She glanced up and smiled, remembering her naiveté. "My plan was to be a pianist, like my mother."

Jenny smiled but remained silent.

"I auditioned at a gathering much like the one at the theater tonight. Fancied myself a child prodigy." She chuckled. "They did not. Something about a lack of discipline. They were right, though it was devastating at the time. My backup plan was singing. I was tall enough to pass for legal age, so I could get a job in a club, but it was hard to get your foot in the door, and by that time, I had run out of money."

She rubbed her forehead, as the memory of her desperation and the point of her monologue merged to bring the past to bear on the present. She traced the embossed flower design on the tablecloth with her finger. The pretty, delicate pattern was a stark contrast to the wreckage her life had become. She couldn't change the paths she'd chosen. She could only hope Jenny would forgive her for them.

"I met up with a fellow who promised to take care of me and open those doors." She focused on a flaw in the white material under her hand, rubbing its defect as if she could smooth it away. She likened it to her fateful decision when she sacrificed her childhood for the promise of a future. For Jenny's sake, she wished those wounds healed as well.

Jenny reached out and stilled her hand. "Kathryn."

Defensive blue eyes snapped up, still lost in the moment. "I was desperate. Angry. Afraid. I wasn't going back. I would have done anything, and I did."

Jenny leaned closer and took her hand in earnest. "You don't have to go on."

Kathryn questioned her tone. "You have to know, Jenny. It's important."

Jenny tightened her grip. "I do know, Kat. I've known for weeks."

Kathryn pulled her hand away as her brow knit in confusion. "That's impossible. No one knows. Not even Smitty."

The look on Jenny's face was one of apologetic guilt as she explained that the discovery came quite by accident, when Rico offered her a copy of her police record during the gun incident. It chronicled several arrests for prostitution and a smattering of other minor charges, spanning a relatively short period of time during her youth.

The explanation made sense, but the breach of privacy had her on her heels. "I was a minor. Those records are sealed."

Jenny nodded. "I know. I'm sorry. I shouldn't have read them."

Kathryn was more shocked than angry. Relief wasn't far behind. Jenny had known for weeks and was still here, still wanted her, still loved her. How could this be?

"And what else do you know?"

"Breaking and entering, trespassing as a juvenile, all dismissed, and most recently, caught in a gambling sting, related to your work with Forrester, I imagine. That's all."

Kathryn nodded, still not quite able to wrap her brain around the fact that Jenny knew and it didn't seem to matter. Not everything was in a police report, however, and not every decision was made out of desperation.

"When I lived in Paris—" She hesitated but knew she had to continue. "I couldn't make it as a singer." She looked Jenny in the eye, knowing this time it would be harder to forgive. "I did the same."

Jenny accepted it with downturned eyes, pursed lips, and a slightly raised brow.

"It was easy, and I was good at it," Kathryn added defensively, suddenly feeling judged.

Jenny looked up, obviously surprised at the animosity. "What do you want me to say to that?"

Kathryn paused. What did she want her to say? She expected her to be repulsed. Of course, who wouldn't be? But Jenny wasn't. True to her word, apparently it didn't matter. Kathryn pulled in her ball and chain of self-recrimination and questioned her own revulsion. That part of her past had never bothered her. She never viewed her body as some sacred temple to be valued and protected. She learned early on that her body was power, a means to an end, and in that regard, it never failed to deliver. She enjoyed wielding that power: the thrill of the seduction, the triumph and satisfaction of her victim's surrender. But then Jenny came along, bringing goodness and laughter and unfamiliar concepts like love and forgiveness—it made her feel dirty. Her whole stinking life felt dirty. She covered the flaw in the tablecloth and closed her eyes. "I've never been ashamed of that before."

"You did what you had to do to survive, Kat. There's no shame in that."

"Isn't there?"

"Situations change. You're no longer in that place, and you are no longer that person."

"Look closer, Jenny. I haven't changed."

"You know that's not true."

"If I have sex for money, I'm a whore. If I have sex for the good of my country, I'm a hero? How does that work?"

Jenny looked away, and Kathryn could tell she was perplexed and annoyed. She couldn't blame her. She'd made it as easy as humanly possible for her to confess, and she'd accepted her choices without judgment, but Kathryn still couldn't believe Jenny wasn't shocked and disgusted. Before she could right the wrong, Jenny's patience reached its end.

"Why are you picking a fight with me? Would you rather I crucify you?"

Kathryn didn't answer, but at that moment, crucifixion seemed a lot easier than being in love. What made her think she was equipped for such an intimate pact? She got up and poured her tea into the sink. It disappeared down the drain, and she wondered if her elusive relationship was destined to follow.

Jenny rose aggressively. "Do you want a fight?"

"No," Kathryn said, as she breezed past on her way to the living room to regroup.

Jenny followed her. "Are you sure? Because I could stamp my feet and throw things if you like." Kathryn stopped and turned as Jenny carried on. "I could dramatically storm out of here, slamming doors as I go, but these shoes are killing me, and I don't have my car." She put her hands on her hips as if to say "Your move."

"Take mine," Kathryn said without hesitation. "Keys are by the door. Smitty will pick me up in the morning."

Jenny stared in disbelief. After all they'd been through—even after declaring their love—it seemed they'd made no progress. Kathryn was going to let her walk out the door. She'd lost count of how many times the woman had rendered her speechless. She'd been reduced to sporadic bouts of dazed blinking.

As if she finally realized how absurd the turn in their evening was, Kathryn's apathetic expression slowly morphed into an amused grin. She put a hand on her shoulder and then cupped her cheek. "I'm really sorry."

Jenny covered Kathryn's hand with her own and exhaled a sigh of relief. Kathryn would drive her mad yet. "What just happened, Kat?"

Kathryn shook her head. "I told you I was insecure. You didn't believe me."

Jenny believed her now. She kissed Kathryn's hand and tugged her toward the bathroom. "Come on. It's late. Let's have a soak and hit the sack." She kicked off her shoes and started down the hallway, unbuttoning her blouse as she went. "If I know the sun, it's going to rise tomorrow and we'll have a brand new day to argue about how much we love each other."

CHAPTER TWENTY

Kathryn propped herself up on her pillow and stared at Jenny's sleeping form. Moonlight suffused the room with an ethereal glow that lit the soft outline of Jenny's profile. Kathryn eyed the gentle curve of her lashes, the classic slope of her nose, and her beautiful lips, parted in sleep. She had to be the most good-natured, tolerant person she'd ever met, but even saints have their limits, and Jenny had reached hers. Despite the jovial end to their evening, Jenny was bathed and on her way to bed with barely a word. Kathryn followed meekly behind, sensing she'd reversed field once too often.

Repeated questions about the silence brought on repeated assertions that she was just tired, but Kathryn knew there was more to it than that when Jenny gave her a platonic kiss goodnight and promised she'd be ready for round two in the morning. Kathryn felt terrible. She'd reduced her lover to a prizefighter and their love affair to a sparring match. She didn't know enough about giving or letting go to make Jenny happy. She knew that about herself, but it never mattered before.

She briefly wished their affair were relegated to just sex, per Jenny's original proposal, but it had never been just about sex for either of them. The memory of how it felt to make love, when all she'd known was meaningless sex, left her wanting more. Needing more. That need filled her heart, overwhelmed her senses, and displaced selfish thought until all she wanted to do was give. Why then, when Jenny was ready to offer the same, did she sabotage the opportunity?

A tear fell when she realized she was afraid. She feared the longing in her soul. It made her vulnerable, and she needed strength for what lay ahead. This love affair would end, sooner rather than later, and it would hurt both of them. Her pain she would absorb, but she didn't want that for Jenny. She should stop this now while Jenny still had a way out. Maybe she'd found that way out tonight. Maybe she was done and her comment about round two in the morning was the final blow.

Kathryn ached to reach out and touch what she'd thrown away, but when she lifted her hand toward Jenny, she imagined her touch like that of a succubus, sucking the life and joy from her lover until nothing was left but eternal damnation. She returned her hand to her pillow and looked away, realizing it had become a self-fulfilling prophecy.

She stared out the window at the moon, trapped behind the tangled limbs of the lone tree on her block. She likened it to her heart: aching to escape but unable to find its way clear of the mire. She didn't know what to do. She couldn't let Jenny go, but she couldn't keep her either. Maybe Jenny would do the hard work for her and end things. She bit down on her raw emotions and let the silent tears fall.

Jenny felt a tear brush her shoulder. She looked up into Kathryn's pained face and caught the next tear before it fell with a gentle hand to her cheek. "Oh, Kat. Is it so terribly hard for you?"

Kathryn swallowed and wiped the emotion from her face with an impatient hand. "I'm sorry. I didn't mean to wake you." She rolled onto her back with an apathetic sniff and stared at the ceiling.

Jenny rolled toward her, placing a hand on her bare shoulder. "Talk to me. What's wrong?"

She heard Kathryn swallow again before she spoke. "I wish I was better for you. Cleaner. Stronger." She paused. "You deserve that. You deserve—"

"Kathryn—" Jenny sat up, realizing she couldn't defeat Kathryn's Pollyanna image of her as a naïve innocent needing protection from her deep, dark past. "This is madness. You can't change your past, and I'm not asking you to. I accept you for who you are. I don't know what the hell—" She stopped and exhaled, closing her eyes against her frustrated outburst.

"You asked me what was wrong," Kathryn snapped, as she sat up and tried to throw off the sheets to escape.

Jenny stopped her retreat with a quick slide to Kathryn's side of the bed and a firm hand on her shoulder. She sensed they were at a crossroads. They would move forward from here, or this would be the end. She didn't want it to be the end, but something had to give. She moved in from behind and offered her apology in a tender embrace. Kathryn accepted it, albeit stiffly, and Jenny waited to speak until she felt Kathryn's frustration subside. She laid her cheek on her shoulder blade, willing her to let her in. "Are you afraid?"

Kathryn released a controlled exhale. "I don't want to hurt you, Jenny."

Jenny repositioned herself so that she was facing her and cupped her cheek in her hand. She could see just enough of Kathryn's eyes in the moonlight to know she was looking at her. "Honey, the only thing hurting me is you trying not to hurt me."

She saw Kathryn's acceptance in her downturned gaze.

"You can't live like that, Kat. You certainly can't love like that." Jenny paused. Moment of truth. "I can't love like that."

That got Kathryn's attention, and her eyes snapped up, widened in panic.

It broke Jenny's heart to see Kathryn's fear, but this was supposed to be the easy part. You both declare your love and the honeymoon phase begins. Kathryn was standing in her own way. Jenny couldn't just ignore that and expect it would change.

She looked deeply into Kathryn's eyes and hoped she could see all the love she had for her there. "As much as I love you, I can't go on like this."

She swore Kathryn stopped breathing, but she could see her pulse pounding in the hollow of her throat. She did what Jenny expected her to do. She raised her chin and became defensive. "What are you saying?"

Jenny shook her head, weary of the pattern. Kathryn was closing up again. They were never going to make it without trust. "Give us a chance, honey, please. We love each other. This is ridiculous."

After a few defiant beats, Kathryn bowed her head, her face like stone under Jenny's hand.

"I don't know how to love," she finally said in a voice heavy with regret.

Jenny leaned in until their foreheads touched, relieved she'd gotten through. She stroked Kathryn's hair, trying to ease her self-doubt. "You said you loved me. Do you?"

Kathryn quickly raised her head, obviously finding the question absurd.

"Yes," she said, strong and confident.

Jenny suppressed a thankful smile. "Then you know how here—" She put her hand over Kathryn's heart. "You just have to *learn* how here." She gently kissed her tortured, misguided head.

"Ah," Kathryn drew out, "there's the rub."

Jenny smiled. "Well, let's not bring rubbing into this just yet."

Kathryn exhaled a chuckle but fell silent again. When she spoke, it was in a whisper. "Do you have the patience to teach me?"

Jenny's heart melted when Kathryn dropped her guard. She reached out and took her hand. "Do you have the courage to let me?"

Kathryn raised her eyes. Did she have the courage to love? She didn't know, but she knew she didn't have the courage not to. Jenny had stolen her heart while she wasn't looking and held it ransom with her persistence. Her normal checklist of how and why was lost in the realization that she had no choice but to surrender. Action absent an alternative was blameless, and, suddenly, falling in love was acceptable, and now that it was acceptable, a necessity. Miracle of miracles, she was getting yet another chance, and she was going to take it—no, she was going to give.

She brought Jenny's hand to her lips and kissed it before bowing her head and pressing her cheek against her palm in a silent thank-you. Whatever brought her to this absolution, this person, this place, where the past had no power, it humbled her. Speech failed her, so she did the only other thing she could do—she sought Jenny's lips instead. Her kiss was tentative at first, sure of herself and her intentions, but not of the breadth of Jenny's pardon.

Jenny quickly dispelled any reservations when she eagerly accepted her answer. The ensuing kiss delivered her message more succinctly than words ever could.

Kathryn took Jenny in her arms and eased her back on the bed. Healing, desire, and need took over, and Jenny's throaty response to her body weight settling above her and the weight of her breasts caressing her rigid excitement blinded her to everything else.

Kathryn didn't know what had taken her so long to find her way home, but whatever it was deserted her like a restless bird in the face of an open cage, when fear turned to trust and years of carefully crafted defenses crumbled.

She felt free, unencumbered, caring only for the woman in her arms and the overwhelming need to have all of her and give her everything. This was what it was like to adore someone, she realized. Her whole body craved Jenny's attention, and the emotional awakening heightened the need to touch and be touched. Her usual appetite for aggressive sex, normally fueled by anger, was replaced by an urgent desire to give her lust, her body, her heart, her soul. Her longing verged on desperation, and it was reflected in her hungry kiss. Jenny was taking it, and giving in kind, but the reckless abandon frightened Kathryn in its intensity. She was losing herself, losing control.

She pulled back, her breath uneven, her eyes dark and searching for the mystical power that had bewitched her so completely. Jenny had never seemed more beautiful or inviting.

Jenny's labored breathing caught as she questioned the faltering action. For a moment, she feared the worst, and she reached up and tucked Kathryn's long hair behind her ear to reveal her face in the moonlight. To her relief, behind the raw passion, she saw purpose, vulnerability, and awe. "I love you," Kathryn whispered to her. She sounded surprised. Under their heaving chests, Jenny swore their hearts were beating as one, and she smiled. "I know."

After another passionate kiss, Jenny was left gasping for more as Kathryn slid lower, dragging her cheek along her chest and then across an erect nipple.

Jenny tangled her fingers in Kathryn's hair and moaned her approval as warm lips enveloped the most sensitive part of her breast and strong hands possessed them. She sucked in a sharp breath as playful teeth and then a soothing tongue teased her nipple.

She clutched Kathryn's back and moaned her approval. "God, yes, don't stop." Being wholly possessed was intoxicating. She was never one for rough sex. It always came across as demeaning and vindictive, but Marcella was her only experience with it, so she considered the source and realized this was decidedly different. Kathryn's insatiable need for her set her body aflame with heightened desire, and she found the more forcefully she consumed her, the more she wanted it, wanted her, and wanted to return it in kind.

Kathryn slid her body the length of her open thighs, painting a trail of kisses down her heaving abdomen. Jenny pulled on Kathryn's retreating shoulders. "I need you here," she said, guiding Kathryn back to her mouth. Their bodies became a writhing puzzle of entwined limbs. She wanted to see Kathryn's face, see the depth of her wild desire.

Kathryn quickly retraced her path up her body and captured her lips in a kiss so desperate that Jenny knew Kathryn was hers, body and soul. They were connected like never before, and she drank in every unspoken word from Kathryn's lips until love was a given and passion stole her reason. She needed to feel Kathryn's surrender, her trust, her acceptance. She wrapped a leg tightly around the small of her back and reversed their positions. She looked down into Kathryn's eyes, thankful to find not only a willingness to submit but understanding as well.

She was on her knees, straddling Kathryn's undulating hips. She leaned forward and resumed their passionate kiss, but her lust was raw now, and the throbbing at her center became an aching need. She stopped kissing long enough to say "Touch me."

Kathryn slipped her hand between her parted thighs and slowly glided her long fingers through her wet, swollen folds. Jenny moaned from deep in her throat and her mouth fell away from their kiss. "*Yes*," she uttered in a breathless whisper. Gentle but firm strokes pulled sounds from her that grew more and more insistent until she couldn't hold on any longer. "Inside. I need you inside."

Kathryn slipped her fingers deep inside, and a wave of pleasure shuddered through her body, eliciting an unintelligible cry that ended in "God, *yes!*"

Kathryn didn't move for a beat, for which Jenny was thankful, because she would have come on the spot, and she wanted this feeling to last. She attempted to resume their kiss, but Kathryn started drawing her fingers in and out in a slow, steady rhythm, and Jenny went weak with every deliberate stroke. Her forehead fell limply onto Kathryn's shoulder, and she just rocked and moaned with the languid waves of pleasure.

She was quickly losing coherent thought and the ability to reciprocate. She lifted her head to protest but was stopped by the sight of Kathryn's face, so open and giving, eyes filled with desire and a longing to please. There was nothing to do but let her take her.

. . .

Kathryn sensed an impending objection and slowed her movements, but Jenny passed on the chance to complain. The rapture in her half-lidded eyes sent the message her voice could no longer convey.

Kathryn eased out, recognizing that Jenny wasn't quite ready to climax. She slid her fingers along her slick folds, pressing and teasing until staccato affirmations became one long, pleasurable moan and she begged to be filled again. Kathryn denied her, taking perverse pleasure in her delicious torture, wringing out every ounce of erotic delight until guttural sounds of pleasure gave way to unabashed pleading.

Kathryn knew there was a fine line between a merciless tease that enhanced pleasure and a premature orgasm that muted it, and she read Jenny perfectly as she slipped her fingers into her again and gave her what she wanted.

Jenny cried out in relief, and her vocal appreciation grew with every plunging stroke. She sat up straight and thrust her hips forward to take all Kathryn had to offer. Kathryn intensified her pace, giving her no reprieve from pleasure.

Jenny reached back and clutched Kathryn's raised thighs. She threw her head back and drove her hips forward, faster and harder, as Kathryn ground deeper and deeper into her. She gave her weight to Kathryn's hip and hand, and they became one with the fluid rhythm that matched their hastened breathing.

With each thrust, Jenny's passionate cries intensified, and Kathryn knew she would come soon. Kathryn felt her own release building, and her gasps and moans joined Jenny's as they pushed each other to the height of pleasure and into madness.

Jenny reached for her, still trying to participate, but Kathryn stopped her. "*No.* Just feel me loving you."

Jenny gave in and just held on.

Kathryn slowly pressed her thumb to Jenny's swollen center, eliciting a cry that resonated somewhere between pain and pleasure.

Jenny bucked her hips to escape the intensity. "Not yet," she managed between gasps and tried to reach for Kathryn again.

Kathryn ended that effort when she made a final deep plunge and

Jenny had taken all of her. She curled her fingers inside, pressing hard against the ridged wall beneath the pads of her fingertips. Jenny cried out at the intense pleasure and arched her back as her body strained to remain upright.

Kathryn massaged the spot and watched Jenny lose herself to unrestrained gasps of rhythmic pleasure. She was beautiful, lost in ecstasy, and Kathryn felt a warm rush of desire as the engorged flesh between her legs ached for release.

Jenny rode her, harder and faster, while her cries rose into a crescendo of bliss. Jenny's arching body at the end of her hands brought Kathryn to the edge of her climax. "Come with me," she urged desperately, as she was losing control. "Come—"

They cried out their release together, and Jenny clutched Kathryn's hands to her as she rode out the spasms. Soon, heavy breathing and involuntary whimpers on every exhale turned into sighs of gratification as Jenny collapsed at her side. Kathryn reflexively settled her arm across Jenny's hips, and neither could manage words or further movement for a few heart-pounding moments.

Jenny licked her dry lips as her breathing slowly evened out, and she rolled toward her. "God, you're easy," she said with a chuckle, referring to her lack of participation in Kathryn's release.

Kathryn grinned between ragged breaths as she welcomed her into her open arms. "I figured I'd better make something easy. Heaven knows nothing else has been."

Jenny rested her head contentedly over Kathryn's still wildly beating heart. "That's all over. We're together now."

Kathryn hesitated, wondering if it really was that easy. She felt Jenny's lashes tickle her skin when she opened her eyes and waited for a reply.

She lifted her head and looked up. "That's all over now, right?"

"We're together now," Kathryn said with a kiss on the forehead.

She knew she couldn't promise smooth sailing ahead, but they were together, and they would meet the roadblocks head on, side by side, from now on. They had shared so much in the past few days. It seemed she'd known Jenny a lifetime. She felt safe in her care, safe in her arms, safe in the knowledge that this was someone she could trust with her heart. *We're together now.* She smiled. She felt lighter, unburdened, if only for these few moments. She turned her head toward the window to give hope to the entangled moon, but it was gone—freed like her heart—pulled from its trap by a force of nature it could not deny. Kathryn kissed her force of nature on the head and whispered, "I love you, Jenny."

Jenny lifted her head and slid her body forward until she was hovering over Kathryn's face. "I love you too." She reached out and stroked her face. "Do you know, Kathryn? Do you know I would never hurt you? Do you know you're safe?"

Kathryn knew there were no guarantees, but Jenny was looking into her soul, promising everything, and there was nowhere to hide from her most fervent wish. "Yes."

Jenny kissed her, sealing her words *and* their fates. The kiss slowly turned from promise to passion, reigniting a slow-burning desire, as Jenny caressed and kissed her way down Kathryn's humming body.

"God, I *am* easy," Kathryn said with a chuckle and surrendered utterly.

CHAPTER TWENTY-ONE

Smitty climbed the stairs to Kathryn's apartment and wondered what awaited him upstairs. He wasn't accustomed to running afoul of her, but ever since Jenny Ryan entered their lives, it had happened far too often for his comfort. Kathryn's personal happiness was important, but it was only a matter of time before it affected her professional life, and that was unacceptable, for obvious reasons.

"Jenny Ryan," he groused under his breath as he got to the landing.

What was the kid thinking? Did she really think she could come between them? Smitty shook his head at the notion. That would never happen. They had shared things Jenny couldn't even begin to comprehend. Kathryn had been angry, that much was certain, but she was not an unreasonable woman. Surely she had to know he was only looking after her best interests? Of course she would. In the light of a new day, everything would be forgiven. Just like always.

He was expected, so he wrapped out his customary knock on the door and let himself in. "Hi ya, doll," he said cheerfully.

"Good morning, Smitty," Kathryn offered indifferently as she exited her bedroom and headed to the kitchen.

So much for being forgiven. There was no *hi, handsome,* no kiss on the cheek, just a dismissive *Good*—

"Good morning, Smitty," Jenny parroted, as she came out of Kathryn's bedroom buttoning one of Kathryn's crisp white shirts over her skirt.

He glanced at Kathryn's back and then to the smiling blonde and ground out a slightly off-balance, "Morning."

He didn't know why he was surprised to see Jenny. He should have known something screwy was going on when Kathryn ditched his tail the night before. He knew she had a gig with Tommy Wallace in the city, but he hadn't considered that she would dodge his protection, so he didn't ask where, expecting just to follow her. He would not make that mistake again.

"What, do you keep him in the cellar, Kat?" Jenny said with a smile.

"There's an idea," Kathryn said, as she deposited her cup in the sink.

Smitty took off his hat and tossed it on the kitchen table and glared at her. Jenny noticed something was amiss and looked to Kathryn, who tried to pass it off as nothing, as she offered a smile on her way to the bathroom to brush her teeth.

"Are you still in the doghouse, Smitty?" Jenny whispered.

"Like you didn't know I would be," he said sternly.

"What?"

He moved in menacingly close. "Why did you tell her I told you about overseas?"

"Because you did, and I'm not going to lie to her."

He didn't like the accusation. "Oh, and *I* do?"

"Did you?"

She had him there, which made him angry. "Do not play games of manipulation with me. You will not win."

Jenny was undeterred by his threat and mustered her own menacing glare. "Kathryn is not a game to me."

Kathryn came out of the bathroom rolling down her sleeve. "Problem?"

Jenny looked to Smitty and tilted her head, letting him decide how it was going to be.

"No problem," he said curtly.

"Good," Kathryn said, absorbing the obvious lie as she passed.

Smitty offered a parting glare to Jenny before following his partner into the kitchen. "Rumor has it Forrester is coming back to town this week," he said casually, knowing the news would shake Jenny from her high horse.

Kathryn appeared unfazed as she emptied the filter cup from the coffeepot and replied with a bored, "Okay."

Smitty knew she was upset about it because she wiped an already clean counter with the dishrag until she had gathered herself sufficiently and then turned. When she finally looked at Jenny, her tight mouth and creased brow gave her away.

The phone rang, breaking the tense silence, and three sets of eyes snapped to the black unit on the small corner table next to the refrigerator. Taking note of the present company, they all knew it could only be one person. Kathryn dragged the phone and its long cord into the living room.

"Hello," she cooed sweetly into the handset.

Smitty and Jenny cast glances at each other and then stared vaguely at their feet as they listened to Kathryn's side of the conversation in the other room. "Oh, Marc, that's wonderful," they heard her say.

Jenny wasn't interested in enduring Smitty's triumphant smirk, one she was sure was there without looking, so she left the kitchen and headed down the short hallway to the bedroom. She glanced at Kathryn on the couch in the living room as she passed.

"Yes, darling," Kathryn said into the phone as she tucked her long legs under her while leaning on the sofa's oversized arm.

Jenny watched with amazement as Kathryn transformed into a pining mistress before her eyes. With a voice sickeningly sweet and her body language vulnerable, she cradled the handset like it was a lifeline to the man on the other end and she would drown without him.

Jenny sensed Smitty staring at her from the kitchen archway, and she gave him what she knew he wouldn't expect—a smile, as if she were proud of Kathryn's skilled acting. She continued toward the bedroom to gather her things, surprised that she didn't find the triumphant smirk on his face that she'd expected. Instead, she found solemn compassion and sympathy.

She circled Kathryn's room, looking for a wayward earring, and tried to put Kathryn's submissive image out of her mind. She found the earring behind a bottle of perfume on the vanity, where she had tossed it in a fit of frustration, along with its mate, the evening before. How quickly frustration had turned into the most beautiful night of her life, and how quickly the morning was stealing it away. She looked at her annoyed reflection in the mirror as she listened to the rise and fall of Kathryn's soothing voice luring Forrester into a false sense of dependency.

Jenny scolded herself for being annoyed, as Kathryn's forewarning of "Can you handle the business end of my life?" suddenly filled the room, making it hard to breathe. She promised she could, and now it was time to make good. She sat on the edge of the bed, the bed where they made love until the early morning hours, the bed where they held each other, shared their tears, bared their souls, the bed they made just an hour ago with full hearts and affectionate glances as they bathed in the peaceful serenity of their intimate sanctuary.

She closed her eyes and tried to harness the memory—something, anything—to give her the strength she'd need to show Kathryn she was up to the challenges they would have to face. If Kathryn felt half the sense of loss and anger she was feeling at the moment, she would need her to be strong, and that's what she swore she'd be. For Kathryn. For Love.

She didn't hear Kathryn hang up the phone, nor did she hear the floor creak as she stood in the doorway, silently watching, but when she opened her eyes, there she was. Jenny stood up, pretending to look for something. "I lost my earring," she said unconvincingly as she held it up. She was doing the best she could, but Kathryn saw through it.

Kathryn shut the door and crossed the room, gathering her into her arms. "I'm sorry."

"Don't do that," Jenny said. "Don't apologize. I'm okay." She backed off their embrace and clipped her earrings on, trying to be strong and understanding. "When?"

"Tonight. He's picking me up at the club after the show."

Jenny silently cursed the bastard. Disappointment made her movements stiff and abrupt. She scanned the room again to distract herself. "Where the hell's my watch?"

Kathryn picked it up from the nightstand, but instead of handing it over, she took her in her arms. "I'm disappointed too, honey. You don't have to play it tough."

Jenny melted into Kathryn's chest, exhaling her disappointment. "Now that I've got you, I don't want to let you go."

"I know the feeling."

They stood in the middle of the room, lost in the sway of their embrace, enjoying a moment removed from the unrelenting march of time.

The unrelenting march of time made itself known in the form of Jenny's incessantly ticking wristwatch in Kathryn's hand.

"I've got to go," Jenny mumbled into Kathryn's shirt collar.

Kathryn nodded regretfully and pulled back. She cupped Jenny's face and gazed deeply into her eyes. "I need to see you this afternoon. Will you take a late lunch? I know a place we can go."

"You just tell me where and when."

After a self-conscious goodbye under Smitty's watchful eye, Kathryn gently shut the front door and then moved to the apartment window to watch Jenny step onto the sidewalk and cross the street. Never had she imagined she could be so consumed with another human being, *by* another human being. Just a few short hours were all they shared, but in those hours, she had found more honesty and more emotional truth within herself than ever before. She was overwhelmed, reduced to tears more than once, and positively dumbfounded by the ease with which her soul entrusted its care to another.

Through it all, Jenny never faltered, never shied away from the raw display of pent-up emotion and relief that came with the dissolution of her carefully crafted defenses. Jenny seemed to thrive on it, to grow stronger, more confident. Kathryn had been freed by Jenny's compassion and sated by her desire. Love was nothing like she'd imagined. Her fear of feeling exposed and vulnerable proved unfounded, as she felt protected in Jenny's arms—safe, as promised.

She continued to gaze out the window until Jenny disappeared from sight, and she realized that nothing had really changed. Her guilt still lurked just below the surface, and her past still shaped her future, perhaps even condemned it. But somehow things were different. *She* was different. Braver. Stronger. Hopeful. Loved.

She heard Smitty move behind her and her mood quickly shifted, as she was brought back to the present and what lay ahead. She turned to face him with fury in her eyes. "You didn't have to say that in front of her."

Smitty held out his hands as if clueless. "What?"

"That Forrester was coming back to town."

"Well," Smitty said indignantly, "she'd better get used to it. You've got a job to do."

"She doesn't need to be reminded of my job, and neither do I."

"Kat—"

"Couldn't you give us just one fucking morning to be happy?" she shouted, eyes gone grey in anger. "Is that too much to ask?"

Smitty balked at her intensity, and the curse, which she knew he could count on one hand the number of times he'd heard come out of her mouth since he'd known her. She regretted that her outburst revealed how serious things had become with Jenny.

"I'm sorry, Kat, but she'd have to know sooner or later."

"She certainly didn't need to hear it from you."

Kathryn would have spared Jenny the news until after their

midday rendezvous, hoping to spend as much unspoiled time as possible with her before they had to face the reality of their responsibilities. Their time together was always precious—with a war raging, everyone's was—but never before had she felt the pressure more acutely than when she watched Jenny walk away from her, taking with her the fragile calm before the storm.

"Don't shoot the messenger," Smitty argued in his defense.

Kathryn collected her things and headed out the door. "Don't give me any ideas."

"Okay," Smitty began, unable to stand the silence any longer as they rode to the training center on Long Island, "I made that crack about Forrester out of spite."

Kathryn was unimpressed by the confession.

"I did it to knock her off her high horse, not to hurt you."

Why he thought that would appease her, she had no idea, but he was digging a hole he'd never get out of.

"I just didn't realize—"

"Now you do," she interrupted sharply.

Disparaging remarks about Jenny and lectures about the pitfalls of their relationship were unnecessary and beyond repetitious. Did he think her so fickle or incompetent? She could handle Forrester blindfolded—a look here, a touch there, a tender word, a well-timed tear. He was putty in her hands. Loving Jenny wouldn't change that. One thing had nothing whatsoever to do with the other.

His lack of faith in her stung, and his jealousy was pointless. They were professionals in a dangerous business. She didn't have the energy or the inclination to entertain his sophomoric indulgences or his doubts.

To hell with his misgivings. And for the moment, to hell with him.

Kathryn sat in Colonel Forsythe's office for a one-on-one conversation about her request for field training.

"I've looked over your request, Kathryn," Colonel Forsythe said gently, flicking the corner of the folder under his hand with his forefinger.

She straightened in her chair as the contemplative flicking stopped and he took a final look through her file and then closed it.

"What makes you think you're ready for this?"

"I can do this. I can."

He stared at her, waiting for a better explanation.

"I've been in the field and I know how to impart that knowledge to others. We're always shorthanded on agents in the specialty ops, and I know my experience is valuable." She could see she wasn't telling him anything he didn't already know. He wanted something deeper, more personal. She appreciated his position and gave him what he wanted. "The nightmares have stopped, and I haven't had a flashback in—" She glossed over her recent breakdown with a dismissive wave of her hand. "I don't know how long, and I'm ready. I'm not going to fall apart, I'm not going to screw up, and I'm not going to risk the safety of those kids on some reckless scheme that—"

"Whoa, whoa, whoa," the colonel interrupted as he held up his hands. "I'm not asking you to defend yourself, Kathryn. I know you're ready. I want to know why *you* think you're ready."

She paused, sorting out her answer. "I've been away too long. Hiding. It's about time I pulled my weight again. I owe them that."

Colonel Forsythe smiled sympathetically but disagreed. "You haven't been hiding, you've been healing. You do more than your part, and you don't owe those boys anything. You did nothing wrong."

"I didn't die. That's what I did wrong."

He was silent for a moment and turned his focus to the file under his folded hands. "That's a tough call, Kathryn."

"Yes, sir, it is."

She appreciated the fact that he didn't have a blanket denial for her statement. He could be counted on to deal with the reality of any particular situation. She failed at her first responsibility on that fateful mission, and it cost those boys their lives. No one could dispute that.

"Moving on." He opened the folder in his hands again, but Kathryn sensed he really wasn't looking at it.

"We realize you've had idle time in the past," he said, "and while it's true Forrester has been conducting most of his activities elsewhere of late, we feel your plate is full at the moment, so I'm denying you active field training."

Kathryn took the blow in silence and turned her focus to the corner of the large oak desk, as her bitter disappointment smoldered like the cigarette butt in the ashtray.

"Understand, your abilities are not being questioned here. It's a matter of priority. We'll review your request again when your current assignment has reached an end."

"The war could be over by then," Kathryn complained, suddenly faced with the realization that she may never see action again, which meant no opportunity to exorcise her guilt.

Colonel Forsythe looked up, understandably confounded by her complaint. "Then so be it, and amen."

Kathryn realized how absurd her protest must have sounded and mutely nodded as she looked down and wondered where she got that smudge of dirt on her knee.

"You're very important to us, Kathryn," the colonel said, "and you're doing exceptional work with Forrester. You should be proud of your service."

She resisted, releasing a disgruntled chuckle as she brushed off her slacks.

"That being said," Forsythe continued, turning his attention to the open file in his hands, "you are an experienced operative, and as you've pointed out, that's a precious commodity around here."

She raised her eyes, a slow, hopeful smile forming on her lips.

"We'd like to have you sit in on some specialty training with our next class. There will be two instructors to take care of the bulk of their preparation. It won't require a lot of time on your part. Impart your experience, that sort of thing. You know the routine." He paused as he closed the folder. "Situation permitting, of course. Forrester is still your number one priority."

"Of course." Kathryn did her best to suppress a grin.

He slid the folder across his desk in her direction. "Here is the proposed team. They're heading to the Farm in D.C. for basic, but we expect them to make quick work of that."

She reached out and pulled the folder to her. "Thank you, sir."

"Don't thank me yet, and don't get excited by the eighth name on the list."

She opened the folder and quickly scanned the first page. Number eight: *Jenny Ryan*. She knew her breathing caught, and she did her best to mask her rising panic as she handed out a levelheaded protest. "You promised to keep her out of this."

"I told you I wouldn't get her into anything she wasn't ready for. I also told you I would oversee her training. She was slated for Branson's team upon her return, but when you put in, I thought you might like to evaluate her. I know I can count on you to give a fair and unbiased assessment of her abilities."

"How do you know she'll pass basic?"

Forsythe leaned back in his chair and lit a cigarette. "Do you think she'll wash out?"

She gathered herself quickly. It wouldn't be wise to be so transparent about her feelings for her new student. "No, sir. I'm sure she'll do a fine job."

He grinned proudly and tossed his spent match into the ashtray. "Our thoughts exactly. She's a very creative young woman. We'd like to see how that translates into spur-of-the-moment decisions."

Kathryn held her tongue. She had been the recipient of many of Jenny's spur-of-the-moment decisions and knew she was quick on her feet, which didn't bode well for keeping her out of harm's way.

"We have no specific plans to utilize her in the field right now. We just want to see what she's capable of."

"Of course. I understand." It was the beginning of a path to danger that would not end until the agent was dead or the war was over.

"Her instructions are in the folder. I thought you might like to deliver the news to her."

"Yes, sir. Thank you."

"Thank you, Kathryn." He extended his hand. "Welcome back."

"Good to be back, sir." She grasped his hand firmly and smiled, not sure she meant it anymore.

CHAPTER TWENTY-TWO

Jenny smiled as she fondled the nondescript key in her hand. When Kathryn said she knew a place they could go, she had no idea it would be a penthouse apartment in one of the priciest high-rises on the eastside. She shook her head with a chuckle as the private elevator glided to its destination and deposited her a few feet away from the luxury loft's double-entry doors.

She pocketed the torn envelope and slip of paper in her other hand and raised her brow, remembering the doorman's knowing but impeccably professional smile when he handed her the sealed envelope containing the key and note.

She was to let herself in and make herself at home. Kathryn would arrive shortly. She unlocked the door to the apartment and entered slowly.

"Holy smokes," she said in awe when the large sunken living room opened up in all its opulent glory before her. The sun streamed in the huge floor-to-ceiling windows on the far wall, and the first thing Jenny noticed was that it was a modern apartment, recently renovated, it seemed to her, or never lived in. It was too neat, too clean, devoid of the personal clutter that usually marked an inhabited dwelling.

Flowing angular lines of gleaming chromium and white leather furniture, conveying more style than comfort, dotted the room, accented by stylized sculptures and large contemporary paintings on the expansive walls. There was a bar on the left side of the room, stocked with every type of liquor imaginable, all neatly lined up in bottles on shelves above the counter. The room was perfect for a cocktail party. She could almost imagine a popular tune being played on the white grand piano in the corner and people in fancy dress mingling with drinks in hand as they chattered on about the day's events.

She slipped out of her shoes after she entered, keeping the light-colored carpeting in the same immaculate condition in which she'd found it. She deposited her jacket and purse on the arm of the white couch before being drawn to the window to gaze at the bird's-eye view of the city. A few blocks north was The Grotto, and a short cab ride west was headquarters. It was the perfect location. "Top o' the world, Ma," she said, imitating James Cagney.

It was the tallest building on the block, and the streets below were a steady stream of movement. Traffic flowed like a metallic river, with no beginning or end, and the people floated along like insignificant specks on the surface of the tide.

From her lofty perch, Jenny couldn't hear the honking of the cabbies or the bustling crowds. She was far removed from the organized chaos below. Rationally, she knew it existed, just like she knew there was a war going on, with thousands dying every day, but it all seemed so peaceful from where she stood, and it lulled her senses into an odd state of denial, suspending such things as worrisome thought and the passage of time. She was mesmerized by the flowing streets below, silent in their journey and steadfast in their mission. For the moment, she was no longer one of them. She was a watcher, oblivious to their plight. *Is this what it's like for God,* she wondered, apathetic as He looks down, so far removed from His creation and their woe? Jenny scoffed at the thought, and her God complex, what with the state of world affairs seriously testing her already dubious belief in such a fellow.

She let the translucent drape fall from her hand and wandered aimlessly through the apartment. It consisted of a large main living area and a kitchen and bedroom on opposite sides from each other. She went through the swinging door to the kitchen first and found it fitted with the latest appliances, again, obviously never used. The refrigerator was on and cold, but, like the feel of the apartment, empty.

She leaned on the counter with her hand on her hip. Who could own such a place? It had to cost a fortune in renovations alone. The answer struck her, and it didn't take long for worrisome thought to find its way back to her. *Forrester*. She quickly removed her hand from the counter and rubbed it, as if it were dirty. A chill skittered up her spine, and it seemed like the walls were closing in on her. She quickly left the sterile kitchen and gravitated toward the warmth of the sun at the large living room window. She wished to feel like God again, to lose rational thought and rise above it all, but as she guided the drape to the side and looked below, she found herself gripped by a wave of vertigo instead. She turned away, putting a hand to her forehead.

"Get a hold of yourself, Jenny," she muttered.

Kathryn would be there soon, and it wouldn't do to waste their valuable time on silly insecurities. So it was Forrester's apartment. So what? She steeled herself to the notion, reminding herself that beggars cannot afford to be choosers, and he was merely the means that would enable them to be together. If she had to work things out emotionally about it, now wasn't the time. She would save that for later. Much later. She wouldn't let him taint their precious hours together.

She took a deep breath and decided to test her resolve by visiting the bedroom. When she pushed open the partially closed door, she was pleasantly surprised and exclaimed, "Oh." This room was very different from the rest of the apartment. It was decidedly masculine, with dark walls against a warm, cherry bedroom suite in the mission style, but personal photographs dotted each surface and beautiful old master-style paintings of figures decorated the walls. She was drawn immediately to an eight-by-ten black-and-white photograph on the dresser. It was a man and a woman, captured from the shoulders up at the moment it seemed that a punch line had been told. The man was young, with dark Cary Grant good looks and a million-dollar smile to match. He was laughing, his head pressed against the temple of the beautiful woman beside him. She was in on the joke, too, her nose wrinkled in laughter, her eyes closed. The expression was foreign, but she'd know that face anywhere—it was Kathryn.

Jenny was struck more by the joy on Kathryn's face than the obvious affection for the man with his hand on her shoulder. She wondered who he was and why Forrester had the picture so prominently placed.

She might have been jealous given more time, but a key in the lock propelled her and her thoughts into the living room and into her lover's arms.

Kathryn greeted her with a vigorous hug and an audible sigh of relief. "Hi. I missed you. Sorry I'm late." She backed off. "How long have you got?"

Jenny snuggled back into her arms. "I have all afternoon," she said proudly before releasing her hold so that she could see her face. "I've taken the late shift to accommodate your schedule at the club. We'll have every afternoon you can get away."

"Well," Kathryn drew out with an appreciative grin as she tossed the leather folio and her clutch to the side table. She kissed Jenny on the lips and whispered a sincere, "Thank you." She removed her shoes and straightened and, for the first time, noticed the room. "Wow."

"Have you never been here before?" Jenny asked, as she followed Kathryn into the room.

"Not since it was redone."

Jenny watched her take in the apartment with great interest. She seemed to have some affection for the place and was mildly amused at its transformation.

"Goodness," she said with a chuckle as she stuck her head into the immaculate kitchen.

Jenny didn't know what was so funny, but she really didn't care when Kathryn took her hand and silently led her across the living room to the bedroom. She stopped as she entered the room, no longer amused.

"Oh, this is perfect," she said reverently. "He's going to love it."

Jenny couldn't help being disturbed by Kathryn's response to the room, so she had to ask. "Forrester?"

"Forrester?" Kathryn parroted, as if she hadn't heard the name in a hundred years.

Jenny knit her brow. If it wasn't Forrester's place—?

"Oh," Kathryn drew out, as she put an apologetic hand on Jenny's shoulder. "I'm sorry, I wasn't thinking. The place belongs to Nicky."

Jenny exhaled in relief. "Thank God."

Kathryn smiled and kissed her on the head. "Bless you for the brave front. Forrester's not going to touch us here, I promise." She gathered her in a tender embrace. "No one's going to touch us here."

Jenny gladly accepted Kathryn's promise and the club owner's generosity. "I'll have to thank Dominic next time I see him."

"Actually, it's Luc's apartment now. Nicky's son. It was a birthday present, complete with a renovation."

"Some present."

Kathryn agreed with a throaty chuckle. "He hasn't seen it yet, but it'll be waiting for him when he comes home. He's going to love it."

The ensuing moments of silence saw the mood go from wistful to melancholy, as the possibility that he might not come home from the war loomed like a dark cloud over both of them. Jenny wasn't going to let that linger. Kathryn had said no one could touch them here, and Jenny would expand that to include no *thing*—especially the war. She looked at the happy young man in the photograph.

"Is that him?"

Kathryn turned, and her face lit up immediately. "Oh, hey! Look at us." She went right to it and picked it up. "Gosh, I remember that." She ran her fingers across his smiling face.

Jenny marveled at the adoring expression on her face. "What was so funny?"

Kathryn released a girlish giggle that was new to Jenny. "Nicky said it looked like we were taking our engagement photo."

Jenny was stunned into silence, and her brow lifted in surprise.

Kathryn didn't look at her, but she placed a comforting hand on her shoulder, sensing the reaction. "He was kidding." She ran her finger over the picture as if she could tousle Luc's wavy hair.

"I guess you two are really close for him to say that."

"Oh, Nicky would love it if we married."

Jenny couldn't believe how casually Kathryn said such a thing. Was it a test? Did she want to make her jealous? "Would you?"

Kathryn gently put the picture back in its place and took her hand. "I don't think his boyfriend would approve."

Jenny blinked. She looked again at the room as if seeing it for the first time. The photographs were mostly of young men. The paintings on the walls were the same. She closed her eyes and broke into a grin. "Oh, jeez."

Kathryn chuckled and rubbed her back. "He's devastatingly handsome, isn't he?"

"I'll say." Easy to admit now that he wasn't a threat. She buried her face in her hand over her misplaced jealousy. "How embarrassing."

Kathryn laughed and gathered her into her arms. "I love you."

Jenny looked up, suddenly serious. "I love you too."

Hours that had seemed so long when spread before them passed without notice until they had run their course. How quickly time had dutifully marched on, and Kathryn cursed it, wondering if it would ever be their friend.

Kathryn dressed after her shower and mentally prepared herself for the job ahead. She had a meeting with Forrester later that evening, and she had to tell Jenny that HQ had tapped her for field training. Jenny would be pleased, she knew, but she was not, and she had to hide her apprehension.

"How are you doing?" Jenny asked, as she came from behind and put her hand on the small of her back.

Either Jenny was getting far too good at reading her, Kathryn lamented, or she was losing her ability to disguise her feelings. Neither was comforting. "I'm missing you already," she answered. It wasn't a lie, but it wasn't the whole truth either.

"Mm," Jenny agreed, as she settled herself on the arm of the sofa. "When will we see each other again?"

"Unfortunately, I haven't any idea."

Jenny's regret showed in her downturned face and deflated shoulders.

"But," Kathryn said with excitement she didn't feel, "I do have some news that will make you smile."

"That'll be a neat trick, considering."

Kathryn retrieved the leather folio and extracted some paperwork. "Colonel Forsythe has asked me to give you this."

Jenny took the papers, her brow knitting in concentration as she scanned the first page. She looked up, cautiously hopeful. "Does this mean—?"

"You've been accepted for field training."

It took a few seconds for the impact of the words to sink in, but soon Kathryn found her arms full of a joyful blonde. Jenny backed off to look at the rest of the paperwork, which consisted of forms to sign, schedules, and rules and regulations. She processed it all, smiling from ear to ear. She looked up with adoration.

"Did you do this?"

"Oh, no," Kathryn said, perhaps too vehemently. "That's from upstairs. You earned it." She managed a grin, for fear her dismay was showing.

"I can't believe it," Jenny said, still grinning.

"These are your instructions on how to approach the center." Kathryn handed her a yellow slip of paper. "And here are directions."

She scribbled them on a piece of notepad paper as she spoke and ripped it out, handing it over as well. "Your name will be at the gate."

"Oh. That's what goes on over there," Jenny responded, recognizing the name of the sprawling Long Island estate.

"Yeah, just saving the free world," Kathryn said, as she forced a smile and screwed the cap on her fountain pen.

Committing the directions to memory, Jenny frowned and turned the note over like she would find something more on the back. "That's it?"

"You were expecting?"

Jenny shrugged. "I'm just surprised it's that easy. I thought I'd be blindfolded and taken to some top secret location or something."

Kathryn grinned seductively. "Well, if you're into that sort of thing, I'm sure I could arrange it."

Jenny raised a brow in approval.

Kathryn faltered at the hungry look in Jenny's eyes but quickly recovered and patted her on the shoulder. "You've seen too many movies."

Jenny chuckled and studied the directions one more time before folding them up. She started putting the note in her pocket but held it up instead.

"Shouldn't I eat this or something?"

Kathryn smirked at the teasing question, reminded of her stern admonition to *remember it in your head or don't remember it at all* while giving Jenny her orientation tour at headquarters.

"I deserve that," Kathryn said. Jenny's gruff welcome to the OSS seemed a lifetime ago. "You've actually got a week before you leave. When you report tomorrow, it'll be an overview, some preliminary information ... just to make sure you know what you're getting into."

"Leave?" Jenny scanned the paperwork, and her shoulders drooped when she realized she and Kathryn would be separated for two weeks. "D.C."

Kathryn nodded.

"And then?"

There was fear in Jenny's eyes, and Kathryn knew she wondered if this meant immediate placement and the effective end of their relationship.

For some, they would continue training elsewhere, but not Jenny. Not yet. "Then you come back to me and I don't let you out of my sight for a week."

Jenny looked up from her paperwork and smiled. "Just a week?"

"Well, I don't want to be greedy," Kathryn joked, doing her best to stay positive. "Uncle Sam will have his way with you and then you'll come home, where you'll be taking some specific training with us at the center."

"Us? Will you be involved in the process?"

"As it stands now, if you make the team, I'll be one of the instructors evaluating you as you go through your tactics course."

"Oh," Jenny said as she nudged her, "I'm a shoo-in. I know the evaluation instructor."

Kathryn pretended to smile, but it was anything but funny to her. She knew Jenny wouldn't need any favors to get through training, and she shuddered to think of what came after.

Jenny looked her up and down. "Hm. That's not a very convincing smile."

"I'm sorry. I know you'll do great."

"But," Jenny drew out.

Kathryn vowed to work on her acting skills. She certainly couldn't afford to be so transparent with Forrester. Finding her deceptive proficiency lacking, she decided the simple truth would suffice.

"I'm sure you understand why I'm not jumping for joy that you may become a field agent."

Jenny put her arms around her waist. "I do, but on the positive side, I'll be learning from the best, so you certainly can't say I'll be ill-prepared."

Kathryn looked away. That wasn't the point. That wasn't the point at all. There was no preparation for the realities Jenny would face in the field.

Jenny tightened her grip, and Kathryn could see by the serious look in her eyes that she understood her anxiety completely.

"We all have to do what we can, honey. If it turns out I'll make a good field agent, then it's my duty to do all that I can to help our side win."

Jenny was right, of course, but the thought of her in the churn of war, of her losing herself to the inhumanity of it all, of, God forbid, losing her, was unbearable. She stuffed down the unthinkable and agreed numbly with a curt nod of her head.

She understood the cost of winning a war, and Jenny, in her uninitiated way, did too. They would part in a few minutes, and she regretted that grim thoughts of the future would taint what was a glorious afternoon spent in each other's arms.

Jenny, to her credit, would not leave it that way. She reached out and smoothed a growing crease between her brows with loving fingers. "I'll be thinking of you every minute until I see you again." She trailed her hand along Kathryn's angular cheek and slid her hand around her neck, bringing their lips together.

The kiss held more desperation than passion, as both women were aware that it could be their last for an undetermined amount of time. They pulled back and looked into each other's eyes. There was no need for words. It was time. Jenny retrieved her purse and jacket from the couch and attempted to return the key. Kathryn wordlessly closed her hand around it, letting her know the key was hers to keep —a promise they would be together again soon. She led her to the door and shared one more parting kiss. She did not open her eyes when they separated.

"I love you," she heard Jenny whisper.

"I love you too," she replied, and then she heard the door open and softly close. She stood motionless for a few moments, eyes still closed, as Jenny's retreating footsteps on the polished hallway floor accentuated the loss she was feeling. She put her ear to the door and strained to hear the sound of the elevator doors closing, signaling the end of one part of her life and the beginning of another.

. . .

Smitty watched Jenny leave the building in the company of a man he did not recognize. If he didn't know better, he would swear they knew each other, might even be a couple. It was Jenny's easygoing personality. She could befriend a perfect stranger in a matter of seconds, as she did here, obviously taking care to cover her rendezvous with Kathryn. They walked side by side down the street until the man tipped his hat and turned the corner. Jenny waved to his back like they were the best of friends and hailed a cab.

"Well done, kid," Smitty muttered, as he glanced at his watch and went back to his paper. There would be no need to look up again for another ten minutes, when, like clockwork, Kathryn would emerge alone and walk the few blocks to the club. He'd seen no sign of anyone keeping tabs on their whereabouts, but they were smart to be careful, and he was at least relieved to see that his partner hadn't lost all sense of propriety.

She'd given him the cold shoulder all day, refusing to acknowledge his attempts to apologize. She finally told him to drop it, and he could tell from her tone it would be for the best. Even the news that HQ had cleared her for special service at the training center didn't buy him a reprieve from the doghouse, and when she told him Jenny was in the next rotation for the Farm in Washington, D.C., he understood why. Her mood was no longer about him. Nothing he could say would comfort her now, so he left her with her thoughts. It had begun, and they both knew what that meant.

CHAPTER TWENTY-THREE

"When did you fall in love with me?" Jenny had asked as they lay together in Luc's penthouse apartment, both contented and relaxed after their lovemaking.

"When you gave me the middle finger salute at the club," Kathryn joked with a grin.

Jenny chuckled. "Gosh, we've wasted a lot of time then."

Kathryn kissed her hand gently and held it to her chest, recalling the exact moment when Jenny had wrapped herself around her heart.

"When you took my hand in the car, after the accident," she said seriously. "I felt like everything was going to be okay ... as long as you didn't let go." She looked into her eyes, thankful. "And you didn't."

Jenny squeezed the fingers entwined with hers. "And I won't."

Kathryn smiled at herself in the mirror as she sat alone at the vanity in her dressing room at The Grotto and remembered her afternoon. She tried to get Jenny out of her head, to let her go, to become Forrester's mistress. This was her job. Her purpose. Catch the bad guys, win the war. But she didn't want to let go. Not yet.

She closed her eyes as her heart filled with the memory. She didn't want to see her reflection any longer. Her low-cut halter dress, the jewelry Forrester had given her, her perfect hair, and her impeccable makeup were lies. They were trappings of a role she used to implement without a thought but now suddenly despised. She wanted to be in love again, lost in someone else's longing for her, driven to distraction by unfamiliar feelings of joy until she hadn't a care in the world.

Their lovemaking that afternoon was a sensual exploration of two connecting souls. They reserved passion for another time, as desire burned just below the surface of their slow surrender into emotional trust and discovery. They watched each other respond to each kiss and measured caress until the sensations stole their ability to focus, and in their blind devotion, they became one. Release was as much emotional as physical, and never before had Kathryn known such contented bliss.

Through her dressing room door, the sound of the trombone player practicing his solo downstairs in the club brought her back to the present, and she opened her eyes to see her flushed face in the mirror. She put her hands to her warm cheeks, took a deep breath, and released it slowly. "Enough," she whispered. She had a show to do in less than an hour and Forrester to deal with after that.

She sat perfectly still for a few minutes as she let her memories drift away—let Jenny drift away. Thoughts of her assignment to Forrester polluted her head like a muddy tributary flowing into a clear spring-fed river. She had just discovered love—just discovered herself in love—and already it was slipping away, the light giving way to the darkness.

She stared at her lips. Victory Red. Even that reminded her of Jenny. *For when you feel bold,* she had teased. She didn't feel bold. She felt empty, robbed. It made her angry. She plucked a tissue from the box beside her and wiped the color from her lips. She opened the top drawer of the vanity and selected another color that was deeper, darker, dangerous. That's how she felt. Her mouth almost curled into a sneer when she read the label: Vixen. How appropriate. Forrester had cost her something, and he was going to pay.

She gleefully applied the color and fixed it with powder before pressing her lips together. A knock at the door followed by a muffled "May I come in?" interrupted her routine.

She checked her reflection. Marc Forrester was early. She traced the arches of her eyebrows with nimble fingers, reiterating their perfection, and smiled with predatory approval.

"Of course," she replied cheerfully as she stood and smoothed her long gown over her hips. She was back, or, sadly, it occurred to her, she'd never really left.

Jenny sat at her desk in MO and rubbed her eyes, frustrated at her lack of progress on her propaganda article. She couldn't concentrate. She looked at her wristwatch. It read ten p.m. Kathryn would be with Forrester by now. His hands would be on her, maybe his lips, and who knows what other indignities she would have to suffer at his whim. She was getting a headache. Coffee, that's what she needed. She had four more hours left in her shift and was determined to finish before she left. Forrester had already taken Kathryn away from her. He would not affect her work too.

She stood and tossed her pencil onto the pile of research reports about the German retreat in North Africa and then weaved her way through the busy office. The night shift was just as hectic as the day shift, she noticed. War was a twenty-four-hour nonstop business.

The coffee was a much-needed boost, and she closed her eyes as she took a sip and leaned against the wall, waiting for the drink to work its magic. She hadn't gotten much sleep lately, not that she was complaining. Last night was well worth the tired eyes and dull throbbing in her head. This was usually her bedtime, but she was glad she was working. She was pretty sure she'd be downright insane if she were at home, just staring at the ceiling, imagining the worst.

"Hey!" a coworker called out as he joined her at the refreshment station. "Congratulations!"

"Hi, Jim. For?"

"For making field agent. We'll miss you around here."

Jenny wondered how he found that out. "Thanks, but I haven't made anything yet."

"Oh, please," he said with a dismissive wave of his hand. "Everyone knows you're slated for bigger and better things around here." He poured his coffee and patted her on the shoulder before walking away with a smile. "Go get 'em."

Jenny stared at his retreating back and then around the office and finally into her coffee cup, wondering how these things got out. Not that she minded he knew—she was secretly proud they felt her worthy of consideration—but this was supposed to be covert central, and office gossip of that sort seemed totally out of place. She shook her head and shrugged as she topped off her cup, but then remembered she'd been privy to office gossip about Kathryn not five minutes after she'd entered the office for the first time, so perhaps it wasn't all that unusual. She chalked it up to human nature and headed back to her desk.

CHAPTER TWENTY-FOUR

Kathryn surreptitiously glanced at the watch face turned to the inside of Marcus Forrester's wrist as he lit her cigarette. He wore it that way for just that reason, so he could check the time without being noticed. It was ten forty-five, and although Kathryn had already spent several hours with the man, she could tell her night was just getting started. She inhaled deeply, savoring her first cigarette in weeks, having given up the habit in deference to Jenny's non-spoken aversion to it. She was glad to have one right then, if for nothing else than to interrupt the incredibly boring monologue she was enduring from one of Forrester's associates. Forrester winked at her as he closed his lighter, and she smiled a thank-you on her eventual exhale. Forrester put his arm around the mercifully silenced man's shoulders and led him away toward another group of equally boring men. Kathryn stood alone and took another welcome drag on her cigarette, vowing never to say "How interesting" to a chemist again.

They were in the obscenely extravagant home of a real estate magnate who was courting Forrester in a blatant attempt to lure him into padding his empire. Forrester had no use for the man's capacity to buy and sell property. He just wanted to exploit the connections that seemed to gravitate to the wealthy and bored.

As far as Kathryn could tell, Forrester's business seemed legitimate for a change. He was seeking investors in a new manufacturing plant and putting them together with the men whose companies would benefit from its production. He was an expert at such marriages, and Kathryn had little to do, as it appeared she was present merely because he wished for her company.

She turned her back on the group and moved to the large archway leading to the next room, where she leaned on the doorjamb and watched the couples dancing to the slow, soothing rhythm of the live band. It was a relatively small affair. The seventy or so people just barely filled the cavernous ballroom. It was somebody's thirtieth birthday. Friends gathered from near and far, creating quite the international mix of directionless heiresses and hopeful playboys anchored by old money couples and ambitious businessmen like Forrester. Kathryn sighed into her coupe of champagne and looked up in time to see the man playing the piano eyeing her seductively. She ignored it, glad for his sake that Forrester didn't see him.

Kathryn didn't know what had happened to Marcus Forrester in the week he was away, but he seemed off-balance, as though he needed assurance, of what she wasn't sure. He came to the club early, with two dozen red roses in tow and a smothering hug that he seemed to think better of once he released it. He was nervous and uneasy. He sat on the edge of the bed in the dressing room and squeezed his knuckles until they cracked, the macho equivalent of wringing his hands.

Kathryn pulled up a chair and, facing him, took his restless hands in hers. She didn't speak. Instead, she let her intense gaze peel away his faltering resolve.

"I need you," he finally said.

Kathryn played the good little mistress and said, "I'll help you in any way I can, Marc. I've told you that."

He stared at her, desperation seeping into his eyes. "*I* need you," he repeated, clarifying his statement.

The confession took Kathryn by surprise, and it occurred to her that "I need you too" would be the expected response, and a prudent one at that, but as she practiced it in her head, it didn't sound very convincing. She saw vulnerability in his eyes, and she was going to make the most of it. The closer she could get to him, the more information she could get, and the more information she could get, the sooner her assignment would be over, and the sooner her assignment was over—well, she didn't know, but it involved spending more time with Jenny, and that was worth anything she had to do.

She swallowed her perceived shock and then feigned delight as she slowly leaned in and kissed him full on the lips. He didn't protest. In fact, he seemed pleased with her answer and pleased with her method. Thankfully, he asked for nothing more to prove her continued devotion. She was surprised to find it was easy—giving away meaningless kisses, holding his clammy hands. He was showing weakness, and she reveled in it.

"I don't love you," he warned when she pulled back.

Kathryn let confusion, then hurt, play across her face for the briefest of moments, and then looked him right in his lying eyes and saw that he was hers. "I don't love you either."

Slow grins broke across both their faces, and Forrester took the initiative for the first time and leaned in for a kiss. Kathryn obliged and then pretended she wanted more when he broke away. He put his palm on her cheek and let her kiss it as she leaned into his touch.

He closed his eyes. "I'm sorry I can't—"

Kathryn saw his sexual inadequacy eating at him. "It doesn't matter, Marc," she promised, covering his hand with hers. "Truly ... it doesn't."

He opened his eyes and suppressed a smile, as relief pulled at the corners of his mouth. "Have you a lover?"

She didn't hesitate, eager to prove Jenny was not a threat and that she had nothing to hide. "Yes." She thought she saw the briefest flash of jealousy in his narrowing eyes.

"A man?" he asked cautiously.

A definite flash of jealousy. "No."

He grinned in approval. "Your young friend."

Kathryn smiled involuntarily but caught herself before her infatuation became too obvious. "Yes."

"Good," he said, as he dropped his hands to his knees and sat up straight. "Very good. It's perfect then."

That inherent bit of arrogance in a man always amazed Kathryn. They would duel to the death over another man but saw no threat in another woman. Even Forrester, with no sexual ability whatsoever, found the primal trait inescapable.

"Yes," she said with a smile. "Perfect."

Kathryn was restless as she deposited her spent cigarette into a cut glass ashtray. There was nothing for her here. There were no mysterious scientists or cryptic conversations about dastardly deeds, only uptight businessmen and their insipid wives, hanging on their husband's arms like window dressings, nodding their heads and laughing at each bad joke like the good little trophies they were.

A tall, elegant woman across the room caught her with her disdain showing. They looked each other up and down with equal scorn until their eyes met and they both smiled, finally breaking into complimentary full-faced grins when they acknowledged they were partners in disgust. The woman broke her gaze with an exasperated eye roll before she tightened her hold on her husband's arm and tossed her head back in forced laughter.

Kathryn chastised herself for judging her. She, more than anyone, knew that life supplied its own judgment, passing its sentence or reward in the form of a consequence for every action. She wondered if she would be blessed or cursed by her actions tonight.

She sensed Forrester approaching before he actually put his hand on her back. Warm lips on her neck followed, and she demurely leaned into his embrace, smiling.

"Finished with your business?" she asked.

"Mm," he hummed into her ear. "Hasn't been much fun for you, I'm afraid."

She turned in his arms and straightened his tie. "And what are you going to do about it?"

He looked into the ballroom and asked if she wanted to dance. She grinned in agreement and deposited her glass with the nearest server, happy to note that the leering piano player had been replaced.

Forrester was a good dancer at least, and she closed her eyes and pretended to get lost in the moment, pressing her cheek tenderly to his as she mindlessly hummed the tune in his ear.

"I love this," he whispered.

She smiled. He was under her spell. "You should come home to me more often then."

He held her tighter. "Perhaps I should never leave you at all."

Kathryn stopped dancing and looked him in the eyes. "Don't tease me, Marc."

He paused, as if wary of his next statement. "What if I'm not?"

Kathryn let him twist on her reaction for a beat and then hugged him. He accepted her enthusiastic response with a relieved laugh and then kissed her on the cheek before resuming their dance.

They were applauding the band after a three-song set when a server approached Forrester and directed him to a phone call, which he took in the next room. Kathryn didn't know what she had just committed to, but her plan to get closer seemed to be working.

Alone again, she turned to leave the floor and walked right into the chest of the amorous piano player. He was a tall man with mousey brown hair that was parted at the side and brushed straight back into Brylcreemed perfection. He looked like a young man when he was sitting at the piano leering at her, but face to face, the permanent smile lines around his soft hazel eyes betrayed his maturity. Kathryn apologized as she attempted to side-step him on her way to the next room, but the band began to play a tango, and he took her in his arms.

"What are you doing?" she said, as her eyes flashed across the room to where Forrester would emerge at any second.

"The tango, with the most beautiful woman in the room," the man said with true playboy swagger.

A thick French accent infused his words, and his arrogance annoyed her. He had to have seen her with Forrester and could see they were a couple.

"You're flirting with disaster," she warned.

He smiled and pulled her closer. "Hello, Disaster, my name is Thierry."

Kathryn bristled as she glanced once more across the room, knowing this man could not only ruin her progress with Forrester, but he could endanger his own life as well.

"I mean it," she said, making her implication perfectly clear.

The man was undeterred. "Well," he said, looking around briefly to acknowledge her fear, "if this is to be my last dance, I shall make the most of it."

Kathryn tried to push away. "You don't understand—"

Marcus Forrester appeared in the doorway, and Kathryn stopped struggling when she saw him. She tried to look helpless and let him know it was not her idea. He got the picture, but true to their odd relationship, he didn't seem to mind. He casually lit a cigarette and nodded in approval, putting his hand in his pocket as he rocked back on his heels, awaiting the performance.

Kathryn turned to her triumphantly grinning dance partner, and she seethed at both men for their conceit. The tall man wrapped one arm around her back and gently lifted her hand in his. She automatically assumed the proper position and draped an arm across his shoulders. The man accepted her submission by pulling her into a close embrace. Kathryn could feel the tension in her back and neck, and she wondered what the hell she was doing. She used to love the trap, the surrender, and the victory. Her anger accomplished nothing. If Forrester wanted a show, he was going to get one. If this stranger wanted an intimate tango, he'd better be up to the task, because bruised shins and a kneed groin were all he would get if he wasn't. She wouldn't even have to do it out of spite. It was just inherent to the dance if done badly. She stifled a smirk, as she had to admit, it would give her a perverse thrill if he faltered.

Their dance started slowly. They were two strangers, unsure, testing each other and their abilities. He retreated to an open embrace, and her arm slid across his broad shoulders and down his arm, where she lightly gripped his bicep. A sliding step to the side, then backward, then forward, and so the introduction went until he slipped the toe of his shoe beneath the arch of her right high heel and lifted her foot as they turned together, pivoting on her firmly planted left foot. She curled her leg around the inside of his as he turned her body across his, and her trailing foot caressed his calf on its way to the floor. The man showed her he knew his stuff, and she proved she could easily adapt to his style.

They were face to face, close, but not touching. Where he led, she followed. His intensity matched hers, and soon the contest was on in a calculated game of precise movements, deceptively simple in their complexity.

The music was lively, and two bodies twisted in unison like trees in a swirling wind. Steps forward, steps back, heels flying, bodies turning, legs stepping over, between, around each other, limbs moving like separate entities yet weaving together as part of a fluid whole. The staccato violin plucked out the tempo, and melodious notes rose and fell from the pushed and pulled bellows of the bandoneon.

The graceful man's hands held and caressed her as they moved in perfect harmony and rhythm. He pulled her body to him. He pushed her away. He took the utmost care and knew exactly where to place her when he led her into a backward lean, and he made sure her effort was minimal when he tenderly welcomed her return. They were no longer combatants but a couple. Kathryn enjoyed the challenge and her partner's expertise. His arrogance was well-founded, and she forgave him for it. The tango was a dance of confidence, after all.

The first energetic song of the set ended and seamlessly blended into a sultry tango waltz that would find them closer than ever. The man closed the distance between them, and she turned her face toward his chest and slid her hand across his shoulders until it weightlessly touched the back of his neck. He pressed his cheek to hers, and she closed her eyes. In their close embrace, there was no thinking. She trusted his lead, and his body told her where to go. Two became one, gliding across the floor with ease, pushing, pulling, turning, heels and toes dragging and pausing in time to the music. It didn't matter who he was. She got lost in the music and the language of their bodies moving in concentrated sensuality.

The song ended and the final song of the tango set began, but neither moved. Kathryn looked to her partner and was not surprised to find desire in his eyes. The tango was an intimate dance if one allowed it to be, and, clearly, he had. Their mouths were dangerously close, and she sensed he was about to do something they would both regret. She stilled his advance with a hand on his chest and said, "Thank you," effectively ending their brief acquaintance.

He paused in disbelief, as if a kiss would only be natural. "But we have not yet finished our dance."

"Thank you," she repeated, as she glanced over his shoulder at Forrester's intense stare. Perhaps they had already gone too far.

"I am sorry," the man whispered before they parted. "I am not usually this forward. I blame your beauty and the champagne." He bowed his head, asking for forgiveness.

Kathryn neither accepted nor refused his request. She simply looked at the floor and then shifted her eyes to glance over her shoulder, a subtle gesture that brought Forrester's presence to their intimate embrace. "Watch yourself."

She extricated herself from his grasp and went to Forrester's side as the murmuring crowd applauded their dance. He welcomed her with a smile and a kiss on the cheek, but she was unsure if he really meant it.

"I'm sorry, darling," she began. "He just—"

Forrester slipped his arm around her waist, claiming ownership once more. "Nonsense. That was very beautiful." He paused, taking in the tall man adjusting his shirt cuffs, then turned back to her, regarding her fondly. "Very sensual ... sexual." He smiled. "Thank you."

She would never figure this man out. "You're very welcome."

He caressed her back as if she had no need to fear him, and she turned for a parting glance at her dance partner in time to see his back weaving through the crowd. His escape was not as macho as his approach to the tango, but smart, and she applauded him for his judgment. She caught Forrester nodding to his gorillas on the sidelines and squeezed his arm, whispering tersely, "Marcus, no. He's harmless." The gorillas continued discreetly on the man's heels. She tightened her grip. "Marc, please."

He attempted to calm her by patting her hand. "I just want to know his name, that's all."

Her heart pounded in concern for the elegant dancer's life, and she gave Forrester a doubting look.

"That's all," Forrester promised. He continued patting her hand as he surveyed the room and gave a final squeeze. "I believe I'm through here. Shall we go?"

Kathryn nodded and offered a worried glance over her shoulder. It was all she could do for the retreating man now.

Jenny sat on an examining table in the infirmary at the training center and pressed a cotton ball to the needle hole in her forearm while the nurse secured it with a piece of medical tape. "All set, Miss Ryan," the portly woman said with a smile. "Welcome to the big show."

Jenny rubbed her arm when the woman turned her back. "Thanks."

The nurse's procedure was more like a bloodletting than a blood test. One more clumsy jab with a needle and Jenny was going to insist on drawing her own blood.

The kindly doctor came in next and handed over her papers, officially ending orientation day at the training center with the completion of her physical. She slid from the examining table and swore she stood a little taller. She beamed with pride as she inserted her medical slip into her folder. It joined oaths of secrecy, letters of denial, releases from responsibility, and her crisp new ID tag to add to her growing collection. It seemed you needed a separate tag for everything in the OSS. She felt like a used watch salesman, but with ID tags instead of timepieces.

She left the wooden building and stepped out into the noonday sun. Kathryn was at the center somewhere. Jenny had seen Smitty's car in the parking lot, and wherever Smitty was—

Jenny took in the grounds and finally saw Kathryn in the distance. She wasn't sure it was her at first. She'd never seen her in casual mechanic's garb, but there she was, sprawled out on the gravel in a light blue mechanic's jumpsuit, with a smattering of tools between her spread legs like a child playing jacks. A German motorcycle sat a few feet to the side, and Kathryn had what Jenny assumed was a carburetor in her hands, turning the thing over and shaking it until a screw fell out.

"There you are, you little bastard," she heard her mutter to herself.

"Hey, lady," Jenny called out as she casually approached. "I hear they have mechanics to do that for you."

Kathryn looked up, and a concentrated scowl quickly turned into a broad grin. "Hey!"

Jenny sensed Kathryn was about to hop up and take her in her arms, but her body relaxed and she set the grimy engine part beside the tools between her legs and squinted into the sun over Jenny's shoulder. "I can't really call Bob the mechanic if I'm in the field, now can I?"

"Ah," Jenny drew out, "good point."

Kathryn's hair was tucked haphazardly underneath a large billed cap that sat back on her head, and her black steel toe work shoes peeked out from under her rolled up pant legs. Her short white socks made her alabaster skin seem tanned in comparison. She wiped her face with the back of her hand and promptly deposited a black streak across her beautiful cheek. Who knew a grease monkey could be so sexy?

Jenny shuffled to the side, shading Kathryn from the sun. Noting her professional demeanor, she appropriately followed suit. "So, how are you?" It wasn't a personal question but one an acquaintance might ask another if they met unexpectedly on the street.

Kathryn smiled her approval and briefly cut her eyes to a soldier who was taking in their exchange from a distance. "I've been well. Busy."

"Good."

Jenny absentmindedly scratched at the tape pulling on her arm through her long sleeve shirt and then stuck both hands in her pants pockets. She bounced slightly on the balls of her feet, at a loss for useless small talk when her heart was craving intimacy and some reassurance that their connection was still intact. She had an unending list of questions for Kathryn about her reunion with Forrester, but, more importantly, she had personal questions, like *Do you want me as badly as I want you right now?* She took a deep breath, trying to gather herself. Kathryn seemed fine. That was all that mattered.

The morning had left Jenny with a new appreciation for Kathryn the agent. Maybe it was the hard realities of "hazardous duty," as they called it, or maybe it was the moment she put pen to paper and felt that she had just signed her life away, literally. She had always considered her life her own, but now it belonged to someone else—her government, in service to her country. It was as it should be, she supposed. After all, she'd spouted the rhetoric often enough. There was a price to pay for freedom, and now her country was asking to collect. What had once been abstract ideology had now become reality, and she felt the weight of the responsibility and a sense of her own mortality as never before. She knew Kathryn understood this burden, and it made her long to be with her, to find comfort in her arms. Solidarity among spies.

Kathryn's trepidation and desperation had become so clear. Jenny felt closer than ever to her, and, oh, how she wished they were alone together somewhere instead of posturing in a very open, dusty courtyard, keeping their distance like two star-crossed lovers, hoping their rival families wouldn't discover their secret. If she thought their time was precious before, she realized she had no idea just how much. Suddenly, their time together seemed depressingly finite. Days? Weeks? Months? Their relationship had instantly burgeoned in importance and intensity. Their separation was no longer an inconvenience. It was a thief, steadily stealing what little time they had left. Once upon a time, she knew it would have made her cry, but now it just made her angry and determined to be strong. Time would not defeat them, nor would distance. Whatever was in store for them, love would bind them always. Nothing could take that from them.

"Are you still excited?" Kathryn asked.

Jenny knew she understood the turmoil the awful truth brings. "Excited ... nervous ... afraid."

Kathryn remembered the feelings well. She also remembered that no one ever knew the true meaning of those words until they were in action, running a deception, or running for their life. She allowed Jenny her homegrown interpretations. She wouldn't have them much longer.

Kathryn noticed a bloodstain on Jenny's sleeve and pointed at it. "What happened?"

"Oh, for—" Jenny rolled up her sleeve, revealing a bloody cotton ball hanging from a piece of medical tape. She pushed the loose end back onto her skin. "During my physical, Nurse Whatserhoozits in there took my blood with a needle I swear was as big as a soda straw." She rolled down her sleeve and chuckled. "You would've been on the floor, I fear."

Kathryn smiled, acknowledging her aversion to blood. She watched Jenny's hand as she deftly buttoned her sleeve, and she remembered the night of the accident, when she'd just barely managed not to pass out. Jenny had offered the same hand that night, and Kathryn held it like it was a conduit to the outside world, a means to escape. She briefly thought about how far they'd come since that night, but then realized it wasn't so far, really, as she longed to take that hand again, wanting to escape, if only for a few moments.

Jenny must have sensed the melancholic shift in her mood and tilted her head. "What is it?"

Kathryn knew there was no point hiding her emotions from Jenny, so she abandoned her casual front for a simple desire. "I need to see you."

She saw a brief wave of surrender in Jenny's eyes and body language, but Jenny recovered quickly.

She glanced at Branson leaning against one of the classroom buildings and lowered her voice to an intimate whisper. "Are you okay, baby?"

Kathryn smiled. She'd been called baby many times, by everyone from friendly, fast-talking jive musicians to disrespectful Joes, but no one had ever filled the word with such love. Jenny looked worried, but it wasn't necessary.

The night with Forrester was nothing Kathryn hadn't endured before, and the argument with Smitty on the way in from the estate was disturbing in its intensity and outcome but nothing Jenny needed to know or worry about, especially since it was about her —again.

Kathryn shook her head and decided not only was she Jenny's baby, but she was uncharacteristically being a baby as well.

"I'm fine," she said, "just spoiled."

"Sure?"

Kathryn nodded and rearranged the tools in front of her. "We can't be together today, and that makes me sore."

Jenny paused and eyed Branson again. "Tomorrow?" she whispered.

"I'll make sure of it."

"Same place and time?"

"I'll send word if something changes."

Jenny stared at her adoringly for a beat and then pantomimed a smudge on her cheek. "You have a—"

Kathryn pulled a red rag from her back pocket and wiped her face clean. "Thanks."

Jenny quickly scanned their surroundings. "I love you."

Kathryn looked up and smiled, unable to feign indifference at such a heartfelt declaration. "I love you too."

Jenny chewed her lip, and Kathryn sensed she'd better save them both from their faltering resolves.

"So, we'll see you back here in a few weeks, then," Kathryn said loudly for the benefit of their voyeur.

"Yes, ma'am, I'm looking forward to it."

"See you then."

"Bye."

Kathryn tried hard not to watch Jenny walk away. She decided she would never watch her walk away again. She stuffed the rag back into her pocket and picked up the carburetor, pretending to give two hoots about whether the machine ever worked again. She heard footsteps approaching from the side and frowned. She knew who it was, and, frankly, she was in no mood.

"Take it somewhere else today, Branson."

"Cute little protégé, Hammond."

"Jerry—" She dropped the engine part with a clank and looked up in time to see Smitty's imposing form arrive.

"Beat it, asshole," Smitty said with a clenched fist, ready to make it happen.

"Take it easy, Johnny. Just enjoying the view."

Smitty didn't have to tell him twice. The man slinked away without a backward glance, whistling a tune as if nothing had happened.

"Asshole," Smitty muttered again before softening his stance. "I'm heading over to the mess for some chow. Can you take a break?"

Kathryn declined, holding up her greasy hands as an excuse. "I've got to get this thing put back together."

"Okay." He stood motionless for a few seconds. "Can I bring you back a sandwich?"

She knew he was still trying to test their shaky ground, so she took pity on him. "Sure."

"Great," he said with a smile and turned to walk away.

"Say, Smitty?"

He stopped and turned. "Yeah?"

"Did you have a blood test as part of your physical?"

"No. Why? Wanna get hitched? After all, we already fight like an old married couple."

Kathryn grinned. Sad, but true, but hopefully things would be different from now on. "Just curious."

He shrugged and continued on his way. Kathryn picked up her project and mumbled, "Neither did I."

Kathryn's week went by quickly. Forrester spent his days at the office and most evenings on the phone in his study. No strangers came to the house for meetings, and there were no major functions to speak of. It appeared that whatever deals had to be rearranged because of Charles Lawrence's betrayal and death weren't quite settled, and the center of the storm seemed to be out of town. Taps on Forrester's phones pointed to Chicago, and agents on the other end confirmed a flourish of new activity. Communication with overseas contacts had increased as well, and the sense that something was going to break soon was the consensus reached by all involved.

Through it all, Kathryn bided her time, waiting for any slip—a misplaced note, an overheard phone conversation, a murmur in his sleep—that would finally give some clue to the mystery that seemed to consume Forrester of late, above all else. They had been sharing a bed since his return, something she initiated and he readily agreed to, but it was strictly nonsexual, of course. She knew if he got used to having her near, he would miss her more when she was not. Her plan worked, as an emergency trip out of town for the weekend had him lamenting their separation. It wasn't hard to convince him to take her along. It was the perfect opportunity to add to the list of players in his little scheme. He was getting lax about working at the house. He'd started bringing home a locked briefcase every night, which Smitty had no problem breaking into while Kathryn kept her assignment occupied.

The documents Smitty photographed with his tiny Minox camera were filled with pages of handwritten scientific formulas and attached correspondence about what appeared to be a biological weapon. The letters all had the same theme. Something was missing or as yet undiscovered. Something important. This would back up what Kathryn had heard the night Charles Lawrence attacked her. The word *reservoir* appeared over and over, and it was obvious that negotiations for this vital piece of the puzzle were ongoing.

Kathryn couldn't get *biological weapon* out of her mind. It reminded her of the file Colonel Holmes had given her on the Ryans and their work in biological warfare. For one panic-inducing moment, she suspected Jenny's meteoric rise through the OSS ranks was no mere coincidence and that, somehow, they would draw her into that world as well. But that was ridiculous. Jenny wasn't a scientist and had no idea what her father was doing.

Lying on her back on a cold stone floor, Kathryn watched the men take Jenny away. One man on each arm dragged her out of the room as she kicked and struggled to escape. The whole thing happened in slow motion. Jenny screamed her name, but it was so drawn out that it sounded like she was in a tunnel of cotton. Kathryn didn't move. It wasn't that she couldn't move, or that she didn't want to—she just felt empty. She was finished. She had failed, and there was no reason to fight. Jenny was finished too. She just didn't realize it, or she was too stubborn to admit defeat. She smiled ruefully. That was so like Jenny—a fighter to the end, even when it was hopeless. When she was out of sight and the muffled screams receded, Kathryn sensed men standing over her and felt the end closing in. She slowly turned her head and looked into the eyes of death. Welcome.

"Are you all right, Kathryn?" Forrester asked as he took her hand.

His touch and the droning of the small private plane's engine as it taxied for takeoff shattered the memory from the night before and made her open her eyes. "Mm," she said, as she turned to him and squeezed his hand. "Just tired this morning."

"You were very restless after your bad dream last night."

"I'm sorry, darling. I didn't mean to keep you up."

"Since I was the subject of your discomfort, I feel it is I who must apologize." He kissed her hand. "You needn't worry, dear. Nothing is going to happen to me."

She smiled and nodded as the plane reached takeoff speed and lifted them toward the sky. She'd awakened in the early morning hours, bathed in a cold sweat, surrounded by Forrester's arms. She recounted her dream but made him the victim, thankful she hadn't called out Jenny's name in her delirium. She also told Smitty, who tried to comfort her by saying it was just a dream. She agreed, and that was the problem. It was just a dream, but it should have been a nightmare. She let them take Jenny. She didn't fight. She didn't care. She just let them take her. It frightened her. Why would she do that?

She closed her eyes again and rested her head against the headrest. Smitty was right. It was just a dream. A perfectly rational manifestation of the lack of control she felt in regard to Jenny's safety, especially since she'd left for basic at the Farm in D.C. Jenny had gone from innocent bystander to OSS agent on the verge of fieldwork, and now Kathryn found herself a helpless bystander as her lover was pulled inexorably toward her destiny. Jenny would be a changed person when she returned, and Kathryn could only hope that destiny would take pity on them and, when all was said and done, they would be together in the end.

Kathryn admired her new manicure as Smitty drove her to the club. Her days would now consist of evenings working at The Grotto, nights and mornings with Forrester, afternoons devoted to OSS business, or *womanly* pursuits, such as the beauty parlor or shopping—just to keep the accounts Forrester set up for her active—or preferably, her new favorite pastime, Jenny, when she returned home.

Smitty didn't like the Jenny part. He'd made that perfectly clear that morning, informing her that Forrester had charged him with providing an accurate account of her afternoons, and other than cover stories to hide OSS activities, a dance card full of blonde would not sit well with the possessive industrialist.

Forrester was fine with her relationship with Jenny, Kathryn insisted, but Smitty accused her of jeopardizing her assignment because of her inability, or unwillingness, to "lay off the kid," as he put it, while Forrester was in town. She, in turn, accused him of jealousy, which he denied, claiming Forrester was a red-blooded man with a beautiful woman under his thumb, and no matter what Kathryn believed, no one was that understanding. Kathryn took offense to Smitty's insinuation that she didn't know how to handle Forrester, and it just went downhill from there, with both parties shouting at the top of their lungs, as the tensions of the past few days unloaded like a sprung clock mechanism until Smitty finally just pulled over. Their unrestrained grievances had their hearts pounding in anger, but when the car finally skidded to a halt, they found themselves in sudden silence, as if the forward motion had been fueling the discord.

"I know you're worried," Kathryn finally said into the tense silence.

Smitty didn't have to answer. It was a given.

"But what happened to trusting me?"

Obviously, Smitty's faith had been shaken, but he calmed down and rethought his approach. He scrubbed his face with his hand and conceded he'd never seen Kathryn so smitten, pointing out it was his job to see that it didn't interfere with the assignment, not to mention her safety. Kathryn accepted his position, understood his concern, and they both apologized for letting things get out of hand.

Kathryn could tell Smitty felt relieved, but things had changed for her that morning. She knew Smitty had to do what he had to do, and although he could be sympathetic to her need for Jenny, his devotion to duty wouldn't allow him to overlook every possible pitfall. She was devoted too, though, and her continuing efforts with Forrester surely proved that. It was probably the only reason Smitty had kept his concerns to himself. He was brass's canary in a coal mine, after all. If something was wrong with her or her performance, he would be the first to know and would warn her superiors about it. She liked to think it was their friendship that kept him from reporting his misgivings, or maybe he weighed the time invested in the case verses starting over and found that as long as he could contain her and reason with her, the risk was worth it. The truth was probably somewhere in between and the only thing they could agree on at the moment. True to the depth of their relationship, Smitty knew her well and still sensed the ever-widening chasm between them.

"Don't run from me, Kat. I'm here for you." She didn't respond, and he was incredulous. "I can't believe I have to say that to you."

He didn't. He shouldn't. She bowed her head and closed her eyes, trying to process her emotions. She reached out and laid her hand on his thigh to ground herself, to be forgiven, to find their friendship again. His hand covered hers immediately, and she was shocked by the urge to pull away. Smitty was becoming synonymous with Forrester and just as suffocating.

It wasn't fair, the association or her wrath. She opened her eyes and stared at her friend. He loved her beyond reason, had saved her life on many occasions, with no regard for his own, would always be there for her, and would always understand and forgive. He smiled. His boyish grin was worn but not defeated. For the first time, she found no comfort there. She found only a reminder of pain and anguish and a future spent wallowing in self-imposed restitution.

It broke her heart, and it frightened her. She'd never been without him and couldn't remember not needing him or counting on him. Even with their ups and downs, he was a constant, her strength.

She would always love him, more perhaps than she was willing to admit, but he was no longer a refuge, no longer home. She turned her hand palm up, accepting his fingers into hers, and she closed her hand tightly around them. He mistook it for a welcome home, and she let him, and then silently said goodbye.

CHAPTER TWENTY-FIVE

*J*enny sat on a crowded train heading home from her two weeks in Washington, D.C. She was exhausted, but the thought of seeing Kathryn again had her running on pure anticipation. The last half hour of the ride seemed the longest—so close, yet so far away. A soldier had kept her company for most of the ride, but he had fallen asleep on her shoulder. She was thankful for his normal conversation while it lasted. After two weeks of hiding everything about herself and receiving the same nondescript banter from her fellow recruits as part of their training, his life story was a welcome open exchange. He apologized for going on and on but explained he was shipping out and just wanted to leave something of himself at home, even if it was only in the memory of a total stranger. He wanted her to remember him as a kind, loving man who had never harmed another living thing. He got a faraway look in his eyes and said he was afraid that would all change soon. He went silent as he considered his future, his thoughts weighing him down until he snapped out of it and smiled, cracking a joke about being nineteen going on fifty.

"Lighten up, Wasilewski," a soldier complained from across the aisle as he slapped his buddy in the arm. "Dames don't dig that noise." He winked at Jenny.

Wasilewski blushed. "Sorry."

Jenny took his hand, ignoring his friends. "What's your first name?"

"Francis."

His buddies across the aisle broke out in a mocking whisper, *Francis, Francis.*

"Frank," the soldier said, chagrinned.

Jenny turned in her seat so she was facing him and put her other hand on top of his. "Francis," she began sincerely, "I'll remember you —" She swept her eyes over his face. "Just like this ... young, beautiful, kind, and gentle." She squeezed his hand. "I won't ever forget this about you. I promise."

He was quiet for a moment, absorbing her words, and then emotion filled his eyes and voice as he whispered, "Thank you."

Wolf whistles came from his rowdy friends, and slaps on the back were accompanied with urgings to "Kiss the girl, ya dope!"

He didn't. He ignored them and slid down in his seat, where he promptly fell asleep with a contented smile on his face.

As the soldier slept, Jenny looked around the train. She saw the world with new eyes—an undercover operative's eyes. She noticed specific details like never before. Her intensive training not only taught her to hide telling traits about herself, but it also taught her to pick up on clues from the people around her. If you looked hard enough, you could uncover where each person came from, where they were going, and why. It was an automatic curiosity now, an ongoing game of honing her skills. It wasn't hard, not among the general public, who had nothing to hide. Most wore their purpose on their faces, revealing intent in their body language. There was the older mother, clutching a handkerchief and imagining each soldier as her own boy, safely on his way home to her; the disgruntled office worker turned to the window in hopes that no one would ask him why he wasn't in uniform; and the exhausted woman with grocery bags on her lap, her work boots giving away her factory job.

It was the people she couldn't read that gave her pause and made her suspicious. Maybe they were like her. Maybe they were judging her every move, waiting for a clue to use against her. Well, she wasn't going to give it to them. Her instructors had said she excelled at her ability to become someone but to reveal no one.

They gave her a name when she arrived in Washington: Spitfire. And a number: 698. This was her new identity—her *only* identity. Jenny Ryan ceased to exist as soon as she walked through the white columned portico of the aptly named Farm. It reminded her of Tara, and she half expected Scarlett O'Hara to appear at the door and scold them all for their silly little war games.

In a world where the tiniest detail, such as the hand you use to hold your fork when you eat or the stitch you use to sew on a button, can reveal your country of origin, she was taking no chances. She became someone else, so much so that she pushed Kathryn out of her mind and immersed herself completely in her new world.

While she was there, she was friendly, so as not to seem guarded —something that could give you away as easily as a slip-up—and she tried to be as ordinary as possible. She played poker badly, and didn't swear once, trying very hard to be what she assumed the group around her would consider the typical woman. That part was easy. She could play simple games of manipulation, but she wasn't prepared for the physical reality of an agent's life. She was left exhausted and on edge by grueling early morning workouts over rough terrain, violent hand-to-hand combat training, and mock missions that would bring brief jail time should they run afoul of the law.

Before she could recover physically, there were nights of mind-numbing mental exercises, which included memory tests done over and over until it became an acquired skill, and frustrating code problems that she swore had no answers and were merely there to drive her insane. She rated herself average in most of these tasks, even though her superiors claimed success and a job well done.

She was one of three women in the group, and male chauvinism was pervasive at the beginning. Fortunately, the instructors pointed out a woman's skill at manipulation gives her the advantage in certain situations, and it goes a long way toward achieving their desired goals. Jenny wasn't sure this was a compliment to women, but in the end, it didn't matter. Their hard work earned them their well-deserved respect.

More training would come, but for now, Jenny was happy to be on her way home. She took the quiet time to find herself again, to fill her mind and heart with Kathryn. With every new experience in the OSS, she gained more respect for the woman who bore the weight of her job so gracefully.

The train pulled into the station, and Wasilewski was unceremoniously awakened by a hat flung at his head by one of his pals.

"Rise and shine, lover boy!"

He scrubbed his face with a groan and sprang to his feet when he saw Jenny struggling to reach her bag on the shelf above the window.

"Here, I'll get that." He pulled it off the shelf and set it on the seat.

"Thank you."

"Aw," cooed his buddies.

The soldier rolled his eyes and secured his hat. "Well," he drew out shyly as he stuck out his hand, "I sure do thank you for the ear."

She ignored his hand and gave him a hug, which he readily returned. "You're welcome, Francis." She pulled away and kissed him on the cheek. "Be careful, and good luck."

"Gosh," he said, blushing.

Jenny smiled and reached up to wipe her lipstick from his skin.

He stilled her hand with a grin. "Leave it, if you don't mind." He thumbed over his shoulder toward his friends. "Let 'em eat their hearts out."

His group began filing out, and he was swept away in their wake, as slaps on the back and friendly nudges pushed him along. Jenny knew she'd never see him again, but she smiled, knowing that for a few brief hours, she gave him comfort, and for the rest of his life, he would know that all that was good in him would live on in her—a kind of immortality in a very mortal world.

. . .

Jenny briefly stood on her suitcase as she scanned the crowded train station concourse, using the higher vantage point to try to catch a glimpse of Kathryn's tall frame. They'd had no contact for the past two weeks, but before they parted, Kathryn had promised that, come hell or high water, she would be there the minute she stepped off the train. The station looked very much like hell, Jenny observed—people were scattering this way and that, like cats on a hot tin roof—but she didn't see any high water, so she kept looking, sure that Kathryn wouldn't break her promise.

It only took one sweep of the concourse to bring a smile to her face. There was Kathryn, dressed in a bold white suit and broad-brimmed hat, with a rich navy blue shirt and matching gloves, which stood in sharp contrast to the gray sea of blurred figures swirling through the station. Jenny watched her tuck her clutch under her arm as she lifted her chin and got on her toes to peer over the crowd, searching.

Jenny grabbed her suitcase and quickly mapped the shortest route through the crowd to her destination. She was jostled and stepped on, but she wouldn't be swayed from her path. She could no longer see Kathryn for all the men's thick shoulders and ladies' hats, but she wouldn't need to, as suddenly the crowd parted like the Red Sea and she was face to face with a broadly grinning tower of a whole lotta wonderful.

"Hi, beautiful," Kathryn whispered as she took her into her arms.

"God, I've missed you," Jenny said into Kathryn's chest.

They embraced for as long as they dared in public, both keenly aware of their surroundings and the necessity for discretion.

Kathryn released her and picked up her suitcase. "How was your trip?"

"It was fine. Exhausting. Exhilarating. Enlightening. Fine."

Kathryn smiled. "That sounds about right."

As they weaved through the station, it seemed every couple they saw was in a passionate lip lock, oblivious to the world around them. Jenny bit her lip and let out a frustrated groan, as she longed to do the same. She knew Kathryn echoed the sentiment as they both simultaneously glanced toward the ladies' bathroom.

The line stretched out the door and along the wall. No privacy there. She looked hopelessly at Kathryn, who put her hand on her shoulder, indicating she shared her frustration. She briefly scanned the station for some place to go—a storage room, a dark corner, some place that would afford them the same luxury of expressing their love that the couples around them enjoyed and most certainly took for granted.

That particular luxury was not for them this day, so they left the station and headed home in Kathryn's car.

CHAPTER TWENTY-SIX

"Kat, I love Bernie, but I haven't seen you in two weeks," Jenny said when she realized Kathryn had driven her to the photographer's apartment instead of her house.

Kathryn turned off the car and was silent, the seriousness of the moment obvious in her suddenly drawn face.

"Kathryn, what?"

"Cal was killed last week. We just found out about it around here a few days ago."

"Oh, God. Bernie."

Jenny didn't hesitate and was out of the car and running to his door before Kathryn could utter another word. She was met at the door by a young man Kathryn didn't recognize, but from the terse exchange, Jenny knew him well.

"He doesn't want to see you, Jenny," the young man said.

"Get the fuck out of my way, Robert!" Jenny said as she pushed by him.

Kathryn approached slowly, stopping at the steps. Robert stepped outside and descended the stairs until he stood beside her.

"How is he?" Kathryn asked.

"Not good, and she's not going to make it any better. He's pretty sore at her."

Kathryn knew exactly what he was talking about. She got an earful from Bernie when she couldn't say why Jenny hadn't returned his calls.

Kathryn and Robert could hear the accusations seeping from the open windows of the row house. Robert sat on the step. He removed a handkerchief from his pocket and spread it on the concrete for Kathryn to sit on. Kathryn unbuttoned her jacket and sat down beside him, as shouts drifted into the street.

"I needed you, Jenny, and where were you? I have always been there for you! *Always!*"

"I know, Bernie, but—" Jenny tried to reach for him but he pulled away. It was the first time he'd ever turned his back on her. "Bernie, please ... I'm here now."

"I don't need you now!" he shouted as he shoved some folded shirts in a suitcase. "I needed you yesterday, and the day before that, and the day before that!"

Jenny knew she'd let him down, but there was nothing she could say.

"I haven't seen you in weeks!" he continued. "You're always so—" He bit down on a curse. "Busy!" He threw open the top drawer of his dresser and retrieved some socks.

Jenny watched him slam drawers and throw once neatly folded clothes haphazardly into his luggage. "Where are you going?" she asked quietly.

He stopped mid-toss and stared, incredulous. "I'm going to Cal's funeral! Where do you think I'm going?" He shook his head and slammed his case shut. He turned and straightened, pulling his bag off the bed in one smooth motion. "Welcome home, Jenny. Now go play with your girlfriend. I don't need you anymore."

His words pierced her heart like a knife blade. She grabbed his arm as he attempted to pass. "Don't say that, Bernie."

He stared at her, tears welling in his eyes. "Hurts, doesn't it?" He continued out of the room, leaving her in stunned silence.

What had she done? She couldn't tell him the truth, and she had no stomach for more lies at the moment. She was sorry now that she ignored his messages that were forwarded to the Farm, but at the time, she reasoned she would be home soon enough. Surely, he could wait. Bernie could always wait. It pained her to admit it, but he was right. She'd taken him for granted. She'd pushed him aside and was oblivious to the pain it caused him.

She straightened her jacket and braced herself for more of the ugly truth. She tentatively stepped into the kitchen, where he was leaning against the counter, staring out the window, arms outstretched and back to her. He knew she was there and said nothing. She closed the gap between them and placed a hand on his tense shoulder. He didn't shout, and he didn't pull away, so she gently embraced him from behind, laying her cheek between his shoulder blades.

"I'm so sorry," she whispered. "About everything."

He lifted his chin, still defiant, but at least was willing to respond civilly. "I've missed you, Bug."

He called her Bug, and she was relieved. She closed her eyes in thanks and held tighter. "You must have—" She grinned. "You called Robert."

She could hear a smile break from his lips, and he relaxed as a laugh rumbled through his back. The laughter quickly turned into sobbing, and she found herself supporting his weight as he turned and went limp in her arms. They both slid to the floor, and Bernie poured out his pain and grief as he crumpled into a ball with his back against the kitchen cabinets.

Jenny held him to her chest and rocked him gently. "I know, sweetie. I'm so sorry."

She was sorry for more than just Cal. She was sorry she'd let their friendship drift so far away, and she knew he cried for the same. Things would be different now that she was back. She swore it.

Jenny left the house with a new appreciation for the word sacrifice. She was just beginning to comprehend the far-reaching grasp of her commitment. She ached to tell Bernie the truth and wondered whether she could ever truly heal the wound she'd inflicted on their friendship without it.

"Thanks, Robert," she said sincerely, with a hand on his arm as she passed. "Sorry."

"Not a problem," he called to her back.

"Are you okay?" Kathryn asked, as they walked side by side to the car.

"Not really," Jenny said, as they both got into their respective sides of the car.

Kathryn put the key in the ignition and took her hand. "I'm so sorry, honey."

Jenny shook her head and exhaled in disbelief. More than just her relationship with Bernie had changed. *She* had changed. She felt strangely empty, unable to feel for Bernie and his loss. It was as if it wasn't real and she had just awakened from a bad dream. Was it that easy to lie to yourself? Can a person just shut off the cold, hard slap of reality in a desperate attempt to retain some semblance of normalcy? Jenny looked into Kathryn's concerned eyes, eyes that had seen so much pain yet still managed to illuminate a soul that had so much to give, and decided, yes, a person can.

Kathryn gazed helplessly at Jenny. This was just the beginning. She saw something in her eyes, something she recognized, and something she would have done anything to spare her from. This path was hard, and it was only going to get harder, but each person dealt with it differently. She could be there for her, comfort her if she could, but the rest would be up to Jenny. She tugged on her hand.

"Come on, I'll take you home."

"No," Jenny said quietly.

Kathryn offered a questioning glance.

"Let's run away instead."

Kathryn nodded in complete understanding and started the car.

She drove them to Luc's penthouse apartment in the city—their safe house. There, the world would stop simply because they wished it, and Kathryn could tell that Jenny very much wished it. She had been understandably quiet on the ride over, and Kathryn didn't push for her thoughts or try to distract her from them. Jenny had a lot to process, and how she dealt with the burdens of her new responsibilities would be the key to her success or failure.

She sensed Jenny felt better just being in the penthouse. The surreal surroundings, the sublime memories of their intimate afternoons together, and the news that Forrester was out of town until the end of the week all muted the sharp edge of reality. Kathryn was glad about Forrester. Jenny would need all the attention she could give her. She would find her way—everyone does—but these first few hours, these first few days, would tell a lot about her ability to adjust, and as distasteful as it seemed to Kathryn at that moment, part of her job was to assess Jenny's mental state upon her return and report her findings to brass.

Tonight wasn't about assessment. It was about support, and Kathryn waited patiently for Jenny to come to her. They moved about the apartment, engaging in pleasant small talk as they settled in. Jenny said nothing about the tragedy that had befallen her friends. She was doing her best to honor their sanctuary and push the day out of her mind, but guilt had a way of seeping into the best of intentions and derailing the simplest of plans.

"I want to forget about Cal and what happened with Bernie," she said after a long, contemplative silence. "Just for a little while." She tugged off her earrings and placed them on the long bathroom counter. "Is that wrong?"

"You do what you need to do, honey. There is no right or wrong in that." Kathryn nudged her. "I think you told me that."

Jenny smiled weakly in agreement as she shed her shirt and then unzipped her skirt.

Kathryn followed suit, removing her hose and dropping her skirt. When she began to unbutton her blouse, Jenny took over.

"I'll do that." She guided the material off Kathryn's shoulders and concentrated on her hands as they traveled over her skin.

Kathryn could see Jenny shutting down emotionally. She didn't look her in the eyes. Instead, she concentrated wholly on her task, as if peace could be found in the mindless pleasure of their proposition. She kissed Kathryn's breasts as she removed her bra and whispered, "You are so beautiful."

Kathryn let her go on seducing her, giving her what she thought she wanted, but Kathryn knew that wasn't Jenny. She never ran from anything, and she wouldn't run very far from this. She would break. It was just a matter of how and when.

Jenny turned her waiting mouth upwards. "I want you."

When Kathryn covered her mouth with her own, Jenny drank desperately from her lips. This is what she needed. Kathryn would bring her back to her senses. She would find herself in their love, and she would break through the dark shroud suffocating her.

"I need you," she said between kisses.

"I'm here."

"Need you," she repeated, as kisses weren't enough and she devoured Kathryn's body, starting at her neck and hastily working her way down her tall frame.

Kathryn let her take what she wanted, but it wasn't enough. Desperation turned to anger, as she wondered why she couldn't feel anything. She was with the most beautiful woman she had ever known, the woman she loved, and she felt nothing. How could this be? She tried to focus on Kathryn's warm skin beneath her hands and lips. She pulled at Kathryn's garter belt, uttering a frustrated curse when she couldn't remove it fast enough. Kathryn took care of it as Jenny shed her slip.

With clothes no longer an issue, Jenny went in search of her misplaced desire. She grasped Kathryn in a desperate embrace and resumed what she hoped would become a passionate kiss. She felt no passion in the kiss, and it frightened her. The harder she tried to feel something, the more disconnected she became.

"Kiss me, Kat," she demanded, as if she were the problem.

"Jenny—"

"Kiss me, Kathryn!"

She looked Kathryn in the eye for the first time since they arrived at the penthouse. She could tell Kathryn saw not only her fear but her anger as well. Kathryn cocked her head, obviously knowing it would do no good, but kissed her fiercely anyway. Jenny moaned as if she felt it—it was her favorite kind of kiss from Kathryn—but eventually pushed away in frustration.

"Damn it!" she said, as she turned her back and put her hand to her forehead. "What the fuck is wrong with me?"

"There's nothing wrong with you," Kathryn said, laying a comforting hand on her shoulder.

Jenny shrugged it off. She didn't want comfort. She didn't want pity. She wanted Cal alive again. She wanted her relationship with Bernie whole again. She wanted the war to be over. She wanted to be stronger, braver. She leaned on the counter and bowed her head.

It wasn't Kathryn's fault. It wasn't anyone's fault. She had to pull herself together. What she was feeling was normal. She just had to give herself time and allow those who loved her to help her.

She took a deep breath, let it out, and felt Kathryn's hand slide gently onto her back.

"I'm sorry, Kat."

Kathryn moved closer, and Jenny turned into her arms for the loving embrace they longed to share at the train station.

"I'm so sorry."

Kathryn kissed her head. "It's okay, honey. It's going to be okay."

Jenny let Kathryn comfort her and believed what she said, because if anyone knew about overcoming adversity, she did. At least she could feel Kathryn again. She could feel the love in their connection. She thought she'd cry in relief, but the tears never came.

Kathryn ended their embrace with a loving kiss and led her into the shower, where she gladly washed away the day.

. . .

Jenny stared at the stream of lights below as they sat on a ledge in the rooftop garden of Luc's penthouse and looked down on the busy city. She felt safe with Kathryn's arms around her and more like herself than she had in the last two weeks. Certainly more than she had in the last two hours. The height no longer made her feel omnipresent. She felt very human, and very fragile. Maybe it was the woman pressed against her back, the fact that she needed her so. Her touch and her presence gave her strength and confidence that she could face whatever lay ahead.

Kathryn had been so good with her, so patient and gentle. She knew she understood what she was going through, and she understood that she was fortunate to have someone who cared enough to see her through it. Kathryn hadn't been so lucky, and her penchant for running was the unfortunate result. Jenny kissed her hand and wished that she had been there for her. Kathryn kissed her head in return.

"You don't have to do this, Jenny. The program is voluntary."

Quitting wasn't an option, and Jenny ignored the offer. She just had to get in touch with her emotions so she could better prepare to face the future.

"I wanted to cry today," she began. "For Cal. For Bernie. For his loss, for the pain I caused him. But the tears wouldn't come. It's like I've lost something ... but I don't know what."

Kathryn held her tighter. "You're just tired."

Jenny *was* tired, but she knew that wasn't it. Shutting out a tragedy was one thing, but losing her connection with Kathryn was another. Apparently, emotions are a package deal. You don't get to pick which ones to experience and which to ignore.

"I was afraid. I don't ever want to lose you like that again."

"You didn't lose me."

Jenny stared mindlessly at the streets below. Tomorrow they would be part of that world again, and somewhere, to someone, they would be as faceless and insignificant as the meaningless patterns of light dissecting the night.

"Everything is going to change now, isn't it?"

Kathryn held her tighter but didn't answer. She didn't have to. Things already had.

Kathryn and Jenny's story continues with *In the Shadow of Truth* (Shadow Series Book 3), available for preorder now at your retailer of choice. Projected release date, late 2022.

If you enjoyed this book, please leave a review so that other readers can discover Kathryn and Jenny as well.

Visit jeleak.com to sign up for my newsletter and receive updates on new releases, works in progress, blog posts, giveaways, and more!

AUTHOR NOTES

My characters are not based on any particular real-life individuals; however, the Office of Strategic Services (OSS), for whom Kat and Jenny work, was a real wartime organization established in July 1942 by President Franklin D. Roosevelt, based on the British intelligence Special Operations Executive (SOE).

The New York City offices of the OSS were headquartered in the International Building at Rockefeller Center. For expediency in my story, I housed several divisions there, but, in reality, the OSS had offices scattered throughout the city, in various buildings. Morale Operations, where Jenny works, was indeed housed in a building off Times Square. The British Security Coordination (BSC), part of the British Secret Intelligence Service, was also housed in the International Building at Rockefeller Center.

OSS Director William Donovan called his recruits "Glorious Amateurs," but the contributions of these brave men and women of the intelligence services are immeasurable, and without them, the war could have had a very different outcome.

Historical fiction propels the reader into a story set in the past. Today, that time period's values and morals might be considered old-fashioned or uptight, but this was the reality for our characters. In some ways, the core of their struggle is still our struggle today. Science progresses, attitudes change, even maps and boundaries change, but the human heart still loves who it loves. Some things are timeless.

ACKNOWLEDGMENTS

Writing may be a solitary exercise, but support, encouragement, and sometimes a loving kick in the ass are all integral parts of what eventually becomes a book in your hands.

I would like to thank my wife for her patience and unfailing belief in my story. Her love and support is the reason that this series has become a reality. To the moon and back, baby. You mean everything to me.

To Pam Greer, my editor and bestie, I love you dearly. I am forever grateful for your friendship and your willingness to pour over my words ad infinitum with the same enthusiasm as the first day you read them. Your love, input, encouragement, and tolerance as I whined about "my vision" made me better at my craft. I've learned so much from you, and I would look like an idiot without you. You're aces, doll.

To my dearest friends—my TRIBE—you are all magnificent. You've been with me since the beginning, listened to me blather on about the never-ending "writing project" with nary a complaint, and cheered with relief when it was finally done (amen). You've helped me in so many ways and never failed to lift me up when I doubted myself. Thank you from the bottom of my heart. I love you all.

To my Beta readers, your honesty makes me a better writer, and I am grateful for your input.

To my ARC readers, thank you for reading, and thank you for your reviews. It means the world to this indie author.

ABOUT THE AUTHOR

J.E. Leak was born in Washington, DC, and grew up on the beautiful South Jersey shores of Long Beach Island. An antiques conservator by trade, she has always been fascinated by history and the stories objects could tell if they could speak. When she isn't bingeing 1940s noir films, she's writing or photographing nature on the spring-fed azure rivers of Central Florida. She has an Associate of Science degree in graphic design and is a devoted night owl.

In the Shadow of Love is the second novel in the Shadow series.

 facebook.com/JELeakAuthor
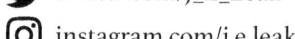 twitter.com/J_E_Leak
instagram.com/j.e.leak

ALSO BY J.E. LEAK

Coming Soon:

In the Shadow of Truth (Shadow Series Book 3)

In the Shadow of Victory (Shadow Series Book 4)

Visit jeleak.com to sign up for my newsletter and receive updates on new releases, works in progress, blog posts, giveaways, and more!

I am part of iReadIndies, a collective of self-published independent authors of sapphic literature. Please visit iReadIndies.com for more information and to find books published by other iReadIndies authors.

Printed in Great Britain
by Amazon